# BROKEN SKY

## SKIES OF CYRNA
### BOOK ONE

## MORGAN K. BELL

*In memory of Jessie Wintle, who always believed in her students and taught us to believe in ourselves*

CHAPTER ONE

# THE NEWCOMER

"Okay." Dorian Valmont drew in a deep, terrified breath. "We're doing this."

Frostvale Skyport was a teeming hive of organized chaos. Aeronauts and dock workers rushed back and forth, shouting commands and hauling crates. The docks were a well-oiled machine, every part in good repair, every person knowing their job and how to do it.

Everyone except for Dorian.

*What am I doing here?*

He looked up in awe at the massive skyships tethered to the docks, gossamer aether sails glistening in the winter sunlight. They were beautiful, Dorian thought. Beautiful and terrifying.

«Are you sure you want to do this?» Dorian's bonded demon, Hematite, seemed every bit as afraid as Dorian.

"Not really," Dorian admitted.

But alongside his trepidation, Dorian felt frantic, desperate hope, so ephemeral that it tried to dart away the second he tried to reach for it. A chance, albeit razor-slim, at a better life. A chance at any life at all.

"This is the one," Dorian said, confirming the dock number on his note from Lord Bradford. "Skyship *Phoenix*." Dorian took several more breaths and continued, "Right. Okay. We can do this."

With forced confidence he did not truly feel, Dorian ascended the gangplank and took his first steps into an unknown future.

It took every ounce of Tai Lunstrum's willpower not to throw her crew-mates off the docking platform.

*Murder*, she reminded herself. Throwing them overboard would be murder. They, unlike her, would not survive a fall from the platform. Wingless folk were so fragile.

"Seven crystals." Her voice came out in a low, steady growl. "Scarcely a moon since we left Pazarae, and you've burned through seven crystals."

"Come off it, Tai." Zachary Falgar leaned lazily against the skyship's railing, the slight breeze tousling his sandy hair. "You know what it's been like. Three Voidstorms in as many weeks! Weather like that, we're bloody lucky it was only seven. No need to ruffle your feathers."

Tai *did* ruffle her feathers, impatiently twitching the raven-dark wings on her back. "A Voidstorm's no excuse to push the engines past the shatter point!"

Falgar sneered. "And you'd prefer what, exactly? Just let the storm winds knock us out of the sky?"

Jakob Sullivan, the other aeronaut, quickly stepped in and spread his burly arms. "It's my fault," he said. "We had that shipment of Toreenish porcelain, and I thought it prudent that we prioritize a smooth ride, even at the expense —"

"I don't care whose fault it is," Tai said, hands balled into fists. "If a shattered crystal blows in the Linking, it's everyone's problem.

We could all get sacked for this! Void, we're lucky we didn't get killed!"

Falgar rolled his eyes in a long, exaggerated fashion. "But we didn't get killed, and if we're sacked, we'll find different jobs. If Xander lets us go over something so trivial as one lousy blown crystal, he doesn't deserve to call himself captain."

Tai glowered. "It wasn't one crystal, it was seven. And anyway, that's easy for you to say! Maybe every captain in Aeris is lining up to hire you, but me, I..." She took several breaths, trying to quell the panic. When Captain Xander found out about their burn rate, he was going to kill her. He was absolutely going to kill her.

At that moment, the sound of footfall echoed across the skydock.

"Captain!" Tai spun around, raising her hand into a hasty salute.

Falgar snorted a laugh, while Sullivan, clearing his throat, said, "I, um, don't think that's the captain."

Tai stopped. A round-faced young man, perhaps within a year or two of her own twenty years, stood at the top of the gangplank. He tugged nervously at the fine silk ruffles at the ends of his sleeves. An aura of pale blue flame flickered in her peripheral vision. *Demonfire.* Strong demonfire, if she wasn't mistaken.

*No,* she thought. That was *definitely* not the captain.

"Ah, hello." The newcomer ran a nervous hand through his crop of reddish brown hair, gazing up in awe at the hovering skyship. "Is, ah, is this the skyship *Phoenix*?"

Falgar tried and failed to stifle a laugh. "Get a load of this cream-puff. Get lost on the way to the ball, rich boy?"

"Falgar," Sullivan said reproachfully.

Tai fixed Falgar with a level gaze. "Kindly refrain from scaring away the customers." She forced what she hoped was a welcoming smile onto her face, and continued, "Apologies, Sir. Some aeronauts don't think their job extends to common politeness or decency. But you'll find no ship faster or more reliable than the *Phoenix*. How much cargo space is needed today?"

The boy appeared well-dressed, well-fed, and, most incredibly, demon-possessed. Shrewdly, Tai thought that if she landed a lucrative contract, that might be enough to make Captain Xander forget about the aether crystals. Maybe.

The boy gaped at her with an open-mouthed, wide-eyed expression reminiscent of a skypuffer. Tai cocked her eyebrows, and the newcomer must have realized he was staring because he reddened and quickly averted his gaze. "Sorry."

*Rich contract, remember, rich contract.* Biting back her annoyance, Tai continued, "If you'd like to have a look at our cargo hold, you'll see we have several options--"

The boy shook his head. "Sorry," he said again. "I... that is... I'm not here to transport cargo."

"Oh." Tai felt her wings droop of their own accord. "Well then, um, what can I help you with?"

Blue demonfire intensified for a moment, and the boy nervously thumbed a gold chain around his neck. Tai noted a dragon pendant clutching some kind of round, red stone.

The boy shuffled his feet awkwardly, his flushed round face resembling his necklace. "I... I, ah, the thing is... I'm supposed to join the crew." He exhaled the last bit in one nervous breath.

This time Falgar didn't bother to hide his laughter. "Join the crew? You? Void Eternal, boy, shouldn't you, I don't know, be off ordering some peasants to bake you a fancy cake?"

"Falgar!" Sullivan's admonition came out like a hiss.

"I'm sorry, I'm sorry," Falgar sighed. "But really. An aeronaut? Him?"

Tai scowled at Falgar, then turned her attention to the boy.

This soft young man with his smooth hands and silk shirt didn't look like he'd done an hour's hard labor in his life. But, well, looks could be deceiving. Tai herself was proof enough of that.

"Have you ever flown a ship before?" she asked in what she hoped was a polite tone.

The boy clutched his leather rucksack like a child's toy and stared resolutely at the ground. Tai supposed this was better than staring at her wings. "No, ma'am."

"Then I'm afraid—" she began.

"Please!" the boy looked up, imploring. "Please, I've got a letter from Lord Bradford, I'm to... I have to..."

Tai felt her frown deepening. "If it's a career in aeronautics you desire, perhaps you can apply for an apprenticeship with the Shipping Authority in Tremaine."

The boy shook his head. "No, no, that's not... that is... I'm sorry. Is Captain Xander Kane here?"

"The Captain is busy," Tai responded.

"That's right," came the gruff voice of Captain Xander as he ascended the gangplank behind the newcomer. "Busy captain, coming through. What's all this about?"

"Captain!" For all that Tai feared him a moment ago, she was glad to see him now. "It's this boy, Sir, he says he wants to join the crew. I don't know what to tell him."

"Captain," the boy said. Shaking with nerves, he almost dropped his rucksack. He fumbled, caught it, and produced a small sealed envelope. The paper was white and crisp. It looked expensive.

Xander grunted as he took the letter. His eyes scanned it, then looked at the new boy, then back at the letter, then the new boy again. For a moment, something like dismay crossed the Captain's face, but he hid it quickly.

"So," Xander finally said. "You're Cyrus Valmont's boy, then, are you?"

"Ah!" the nervous boy replied. "Yes. That's right, Sir. I'm Dorian Valmont, Sir."

Tai drew in a sharp breath. Even she'd heard of Cyrus Valmont. This boy was his son?

"And the demon?" Xander asked.

"Hematite, Sir." For a moment, the blue light intensified, and a large lizard-like creature joined them on the dock, a mane of blue fire cloaking the burnished silver-black hide that gave the creature his name. Tai had seen wild demons fluttering around the forests of her homeland, for all that the border guards tried to keep them out. But those were small, flickering things. This creature was enormous. Powerful. Solid. More than a little intimidating, if she was honest.

"Hematite," Xander repeated, for a moment taken aback. "A pleasure."

The demon twitched his tail back and forth, and although Tai was no expert on demonic body language, she got the impression the feeling was not mutual.

Xander coughed and ran his hand through his shaggy brown hair. "Well, all right, then. Let's show you around, shall we?"

Tai blinked. "Wait. He's... hired? Just like that?"

"Everything looks in order," Xander shrugged.

"But sir!" Tai protested. "He says he's never flown before. Surely, we should give him some kind of test, or an interview, or..." *Or the myriad of trials you put me through to get my position on the ship.*

Xander, however, shook his head and gestured at the newcomer. "He's Cyrus Valmont's boy."

*So.* That was how it was, was it? This boy, this rich, spoiled, inexperienced youth, was to be hired on the strength of his family name alone?

Xander, however, gestured for the Valmont boy to follow him belowdecks, leaving Tai to stare at their retreating backs in disbelief.

Dorian's heart beat a frantic staccato as he followed the captain up the gangplank. Well! He was here. That was something. A few short hours ago, he wasn't sure he'd live to see the evening. Now, he was on a skyship. A *skyship*, Ancients help him.

*What am I doing?* He tried to swallow back the anxiety rising in his throat. *What. Am. I. Doing?*

The plan already sounded far-fetched when Bradford laid it out for him that morning. Now, it seemed ludicrous beyond comprehension. He didn't know the first thing about skyships! What was he thinking? Dorian was no Tovian Eagleheart or Lord Zekador, to live an adventure out of the Epics.

«I do not like this,» the demon Hematite repeated for the hundredth time this past hour. «If we had only a few more days to plan, I could have thought up a thousand better ways to stay alive. But I do not like this.»

Dorian didn't like it either, but they didn't have a few more days. They had to leave Adenthul now. «Let's just pay attention to the Captain,» Dorian said, «Before he decides we're too incompetent to bother with and tosses us overboard.»

«I have met the human Xander Kane.» Hematite said. «I may not like him much, but I doubt he'd resort to actual murder.»

«It's just a figure of speech,» Dorian said. Xander might not want Dorian dead, but that didn't mean he wanted Dorian on his ship. How long would Captain Xander tolerate an absolute novice?

Dorian ran his hand along the *Phoenix's* polished wood railing. He heard a clucking sound coming from a nearby wire mesh enclosure and concluded that the crew must keep their own chickens. He noted several raised wooden beds on the upper deck as well, probably meant for gardening, though currently, in the winter, they contained only fallow soil.

Various spell sigils shone bright blue against the deck's rich dark wood, culminating in a large circle near the aether engine. Without intending to, Dorian puzzled out what they did. Connection, position, air. Those all made sense. But what was that Greater Sigil of Zekador in the center? Some sort of connection between the physical and spiritual realms?

«This is not the Grimoire,» Hematite said. «You do not need to decipher the inner workings of every random spell.»

Dorian almost smiled. «Perhaps not.» But figuring out spells had become second nature. He felt a regretful pang at the reminder that those golden afternoons with Saedra were now over. At least he still had the Grimoire. It weighed heavily in his rucksack.

Biting his lip, Dorian examined the rest of the deck.

On the back of the ship — *aft*, he seemed to recall — the gleaming brass aether engine glinted in the sunlight. At the front — *fore*? Or was it *bow*? Gods, he wished he knew anything about skyships — a wooden bird decorated the masthead. He supposed that was where the ship got its name. But with its conical, stinger-like engine, and the gossamer sails jutting out the sides, Dorian thought the ship looked more like a bumblebee than a phoenix. The squat, round little vessel didn't look like it ought to fly at all. Rather like Dorian himself, he thought wryly. But unlike Dorian, he was sure the ship could fly just fine.

*Gods.* Dorian used to dream of this. A life in the sky, like a hero out of a legend. But those were just boyhood fancies. His demon was right. He didn't belong here. He belonged at home by the fireside, enjoying a warm bowl of stew, a cold mug of cider, and a thick book of Ancient sigilwork.

*What am I doing here?*

"... Has the capacity for up to twelve crew, but I like to keep things minimal, so we've only four at the moment. Five, now, with you here, I suppose. Regardless, you'll get your own cabin." Dorian realized, to his embarrassment, that the captain had been talking for several moments.

"Oh," Dorian said, clutching his rucksack and hoping the captain didn't notice his distraction. "Oh, that's good."

"Not enormous, but it'll be yours," Xander said. "Over here's the head."

"The head?"

"Toilet, for the uninitiated. Try not to flush anything bigger than a small wad of tissue, else it gets cranky. You clog it, you fix it. Aether-heated tank isn't the biggest, and there's five of us here now, so try to keep showers to less than five minutes."

Dorian poked his head in the lavatory, wincing at just how tiny it really was. The baths in Callahan Manor could have held a dozen of these.

"Common area's over here, and behind that is the galley," Xander continued, either oblivious or choosing to ignore Dorian's discomfort. "Cooking is part of the usual chore rotation. You, ah, can cook, can you not?"

"Ah, yes, sir," Dorian said, straightening slightly.

"Mmm," Xander grunted. "Well, that's something. Ever worked on a skyship before?"

"No, Sir," Dorian said. He wished he could give a different answer.

"Ever flown in a Linking?"

Dorian felt his face redden. "No, Sir."

"Ornithopters? Gryphonback riding? Skimmers?"

"Sorry, sir." Dorian stared resolutely at the toes of his boots, barely visible beneath his soft stomach. *What am I doing here?* Xander was going to kick him off the ship, he just knew it, and then he'd really have nowhere to go.

Xander shook his head. "Well, then, what skills do you have?"

Dorian swallowed. "I can read and write and can keep ledgers. I've passed core competency in standard spellcasting."

When he said it out loud, it seemed a depressingly paltry resume.

"I can also do chores, and things," he added, in a desperate grab to make himself seem less pathetic. "You know. Swab decks."

«Swab decks?» Hematite sounded half way between amused and horrified. «Do you even know what swabbing decks means?»

Dorian winced. In truth, he had no idea. Wasn't it just a fancy word for scrubbing?

"I can scrub decks," he amended. *How hard could it be?*

"Well, I suppose that's a start," Xander sighed.

The captain wore a neutral expression, but Dorian could see it there, in his eyes, the familiar disappointment. The look people got when they compared Dorian Valmont to his father. When he was alive, Cyrus Valmont had been handsome, charming, athletic, and brilliant. Everything Dorian wasn't.

"Something the matter?" Xander asked.

"Nothing, sir."

"I'll start you out on chore rotation," Xander said, "But I'll expect you to learn as you go. I can't afford to pay a cabin boy, but you'll get free passage. That's the best I can offer."

"Oh," said Dorian, who hadn't been expecting pay at all. "That's, um, more than fair, sir."

"Also, I'll be teaching you the sword."

Dorian stopped in his tracks. He felt the blood draining from his face. "The... the sword, Sir?"

Hematite's mindvoice came upon Dorian like a gut punch. «I cannot allow this.»

Dorian wanted to agree with the demon. He'd take any excuse to get out of it. «I don't think it's really up to us,» he said glumly. «He's the captain, after all.»

«What my Lord Meroneth would think,» Hematite moaned, «To know that I have allowed my host to climb on board a skyship and learn the sword! I am supposed to protect you, not help you to get stabbed!»

"Mmm," Xander confirmed, unaware of the telepathic argument going on in Dorian's head. "Dangerous place, the skies. Pirates, you know. And, well. What Callahan wants, Callahan gets. Particularly regarding those he wants dead."

Dorian gulped. *Callahan.*

«Maybe the captain is right,» Dorian reluctantly told Hematite. «You'll have an easier time keeping me safe if I can at least protect myself.»

But even as he said it, it seemed ludicrous beyond imagining. The sword? He couldn't learn the sword! He'd never picked up a sword in his life!

To Xander, however, he simply nodded and said, "Ah... yes, Sir. I suppose that's the case, Sir."

Oh, Gods and Ancients! What was he *doing* here?

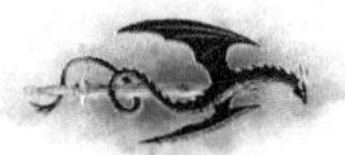

Captain Xander Kane sank into his threadbare armchair, propping the leather-bound sketchbook in his lap. He flipped to the first blank page, nibbled absently on the blunt end of his pencil, and began sketching.

*Sweet gods above, what a day.*

Xander made a habit of avoiding Frostvale, if he could get away with it. But the *Phoenix* was, technically, registered there, and he had to renew registration every seven-year Cycle. Most of the time, it was simple. Pick up supplies, fill out the paperwork, avoid the scrutiny of the local town lord.

But on this, his third visit, he found something he hadn't expected.

Cyrus Valmont's son. Cyrus Bloody Valmont's bloody son was in Frostvale, possibly had been in Frostvale the whole time, and now he was on Xander's bloody ship. *Gods and Ancients above,* he needed a drink.

Xander put the sketchbook aside, and, holding his pencil between his teeth, procured a crystal decanter and matching tumbler from the cabinet. He poured himself a measure, then took up his sketchbook once more.

There, in smooth pencil lines, he drew the Valmont boy, round face downcast, eyes averted. Xander fancied himself a skilled artist and took pride in his memory and attention to detail. He found he could usually draw an accurate likeness of anyone. Behind the shy, awkward boy, he drew another figure, stocky and reptilian, gunmetal skin swathed in flame.

Hematite. Fifteenth Degree Demon.

Demons weren't exactly unheard of among the upper echelons of

Aeris. But Hematite wasn't just any demon. Xander recognized Hematite.

Taking another sip of whiskey, he turned the pages back to the oldest drawing in the sketchbook. Xander's technique was rougher, back then, a little more sketchy, but he still captured his subjects with accuracy and detail.

Cyrus Valmont stood to the far left of the page. Xander supposed he could detect some resemblance between the man and the boy. The shape of their noses, the set of their ears, their copper-colored hair. Not to mention the flickering blue light of demonfire, just in his peripheral vision. *Hematite.* What were the bloody odds?

And yet, despite these similarities, Xander found it difficult to imagine two people more different than Dorian and Cyrus Valmont. If Cyrus was an untamed gryphon, then Dorian was a frightened dormouse.

In the image, Cyrus stood just how Xander remembered him, with a confident, relaxed posture, muscular arms crossed, staring with passion and determination at some unseen point in the distance.

*How young we all were. Gods know I could use your advice now, old friend.*

Xander took another long swig from his whiskey tumbler before returning his attention to the old drawing. Xander's sister stood in the middle of the image, wide eyes shining with hope and promise. Now, she was missing, possibly dead. *Better be dead,* an uncharitable part of him thought, or else better have a bloody good reason for abandoning her family. He pushed those thoughts aside, dismissing them as unworthy. He wanted her to be alive. Of course he did. But Gods Above, what a mess she left them all in.

Sighing, he then inspected the man to her right. Janus Callahan. Janus Bloody Callahan.

"Secured yourself a crown, now, did you? You always were the most ambitious of us."

Xander himself stood behind the others in the picture, slightly off to the side. Part of the group, and yet separate. Not nearly as handsome as either of the other two men. He always tried to be objective in his creations.

Xander shook his head sadly and took another drink. This was all as much his doing as anyone's. He'd known of the Valmont boy's existence, naturally. But did Xander ever seek the boy out, or see to his wellbeing? No. Of course not. He'd barely thought about him at all.

Xander supposed he ought to be glad the boy seemed well cared for. Callahan fed him and clothed him and sheltered him. Rather lavishly, even.

But not all needs were material, and not all scars showed on the surface. Xander thought he recognized that morose, haunted look in the boy's eyes.

A knock sounded at the door, snapping Xander out of his reverie. He closed the sketchbook and set it aside on the end-table.

"Enter," Xander said.

The wooden door slid open, and in walked Tai Lunstrum. Xander schooled his face into an expression of practiced patience. A good, diligent worker, that one. But by the gods, would it kill her to lighten up sometimes?

"Sir," she said with a crisp salute.

"You don't have to do that," Xander said. "This isn't a warship." He felt his face twist into a mischievous smile. "What's this I hear about you going through seven aether crystals this moon?"

The girl visibly paled. "Forgive me, sir," she said, lowering her head. "I tried to tell the others — tried to get them to fly more carefully, but there were those Voidstorms, and Sullivan said something about Toreenish porcelain, and there's no reasoning with Falgar, and I... and I..."

Xander smiled ruefully and shook his head. Their burn rate wasn't Tai's fault. Indeed, it would have been much worse, if not for her expert engine maintenance. She was the best bloody skyship mage he'd ever hired. He just wished she wouldn't hold herself so far apart from the others.

Offering neither praise nor admonition, Xander re-filled his whiskey from the decanter. "Want some?"

"No, thank you." She ruffled her wings in vague indignation.

"What can I do for you, then?"

"Right. Sir. I was just wondering... that is..." she stood straight, drew in a deep breath, and let it out. "I was wondering if it was wise to let someone like that boy on our ship. Sir."

Xander cocked his eyebrow. "And you are now the arbiter of who should or shouldn't be on my ship?"

Her wings fluttered in obvious discomfort, but she stood her ground. *Admirable.* "Apologies, Sir. It's not that." She drew in another deep breath. "At least Falgar and Sullivan can fly. Captain, he said he's never worked on a ship before. We already decided against taking on untrained apprentices back in Westfall. Are we really—"

Xander cut her off with a wave of his hand. He ought to have expected this, he realized in retrospect.

"The boy's father was one of the finest aeronauts I've ever known."

Tai straightened. "So you are only hiring him based on his family name?"

Xander let out a long breath. "Perhaps," he admitted. "But I owe his father a favor. He's dead and I can't repay it, but I can repay the son. Can you understand that, at least?"

Tai cocked her head sideways, considering. But then she shook her head. "I'm sorry, Captain. But it just isn't right. He has a fifteenth degree demon, for the Ancients' sakes. I've heard horror stories about the havoc demonic energy can wreak on a Linking."

"That's just superstition," Xander said. "I heard the Ancients actually considered it good luck to keep a demon or two on a ship."

Tai shook her head. "Now who's being superstitious?"

Xander sighed. Folding his hands, he said, "I've been known to hire crew who were, shall we say, unconventional." It was a cruel thing to say, and he knew it. But he also knew it was the only thing that would make her see reason.

Tai opened and closed her mouth several times, evidently trying and discarding several arguments before ultimately lowering her head in defeat. "I... suppose that's true. I... apologize. I was out of line. You're right. You're the captain." But in a quieter tone, she added, "I just hope you know what you're doing."

She spun towards the exit and left without waiting for him to respond, and Xander refilled his whiskey once more.

"I hope so too, Tai," he said to the empty doorway. "I really hope so, too."

Tai was right. Xander shouldn't let an untested, inexperienced, possibly spoiled youth onto his ship just for the sake of his family connections.

But what bloody choice did he have?

He flipped the sketchbook back open, back to the drawing of Dorian's father.

In the picture, Cyrus wore a pendant, a gold-wrought dragon encircling a smooth round stone. The boy, Dorian, wore one just like it. A dragonstone.

But while most dragonstones were dull, matte gray, Dorian Valmont's shone vivid scarlet. Xander had seen a dragonstone change its color only once, and that was only for a moment.

Xander had a hunch, and if that hunch was correct, then there was much, much more to the Valmont boy than met the eye.

# CHAPTER TWO
# A TROUBLED MARKETPLACE

Tai twitched her wings in annoyance as she tied the line to the dock.

One week. One week since they departed from Frostvale and picked up that new boy. One week to make Tai think she was going to go out of her mind. Dorian Valmont knew nothing about life on a skyship. He complained, he got in the way, he contributed almost nothing of value. Why in the Void had Xander insisted on hiring him?

She joined Captain Xander as he stared out at the town below. "Crimsonrock," he said. "Second biggest city in Kasanarae. They crowned a new king recently, and he and I have never seen eye to eye." At this, the new boy, Dorian, shuddered. "But I've got a lucrative contract with some wine merchants, and gods know we need the money. Sooner we're airborne again, the happier I'll be, though. Falgar, Sullivan, you come with me to help load our clients' cargo. Lunstrum, find Valmont and take him into town to replenish supplies."

"I can get supplies by myself, Sir," Tai protested.

"I know you can," Xander said. "But he needs to see how we do things around here. That's an order."

Tai glowered, but knew better than to argue.

As soon as they reached the market, however, babysitting the new boy became a secondary concern. Something was wrong in this town. No crowds mingled the cobbled streets of the market square. No young lovers met on the stone fountain benches. No merchants hawked their wares. Instead, the sellers stood in their stalls like caged animals.

The market stalls' silk awnings hung dusty and threadbare as the scant few shoppers darted about nervously between them. The last time Tai and the crew landed in Crimsonrock, they encountered a busy town full of cheerful commerce. What she saw now provided a stark and drastic contrast.

"Please!" came a frantic voice from among the market-goers. "Please, if anyone could spare some change... any amount helps, please, I'll take anything!"

*Beggars*, Tai thought. There never used to be beggars in Crimsonrock. She straightened her shoulders and looked away, trying to ignore the man's desperate cries.

"He sounds so desperate," Dorian said.

"I know, it's terrible, but we can't help every poor sod in the world," Tai said. "Come on, let's go get supplies before Xander—"

She cut off at the sound of a strangled cry. The beggar staggered backward, eyes wide as two burly men in chain mail surrounded him on either side.

"No, please, please, I still have three more days!" the beggar cried.

"Where's Beckett's money, Owyn?" the soldier demanded.

"Beckett," Dorian repeated, his voice a choked whisper. He'd come to a full stop now, gazing at them with wide, horrified blue eyes.

"Come on, Dorian," Tai said, tugging his arm.

"They're hurting him," Dorian said. His hands clenched and unclenched into fists, his expression helpless, stricken.

"I know," she said, "But there's nothing we can do."

Tai didn't need Kassoria's gift of foresight to know what would happen if soft, pampered Dorian picked a fight with these toughs. But Dorian stood rooted in place.

"I... I have it! I mean. I will have it. The terms of the loan were..." the frantic-looking man swallowed several times. "I still have three more days."

"I know you do." The second enforcer shoved the beggar roughly in the stomach. "This is just a preview of the treatment you'll get in three days' time. Just remember. Beckett will have his money. Even if he's got to take it out of your arse."

The other soldier laughed cruelly and the two of them stalked away.

Before Tai could stop him, Dorian rushed up to the man and helped him to his feet. "Are you okay?"

The man, who Tai recalled was called Owyn, grimaced. "I've been better if we're honest. But I still have three more days. I can figure something out."

Dorian's blue eyes shone with a combination of pity and anger. "This Beckett wouldn't happen to be Lars Beckett, would it?"

"The very same," Owyn said. "My wife warned me not to take own a loan out from the king's own master of coin, and yet, did I listen?" He gave a weak laugh that was almost a cough. "Just, there has been little work since King Callahan closed the border to Thlarknians, and my daughter Claribel has possession sickness... ah, but you don't need my entire life's story."

Dorian shook his head ruefully and dug his hand into his belt pouch. A moment later, he procured a gold coin. An entire gold coin.

"What are you doing, Dorian?" Tai hissed from the corner of her mouth.

Owyn gazed wide-eyed at Dorian as if he were Lord Zekador

himself coming down for the Gifting of the Mystic Moon. "You are kind, but... I cannot accept this."

Dorian shook his head. "Take it. Lars Beckett used to be the banker in the town where I grew up. I'm well familiar with his predatory policies."

Owyn looked down at the gold coin as if it contained the secrets of the universe. "With this, I can... can buy some time. To get back on my feet, at the very least. Thank you, kind sir. Truly. Nahiira's blessing be upon you."

"He was probably making all that up about the sick daughter, you know," Tai told Dorian the moment they were out of earshot. "And what were you doing flashing that kind of coin? Do you want to get pickpocketed? Besides. I know you come from money, but you are aware Xander isn't paying you, right?"

Dorian's face reddened, and he scratched his neck. "You saw what those soldiers were doing to that poor man. I couldn't make them stop, but I had to do something." His hands curled into fists once more.

Tai's wings lowered, her annoyance already draining away. "It was decent of you," she admitted. This new boy was clueless, but at least he had a generous spirit. She hoped the rough life of an aeronaut wouldn't crush it out of him. "There have been times when I had trouble finding work and had to rely on the kindness of strangers. It's easy to forget that, sometimes."

Dorian examined the remains of his coins. "I should probably save most of this," he admitted, "But there were just a few things I wanted to pick up while we're here."

She looked on, wide-eyed, as he moved between the market stalls, purchasing great gnarled ginger roots and jars of honey, and even a linen sack of Orith sea salt.

"What's all this for, anyway?" she asked.

"For the galley on the *Phoenix*," Dorian said. Blushing slightly, he added, "I just thought it would be nice."

She opened her mouth to say more, then closed it again. It was his gold, after all. She just wished she could be as cavalier about her own gold. *Void Eternal*, these prices on aether crystals!

"Valgren save me," she moaned as she beheld a table lined with shining blue crystals, "I'd hoped to afford twice this much. Xander's gonna have my feathers."

Dorian shifted his weight between his feet. "I, uh, still have some more gold," he volunteered tentatively.

Tai shook her head. "No. Keep it. We'll make do, somehow."

Dorian's brow creased as looked down at their parcels. "I guess in the meantime, we could try to make the ship run more efficiently."

"Oh?" Tai asked. "You know much about aether engine efficiency, do you?"

Dorian's blush deepened. "Well, no. But..." He swallowed. "I was looking at it the other day, and I'm curious why you used the Greater Sigil of Zekador when the Lesser sigils of the physical and spiritual realms would work just as well."

Tai's wings flared. "You have a problem with the way I enchant the engine?"

Dorian spread his arms placatingly. "No, no, not at all... I... Sorry. Wasn't my place. It's true I don't know the first thing about skyships. Just... I've been told I have a talent for parsing out sigils." He stared at the ground, face red, as if even this small amount of self-praise were a bridge too far.

"Dorian," she said, hesitantly.

"Mmm?"

"Why are you here?"

"At the market? Because the captain ordered."

She rolled her eyes. "You know what I meant."

He didn't answer for what felt like a long time. Finally, he said, "I needed to disappear."

She twitched her wing. "You're a criminal?"

The boy didn't exactly look like a hardened delinquent. But then, she supposed it always was the ones you'd least suspect.

Dorian waved his hand. "No, no, nothing like that. Well. Not on purpose. It's..." he seemed to struggle to find words. "You know the new king the Kasani have?"

"Seems like a pleasant fellow." Tai lifted her wing in the Orith gesture of sarcasm. "What about him?"

Dorian took a deep breath. "Well. He, um, sort of wants to kill me."

"Be serious."

The glum look in his eyes told her he already was.

"Wings of the Savior," she swore in Toreenish. Switching back to the Kasani trade tongue, she said, "What in the Void are you doing wandering around a public market square?"

He waved his hand again, and quickly amended, "He thinks I'm already dead. So he's not actively looking for me. At least not yet. But if he found out I'm alive... Well then." he made a throat-slitting motion.

Tai bit her lip. "And why, exactly, does a king want to kill you?"

"It's... a kind of long story."

"We've got a long walk ahead of us."

He reddened, grimaced, and looked away. "I'm sorry," he said, eyes downcast. "I can't."

Tai thought about pressing the issue, but she knew it would do no good. She was becoming entirely too curious about this earnest, foolish boy, who expertly analyzed her sigilwork and freely gave coin to strangers. That would not do. She flared her wings and crossed her arms. "Fine," she said, "Do whatever you want. It's no concern of mine."

Yet even as she said it, she knew it wasn't true. A fifteenth-degree demon, and now the target of a malicious king? Whoever this boy was, Tai had a feeling that he was about to become all of their concerns, and much sooner than she'd like. She hoped Xander letting him on the *Phoenix* hadn't been a terrible mistake.

# CHAPTER THREE

# DRAGONS IN THE LINKING

There was no doubt about it, Dorian thought miserably. Joining the crew of skyship *Phoenix* was *definitely* a mistake.

It was a cool afternoon, but he'd never know it. Dorian's face, flushed with sweat, felt burning-hot even in the chill late winter air.

Another week had passed since they left Crimsonrock, making it two weeks since he left home. An exhausting two weeks, filled with endless hours of scullery, laundry, and, yes, deck swabbing. Which *did* simply mean scrubbing. But Dorian never realized before how exhausting deck scrubbing could be. All of his chores were exhausting.

But worst, worst by far, were the sword lessons.

"Lower your stance," Xander commanded.

Dorian did, and stepped back into a lunge, only to be greeted with an outraged squawk as Henrietta, one of the ship's hens, waddled away in an indignant cloud of white feathers.

"Do try not to trip on the chickens," Xander said patiently as he ushered the bird back into the coop. Mrs. Pennyfeather, the other hen, clucked in a way that Dorian could have sworn conveyed smug disapproval.

"I'd like to see you try it," Dorian muttered to the chicken under his breath.

Dorian knew, logically, that learning to fight was important. That if King Callahan ever caught word that Dorian lived, that he'd need to defend himself. And he supposed a part of him hoped that one day, if he ever encountered someone else being brutalized like that man in the marketplace, that he might do more to intervene.

«You gave him your coin,» Hematite pointed out. «That was far more helpful than putting yourself in danger.»

«Maybe,» Dorian allowed. But he'd hated standing there, terrified and helpless, while Callahan's hired bullies did what they pleased to the poor fellow. He should have been able to do more, Void curse him.

The way things stood now, though, Dorian wasn't sure he'd ever be able to beat King Callahan's soldiers in a fight. Dorian didn't think he could ever beat anyone.

"No, no, no," Xander shook his head, losing patience. "You're doing it all wrong. You have to keep your wrist out, like this."

The captain held out his sword arm in demonstration. The hilt of the wooden practice blade nestled easily in the captain's calloused fingers. Dorian attempted to follow the motion and raised his own weapon. His arm shook, just a little, from the effort of holding it steady.

"Better," Xander said. "Now let's see some more lunges, shall we?"

"Again, Sir?"

Dorian didn't mean to complain so much. Really, he didn't. But he was sore in places he hadn't even known existed. His arms felt like limp noodles. And his legs — he only wished he couldn't feel those. Even walking the short distance across the deck felt like agony.

«I told you,» Hematite said. «This is what adventuring is. Cold, wet, and miserable.»

Well. Dorian didn't feel cold, but he was damp with sweat, and certainly miserable.

"I'm sorry, Captain," he sighed, "My body simply wasn't meant to do this sort of thing."

"That remains to be seen," Xander grunted. "But no matter. I can see you've had enough for today."

"Thank you, Sir," Dorian said, trying and failing to hide his relief.

Exhausted, Dorian made his way over to the water barrel to refill his canteen. He'd never so much appreciated water, sweet, cool, glorious water, before he came on board the *Phoenix*. He eagerly gulped down the contents of his canteen, then refilled it again.

"Have a good training session?" asked his crew-mate Sullivan, smiling.

"Mmmm," Dorian said.

"What do you think of life in the skies so far?"

"It's..." Dorian began, but he wasn't sure how to finish the sentence. *Miserable? Exhausting? I don't belong here?*

"A little overwhelming?" Sullivan suggested.

Dorian nodded with a tentative smile. "Just a little."

"It gets better," Sullivan said. "If you stick with it."

Dorian found that hard to believe, but he forced himself to nod, anyway.

Sullivan clapped him gently on the shoulder. "You'll get there in time."

"Easy for you to say."

Sullivan chortled. "And you think I just emerged from the womb like this?"

Dorian responded with a shrug and an awkward smile. In all honesty, yes. Sullivan was Sullivan. Big and tough and unmovable. It amused Dorian, just a little, to think of a squalling baby Sullivan, already bulging with muscle, like those old paintings of the reborn god Zekador.

"Tell you what," Sullivan said. "Why not come join us in the Linking?"

Dorian gaped at the aeronaut. "J... join you?"

Sullivan nodded eagerly. "I really think you'll like it."

"But I... I don't know how to fly," Dorian gibbered.

Undeterred, Sullivan replied, "One way to learn, isn't there?"

Gesturing for Dorian to follow, Sullivan crossed the deck to the complicated spell circle shining bright blue against the dark wood. Sullivan beckoned to Dorian a second time before disappearing into the circle.

Dorian jumped as his crew-mate seemed to vanish. After nearly two weeks on the *Phoenix*, it still surprised him every time the aeronauts entered and exited the Linking.

"Well?" Sullivan's voice reverberated from the circle. "Are you coming?"

"I can't," Dorian's voice came out as a squeak.

"You can," Sullivan contradicted, his voice almost unnervingly calm.

Dorian sighed. "You're really going to make me do this, aren't you?"

Dorian took a nervous breath and swallowed. With the air of someone walking to his own execution, Dorian stepped into the spell circle and into another world.

Into a *better* world.

Dorian gasped. As soon as he passed through the circle, he floated freely, colorful motes of energy dancing back and forth. Here in the Linking, it seemed like all the colors were brighter. He laughed with delight at the wind rushing through his hair.

The ship floated behind him, ghostly and transparent, attached as if by an invisible tether. A part of him, yet also separate. The arcane symbols of the spell circle shone all around them, glowing brightly. Air and movement, balance and connection. And — *yes* — Tai actually followed his advice and replaced the Greater Sigil of Zekador with signs of physical and spirit energy. Dorian felt a little thrill of pride at that.

Beneath them lay the ever-present blanket of underclouds. Dorian watched in awe as a floating island receded from view, waterfalls raining down on the clouds below.

Dorian felt like a piece of him, missing for so much of his life, suddenly clicked back into place.

"Beautiful," he whispered.

"Isn't it?" Sullivan asked. He swam up beside Dorian with the effortless grace of a seasoned professional.

"Zekador's Pants, Dorian, *you're* in the Linking?" Falgar asked. "You can't even pull your own weight around here, much less the weight of the ship."

"Falgar," Sullivan said warningly.

Tai looked up in surprise, and for a second it almost looked like she was glad to see him there. That surely must have been his imagination, however. A moment later, she resumed her usual scowl and turned fixedly away from him, her black wings flapping steadily to keep her afloat.

"Does it help to do that?" Dorian asked without thinking.

"Of course not," she said, stilling her wings. However, Dorian noticed she started flapping them again a few moments later.

"Right," Xander said, swimming through the air to the head of their formation. "Now we're all here, we maneuver north."

Dorian learned how to swim in a lake years ago, as a child. Flying in the Linking wasn't so different. He moved his arms and legs, and somehow, miraculously, the ship moved behind him. He let out a high-pitched laugh of excitement. "Would you look at that!"

Falgar cocked a single eyebrow. "Ancients, Dorian, for some fancy rich boy, you are such a country bumpkin."

Dorian, however, only smiled. The Linking was far too wonderful to let Falgar's teasing get under his skin.

Dorian soon found, however, that flying the ship was a lot more complicated than swimming in a lake. He felt the strain, the push and pull of the magic. Move here against the air current, and the spell sigils shifted from green to yellow. Catch that thermal updraft, and the faltering sigils glowed strong blue. He'd seen spells like this, but only in books. The magical symbols must depict the strain on the engines. Push them too far into the red, and he'd shatter the aether crystal. Best to avoid that.

For the first time in weeks, Dorian grinned unabashedly. He was moving the ship! Under his own power! Just like a dashing sky pirate from one of the tales. Well. Perhaps minus the dashing part. He expected Hematite to make fun of him, but the demon was unusually silent. In fact, he realized he could barely sense Hematite's presence at all.

*Odd*, he thought, a prickle of unease dampening his enjoyment.

Like swimming through the water, swimming through the air was exhausting work. Before long, Dorian's limbs started burning with the effort. He heaved for breath and wished fervently that he'd thought to bring his canteen with him.

His body protested more and more as the flight wore on. He fell behind, a little at first, then more and more. To his shame and horror, the ship slowed down, too. The spell circle shifted from blue to a sickly yellow green. *I'm holding the others back*, he realized with dismay.

Nobody else in the Linking seemed to be tired. They weren't even breathing hard. For a moment, he allowed himself to just watch them work, so graceful, so competent. *Gods*, how he wished he could fly like them.

The chain of Dorian's pendant tugged at his neck. Right now, the dragonstone, and everything it represented, seemed a heavy burden, dragging him downward towards the underclouds.

*Wait. No.* It wasn't just his imagination. The pendant really was pointing downward, and slightly to the east. He blinked in the direction the dragonstone pointed.

*What in the Void?*

Off in the distance, several brightly colored objects flew in formation. Too large and few in number to be migratory birds, but too small to be more skyships. Ornithopters? This far from land? Unlikely. Was this just a vision brought on by the ambient magical energy?

"Um," he said, trying to get the attention of his crew-mates, "Um, what's that over there?"

They ignored him. Frustrated, he strained himself to catch up with Tai, who was closest. "Um, sorry," he repeated, catching his breath, "But, um, there's something strange over there, and I, um, think you should see it."

"Void's sake," Tai complained. "Jumping at shadows now, are we?" But she fluttered over to see what it was, and her eyes widened in surprise when she saw where he pointed. "That can't be right. Captain! I think you need to see this."

"Oh?" the captain replied, swim-flying over. "What in Zekador's name? Valmont, can you cast a magnification spell?"

"Oh!" Dorian said. "I think so."

Dorian reached for the athame attached to his belt. In his nerves, he fumbled and nearly dropped it, but caught it in time. He didn't know what would happen if he dropped something in the Linking, and he didn't want to find out. Dorian could just imagine his only spell-knife tumbling end over end down to the clouds below. It wasn't like he could write to Stewardess Tahlia and ask for a new one.

Tightly gripping the leather-wrapped handle, Dorian traced the sigils into the air. Location, displacement, physical manifestation. The surrounding air flickered and rippled, converging together in the shape of a lens. What he saw on the other side nearly made his heart stop. It should have been impossible. It *was* impossible.

"Bloody Void," Captain Xander said, sounding almost impressed.

*Bloody Void indeed,* Dorian thought. Six dragons flew in a tight v-formation, gemstone-bright scales glittering in the sunlight. Even more remarkably, the dragons appeared to have humans riding on their backs.

"Dragonauts," Tai whispered. "But how? I mean, they're just legends, right?"

"It's some kind of Illusion," Dorian said, voice quavering. "It has to be."

He scanned for the telltale signs of Illusion magic — blurred edges, over-saturated colors. But the dragons looked solid to him.

"That's no bloody illusion," Xander said. "Void Eternal. She actually did it. Unless... oh, no. No, no no."

Dorian felt a cold prickle on the back of his neck. He'd only known the captain for a couple of weeks, but Xander didn't seem the type to scare easily. The tone of his voice was downright chilling.

"Zoom in further," Xander commanded.

Dorian quickly obliged with a flick of his spell knife. And then, in shock and horror, he dropped his athame. Fortunately, it hovered in front of him and didn't fall. But the knife was the last thing on his mind.

The sight of the lead dragonaut's familiar face, partially hidden by an all-too-recognizable helmet, hit Dorian like a punch to the gut. Captain Xander looked little better.

"Janus Callahan," Xander whispered, as though the name were a curse.

"The king of Kasanarae?" Tai wondered. "What's he doing way out here?"

Dorian's heart pounded in his chest. "He found me." How had Callahan tracked him down so quickly? He'd not even lasted two weeks! Had Bradford turned him in? Why bother helping Dorian at all, only to betray him? Or had the man he'd helped in the market-place passed his description to Lars Beckett, who reported it to the king?

"*No good deed goes unpunished,*" King Callahan's cruel, sardonic tone echoed in his head.

"I thought you said he thought you were dead," Tai said.

"You're telling me," said Falgar, "That the King of Kasanarae is out there," he waved towards the dragons, "On a dragon, because of him?" He gave Dorian a look of utter disbelief.

"Not because of him," Xander said, his voice quiet, grave. "Because of me."

"What?" Tai asked.

"Evasive maneuvers!" the Captain barked.

"But I don't—" Falgar began.

"I'll explain when we get out of here. I said, evasive maneuvers, *now*."

Falgar kicked out his legs to move the ship. But he hadn't gotten far before he turned back towards the others, his face a mask of horror. "They're casting a spell. It almost looks like... Meroneth's balls! They're provoking a Voidstorm! On purpose!"

Black clouds rolled in with unnatural speed, blotting out the sun. Lightning arced across the sky. They had barely an instant to react before a powerful gust of wind slammed the *Phoenix* with the force of a battering ram. Sigil after sigil went straight from blue to red as the Linking reverberated with unstable energy.

Dorian spun end over end like a child's toy gyroscope. "Help!" He gasped to no one in particular as he tried and failed to right himself.

Something strange shifted inside Dorian. The world seemed to slow down. He felt, slowly at first, then more rapidly, Hematite's presence reasserting itself within him.

«I do not believe this,» the demon complained. «Honestly, of all the foolish, most asinine things. I told you that you had no business being in the Linking. And now I must set everything right. Typical human. Always getting into trouble.»

The creature of silver-black sapphire flame jumped out of Dorian and charged the storm head on. Dorian could only watch in awe and terror as Hematite dashed and darted through the roiling clouds. Slowly, miraculously, the storm abated. The faltering Linking sigils returned, not quite to blue, but at least to an acceptable greenish-yellow.

Time snapped back to normal, and Hematite plunged back into Dorian with a surge of ice.

"What in the Void?" Sullivan's eyes practically popped out of his head. "Was that the demon? He just saved our lives!"

Dorian opened his mouth to answer, but before he could do so, another gale force wind rocked the ship. Hematite had weakened the storm, but not banished it entirely. Dorian crashed into Sullivan, and the two of them fell together, careening towards the edge of the Linking. Sullivan swore and grabbed Dorian's hand, and they spilled onto the deck, back in the "real" world at last.

The firsts things Dorian heard were Henrietta and Mrs. Pennyfeather's disgruntled shrieks. Safe in the chicken coop, they'd at least managed not to fall overboard, but he understood their indignation. The deck was a mess.

«Foolish, reckless boy!» the demon Hematite cried out with the frightened anger of an overprotective parent. «What did you think you were doing, entering the Linking during a Voidstorm?»

«I didn't know there was going to be a Voidstorm,» Dorian responded crossly. How in the Void was he supposed to have predicted that? «What did you do back there, anyway?»

«Kept your foolish and reckless hide alive, for which you are welcome, by the way,» Hematite said.

"Well," Dorian said, heart pounding, "Thank you."

Whatever Hematite did, it worked. The *Phoenix* still trembled in the turbulence, but at least now the ship flew true. To Dorian's relief, he saw no sign of the enemy dragonauts. But that gave him little comfort. The *Phoenix* had survived one attack, but Dorian had a feeling worse was to come. Did Callahan know Dorian was onboard? How in the Void had he gotten a dragon? And what did Captain Xander mean that the king was after him, too? Had he fled from the proverbial frying pan only to land in the proverbial fire? He forced himself to take several calming breaths. One thing at a time.

"Thanks for getting me out of the Linking, Sullivan. I never would have — Sullivan? Are you okay?" With some clumsy effort, Dorian climbed to his feet. But the burly aeronaut did not follow suit.

Sullivan clearly wasn't okay. He lay twitching on the deck, right arm splayed out at an unnatural angle. Undeniably broken.

"Oh, no. Oh, Void." Dorian tried to help Sullivan up, but it was no use. Sullivan was heavy with muscle, and Dorian was weak, so weak. *Useless as always.* "Someone help," he called into the Linking circle, fighting back tears. "Sullivan's hurt. I don't know what to do."

Falgar emerged a moment later, eyes wide, face twisted into a horrified sneer. "Void eternal, rich boy. What did you do to him?"

With practiced efficiency, Falgar hoisted the larger aeronaut into a fireman's carry. Dorian could only slump miserably against the railing, panting for breath. He wanted to cry.

Dorian recalled thinking, for a few blissful moments, that he belonged in the Linking.

*Well.* Look what became of that. Hematite might have saved them, but Dorian himself was worse than useless.

Dorian couldn't even make himself process everything that had just happened. Callahan, attacking them from the back of a dragon. Hematite, neutralizing a Voidstorm. All of that felt distant and dreamlike. But one thing stood out to him with overwhelming clarity. Sullivan. Kind, hard-working Sullivan, friendly to everyone, always eager to help, was badly hurt. And it was all Dorian's fault.

"Oh, Ancients," Dorian said. "Not again."

# CHAPTER FOUR
# DEMON IN THE FORTRESS

Dorian scrambled to catch up with his father on the steep mountain pass. He laughed as he ran, delighting in the wind running through his shaggy copper hair.

Groves of golden aspen dotted the verdant hillside, signalling the end of summer at last. As the moon of Ripening gave way to the moon of Stone, the sun shone brightly in a crisp, cloudless blue sky. It was a glorious day, and not just because of the weather. After years of being left in his nurse's care while his father traveled the world hunting Ancient treasure, Dorian was at last old enough to come along.

"Is it true there used to be dragons where we're going?" Nine-year-old Dorian bobbed up and down with enthusiasm.

Cyrus Valmont laughed and ruffled his son's hair. "That's right," he said. "Icereach Castle was one of the great fortresses of the Ancient dragonauts."

"Was it the biggest fortress?" Dorian had to jog to keep up with his father's long stride.

"Not the biggest, no," Cyrus said. "That would've been Grey-stone, in Thlarknia. Though Cloudfire, in Toreen was a near match for size."

"Oh," Dorian said, disappointed. "I'd hoped Icereach was the biggest."

"Icereach still boasts a proud history," Cyrus said. "It was the fortress of Roderick Torvald, the first dragonaut."

"Lord Zekador was the first dragonaut," Dorian protested.

Cyrus laughed. "In the legends, perhaps, but those are only stories. Roderick Torvald was the first *known* dragonaut."

Dorian shrugged. He didn't have time to argue about something as stuffy and boring as religion. Not when there was an Ancient fortress to explore. "All right, well, this Torvald guy. What was he like? Did he come from here? From Adenthul?"

"That's right," Cyrus responded. "Though it wasn't called Aden-thul, back then. All of this was part of the Kasani Empire in the old days."

"How come we've never come to Adenthul before now?"

Cyrus didn't answer for a long time. Finally, he said, "Your nurse doesn't like it."

"Is that why Rowena stayed behind in Kasanarae?"

"Full of questions today, aren't we?" Cyrus gave a strained-sounding chuckle. "And she's your Nurse, not Rowena."

Dorian crossed his skinny, boyish arms. "I will not call her Nurse. I'm nine years old, not a baby. Besides. When are you just going to marry her already? Then she'll be my Mother in truth and I could just call her that."

Cyrus coughed and pointedly ignored the question. Dorian saw Cyrus kissing Rowena three days ago, but he didn't think Cyrus knew that.

"Is it true the dragonauts used to fly to the moon?" Dorian asked, ever quick to change the subject.

"Most scholars think so, though how they travelled so far or what they did when they got there is unclear."

"Sooooo," Dorian extended the word. "Is that why we're coming here now? Portals to the moon?"

Cyrus laughed. "If there were ever portals to the moon, I know nothing of them. But an old contact of mine wanted me to investigate... clues. Within the fortress itself. About the magic that created the dragon bond to begin with."

"Well, everyone knows that." Dorian rolled his eyes. "Zekador sacrificed all his God powers to turn the demons into dragons."

Cyrus snorted. "I told you already. Zekador is just a legend. And besides. If the demons all turned into dragons, why are there still demons?"

Dorian didn't know what to say to that, so instead, he picked a stick up off the ground. "I want to be a dragonaut," he declared. He swung the stick as if it were a sword. "I'll be the greatest swordsman in the world, and me and my dragon are gonna fight for *justice*!"

"Then the evils of the world will have found a formidable foe indeed. Though the dragonauts of old were not just warriors, but scholars and magi as well, so mind you, pay close attention to your studies, yes?"

"Yeah, yeah."

They rounded a corner, and the crumbling fortress came into view. Dorian gasped in astonishment. Two of the four massive turrets had crumpled, and ivy now dominated the stonework. But even thus dilapidated, Icereach Castle was magnificent.

As the uneven dirt hiking trail gave way to a worn stone staircase, however, Cyrus lost all pretense of joviality. He put a worried hand on his son's shoulder. "We're not alone here."

Two handsome gryphons stood tethered to a tree near the castle entrance. The eagle-headed felines looked faintly bored as they watched a dragonfly dart between the shrubberies.

"Zekador's poorly fitting pants, Father," another boy's voice complained. "Why did you have to drag me out to the middle of nowhere? I wanted to go riding, not traipse around some dusty ruins."

"Now Bradford," came a second voice, a man's. "The old fortress is part of our lands. If you're to be lord of Frostvale one day, you must come along on the routine inspections, too."

Cyrus's hand tightened on Dorian's shoulder.

The boy, who Dorian saw was only a year or two older than himself, kicked at the dirt with a polished leather boot. "When I'm lord, I'll hire people to do the boring stuff."

The older man's thin mouth narrowed, but he said nothing. Instead, he spun around and fixed Dorian and Cyrus with a piercing stare. The temperature in the courtyard seemed to go several degrees colder.

"Ah," the man said. "Our guests have arrived."

"Guests?" Dorian blurted before he could stop himself. The strange man made it sound like he expected them. Cyrus squeezed Dorian's shoulder in warning.

The stranger was a stately-looking gentleman, well-dressed in blue leather riding gear. He wore his brown hair tied back in a tight ponytail, receding hairline displaying an impressive amount of forehead.

"Janus," Cyrus said stiffly. "They led me to believe Jameson would be my contact."

"Try to be logical, Cyrus," the man, Janus, replied. "Would you have answered my summons if you thought it came from me?"

"This was a bad idea," Cyrus said. "Dorian, let's go."

"Aren't you the least bit curious about what's in that fortress?" Janus asked.

"Not if you've got anything to do with it," Cyrus said.

"Come off it, Cyrus," Janus said. "I am not the wounded party here."

The curly-haired boy, who must've been Janus's son, rolled his eyes. "Grown-ups," he scoffed. "Always speaking in riddles. I'm Bradford Callahan. I'll be Lord of this entire region one day. That means I gotta do boring stuff, like inspect this castle, but it also means everyone's gotta do what I say."

Bradford extended his hand. Dorian took it, a little uncertainly. Bradford had a tight grip for a boy of only eleven.

"Right," Cyrus said, frowning. "Dorian, you stay out here with the Callahan boy. Try... try not to get in trouble."

Dorian didn't think he'd ever seen his father looking so distraught. But then, his words actually sunk in. "Wait. We're not coming with you?"

"No," Cyrus said, "No, no, I'm afraid it's not safe."

"But we came all this way!"

"I quite agree." Bradford unexpectedly rose to Dorian's defense. "Why drag us all the way out here just to leave us in the courtyard?"

Janus made a guttural sound in the back of his throat. "Because I am your father and you will do as I say."

Cyrus drew Dorian closer to him. "Hate me if you must," he said, his voice a harsh whisper. "But leave the boy out of this."

"You needn't worry, Cyrus. The boy will be perfectly safe with my son."

Somehow, the haughty tone in Janus Callahan's voice made Dorian wonder if maybe he was in danger after all. Just who was this strange man?

Cyrus looked warily at the strangers, then at Dorian. "Very well," he said, with great reluctance. "I changed my mind. Dorian, it's best you stick with me. But stay close to my side, and do not wander off. Am I understood?"

"Yes, father," Dorian said, though it chafed to be treated like a boy no older than five.

"If he's going, I demand to go, too," Bradford said.

"Oh, very well." Janus heaved a long sigh. Dorian swore he could hear the man's teeth grinding. "Come along if you must."

It was a tense party that made their way through the fortress entrance. Bradford had a point. Why had their fathers dragged them all the way out here, only to waffle over whether they should enter the fortress? Something about Janus Callahan's arrival caught Dorian's father off his guard. But that didn't explain Callahan's own behavior.

As Dorian's feet crunched on the dusty cobblestones of the fortress, however, Dorian soon all but forgot strangers. They were walking where the Ancients once tread!

Dorian fantasized he was a famous Ancient dragonaut, going up to the launch platform to meet with his glorious dragon, and take off into the wild freedom of the skies. Still holding the stick he picked up earlier, he swished it back and forth, pretending it was a dragon-hilted sword of old.

"What are you doing?" Bradford Callahan asked.

"Ah. Nothing." Dorian dropped the stick in embarrassment. But he felt a small pang of regret as he left it behind in the hallway.

Cyrus, however, seemed to have a worse time. The further they traversed the empty catacombs, the more agitated he became. He kept scratching his neck in consternation and looking down at his map.

"This can't be right," Cyrus said. "This surely can't be right."

"Trust me, it isn't much longer," Janus Callahan said. "You're the only one who can help us with this. Please understand, I would not have written to you if I didn't desperately need your expertise."

But Janus's reassurances only seemed to increase Cyrus's unease.

Dorian wasn't sure why his father seemed so afraid. The boy, Bradford, was right. The fortress wasn't dangerous. If anything, he decided, it was a bit boring.

Or, at least, he thought it was, until he saw a flickering blue light shining from a side passage. An aether deposit?

"I'm going to look over there!" Dorian didn't wait for a response before sprinting down the corridor.

Cyrus took off after him. "Dorian, wait!"

When Dorian reached the light source, he skidded to a halt, transfixed. A creature the likes of which he'd never seen, lizard-like and swathed in a mane of blue fire, sat alone in the chamber. It had a hairless, slick black hide that seemed to shimmer with silver in the light of its own flames. The creature twitched its tail back and forth, and seemed to flicker in and out of existence.

"Are you... are you a dragon?" Dorian asked in awe.

«A dragon? Me?» the words, laced with mock indignation, sounded clearly in Dorian's head.

"Hematite," Cyrus breathed, staggering into the chamber. He raised his athame, placing himself between Dorian and the creature. He let out a bitter chuckle. "First Callahan and now this."

«A reckoning indeed,» the creature said. «It appears not even the great Cyrus Valmont is immune to the consequences of his actions.»

"Get out of here, Dorian," Cyrus warned. "That's a demon there. My demon, gods curse it."

"Your demon?"

But before Cyrus could explain further, several things happened at once.

First, the ground started shaking. Pebbles danced up and down on the stone floor.

"Meroneth's balls," Cyrus swore. "A skyquake? Now?"

«This is no ordinary skyquake!»

Apparently frightened, the demon's gaze darted rapidly from Dorian to Cyrus, and then back to Dorian. The ground shuddered again, more violently this time. Dorian lost his footing and collapsed onto the uneven stone floor just in time to hear the unmistakable sound of breaking stone. A crack appeared in the ceiling and spread.

Eyes wide with terror, Dorian fought to stand back up. But as if in a nightmare, his body refused to obey, even as dust and then increasingly large chunks of shattered rock fell upon them.

The creature lunged towards Dorian, jumping onto him — no, jumping *into* him. Searing cold surged through every inch of Dorian's body. He must've blacked out, because when he came to, he lay on his back, gazing up at the remains of the ruined ceiling. The rest of the chamber was in shambles, tumbledown remnants of wall and ceiling now obstructing the place where Dorian fell. What had happened? Was he thrown during the quake? Where was his father?

*Oh, sweet Gods and Ancients. "Father!"*

Dorian struggled to stand. His blood felt like someone had turned it into ice. Heart pounding, he staggered over to the pile of rubble where he and his father stood not a moment before.

"F... father," he said again, his voice coming out a choked whimper.

Cyrus Valmont lay unmoving, his face ashen and pale, half covered under an unsteady heap of ruined wall. Dorian removed the stones as quickly as he could. Handfuls of rock and rubble, tossed to the side. He coughed, and he sobbed, but he kept working.

«I am afraid there is no saving him,» the demon, Hematite said.

Dorian blinked back tears, refusing to heed the creature's words. «He was right next to me,» Dorian said. «I was fine, so he should be fine too.»

«No,» Hematite said, «Dorian, listen to me. I have... created a bond between us. With it, I could move you to safety. But I could only save one of you. I am sorry.» To the demon's credit, he at least sounded sincere. But Dorian was in no mood to hear it.

"Father," Dorian sobbed. He picked up Cyrus's hand, searching for a pulse like Rowena once taught him. "Father, come on, you can't be dead."

"He's dead."

Dorian jumped. For a second, he thought it was the demon again. But no. Behind him, short of breath, stood Janus Callahan, his ponytail half undone, his clothes rumpled and dusty. Bradford Callahan stood to the side, eyes wide with horror, clutching his father's torn cape like a much younger boy.

"He's not dead," Dorian said, knowing he, too, sounded childish. "I just have to uncover him. I have to..."

"Come with me, boy," Janus said. He put a hand on Dorian's shoulder, an awkward gesture from someone obviously not used to physical comfort. But perhaps the man meant well.

"I need to find my nurse," Dorian said. He was gibbering now, but he didn't know what else to do. Rowena would know. Rowena

could help him. "Her name's Rowena Selene, she's in Kasanarae —
she —"

"Your nurse will be notified, but she was an employee of your
father's, not... equipped... to rear a child by herself."

"But—" Dorian gaped at the man.

"I know you are distraught," Lord Callahan said, "But we must
discuss your future."

"My... my what?" Dorian's young mind barely processed the
words. The future? His father was buried under a mountain of
rubble. His world had ended. There was no future.

"Whatever differences we had later in life, your father was once
my dear friend." Janus Callahan swallowed as if tasting something
bitter. "That is, I think it best that... that I should be the one to take
you in."

"Take me... in?" Dorian couldn't make the words make sense. It
was as if Callahan was speaking in an unfamiliar language. His
father was dead, and this man, this Lord Callahan, wanted to take
Dorian in?

«This man offers you his generosity,» Hematite said.

As the demon spoke, Dorian thought he caught a flash of blue
flame out of the corner of his eye. Lord Callahan must have seen it
too, because his eyebrows shot upwards. "What have we here?"

Hematite sprung forth, seemingly out of nowhere, and perched
himself on Dorian's shoulder.

"Hematite Bloodstone of the quiet pond." Callahan's voice held
just a hint of mockery. "This boy's awfully young to be a demon host,
isn't he?"

The demon wrapped his tail lightly around Dorian, in what
seemed like a protective gesture.

"He... he saved my life, I think," Dorian put in, not sure why he
felt the sudden need to defend the creature.

"And let your father die," Callahan said coldly. "I see. Well, let us
hope you are worth it. Come along, then."

It was too much. All entirely too much. Sobbing, terrified, Dorian bolted. He knew he wasn't thinking clearly. Where did he expect to go? Back to town? It seemed as good an option as any, and right then, Dorian didn't care about being sensible.

Dorian slipped on a rock and lost his footing, collapsing on the dirt path with a force that knocked the wind from his lungs. Blood spilled from a scrape on his elbow, and tears streamed from his face.

«Please,» said the demon. «Think about what you are doing. How will you pay for passage all the way to Kasanarae without your father's coin? What skyship will invite a scared and dirty unattended child?»

Dorian didn't want to hear the demon's logic. «You should have let me die,» he said. «You should have saved him.»

Janus Callahan hurried down the path, extending his hand to help Dorian up. "Do not make this more difficult than it needs to be. Keep up this reckless behavior, and you'll only get more people hurt or killed."

All at once, Dorian felt the fight drain out of him.

"It was my fault, wasn't it?" Dorian choked back a sob.

If he had not insisted on going into the fortress, if he had stayed in the courtyard with Bradford, if he had not wandered off on his own. If Hematite hadn't tried to save Dorian instead. Then his father would still be alive.

"Perhaps," Lord Callahan said curtly. "But there is nothing to be done about it now."

«Your father would have wanted me to save you,» The demon sent a warm wave of reassurance through Dorian, but Dorian flinched away from it. He didn't want empty platitudes, not from a demon or from anyone else.

"The demon will give you power if you know how to nurture it," Callahan said matter-of-factly.

"I don't want power." Dorian suddenly felt small. "I want my dad back!"

«Even the gods lack that power,» Hematite said sadly. «But as long as you are mine, I shall protect you.»

"Just get on the gryphon," Callahan said impatiently.

"I don't know how to ride," Dorian said. It felt strange to voice such a mundane, practical concern in the face of all the other horrors of the day.

"You can ride with me," the boy, Bradford, offered. "I won't let you fall."

Defeated, Dorian followed the Callahans back to their gryphons. But on that long, miserable flight to the town of Frostvale, Dorian wished with all his heart that he was the one lying dead in that ruined chamber.

# CHAPTER FIVE

# LATE NIGHT PONDERINGS

*PRESENT DAY*

Tai couldn't sleep.

Uncharitably, she felt inclined to blame the new boy, who snored like a Thlarknian mining cart. But that was unfair of her. She'd always had trouble sleeping ever since she left Orith. Besides. She didn't hear any snoring from the adjacent cabin tonight.

She sat up, stretched her wings, and glanced out her small porthole window. No moon tonight, only stars, strewn across the sky like a ribbon of glitter. Even moonless nights seemed impossibly bright for Tai, who was used to uninterrupted darkness.

Tai paused and listened. Not only did she not hear Dorian's snores, but she also didn't hear any breathing or creaking cot springs. Tai suspected she wasn't the only one unable to sleep. Frowning, she jumped down off of her bunk and slid open the cabin door.

Some skyship crews flew in shifts throughout the night, but their crew was small, and an older vessel like the *Phoenix* could use the rest as much as the aeronauts. So every night, Tai and the others cast spell anchors to ensure the vessel didn't drift too far. She checked the safety wards, thin lines of runic light surrounding the hovering skycraft. So far, they'd not detected so much as a pigeon. The *Phoenix* was alone in the empty sky.

Along the wall, the aether lamps set in brass wall sconces glowed a faint nighttime red. But down the corridor towards the galley, a brighter yellow light flickered, accompanied by the telltale sound of rustling. "Found you," she muttered, with the slightest hint of a smile.

Dorian stood in the galley under the light of a single aether lantern, tongue stuck out in concentration as he stirred a wooden bowl of thick, sticky dough.

"Up late, aren't you?"

Dorian jumped and dropped the wooden spoon on the table, splattering gobs of moistened flour across the table.

"Oh... oh no," Dorian said, hurriedly wiping down the mess with the corner of his apron.

"Hey, sorry, sorry, didn't mean to scare you," Tai raised her hands placatingly. "Just... um... what are you doing?"

"Baking a pie," Dorian said. He stared at the ground with the air of someone caught trying to burgle the Crown Jewels of Vatea.

"In the middle of the night?"

"I intended to share it," Dorian said quickly. "I mean. I'm not that greedy. Pie for everyone."

"Oh," Tai said, running an awkward hand through her hair. Here she was, complaining about him nonstop, and here he was, baking pie for the crew. "Oh, sorry. Didn't mean to ruin the surprise."

Dorian scratched his neck. "It's... not a surprise, exactly. I, uh, like to bake, when I'm sad or worried, it... helps me think. But I'm sorry, I, uh, didn't mean to wake you." He grimaced.

"You didn't wake me." Tai sighed, "I have trouble sleeping during the best of times. But is it something I can help with?"

"You can whisk one of those eggs there," Dorian said, pointing at a bowl of Henrietta's fresh brown eggs.

"Oh!" Tai said, smiling despite herself. That wasn't what she'd meant by her offer to help, but whisking some eggs was bound to be a lot easier than solving whatever was actually bothering him.

"So... you're really not upset?" Dorian asked.

"Why would I be upset?" Tai cracked the egg into a small ceramic bowl and disposed of the shell in the compost bin.

Dorian's face reddened. "Well... Callahan used to hate it when I'd go down to the manor kitchens. 'Beneath my dignity as a representative of the household,' he called it."

Tai snorted as she picked up a whisk from the supply shelf and set about whipping the egg into a frothing yellow mixture. "That's stupid."

"Not something you'd want to say to his face." Dorian glanced at her and added, "Actually, you might get away with it, if anyone could."

Tai raised her eyebrows. "And what's that supposed to mean?"

Dorian flushed, perhaps realizing he'd said too much. "Only that you're a bit, ah... nothing. Never mind." Dorian pointedly did not look at her as he set about opening a jar of preserved plums with gusto.

"You're scared of me," Tai said, mouth drawing into a wicked grin.

Dorian made a noncommittal noise that sounded like "Eemph" and dumped the sticky contents into another bowl.

"I promise I don't bite," Tai said. "Much."

Tai hadn't been aware a human face could go as red as Dorian's did. "I... that is... it's just that you're so..." he waved his free hand, "Talented, and confident, and good at flying, and..."

Tai enjoyed needling the boy. "Why Dorian," she said, "Are you flirting with me? I'm afraid I'm focused on my career right now, but it's flattering all the same." She batted her eyes.

Had she thought his face couldn't go any redder? She'd been

wrong. "No!" His voice came out with a choked squawk. "I mean... you're quite pretty... not that I would... but the thing is... I'm already courting someone." He let out that last bit in one frantic breath.

"Oh," Tai said, sitting down and sucking on her proverbial foot. *Well done, Tai.* Taking the joke too far, as always. Just because Dorian was bumbling and awkward didn't mean he was all alone.

Poor Dorian only wanted to bake a pie. It occurred to her far too late that she was probably bothering him. "I'm sorry, I shouldn't have... I can go. "

"No," Dorian said, seeming to regain calm. "I appreciate the help, really. Do you, ah, think you could grate some of that ginger?" He gestured at a gnarled brown root on the table. She recognized it as a spice he'd bought with his precious remaining coin.

"Sure." Tai picked up the ginger and the grater, glad for something to keep her hands busy. "I've never had ginger in a plum pie before."

"It's pretty good," Dorian said, brightening, "At least, I think so." With a sardonic, self-deprecating half smile, he patted his stomach and said, "I know a thing or two about food."

Tai snorted. "I'll take your word."

They worked in silence for a time, him occasionally asking for some crystallized honey or a pinch of salt, but otherwise saying little. *Baking a pie.* She smiled and shook her head. Tai hadn't baked a pie since she and her former lover Kadmin parted ways. But somehow, helping the new boy with his grated ginger felt more natural, more companionable, than baking for Kadmin ever had. She swatted the notion aside like it was an irksome gnat. The last thing she wanted to do was think about Kadmin.

Finally, the pie and mixture were complete, and Tai watched with fascination as Dorian assembled the pieces. He took great care with the top of the pie, molding the remaining dough into a cross-hatch pattern and shaping little dough berries and leaves for decoration.

"That's beautiful," Tai commented.

Dorian flushed yet again. "Thanks," he said. "I could do better with all my tools in the manor kitchen, but I have to say, this ship galley's pretty well equipped."

"We do our best," Tai said.

He placed the pie in the cast iron oven and toggled the knob on the aether range. "Now, the hard part. Waiting, and cleaning up."

Tai nodded and looked with dismay at the pile of dirty bowls and utensils. "I'm afraid there are no servants to pick up after us here."

She meant it lightheartedly, but the despondent expression on his face told her she'd gone too far yet again. *Void Eternal.* Did she always have to say the worst possible thing?

Dorian shook his head. "Lord Callahan might not have liked it, but he couldn't completely bar me from the kitchens. Stewardess Tahlia could. And that's precisely what she would have done, if I'd expected the servants to clean up after me."

"Smart woman," Tai said with a smirk.

She wondered what it must've been like to grow up in a big manor house. True, it was clearly not all fun and games. Dorian wouldn't be here if it were. But Tai's own family hadn't exactly been generous with affection. If you were going to be the purple glowyrm of the family regardless, she reasoned, better that they be a rich family. But then she remembered those dragons, and that Voidstorm, and she gave an involuntary shudder. Tai's family might find her incomprehensible, but at least they never tried to kill her.

"So did it help?" Tai asked, taking a dishrag from the hook on the wall and getting to work on the bowl she'd been using.

"Oh, yeah, thanks," Dorian said. "Truth be told, I hate grating the ginger, so I'm glad I had your help for that."

"I mean baking. You said you did it when you're upset. So... did it help?"

Dorian sighed, wringing his own dishrag out into the washbasin. "I... maybe. I don't know."

Tai bit her lip. She didn't want to pry where it wasn't her business, but taking a risk, she said, "If... if it's something you want to talk about, I promise I'm not as scary as I seem."

She gave him a hopeful smile, which he returned, albeit sadly. He spent several long moments scrubbing the dough bowl with perhaps greater than normal concentration, and Tai thought he would not answer. But then, at length, he said, "I think... maybe it's best... that is, next time we land somewhere sufficiently far away... I should probably leave the crew."

"You can't!" Tai blurted, surprised at the vehemence in her own voice.

He raised his eyebrows. "I thought you wanted me off the ship."

"I... did," Tai admitted, once again feeling shame bubble up inside her. "But... you just got here!"

Dorian spread his hands helplessly. "You saw those dragons. They were after me."

"You don't know that," Tai said.

He shook his head. "If I stay, I'm just putting everyone in danger."

"Sounds to me like Xander knew full well what's happening with this Callahan guy," Tai said. "If he thinks this is the safest place for you to be, then it probably is."

"I don't know. Maybe if I were..." Dorian stared wistfully at the ceiling. But he shook his head again, and then buried it in his hands. "But I'm not, and that's that."

"Maybe if you were what?" Tai asked.

Dorian looked at her, a thousand conflicted emotions creating a miniature storm in his wide, expressive eyes. Gods, she thought, unbidden, he really had gorgeous eyes, precisely the color of the late afternoon sky. But he looked so miserable. Just then, all she wanted to do was embrace him and tell him everything would be okay, to somehow make everything okay. *Ridiculous.* She barely knew him. She had neither the duty nor, most likely, the capability to fix his problems for him. But gods, it hurt to see him looking so distraught.

"The thing is," Dorian began, "For a minute there, when I was in the Linking, it was… I was…" He traced a knot on the tabletop with his finger. The sadness in his eyes gave way somewhat, his brows furrowing into an expression of fierce longing.

"You liked it," Tai guessed. "Flying in the Linking."

Dorian opened his mouth and closed it several times, clearly still searching for words. Finally, he nodded.

Tai paused and folded her hands in front of her, taking in the mouthwatering aroma of baking plums. "If you wanted to become a proper aeronaut," she said at length, "I don't see any reason you couldn't."

Dorian laughed, a bitter, hollow sound. "An aeronaut? Me? Five minutes in that Linking was enough to make my arms feel like they were going to fall off. How in the Void am I supposed to hold my own like a real aeronaut?"

Tai sighed and twitched her wings. "So you're a little out of shape. It happens. Use the training equipment in the cargo hold if it bothers you. It's there for everyone."

For a second, a look of hope crossed his features.

"Listen," Tai said. "I've… been unfair to you. The truth is, I think I was jealous."

Dorian blinked. "Jealous? Why?"

"Xander let you on the ship without question," she said. "Do you know how long it took me to get a job? I had all the qualifications, even some solid experience under my belt. But most crews turned me away at first glance."

"Why would they do that? You're a great aeronaut."

Tai responded with a sad smile. "Thank you. But. Well. How many Orith do you know who work on skyships?"

Dorian blinked. "Um, including you? One. But I, um, also only know one Orith. And only about four aeronauts." He flushed again. "Sorry."

Tai shook her head. "Thing is… there's no magic beneath the underclouds. So my people, we… don't exactly have a reputation for being great at it."

"But that's ridiculous," Dorian said. "You can do stuff with runes and sigils that I couldn't even imagine." He sighed and rubbed the back of his neck. "So here you are, struggling to get any work as an aeronaut. And then along comes me, who's never stepped into a Linking in my life, and the captain just lets me climb on board." Dorian heaved in a deep breath and let it out. "Void Eternal. No wonder you were upset."

"But it was petty of me, and wrong," Tai said. "The thing is... I guess I know what it's like to be judged unfairly based on my appearance. So what I'm saying is, I'm sorry."

He smiled. He really had a pleasant smile. "You really think I could? Be a real aeronaut, I mean?"

She shrugged, wings twitching. "Sure."

For a second, blissful longing crossed his face. But then he shook his head and said, "I'm sure you're just being nice."

"You must not know me very well. I never say things just to be nice." She shook her head and drew in a deep breath, taking in the tantalizing fragrance of ginger plum pie. "Sweet Ancients, Valmont. If this pie tastes half as good as it smells, then there's no way in a million years we're going to let you leave the crew."

Dorian's flushed face blossomed into a genuine smile. It was a glorious sight.

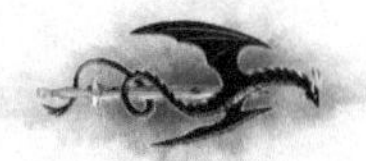

Captain Xander also sat awake late that night, staring at an old beaten leather journal in the guttering lantern light. No matter how many times he turned it over in his head, it kept coming back to the same thing. Janus Callahan had tracked them down on purpose.

The only question was, why? Xander hadn't spoken to Janus Callahan in over twenty years. He supposed the Valmont boy's presence was the obvious answer. Had the young Lord Bradford been less fastidious than he claimed in convincing his father of Dorian's death? Yet while that explanation made the most sense, a troublesome nagging in the back of his mind told him he was missing something crucial.

The thing that worried Xander most was the silence on the aether networks regarding King Callahan's dragonauts. Surely, the *Phoenix* couldn't have been the only ship to encounter them. But the beacon crystals lit up only to convey the same old mundane news about air currents and storm predictions. If Janus's dragonauts weren't public knowledge yet, that was because he didn't want them to be. So the question remained: why were Xander and his crew still alive?

Did the king believe he'd killed them? Perhaps Callahan truly thought the *Phoenix* was lost beneath the underclouds. It wasn't like they could search for any wreckage. Once a ship sank beneath the clouds, it was lost irrevocably. But Xander wasn't willing to stake their continued survival on that level of speculation.

Another possibility took root in Xander's mind and refused to let go. He wished he could dismiss it, because the implications scared him even more than simple, mundane death. What if they hadn't sent the storm to kill them at all? Those dragonauts had seemed in perfect control. What if it had only been a distraction? Janus might well have planned to use the ensuing chaos to take the ship, and its cargo, for himself. He might, at this very moment, be waiting for another chance to strike. *Might, might, might.*

Xander found it difficult to focus on the day-to-day duties of running the ship when he half expected his former friend to appear from behind a cloud with not just a flight of dragonauts, but the entire Kasani Armada besides.

Whether or not Callahan knew Dorian was on board, the king no doubt recognized the *Phoenix* itself. It had been an Order ship once, before Xander ran off with it. Callahan knew full well who Xander was. And he knew what Xander had.

Xander removed the false bottom from his middle desk drawer

and beheld the object hidden there. It looked like an ornate magnifying glass or perhaps a hand mirror; the handle wrought in the shape of two serpentine dragons twisted together, holding a thin sliver of a crescent moon. Within the crescent, however, forming the rest of the moon shape, was a flat, iridescent sheet of aether crystal. Nobody even knew how to form aether into that shape anymore. In Xander's hands, it was a lovely Ancient artifact in remarkably good condition, probably worth a hefty sum if he ever wanted to sell it. But it took a bond to a dragon to unlock its actual power. And, somehow, Janus Callahan had just that very thing.

Xander uncorked his whiskey decanter and poured himself a generous measure.

*Janus Callahan, dragonaut.* Xander didn't want to think about how the king had accomplished that. Callahan's ruthless pursuit of magical knowledge had been the main reason Xander left the Order. But as far as Xander knew, Callahan wasn't part of the Order anymore. He was working alone, or perhaps with the Kasani government. And that meant that he and the Order might, for once, share a common goal.

Xander shook his head ruefully and drummed his fingers on the tabletop. He'd sworn he'd have nothing to do with the Order ever again. To contact them now made him feel like a chastened runaway gryphlet, crawling home with his tail between his legs. But it couldn't be helped. He was in over his head, and they were the only people on Cyrna who might help him.

But as he thumbed through his list of contacts, he wondered if it might not be too late even for that. Were his last bridges burned at last? Who could he turn to? Mother, dead. Father, dead. Elenor, dead. Cyrus, dead. He'd lost touch with Sylvia more than a cycle ago. He'd never bothered trying to keep in touch with Jameson. But Hildegard... Hildegard was still around. As far as Xander knew, she was working as an archaeologist at the ruins of Greystone Citadel. That was only a few days' flight from here.

Xander's stomach churned with a cocktail of conflicted

emotions. *Hildegard*. Would she be pleased to hear from him? Furious that he'd been out of touch for so long? Well, there was nothing more to it. If anyone on Cyrna could get him out of this tangled mess in which he'd found himself, it was bound to be Hildegard Weatherbee.

Before he could change his mind, he downed the rest of his whiskey. Then he procured a fresh sheet of parchment, dipped his quill in the inkwell, and began writing.

*Dear Hildegard,*

*I recognize that it's been awhile...*

# CHAPTER SIX

# THE ARRIVAL FEAST

*ONE YEAR AGO*

Dorian hated feasts.

Oh, he liked the idea, in theory. Good food, good companionship, good times. But most feasts took a good idea and turned it into a miserable experience.

Dorian hated all the pomp and production. He hated his uncomfortable formal clothes, and he hated worrying whether he was using the right fork. Why were there so many Void-cursed forks? After almost ten years of living in Callahan Manor, Dorian still couldn't seem to figure out the forks.

No. Feasts took the simple pleasure of sharing a meal, and turned it into a stressful monstrosity. All things considered, he would much rather enjoy his supper in peace.

"I don't suppose I have to attend?" Dorian asked as he sat in the kitchen peeling potatoes.

"*Tcch,*" Stewardess Tahlia gave an impatient scoff. "What nonsense is this?"

Normally, he got along well with the stewardess. She reminded him of his nurse, Rowena, who he still missed terribly. But today he could tell her patience was running thin. Initially hired to be Bradford and Dorian's governess and tutor, Tahlia had risen through the ranks and was now head of all the manor staff. Usually, she had a light hand with kitchen operations. But it was all hands on deck to prepare for the feast tonight.

"Just... I'm not really Callahan's son." Dorian grimaced as he tossed a curled potato peel into the compost bucket. He wasn't supposed to be down there either, but the kitchen staff clearly needed help, and what Callahan didn't know wouldn't hurt him.

«You really are terrible at acting like a nobleman,» Hematite chided. But the demon didn't really mind. Hematite liked the kitchens. Demons felt and sensed everything their hosts did, after all. Baking bread smelled just as good to Hematite as it did to Dorian. The manor kitchens provided all the warmth and comfort the rest of Lord Callahan's manor house lacked.

"Enough of that, now," Tahlia said, firmly but gently. There was an understanding look in her hazel-green eyes, but she shook her head and said, "You are part of this household, for all that Janus seems to forget it sometimes. Besides. I'm sure the princess of Kasanarae will be quite excited to meet you."

Dorian snorted. "Right," he said, "Lord Callahan's useless nobody ward. That's who every princess wants to see."

No one seemed to explain why the heiress to the most powerful throne on Cyrna was coming to stay here, of all places. Some speculated she was hiding from assassins, while others hoped she might try to broker an alliance through marriage to Bradford. But all those reasons seemed flimsy to Dorian. Assassins could find her in Adenthul as easily as they could in Kasanarae. And surely the crowned princess could do better than the son of a two-bit lord from the Adenthulian hinterlands.

"No matter," Tahlia said. "While I'll not complain about the help, you'd really best go make yourself presentable."

Dorian sighed. "Presentable, right. If I can gain something

resembling grace and poise within the next hour, I'll be sure to do so."

"Believe me. Nobody is expecting you to do that." The temperature in the kitchens seemed to plummet as a dreaded, familiar voice reverberated off the stone walls. The servants all stopped what they were doing and looked up in apprehension. His own stomach twisted in an icy knot, Dorian turned around.

"Good... good afternoon, Lord Callahan."

Tahlia wiped some flour off her apron and swept into an approximation of a curtsey. "My Lord," she said. "What brings you to our humble kitchens?"

"Making sure all is running smoothly for the feast tonight," Callahan replied. His sharp, icy glare turned towards the servants. "Well? Back to work."

There was a flurry of activity while everyone frantically tried to look busy in front of the manor lord.

"And," Callahan continued, "To make sure my ward understands his role here in the manor." He put his hand on Dorian's arm, fingers digging in just enough to let Dorian know he meant business. "A word, Valmont, if you please."

There was, of course, no choice but to follow. Dorian thought he saw a look of concern mixed with pity on Stewardess Tahlia's face as Lord Callahan ushered him into the hallway. Outside the kitchens, the temperature sank ten degrees more.

"I sincerely hope," Callahan said through gritted teeth, "That this is not how you expect to present yourself at the feast tonight."

Dorian grimaced as he looked down at the same woolen shirt he'd worn for the past three days, splattered with flour from the kitchen and a bit of last night's gravy. Janus Callahan's stony gaze fell directly upon the gravy stain, lips pursed into a slight sneer, making his displeasure known.

"I'll, ah, go get cleaned up, sir," Dorian said, staring at the floor.

"Do that," Callahan said. He dug his fingers into Dorian's arm again, harder this time. "And while you are skulking off in the kitchen, ignoring your responsibilities, remember that I took you in when no one else would, and that I can easily retract my generosity. Would you rather be a beggar on the street?"

Dorian felt a surge of fear, partially from Hematite and partially from himself. There were times, in his rare moments of wistful defiance, that Dorian thought perhaps he would do better on his own, outside the cloud of Janus Callahan's cold-hearted tyranny. But Dorian didn't know if he really had it in him to give up those creature comforts that made life bearable. And for his demon, who felt everything Dorian did, it would be even worse. He couldn't do that to Hematite, who had been his only friend, his only source of comfort these long gray years at Callahan Manor.

"I don't want that, Sir," Dorian said, slumping his shoulders.

"Then go clean up for the feast. You may not be my son," Callahan was always fond of reminding Dorian, "But if you embarrass my household in front of the princess of Kasanarae than I swear by all the gods..." His grip on Dorian's arm tightened further still as he trailed off, leaving it to Dorian's imagination what his punishment might be.

"Of course, Sir," Dorian stammered. "I'll go right away, sir."

Finally, finally, Callahan let him go, and Dorian fled like a mouse to his small but comfortable chambers. Callahan was right about one thing. Dorian was lucky to have anywhere to go after his father died. He'd written to Nurse Rowena in secret, once, about a moon after he'd come here. She'd never replied. Perhaps she really never saw Dorian and his father as any more than employers. In the end, Lord Callahan was all Dorian had. He might not be very nice, but Dorian owed it to him at least not to be a total embarrassment.

Unfortunately, it seemed most of the time, Dorian seemed to embarrass Lord Callahan simply by existing. He put on his thrice cursed feast clothes as expected, but he knew it wouldn't be enough. It never was. Frankly, he didn't understand the point. He'd never be handsome like Bradford. Putting on a fancy suit didn't make him look any better, it just made him look like a throw pillow.

Regardless, Dorian arrived at the great hall some forty minutes later, chafing in the restrictive silks, wishing he could be anywhere else. At least he didn't have to sit at the high table with Lord Callahan. Callahan didn't even grant his own son that privilege. The manor lord sat alone, as was his custom, holding himself above, and apart from, the rest. But not sitting with Callahan meant sitting with Bradford and his friends, and they were, unfortunately, almost as bad.

Bradford's best friend, Graigor Beckett, son of the wealthiest banker in Adenthul, laughed and punched Bradford in the arm. "Well, if it isn't your dear brother!" He leaned forward, crossing his muscular forearms and looking down at Dorian with absolute derision. "Demonfire burning strong as ever, I see. Meet me in the training field some time and I can help you banish the beast, eh?"

"Hematite is my friend," Dorian replied, fiddling with the embroidery at the end of his jacket sleeve.

"Friends with a demon, he says." Graigor rolled his eyes and smirked. "You'll claim you want to bed the creature next."

Demonic bonds, of course, did not work that way, but Dorian saw no point in explaining it to Graigor. The burly youth cared less about facts and more about different ways he could make Dorian's life miserable.

"Oh, come now, don't be like that," Graigor whined with mock indignation. "Don't you know those things can kill you?"

Dorian grunted. Even if he wanted to fight Hematite, which he did not, he knew Graigor Beckett didn't actually intend to help him. Graigor only wanted to lure Dorian into the training field as an excuse to taunt him for his obvious lack of athleticism, perhaps even beat up on him a bit. He'd done it before, five or six years ago, when he'd offered to teach Dorian how to ride a gryphon. Dorian had been younger, back then, and more naïve. He knew better than to be fooled again.

"I'm only looking out for the best interests of my dear friend's dearest brother," Graigor said with a knowing smirk.

"He's not my brother," Bradford said, a trifle churlishly. But with a sanctimonious little smirk, he added, "But Graigor has a point. We only care about your well being. We'd hate to stand by and watch as the demon raises you like a cow for slaughter."

"Cow for the slaughter indeed," Graigor chortled. "He's as dumb as a cow, isn't he? Don't just sit there open-mouthed, say something, for the gods' sakes."

"I— " Dorian wanted to stand up for himself. He wanted to tell Graigor Beckett to leave him the Void alone. But the words caught in his throat and nothing he could do would release them. He stared down at the embroidered corner of the tablecloth, face burning with shame and humiliation.

"Come now, be nice!" Graigor's sister, Corynne, swatted Graigor's arm with an elaborate feather fan. "Besides, my dear brother. Cows are the female ones."

Dorian sighed and slumped lower into his chair, wishing he could disappear entirely. «It's going to be a long evening,» he complained to Hematite.

«They torment you because of me,» Hematite replied.

«Nonsense,» Dorian rebuffed the demon. «They torment me because of me. Maybe if I was better at being a nobleman, had better table manners, or if I could run a single lap around the training yard without collapsing...»

«Now you are the one speaking nonsense,» Hematite said. With a telepathic sigh, the demon continued, «I suspect they would find other reasons to act like boorish ruffians. Neither of us should have to change who we are for the likes of them.»

There was a clinging of cutlery on glass, and Lord Callahan stood from the high table. The entire great hall hushed at once. Callahan had that effect on people. The gaunt, balding lord projected an aura of icy solemnity, the sort of thing that caused laughter to falter and die.

Lord Callahan launched into a long and monotonous speech, chastising the people of Frostvale for their numerous shortcomings while imploring them to put their best feet forward for the visiting princess. Dorian, who was well used to Callahan's tirades, yawned and stared at the wrought-iron chandeliers. The cream-colored plaster and dark mahogany beams on the ceiling reminded Dorian of butter in an earthenware crock. Ancients, but he was hungry. When were they going to get to the actual food part of the feast?

"And so," Lord Callahan concluded, his voice cool and emotionless, "I present to you our most esteemed guests."

Callahan swept into a bow, and the great wooden doors to the feast hall swung open.

Dorian had expected an entire retinue, but only one person walked in. A woman, heavily armed and armored. She was taller than Dorian and nearly as big around. While she sported a sizable paunch, Dorian noted bulging muscles visible even beneath all her leather and chain mail. This wasn't someone Dorian wanted to get in a fight with. She wore an elaborate blue and silver tabard over her armor, emblazoned with the silver seven-pointed star of Kasanarae. She had bright, intelligent silver eyes, and silky black hair tied back in a complicated plait.

"Is that... is that the princess?" Dorian wondered.

"Would that we were so fortunate," Bradford said. He gazed at the woman with rapt fascination.

"Must be her bodyguard," Corynne mused. "That's an impressive sword she's got."

"A woman bodyguard?" Graigor asked incredulously.

"Are you going to pick a fight with her?" Dorian wondered.

"Fair point, Cow," Graigor conceded. "Well, Brad, be grateful she isn't the princess. Imagine being betrothed to an ogress like that."

Bradford blinked several times, as if coming out of a trance. "Oh... yes. Terrible." He suddenly became very interested in his wine goblet.

"There isn't any betrothal yet," Corynne pointed out, a little acidly. It was common knowledge that she nursed her own ambitions to marry Lord Bradford.

The guardswoman declared, in a clear, feminine voice, "I am honored to present Princess Saedra Alansae Adrienne Rachelle Penregon Kasani, crowned heir to the proud nation of Kasanarae."

She stepped aside, and the princess herself came gliding in behind her.

Dorian craned his neck to get a better look. In some ways, Princess Saedra looked exactly how he might have expected a princess to look. And yet, that such a person could actually exist took his breath away. She was smaller than the guardswoman, though still curvaceous, her hourglass figure draped in an extravagant gown of dark blue velvet. Her hair, silky black like the guardswoman's, was tied back in a net full of gemstones. Similar stones were sewn into the fabric of her dress, making it look like she wore a sky full of stars.

"Wow," Dorian said.

"Do you know," Bradford said, "I think I preferred the guardswoman."

"Then I'll take the princess for myself, if you don't mind," Graigor chortled.

Corynne rolled her eyes, but then returned her gaze to the princess with a look of almost greedy fascination.

Princess Saedra made her rounds about the feast hall, introducing herself first to Lord Callahan, then the rest of his household and the townfolk.

"Um, hello," Dorian said when his turn came. He surreptitiously wiped his sweaty hand on the side of his silk pant leg before proffering it to her. Her own hand was tiny and smooth, decorated with glittering rings of silver and white. "Ah, Dorian Valmont, your, ah, highness."

Princess Saedra raised Dorian's hand and kissed it, just like she'd done with Bradford's. She met Dorian's eyes, and then seemed almost to look through him, staring intently at his blue aura of demonfire.

"A pleasure to meet you, Lord Dorian Valmont and Honored Demon Hematite Bloodstone of the Quiet Pond," she said.

Dorian's eyes widened at the use of Hematite's full formal title.

«Have you met her before?» Dorian wondered, but the demon replied with a silent negative.

Dorian sputtered an awkward "N... nice to meat you. But I'm not ... not a Lord."

«Not not a lord?» Hematite teased. «So you are a lord!»

«Oh, you know what I meant,» Dorian said. His face burned with embarrassment. But Saedra had already departed, joining Lord Callahan at the high table. *An honor indeed*, Dorian thought.

Dorian remembered comparatively little about the rest of the evening. There was wild boar and rare citrus fruit and entirely too much wine. Bradford, Graigor, and Corynne continued to be unpleasant.

But that was all secondary compared to the princess herself.

As absurd as it sounded, Dorian couldn't shake the feeling that she was watching him. It was ludicrous, of course. Dorian was nobody. He supposed Hematite was an impressive demon for backwater Adenthul, but Saedra hailed from Azure, one of the largest and wealthiest cities in the seven skies. Surely she'd seen a demon before. What possible interest could Dorian and Hematite be to someone like her? Yet every time his eyes strayed towards the high table, there she was, silver eyes right on him, expression thoughtful.

The feast finally ended with some elaborate spun sugar confection, and the waistband of Dorian's silk trousers felt tighter than before. Dorian was eager to get back to his bedchamber and lose himself in an adventure novel until unconsciousness took him. However, Princess Saedra seemed to have other ideas when she cornered Dorian in the hallway.

"I must speak to you," she said, leaning so closely towards him that he could smell her honeysuckle perfume. "Alone, if possible."

Dorian swallowed. "You want to... alone... with me?" He seemed to have lost his ability to form full sentences.

"Strictly business. I'm sure you understand," she said.

"Right, of course," Dorian said, "Business." He wondered what business the princess of Kasanarae could have with him.

"Is there somewhere we may speak in private?" the princess asked.

"Library should be empty this time of night," Dorian said.

"Right," Saedra said. She turned to her bodyguard, the large woman who announced her entrance. "Vivienne, kindly bring the book to the library, won't you?"

"Right away, your Highness," the guardswoman replied with a salute. She eyed Dorian with curiosity before sweeping away.

The library was, indeed, empty. Dorian kindled the aether lamps and politely pulled out a stool for Saedra. The princess made quite a production of arranging her skirts before sitting. She looked so out of place, in her fine jewel-bedecked evening dress, amidst the dusty stacks of books.

"Is that Lady Callahan?" Saedra asked, gesturing to a portrait that hung above the fireplace.

"Erm, yes," Dorian said, noticing the painting as if for the first time. A much younger Janus Callahan stood smiling with his arm around the waist of a pretty, brown-haired woman holding an infant Bradford. She had wide blue eyes and a heart-shaped face and looked at her tiny son with adoration. The family looked so young, and so happy. Dorian found it hard to imagine cold-faced Lord Callahan smiling like that today.

"What happened to her?" the princess asked.

Dorian squirmed uncomfortably on the library bench. "I'm not sure," he answered. "She died before I came to live here."

Saedra had inadvertently just broken one of the chief unspoken rules of life in Callahan Manor — they did not talk about Lady Callahan. Simply mentioning her name was a surefire way to send Callahan into the foulest of tempers. Whatever happened to her, it must've affected the manor lord deeply, for her unspoken spectre to haunt the manor halls all these Cycles later.

"So," Dorian said, eager to change the subject. "How can, um, I help you? Your, uh, highness."

"You may call me Saedra," she said. "I see no need to be so formal while we are working together."

"You can call me Dorian, then." Then, reddening, he added, "But I mean. You probably would have anyway."

Dorian's throat felt dry. He simultaneously wanted more wine, and thought he'd already had far too much of it. Working together? What did that mean? What could he possibly offer to the princess of Kasanarae?

"I, um, I'm not sure what you've heard, but I'm not..."

"You are Dorian Valmont?"

"Er, yes, he's me, that is, I'm him... But I'm not... I don't..."

"You are the reason I came to Frostvale," Saedra said.

He thought surely he'd misheard, some error in translation between Saedra's mouth and Dorian's ears. Not an assassination plot? Not a marriage contract with Bradford? Him? *Him?*

"I'm sorry. What?"

"I most likely will marry Lord Bradford, or at least make a show that I'm considering it," she said. "It would be a good match. An alliance between Kasanarae and Adenthul would benefit us all. But if I'm truly honest, that is only a cover."

"But I'm not--"

Before his perplexed, slightly wine-addled brain could formulate a response, the guardswoman, Vivienne, returned. "Here you go, princess."

Vivienne plopped a leather-bound volume unceremoniously in front of the princess, sending up a cloud of dust. The cover was dyed rich, dark blue, embossed with intricate knotwork.

Dorian ran his hand along the cover before he could stop himself. It reminded him of all the expensive books Lord Callahan kept in his private study, the ones Dorian could never touch.

But Hematite's sudden jolt of surprise turned Dorian's mood from longing to apprehensive.

«That is...»

Dorian drew his hand back. «It's what?» he asked.

«I have seen that book before,» Hematite said.

«Don't suppose you want to be a bit more forthcoming,» Dorian said sardonically.

The demon merely twitched in agitation. Hematite got like this, sometimes, all bothered about things he would not or could not explain.

Saedra waved away the dust cloud, unperturbed. "Thank you, Vivienne. Please guard the door against eavesdroppers."

"Can do." Before she left, Vivienne squeezed Dorian's shoulder and said, "Be nice to her, eh? She's my very favorite cousin. Without her, I'd be heir to the throne, and between you and me, that'd be unbearable."

"You're a princess too?" Dorian practically squawked in surprise. One princess in the manor was alarming enough, but two?

"A duchess, actually," Vivienne said, "But my main role is keeping the princess here alive. She's much more important than little old me."

There was nothing little or old about Duchess Vivienne, but Dorian gave her a shaky smile anyway and turned his attention back to the book that had his demon so agitated.

Once Vivienne was out of earshot, Saedra opened the book to a random page and pushed it to him. "I had hoped," she said, "That I might have your help to read what these pages contain."

The page was upside down, so Dorian rotated it. It depicted a spell circle, a highly complex tangle of sigils and calculations, far beyond his own limited education. Although he couldn't fathom what it did, he found himself keen to figure it out. Connection, sure, and there was the spirit. But what did the energy of thought have to do with the energy of the body? And... goodness, he wasn't even certain he recognized the sigil in the middle. Was supposed to represent a dragonstone? He'd read about those old artifacts, but never ever seen one. His heart pounded. Why did Saedra want his help? He was fine enough at magic, sure, but hardly worth traveling to the middle of nowhere. Saedra had all the magi in Kasanarae at her disposal.

The princess, however, looked at Dorian expectantly, biting her lower lip in eager anticipation.

"I... it's a very complicated spell." Dorian wet the roof of his mouth with his tongue. "I think maybe it has something to do with... with binding spirits together? But I don't... I mean I'm not..."

Saedra clapped her delicate hands. While Dorian still grasped for words, the princess abruptly reached across the table and hugged him. Dorian felt his entire body turn scarlet.

"I... what... "

"I've been searching for so long," she whispered. "So long to find the one who can read this."

"I... I mean... glad I can help," Dorian squeaked nervously, "But surely... surely the Archmage, or someone, maybe the court wizard..."

The princess shook her head. "You don't understand. For me, and for everyone else I've shown it to, the pages of this book are blank."

Dorian blinked. "Blank?" He thought his expression must be pretty blank, too, for all he understood what was happening.

Saedra nodded. "That's right. Blank." she took in a deep breath and let it out. "I have long sought the one person on all of Cyrna who can read these pages. Dorian Valmont, that person is you."

## CHAPTER SEVEN
# GREYSTONE CITADEL

Dorian stared out over the railing, shoulders slumped. From up here, the Thlarknian landscape looked barren and dusty, and the remote village below was hardly any better. Was this really where he wanted to spend the rest of his days?

Mrs. Pennyfeather made one of her disapproving clucks as she waddled past.

"I'll miss you most of all," he reassured the chicken.

Sullivan approached him, his arm in a sling. "Quite some view, isn't it?"

"I suppose," Dorian said, slumping his shoulders.

"Not quite the same view as from the Linking," Sullivan added with a knowing smile.

Dorian grimaced. It was because of him that Sullivan had to watch the landing from the deck, and not take part with rest of his crew-mates. "I'm sorry again," he said. "For getting your arm broken."

"Nonsense," Sullivan said. "I've already said it wasn't your fault."

But Dorian knew that wasn't the case. Sullivan would have never gotten injured if Dorian could fly worth a spark in the Void.

"At any rate," Sullivan continued, "I'll get to see a Healer in the village, so no lasting harm done." The burly aeronaut paused and continued to look out at the approaching landscape. "You don't really intend to leave the crew, do you?"

Dorian sighed. "I don't know."

"I must say," Sullivan said, "That pie you made was delicious. Would be disappointing never to taste your cooking again."

Dorian flushed, but he smiled as well. "Thanks for that. But... maybe it's for the best, you know?"

He thought about the Linking, the vivid colors and the swirling magic. Was Tai right in her assessment? Could he, perhaps, one day become a proper aeronaut? The thought filled him with equal parts hope and longing. But then he thought of Lord Callahan and his dragons. It wasn't fair of Dorian to put the others in danger when he offered so little in return.

«The town might not look like much,» Hematite put in, «But at least you will be safe there. Staying on the ship will only land you in more trouble.»

Maybe so. But when they finally made landfall, Dorian knew he'd much rather stay with the *Phoenix* crew than resettle in this dreary place. The dusty, aged skyport had a general air of long neglect and disuse. There were only three other skyships docked, each chipped and battered behind a thick layer of dust. Dorian wondered how long they'd been tethered there.

"I thought Thlarknians were supposed to be rich," Tai said as she surveyed the desolate skyport.

"In the big cities, maybe," replied Captain Xander. "But Greystone village is as close to the arse end of nowhere you can get while still having a skyport."

"So why did we land in the arse end of nowhere?" Falgar wondered.

"It's not what's in the town," Xander said. "It's what's beyond it."

He gestured towards a forbidding spine of mountains in the distance. "Greystone Town is the closest town with a skyport to Greystone Citadel. But we still have a good hour's skimmer ride ahead of us."

Dorian's breath caught in his throat. "Greystone... Citadel."

He should have known, of course. As soon as he'd heard the name of the town, he should have connected it to the fortress. After all, hadn't he once been able to name off all the ancient dragonaut strongholds by heart? *Greystone, in Thlarknia, the largest and the mightiest.*

"I thought... I mean... aren't we just a shipping company?"

"Indeed," Xander said, smirking. "And it just so happens that we're shipping things out of the old fortress." His brows narrowed into a thoughtful expression as he dusted his hands together. "Righto. Falgar, Sullivan, I'd like you two to go into town for supplies, and see if you can find a Healer about Sullivan's arm. Lunstrum, Valmont, you'll be coming with me. I've already arranged this skimmer for transport."

"Skimmer," Dorian repeated, surprised, and a little fascinated. He'd never seen one of those before. Back home in Adenthul, most people still used gryphon carts to get around.

Xander led them to a row of wooden coaches hovering just a few hand spans off the ground.

"They really run on pure magic," Tai mused. "Seems inefficient, doesn't it?"

"This is Thlarknia," Xander replied. "Middle of the desert, isn't it? Not much food around to feed livestock with. But aether? Aether is plentiful." The captain kicked up a bit of dirt, and Dorian could have sworn it glittered with a hint of blue.

Dorian found the prospect of skimmer flight exciting. But on closer inspection of the vehicles, his enthusiasm waned. These skimmers were in even worse repair than the rest of the ships on the skydock. They'd been painted different colors at one point, maybe.

But most of them were chipped, and all of them were dirty, leaving them all a uniform brownish gray.

The majority of the boxy interior was given to cargo space, leaving only a narrow bench near the front for Dorian and Tai to squeeze themselves in. The inside of the cabin smelled faintly of mildew and old beef stew. Dorian sighed and positioned himself as close to the wall as he could manage lest he encroach on Tai's personal space.

The flight itself was little better. While a skyship like the *Phoenix* soared comfortably through the open sky, the skimmer bumped and jostled at every minor bit of turbulence. Dorian thought this almost might be fun, except that he kept bumping into Tai.

"Sorry," he told her when his shoulder brushed against her wing for the fifteenth time in as many minutes.

"*I* bumped into *you*," Tai pointed out. She looked pale and a little sickly, her brown knuckles turning white as she clung to the window ledge.

So it was, an uncomfortable hour later, that they finally saw their first glances of Greystone Citadel.

"Sweet Ancients," Tai whispered. "It's huge!"

Dorian thought "huge" was an understatement. The dilapidated castle was the size of the entire mountaintop. *No*, he realized, it *was* the mountaintop. Those long-dead Ancient architects somehow turned the entire peak into a fortress. Centuries later, mammoth gray walls and needle-sharp spires loomed over the Thlarknian landscape like a silent sentinel. Bumpy ride or no, it was worth it to get to see this.

"I mean," Dorian continued, staring with wide-eyed fascination, "I knew it was supposed to be the largest of the dragonaut fortresses, but... Wow."

"If ten-year-old me knew that one day I'd be flying here on routine business, I'd've lost half my feathers in excitement." Despite her pallor, Tai's face split into a grin. Dorian admired the way the smile lit up her entire face, then, blushing, hurriedly returned his attention to the fortress.

"You... you like Ancient fortresses?" he asked.

He hadn't known that about her. He realized with a pang that, although he admired her greatly, he didn't actually know much about her at all. This filled him with a surprising amount of melancholy. He found he didn't want to leave the crew before learning all he could about this blunt, bold, talented Orith woman.

"Oh, yes," Tai said, brown eyes shining, seemingly unaware of Dorian's turmoil. "I was absolutely mad for dragons as a child. Collected every dragon-related paraphernalia I could find. My mother thought I was a few stray feathers and a broken branch, but what can we do?"

"Stray feathers and what now?" Dorian asked.

"Oh, sorry, it's just an expression. Probably makes more sense in the original Toreenish. It means... not all there, you know? Proper Young Orith Ladies are not supposed to be obsessed with dragons." Her smile turned rueful. "But that didn't stop me. I wanted to be a real dragonaut. Not just behold the haunted remnants of the past." Her wings drooped slightly, and she added, "Sorry, I know, that probably sounds silly."

"No," Dorian said, smiling sadly as he remembered a nine-year-old boy swinging a stick like a sword. He might've felt the same way about the fortress, once. Before Icereach. Before the worst day of his life. "Not silly at all."

He sat back and resumed staring out the window, equal parts fascinated and terrified of the looming fortress ahead.

Dorian's melancholy gave way to a rising tide of panic as he disembarked from the skimmer. He knew he was being irrational. He tried to tell himself to calm down. But as he walked up the stone path leading to the mountain-sized fortress, his heart seized with dread.

Another Ancient Dragonaut Fortress. Different from the Icereach Castle of his boyhood, and yet in some ways, so very much the same.

Even all these years later, the memory of falling rocks haunted his nightmares. He could've died too, if not for Hematite. Often, he thought he *should've* died.

Hematite, corporeal at his side, shook his head. «We demons are not always given much freedom to choose. But I chose you. Try to remember that.»

Dorian supposed that, weighed against the infinite unknown of death, Dorian was glad Hematite saved him. He wanted to be alive. Really. But *Sweet Zekador!* Cyrus Valmont could've expertly handled everything that was happening — the increased Voidstorms, Callahan's rise to power, the sudden re-emergence of dragonauts. Dorian had never in his life felt more out of his depth. Whether or not he stayed with the crew, how could he grapple with things so far beyond him?

«Is it still your intention to stay here in Thlarknia?»

«I don't know.» He wished everyone would stop asking. He wished he didn't have to decide.

The gargantuan towers of Greystone Citadel bore down on him with all the power and might of ages past. It was like it belonged to the gods, and not mere mortal dragonauts. Unwelcome thoughts shuffled through his mind. What if there was a skyquake here, now? He imagined this giant structure falling down around them, and it turned his bowels to liquid.

«Come now. Stay in the present.» A mindvoice brushed past him like magic on the wind. Not Hematite's voice.

«Another demon?» Gods above, did all Ancient dragon fortresses have demons lying in wait?

«No,» Hematite said. «Not one of us. Something ... else.»

Dorian forced himself to take several long breaths. *Keep it together, Dorian.* Bad enough that Tai and Xander thought he was useless. He didn't want them to think he was off his gryphon, too. So, wearing an expression of calm he didn't feel, he followed the others down the cracked cobbled walkway to the courtyard.

Buzzing, crackling magic in the air made Dorian's arm hairs stand on end. He had never felt this much ambient magic in his life. He could almost taste it, a sharp combination of citrus and cinnamon. His dragonstone pendant thrummed.

"What is this place?"

Dorian didn't realize he'd spoken out loud until Tai answered, "Greystone Citadel." She smirked. "But I thought you knew that already."

*Right. Of course.* He tried to breathe. In and out, in and out.

They crossed a crumbling archway into the main courtyard, and the din of magic surged further still. Dorian felt like there was a swarm of bees nearby. Magic bees. He let out a giddy, involuntary laugh, which caused Tai to look at him askance.

"Sorry." Dorian covered a cough and forced his face into a neutral expression.

Across the courtyard, a massive stone staircase led up to the castle itself. Colossal stone dragons as tall as Callahan manor lined the stairway, most of them chipped and broken, some of them missing their heads.

Dorian wanted to climb those stairs.

«Why in the Void would you want to do that?» Hematite sounded horrified.

«I... don't know.» But whatever the reason, the wide stone steps and the fortress beyond called to him.

"—One of the lead archaeologists for the Order of the Silver Dragon, and a dear old friend of mine."

Dorian blinked.

Just how long had Captain Xander been talking?

Dorian realized he'd completely failed to notice a fourth person joining them in the courtyard. This stranger dressed in sturdy, practical clothes, with a brown hidebound notebook under her right arm. A flyaway strand of auburn hair escaped the confines of her bun and streaked across a hawk-like face. She looked younger than Captain Xander, but Dorian found it difficult to discern her precise age.

"Ah, hello," Dorian said. He wished he'd heard the woman's name.

«Hildegard Weatherbee,» Hematite helpfully provided.

«Glad one of us was paying attention. Wait. Is she related to Tahlia?» He examined the woman again, but if she bore any resemblance to his absent governess, he didn't see it.

"Enough about me, Xander," Hildegard Weatherbee said. "Please, please, introduce your crew."

Xander cleared his throat. "Right. Of course. Well, ah, here are Tai and Dorian. They'll be helping today."

"Ah!" the woman clapped Tai on the shoulder and shook her hand. "Xander said in his letters he'd found a brilliant Orith aeromage." Turning to Dorian, she said, "And you must be Dorian Valmont. Oh, it's good to meet you at last. And Hematite! A pleasure, as usual."

«I always did like her,» Hematite said.

"You two... know each other?"

Hildegard flashed an understanding smile. "I met Hematite through your father. Your parents were both dear friends of mine, once upon a time."

Xander cleared his throat. "To business?"

"Right, right, of course," Hildegard said. "I received your missive, and I think I can help. Jameson and I have been working on a device that renders skyships invisible to scrying techniques. It works based on a combination of Illusion and Meronethian Ice magic. I can show you the sigils if you like."

Xander nodded in approval. "That does sound promising. Will it keep Callahan's goons away from us?"

Dorian looked up in surprise. If this woman had a device that could hide them from Callahan's forces, maybe he wouldn't have to leave the crew after all. It surprised him how hopeful this made him feel.

"Nothing is guaranteed, of course," Hildegard said. "But it will prevent him from dogging your every step, at the very least. I can also help you falsify the *Phoenix's* registration, so you don't show up like a glaring red beacon in every port you land in. But you must understand, I can't do all this for free, even if it is for an old friend."

Xander grunted. "Bloody Order. Ruthless as ever. Very well. Name your price." He put his hand on his coin purse, frowning deeply.

"I've no need for your coin," Hildegard said. "It's your cargo space I'm after."

Xander's posture relaxed slightly. "Well. I am in the business of hauling cargo."

Hildegard nodded. "I've got a bunch of documents I'd like you to take off my hands. Old books, accounting ledgers, that sort of thing."

"Sure." Xander frowned. "But why?"

"To keep them away from Callahan."

Dorian's heart sank. Surely this would only make them more of a target.

Xander seemed to think along the same lines. "Might as well hang a banner from the ship saying 'Free Stuff for Callahan, Please Capture Us.' I doubt your device will be worth a spark in the Void if half of Kasanarae is after us."

"Well, it's not as if you're going to advertise what you have," Hildegard said with a snort. "I'd say you're a far sight safer with my the documents and my cloaking device than you are with Valmont and the Moonglass and no cloaking device."

"Fair enough," Xander allowed. He shook his head and looked up at the cloudless blue sky, as if expecting Callahan's dragonauts to swoop down any minute. "But surely you can't expect me to carry them around in my cargo hold indefinitely."

"Not quite." Hildegard's mouth turned into a thin-lipped smile that was almost a grimace. "I hope that they will eventually wind up in Sylvia's hands."

Xander's mouth fell open. "My — my *sister*?"

"Now, I know you two didn't part on the best of terms," Hildegard began. But Xander waved her off.

"She's... she's alive, then." Xander visibly swallowed. "And... and I suppose you know how to contact her, do you?"

Hildegard let out a long sigh. "That's sort of the problem, isn't it? Sylvia... is more the sort who's going to contact *you*."

Xander snorted. "Then I'm afraid I won't be much help. Sylvia hasn't wanted a spark in the Void to do with me for three bloody Cycles now, and I doubt that'll change anytime soon."

"I'd say just about everything's changed," Hildegard said. She stared pointedly at Dorian and Hematite when she said it.

Dorian did not know what they were talking about, but he wished they'd hurry and finish. Part of him thought maybe he should care about Xander's past and his family, but he couldn't, not now, with the itchy, buzzing magic relentlessly urging him into the fortress.

"You and your thrice cursed Order can fly straight into the Void," Xander said. But then he straightened his shoulders and continued, "But business is business. Lunstrum and Valmont here will help load the documents into the skimmer bed. You show me this miracle device of yours."

"Right this way." Hildegard gestured for him to follow.

The documents, it transpired, were already packed and crated, which at least ought to make their task easier. But Dorian couldn't help feeling let down that they wouldn't be entering the fortress itself.

«Just as well,» Hematite said. «Do you really relish carrying those boxes up and down all those stairs?»

«You and stairs,» Dorian said.

«I cannot help it if I like to be comfortable.» Hematite inspected his silver-black claws.

It probably was lucky they didn't have to move the documents far, because there turned out to be a lot of them. Boxes upon boxes of paperwork, scrolls, and leather-bound tomes. There were stacks of loose paper tied together with twine, and scrolls of vellum so fragile Dorian feared they might dissolve in his arms. There were even some stone tablets. *Stone tablets,* Ancients help him.

By the time they finished moving all the cargo, Dorian was drenched in sweat, heaving for breath, and had long exhausted his supply of water. And yet, the magic thrummed as insistently as ever. He half expected droplets of sweat to bounce off of his goosebump-covered skin.

When at last they'd finished, Dorian tried to take a swig from his canteen, remembered it was empty, and collapsed into a folding wooden chair. "I have got to get in better shape."

"Good work," Hildegard said. "There's cheese and grapes here if you want them."

Dorian popped a grape into his mouth, but the juicy tartness held little appeal. The entire courtyard felt like a hazy dream, like he was watching it from far away, through the end of a long tunnel.

He wished he could follow Tai and Hildegard's conversation. Their eager discussion of magical theory reminded him of his time with Saedra. Except, no, that wasn't right. This was…

He blinked. Now they were talking about the cheese. When had they changed topics? Had he zoned out for seconds or minutes? Dorian needed to get out of here.

«No. You do not need to leave. You need to find me.»

That other mindvoice again. It was clearer now, and more persistent. Dorian knew by instinct that it came from the fortress, like the magic. And it wouldn't leave him alone until he went to it.

He thumbed his pendant and tried his level best to think logically. The fortress was likely unsafe. The building was more than a thousand years old. He could die in a cave-in, just like his father.

But.

*But.*

Whatever this magic pulse was, it didn't feel malevolent. And Dorian wanted to obey it, despite all logic and common sense.

"All right!" he blurted at no one. "All right! I'll go!"

"What?" Tai looked at him like he'd sprouted a second head.

But Dorian ignored her and took off running towards the inner fortress.

"You attach it to the aether engine like this, and these sigils determine what you want your energy signature to be," Hildegard explained.

Tai stared in fascinated curiosity at the device. So this was what they'd come all the way out here for. This was what was supposed to keep them safe. The smooth brass sphere was about the size of a grapefruit, encircled by a band of glowing blue spell sigils.

"And it just... makes our ship look like a Voidstorm?" Tai wondered.

Hildegard nodded. "Or a regular storm, or a pack of wild demons, or even a flight of wild dragons if you wanted, though, given your current difficulties, I'd recommend against the last one."

She picked it up, feeling the thrum of captive magic stored within the device. "It's incredible," she said. "But... but it is it safe? All this messing with magical energy won't... won't turn us into pit wraiths, or something worse?"

Hildegard laughed. "There's no such thing as pit wraiths, my dear. I should warn you, though, that it only affects scrying mirrors and similar techniques. If someone flies right up to you, they'll see your ship just as it is."

"I suppose that makes sense," Tai said, putting the device down.

"Do have some of the cheese, dear," Hildegard encouraged her. "It's very good. Imported from Narea."

Tai picked up a yellow triangle and gave it a dubious sniff. Cattle and goats, unfortunately, did not survive Orith's long-ago descent beneath the underclouds. Even after five years of living in the sky, Tai found the Aerish habit of eating spoiled and curdled animal milk revolting. This cheese smelled like the *Phoenix's* training equipment on the evening before bath day.

Still, Tai didn't want to be rude. So, out of deference to her host, she took a bite. And quickly took a sip of tea to cover the pungent flavor.

"It's…" she began, scrambling to come up with something polite.

Hildegard laughed. "The gruyere is a bit of an acquired taste. Try the havarti. It's milder."

Tai picked up the soft white square and tasted it. An improvement, she supposed, but did it have to be so slimy? Her insides gurgled ominously.

"What do you think of the cheese, Dorian?" she asked, but he didn't seem to hear her. He drummed his fingers on the table in agitation, his expression elsewhere.

"Dorian?"

He stood bolt upright. "All right! All right! I'll go!"

"What?"

Before Tai could say anything else, Dorian sprinted towards the fortress at full speed.

"What the—"

"He can't enter the fortress, it's not safe!" Hildegard's brown eyes were wide with fear.

"Forgotten Void," Tai swore, abandoning her tea and cheese and taking off in his direction.

By the time she caught up, they were both out of breath.

"Dorian!" She clutched a stitch in her side.

"Oh, hello Tai." Dorian stood at the top of the staircase, looking around. His face was red and sweaty, and he panted for breath, but he didn't seem to care.

Without so much as a farewell, Dorian turned around and

started walking off down a side passage. Swearing under her breath, Tai scrambled to keep up.

"Where are you going?"

Dorian came to a stop at the end of the hallway. It was easy to see why. The floor cut off abruptly, with only jagged rock between themselves and the levels below. Above them, lances of sunlight filtered down through cracks and holes in the broken ceiling.

"It's dangerous up here."

Dorian blinked and then shook himself. "Tai. Sorry. I—" he looked around. "Goodness. How far have I walked?" He ran a shaking hand through his sweat-soaked hair.

"Dorian, we have to go. Hildegard told us to stay in the courtyard. Don't you remember?"

Dorian blinked again. "I — don't remember. I — I only came here now because — because of the magic." He blinked several more times. "I have to follow the magic."

Tai bit her lip, her concern increasing. "Dorian, that doesn't even make sense. What magic?"

"The *magic*." Dorian spread his arms. "Can't you feel it?"

"No, Dorian," Tai said. "There isn't any magic."

He didn't give any indication that he'd heard her.

"Come on, Dorian." She touched him on the arm, intending to lead him back to the entrance.

Dorian, however, snatched his arm away. "I can't, Tai. Don't you understand? The magic won't leave me alone if I don't — if I don't —" he shook his head, looked around, and placed his hand on the inner wall, far too close to the broken floor for Tai's comfort. "It's coming from this way..."

"Come on, Dorian, let's go back."

Dorian ignored her and ran his hand gently along a crack in the wall. Tai's frown deepened. Had that crack been there a moment ago?

As Tai watched, the crack spread, not just on the wall, but along the floor as well.

"Dorian!"

"What?" he looked up, but it was too late.

As if in slow motion, the wall crumbled like shards of broken pottery.

*Oh no oh no oh no.*

Tai leapt forward and clasped his hand. It pulled loose, but she caught his silk shirtsleeve instead. "I've got you," she said, and pulled with all her might.

But it did no good. The floor underneath her crumbled, too, and the stone tiles gave way to join their brethren. Tai gave one last desperate heave as the wall and floor dissolved. The two of them tumbled together down in a cascade of rubble.

# CHAPTER EIGHT

# LOST MAGIC

*ONE YEAR AGO*

"I'm sorry," Dorian said, blinking. "Did you just say no one can read this book except me?"

"Indeed," Saedra said.

"But I mean... that can't be. I'm... I'm nobody."

Despite all his bafflement, Dorian felt a small private thrill of excitement. This was something right out of the stories he loved best. Was he about to discover some kind of innate hidden talent before being swept off into a life of adventure and excitement?

«Believe me,» Hematite said. «Adventure and excitement are highly overrated.»

"Your demon," Saedra said. "Hematite Bloodstone."

"What about him?" Dorian turned away from the book and extended his right hand, releasing a wisp of blue flame that resolved into Hematite's reptilian form. At fifteenth degree, Hematite stood near as tall as Dorian. A far cry from the forearm-length creature he'd met more than a Cycle ago.

"I'm sure you're aware by now," Princess Saedra said, "That

before he bonded you, your Hematite was bonded to your father, Cyrus Valmont."

Dorian nodded, grimacing, as he remembered that terrible, terrible day, when Hematite came for Cyrus, but left with Dorian.

"Cyrus Valmont was one of the greatest magical scholars of his time," Saedra explained. "And he wrote his knowledge in this book. But lest it fall into the wrong hands, he enchanted it to appear blank to everyone except for Hematite and his bondmate."

"But my father wasn't bonded to Hematite when I knew him," Dorian said, frowning. "All that was before I was born."

"I can only speculate, of course," Saedra said, "But I'd venture to guess that Cyrus believed he could simply summon Hematite back whenever he needed to view or share the knowledge. Perhaps he'd even done so that day at Icereach castle. But he passed away. And now Hematite is yours."

Dorian fought to swallow the embarrassing lump in his throat. "Is that true?" He asked Hematite.

The demon nodded. «It is.»

Dorian buried his head in his hands. In the years since Cyrus's death, Hematite had become Dorian's friend and champion, a welcome companion in the otherwise lonely and dreary confines of Callahan Manor. But there were days, too many of them, when in his bleakest of thoughts Dorian knew the world would be a better place if Hematite had saved Cyrus instead. The princess's words only seemed to confirm that.

"He was so much more valuable than me," Dorian said.

«Nonsense.» Hematite twitched his tail. «I know you exalt the man, but Cyrus... was not kind to me. I do not believe he saw me as a sapient being in my own right, not like you do. I was a means to an end to Cyrus. An object, to be used and discarded, all in the service of his All-Important Grimoire.» Hematite's blue flames flared, and Dorian got the impression that if the demon could have spat on the book, he would have. «I apologize. I know this must be painful for you. But I can no longer deny the truth. Your father fancied himself some grand hero from a tale, and look where it got him in the end.»

"Yeah well," Dorian said, scowling, now. "Now the book's my problem, isn't it?" He laughed bitterly. "My turn to be the glorious hero." That was certainly a joke. The thought of Dorian engaging in any heroics was beyond ludicrous. Still, there was a part of him that felt a sort of wistful longing at the thought.

«Heroics,» Hematite said with a dismissive flick of his tail. «Self aggrandizement, more like.»

«Perhaps so,» Dorian allowed. He would be helpless on a real heroic adventure. Still, Princess Saedra wasn't sending him off to tame wild dragons. She simply wanted help to decipher a magic book. What could be so bad about that?

«The spells in that book are dangerous,» Hematite warned. «Your father hid them for a reason.»

Dorian frowned and regarded the princess. Hematite had a good point. "Why exactly do you want my father's spells?"

Saedra smiled ruefully. "Suppose that's a valid thing to ask," she said. "Do you know how my mother died?"

Dorian blinked at the sudden non sequitur. He racked his brain for knowledge of current events. "Queen Aithne of Kasanarae… Didn't her skyship crash?" Then, realizing he probably sounded rude, he quickly added, "Ah, my condolences, your Highness."

"I told you to call me Saedra," Saedra said. "But I'm afraid you're right. My mother's royal yacht flew into a Voidstorm. The aeronauts were adept at their jobs, but it was not enough."

"I'm sorry," Dorian said, wishing he could think of something better to say.

Saedra folded her hands, eyes downcast. "And then my brother died less than a year later. There was a skyquake, you see. The third in two moons! Tionel was distributing bread to the poor. Always so compassionate, my brother. But those buildings down in the lower city just aren't meant to handle so many skyquakes. There were no survivors."

Dorian felt a familiar twist in his gut. "I'm sorry," he said again. "My father died in a skyquake too."

Saedra nodded sadly. "You see, we have something in common, then. Both of us lost loved ones in a skyquake. And both of us remain now, feeling wholly inadequate to the tasks they left us. But we are what the world has, neh?"

"I... suppose so," Dorian said, swallowing. "But I'm still not sure I understand. What do you need me to do? What's in this book that's so important?"

"These tragedies were not isolated incidents," Saedra said. "Every single year, there are more and more skyquakes and Void-storms. It can only mean one thing — the magic of Cyrna is failing."

"Failing!" Dorian's voice came out a terrified squawk. Magic was part of everything in Aeris, from the growing of crops to the trans-port of supplies to the subtle movement of the floating lands them-selves. For it to simply stop working seemed unthinkable.

Dorian picked up the book again, running his hand down the page full of complicated diagrams. It was written in his father's hand. He saw that now. How could he have failed to notice before?

"And these... these spells? You think they can save the magic somehow?"

Saedra nodded. "It was your father's life's work. All of his legendary research and exploration was dedicated to the restoration of Aeris's magic." She folded her hands aid said, imploring, "Please, I need your help. All the world may depend on it."

Dorian let out a giddy, nervous little laugh. The world? Depending on him? He was not prepared. But a small part of him was excited, too.

«You have definitely had too much wine,» Hematite chided.

"I'm... not my father," Dorian said, "But I'll help in any way I can."

*THREE MOONS LATER*

"You like her, don't you?" Bradford tilted the wooden library chair backwards and twirled his quill pen in his left hand.

"Who, Stewardess Tahlia?" Dorian asked, raising his eyebrows. "I find her very capable."

Dorian knew he shouldn't push the lordling's buttons. But his time with Saedra made him inclined to be a little more daring. Just a little.

"I don't mean Tahlia, pit wraith." Bradford rolled his eyes. "Princess Saedra. You like her."

"I think she will be a very good ruler one day," Dorian replied.

Bradford made an exasperated *tcch* noise. "You know what I mean. Well. It's not as if someone like you would ever have a chance with the Princess of Kasanarae. But just keep in mind. Princess Saedra is to be my bride, not yours."

"The betrothal arrangement isn't final yet, Bradford," Tahlia Weatherbee pointed out as she swept into the room. "And it likely will never be, if you spend so much time mooning about your would-be fiance's bodyguard."

"Mooning about, I say! You make me sound like some love-struck schoolboy." Bradford crossed his arms in mock indignation.

"Well," Dorian muttered before he could stop himself, "Aren't you?"

Bradford glowered. But he didn't argue right away, probably because he knew Dorian was right for once. Bradford was always making excuses to spend time with Duchess Vivienne, riding their gryphons above the forest, practicing archery in the yard, or sparring with swords and staves.

The only problem was, Duchess Vivienne was not Bradford's betrothed.

Bradford recovered his calm confidence and smirked. "Yes. Well. A king must have a mistress, mustn't he?"

Tahlia's lips narrowed. "Infidelity can be dangerous, even for a king. And besides. If you expect your wife to be faithful, you'd best hold yourself to the same standards." Her nostrils flared. "Either way, I think you'd best focus a bit more on your studies, and less on your love life. Or your brother's love life."

"He's not my brother," Bradford said, but he didn't argue further.

"On that cheerful note," Tahlia continued. "Today we will continue our discussion on Illusion magic."

Besides her other duties in the manor, Stewardess Tahlia was also in charge of Dorian and Bradford's education. She launched into her Illusion lecture with the same swift efficiency with which she did everything else.

Dorian tried to pay attention. He did. But that afternoon, he had a great deal of trouble focusing on Illusion. Not when his thoughts were on the powerful spell he had transcribed in his rucksack. And on how he imagined Saedra would react when she saw it.

Dorian's relationship with Saedra was a professional one. No need to delude himself that it was anything else. Gods knew he wasn't that naïve. She liked him because he was useful to her, for no other reason. But Dorian didn't get to be useful to anyone very often, least of all kindhearted, intelligent, and undeniably beautiful princesses. So, by all the seven gods, he resolved to be as useful as he could be.

Excitement and fear intermingled when he thought about this latest spell. He wasn't sure he should share it at all. He'd rehashed the argument over and over, with Hematite, and with himself. Hematite, and, by extension, his father, had been quite right to hide it away. It was a dangerous spell. Maybe the most dangerous spell he could think of. Dorian believed a more skilled mage could reverse engineer it to fix the world's magic, but as it was now, it could do incalculable harm. But in the end, it was Saedra who would decide what to do with it, and Dorian knew he'd do anything for Saedra.

"Valmont. Dorian Valmont." Tahlia's sharp voice cut through his reverie.

"Ah!" Dorian looked up, shamefaced. "Sorry, Head Stewardess."

"Keep your head on your shoulders or you'll walk straight off the edgecliffs. Since your expression makes it clear you're not paying attention, I shall repeat the question. Recite for me, if you please, the signs of a badly done Illusion spell."

Dorian scanned his paltry notes. "Right, right. Badly done Illusion, badly done..."

Bradford rolled his eyes. "If I may, Stewardess, the signs of a badly done Illusion spell are blurry edges and overly bright or muted colors." He sat back and gave Dorian a knowing smirk.

"Very good," Tahlia allowed, "But that question was meant for your brother."

"He's not my brother." Bradford scowled.

The rest of the lesson dragged on in a similar fashion. Dorian tried to suppress his relief when she finally said they could leave. He shoved his belongings into his bag and rushed towards the exit, eager for his meeting with the Kasani princess.

"Dorian," Tahlia said, when he was just short of freedom. "A word?"

Dorian's heart sank. "Head Stewardess," he said. "About Illusion, I..."

"This isn't about Illusion," Tahlia responded. "Though I find it suspect that you find yourself unable to discuss the basics of Illusion when you've been looking at a book with Illusion on it nonstop for the past three moons."

Dorian froze. It was just his imagination, but suddenly, it seemed like his father's book glowed within his bag, a white-hot beacon. "I'm not... that is... I mean, nothing I have is blurry, or brightly colored, or—."

Tahlia smiled and shook her head. "Ah, so you do pay attention.

Well, fair enough. But I taught you the signs of poorly done Illusion. It happens I've seen an Illusion or two in my day. That one is rather spectacular."

"I… um…" he did not know what to say.

"No matter," Tahlia sighed. "That isn't what I wanted to talk to you about."

"It isn't?"

"No," Tahlia said. She looked grave, older than her forty-two years. "Bradford is not the only one who has noticed that you and Princess Saedra spend a lot of time together."

Dorian scratched his neck. "Saedra and I aren't… we're not…"

"Princess Saedra," Tahlia corrected him. "And I see the way you look at her."

"She's my friend," Dorian said. "I'm allowed to have friends, right?"

Tahlia's expression softened, the lines around her hazel-green eyes crinkling. "Of course you are. If anything, I'm glad to see you are making friends. I just wish to impress upon you how important it is not to come between Bradford Callahan and his wife."

"But she's not… I mean, Bradford's always off with Vivienne Penregon."

Tahlia pursed her lips in disapproval. "Duchess Vivienne," she corrected him, "And I believe I've made it clear I don't approve of that, either. But I cannot emphasize this enough. For you to pursue a romantic liaison with another man's fiance is… dangerous. Extremely dangerous. Especially when that woman is the princess of Kasanarae. Especially," she added, more quietly now, "When that woman's fiance is the son of Janus Callahan."

"All right, all right." Dorian waved his arms in supplication. "I won't pursue a relationship with the royal heir to a powerful nation. There. You happy?"

"Boy, I haven't been happy in near three Cycles," Tahlia replied with a snort.

"Twenty-one years is a long time to be unhappy," Dorian replied.

The words slipped out without meaning it, but he felt bad. Tahlia did everything around here. Dorian was just a ward, and he found Callahan Manor depressing. How must it be for the staff?

Talia's expression softened, and she said, more gently, "Just an expression, my dear, but your compassion does you credit. Just be careful. That's all I ask." She waved him away, letting him know he was dismissed, but she creased her brows in a worried line.

Dorian forced himself to put Stewardess Tahlia out of his mind. He was about to see the princess, after all.

Dorian crossed the sunny orchards, taking in the scent of pink and white apple blossoms. It was a glorious spring day, the first pleasant weather they'd encountered after a seemingly interminable Adenthulian winter. It was hard to take much heed to Tahlia's dire warnings when it was the first day of Spring and the sun was in the sky, and he had a powerful spell to present to Princess Saedra.

"Did you bring it?" Saedra asked. Her gray eyes shone with anticipation. She stood up from where she sat, on a picnic blanket under one of the apple trees. She wore a pink and white afternoon dress to match the flowers. By all the gods, she was lovely.

"I did," Dorian said. His heart raced with nervous excitement. Reaching into his bag, he drew out his carefully copied transcript. It was easy to forget his misgivings when she looked at him like that.

Saedra took the parchment reverently, eager eyes scanning the sigils and circles. Her expression brightened with excitement, a radiant smile lighting her face as surely as the Spring sunlight.

"Oh, Dorian," she whispered.

And then, quite without warning, she leaned forward and kissed him.

# CHAPTER NINE

# THE CATACOMBS

*PRESENT DAY*

Dorian collapsed with Tai in an ungainly pile on the cold cavern floor.

"Oh, oh no, not again." Wincing, Dorian struggled to sit upright, heart in his throat. "Oh, gods, Tai, are you all right? Are you broken? Oh, gods, I broke Tai, didn't I? Gods and bloody Ancients."

Tai stood up, dusted herself off, and stretched her limbs. "You didn't break me." She twitched her wing. "Wing might be sprained. Useless thing. But everything else seems fine. Like they say. Nobody can take a fall like an Orith."

"It's all my fault. Zekador's pants. I broke the bloody wall. First my father, then Sullivan, now you…"

"Stop that. The wall was going to collapse whether or not we were there. That's why Hildegard told us to stay out. And don't worry about me." She shook out her good wing. "Like I said. We Orith are built to handle a rough landing. But *Zekador's Pants*, Dorian. You're human. What about you? Are you okay?"

With monumental effort, Dorian rose to his feet. "I think so. Plenty of padding, see." With a self-deprecating smile, he wiped the dust off his backside and shook his head. He'd taken a beating, no doubt about it, and surely he would feel some bruises in the morning. Perhaps his injury was worse than he guessed, and he'd notice once the shock wore off. But for the moment, he thought he was okay.

"Just once I'd like to visit an Ancient fortress without it collapsing around me." Dorian grimaced and looked up at the distant ceiling, where shafts of light filtered down through the recently upheaved dust. "So. Um. How do we get back up there?"

"Your guess is as good as mine." Tai's mouth was a thin, grim line. She climbed up the pile of fallen rocks, trying and failing to reach the opening in the ceiling.

"Hey! Help! Xander, Hildegard, anyone there? Could use some help here! Maybe a rope?" Tai jumped up and down and waved her hands, but the only response was her own voice echoing back across the cavern.

"They'll come looking for us," Dorian said. "Won't they?"

"Maybe. But we were pretty far in when we fell. Could be hours before they find us."

Dorian bit his lip. "I don't suppose you can fly out of here? Maybe tell Xander and Hildegard where we fell?"

Tai's expression turned rueful. Twitching her injured wing, she said, "No. I'm afraid not." She looked at Dorian, then back at the fallen pile of rubble. "You're taller than me. Maybe you can climb out?"

Dorian snorted. "Do I look like I can?"

"Looks... can be deceiving?"

He shook his head. "Not this time."

Tai sighed and shook her head. "I just wish it weren't so dark in here. Not even enough aether to get some better light." She tapped in frustration at dull crystal on the hilt of her athame.

Dorian laughed, earning another confused look from his crew-mate. "Sorry," he said. "It's just — you really can't feel all this magic?"

Down here, the energy that permeated the courtyard vibrated all the more intensely. Not enough magic? There was magic, all right. An overwhelming surplus of magic. More magic than Dorian could use in a lifetime.

But Tai shook her head. She couldn't sense it.

Grasping for his belt sheath, Dorian retrieved his own athame. He didn't even need to aether-charge it before drawing the sigils for Flame and Light that turned the knife into a makeshift torch.

"How did you do that?"

"I don't know," he answered honestly.

Taking several long breaths to steady himself, Dorian inspected their surroundings. The improved lighting revealed cobweb-strewn wooden shelves littered with broken bits of pottery and petrified foodstuffs. The once-sturdy wooden door hung splintered and crooked on its hinges. Victim, it seemed, of some long-ago fight with a battering ram.

Dorian, who hadn't eaten since breakfast and dreamed wistfully of lunch, felt a moment's empathy for whoever used a battering ram to get into the pantry. His stomach grumbled hopefully, but he knew he'd find nothing edible in this forgotten storeroom.

«Should have had some of that cheese,» Hematite said.

Dorian agreed. But nothing to be done about it now, so he shone his light out the door and into the dusty stone corridor. "Guess the only way out is through."

"I don't know," Tai said. "Doesn't that seem like a good way for a whole ton of crumbling rubble to fall down on our heads?"

«Your friend is sensible,» Hematite said.

Dorian sighed. *Sweet Ancients.* Never mind his memories from years ago. The last five *minutes* should have been enough to convince him of that. But while every ounce of his good sense told him to stay right where he was, he knew the strange magic wouldn't let him. Dorian's pendant thrummed.

"I... think it might have to do with this." Dorian lifted the golden chain and showed her the dragon on the other end. "I think it's connected to this fortress somehow. There's this... this magical pressure, and the pendant is leading me to the source. I... I know it's completely irrational. I shouldn't want to go find the source. But Tai. But if I don't, I..." he swallowed. "I think I'll regret it for the rest of my life."

«I do not like this,» Hematite said, but he also didn't suggest any better options.

"Can I see the pendant?" Tai asked.

Dorian hesitated, but he couldn't think of any reason not to let her. He removed the gold chain and handed it to her. He half hoped the magical pressure would vanish, but it only lessened a small amount. Although, he thought, it *did* lessen. That meant he was right, at least, about the connection.

Tai frowned as she inspected it. "I don't feel any magic like you describe." She handed it back to him, and he looped it back around his neck. "But there was definitely something strange about it. Like an aether crystal that's... blocked somehow. Maybe it's keyed specifically to you."

"Is that possible?" Dorian wondered.

Hematite thrummed with knowing apprehension. «It is possible. But for one of them to... oh, I knew it was a bad idea for you to cast that spell. I just knew it!»

Tai shook her head. "I suppose the choice is to follow this thing or hang around down here. The fortress might be dangerous, but it beats starving to death waiting for rescue."

"It would take me some time to starve to death," Dorian said with a wan smile. "But I take your point. Follow the magic source with me?"

Tai smiled and took his hand. "Got nothing better to do. Lead the way."

If Dorian had hoped for Ancient treasure and lost magic around every corner, he was soon disappointed. The dark, dusty corridors of Greystone Citadel were long, winding, and, it seemed, totally empty.

Each branching hallway led to either a dead end or a cave-in. After an hour's wandering, they were no closer to the source of the magic or a way out. Dorian's legs made their indignation known. He wasn't used to this much walking. And he was cold, too. He'd worked up a sweat above in the scorching desert sun, and now his damp skin shivered in the cool and musty underground. He wished he had a coat.

«What did I tell you?» Hematite complained. «This adventuring is. Cold, wet, hungry, and miserable.»

Dorian certainly wouldn't deny the other three, but he didn't think he was miserable. At least not yet. At least he was doing something.

Tai followed close to his side, careful not to lose the light of the single spell-torch. Despite the chill air, her presence made Dorian feel warm inside.

"Say, Dorian." Tai's voice broke through the sound of their crunching footsteps. "Your woman. Queen Saedra."

Dorian's heart gave a tiny jolt. "She's not 'my woman.' She's the queen of Kasanarae. But. Erm. What about her?"

"What exactly kind of relationship did you have?"

Dorian felt himself redden. "We were — we were —"

"Did you enter her castle?" Tai's brown eyes sparkled in the torchlight.

Dorian shook his head, perplexed. "In Kasanarae? Of course not. We never left Frostvale."

Tai rolled her eyes. "I meant churn butter. Sheath the magic dagger. Put milk on the waffle. Bury the weasel."

"Put milk on the — bury the — bury the what?"

Tai grinned. "*Have sex.*"

"I — ah — that is —"

"Well," Tai prodded, "Did you?"

Dorian coughed and sputtered several more times before nodding a single affirmative.

"Ah! Wonderful!" Tai clapped eagerly.

Dorian's face burned brighter than his spell-torch. The images returned to him. Saedra, laying beside him, soft and graceful, a work of art. He, awkward and ungainly, naked and exposed. *Void Eternal.* This was the last thing he wanted to talk about, here in this cavern, with Tai, of all people.

"Do you love her?" Tai asked.

Dorian's throat felt dry. He tried to take a swig from his canteen, but he'd finished the last of the water hours ago. "I — yes, I think so." He swallowed some saliva to appease his parched throat.

"So supposing you accomplish all your dreams and unseat this Callahan and marry the lovely queen," Tai said, "Doesn't that make you the new King of Kasanarae?"

Dorian gaped at her. "I don't — that is — I hadn't — I hadn't planned that far ahead."

Right now, it felt like enough of a challenge just to stay alive. But supposing a miracle occurred. What then? Dorian couldn't be King. Surely. Could he?

«You would be a bit on the meek side for a ruler, but better than many,» Hematite said.

«Thanks for the vote of confidence,» Dorian replied. Out loud, he added, "I'm just not sure it works that way."

"Hmmm." Tai put a thoughtful finger over her mouth. "Well, she might make you her mistress. Or... what's the word in Aerish for a male mistress? Mister? Like a concubine, but a man. Man concu-bine." She put her hands together. "Mancubine!"

Dorian sputtered a cough. "*Mancubine?*"

«Ah, now this I like,» Hematite said. «All the luxury, none of the responsibility. Dorian Valmont, Mancubine.»

"Meroneth's balls," Dorian replied, burying his face in his hand.

«Your balls, actually,» Hematite said.

Between Hematite and Tai, Dorian thought he might actually die of embarrassment.

Tai was beside herself with laughter. "Imagine you, all gussied up like--" she cut off abruptly.

"What is it?" Dorian asked.

"Up there."

Dorian froze and shone the torch ahead. He saw nothing, but he heard something. A scratching, hissing noise. The buzzing of his pendant intensified. Or maybe that was just his heart racing.

"Pit wraith," Dorian squeaked.

"Don't be silly, those are just legends," Tai said, though her voice cracked just a little.

Dorian proffered his hand to Tai. "Let's not wait around to find out what it is."

Her small, calloused hand in his large, soft one. They hurried away from the source of the noise. His pendant buzzed with greater intensity.

As they progressed, the catacombs became wider, more rugged. The stone hallways gave way to rough-hewn underground tunnels. A way out, Dorian wondered, or deeper in? At least this section was better lit. Luminescent blue aether crystals jutted out of the cavern walls at random intervals. The magic buzzing grew steadily stronger, so strong he thought his bones might jump out of his flesh.

"There... aren't such things as pit wraiths, right? We're not going to... to transform?"

"I sure hope not," Tai said. "Feel any desire for human flesh?"

Dorian forced a weak smile. "Hungry enough to eat a whole gryphon, if we're honest. But not humans."

The scraping noises grew closer. *Scritch, scratch. Scritch, scratch.*

Behind them, there was only the softly glowing wall of aether. There was no way out.

Dorian waved his torch in the noise's direction.

"You don't want to eat me, Mister Pit Wraith!" Dorian's voice shook. "Too fatty. You'll get indigestion."

"Stop that," Tai said irritably.

Dorian had hoped his attempt at levity would ease his growing panic, but his heart kept on hammering to escape his ribcage. He wondered if he might just fall dead right there and save the pit wraith the trouble.

Against his pounding chest, Dorian's pendant pulsed urgently. He approached the interloper.

It was not a pit wraith.

The being before him resembled a glittering sculpture of gemstone. Magnificent scales like rubies glittered in the torchlight. She — he knew it was *she*, somehow — had wings, large and leathery and batlike, with a membrane of spun gold. Golden, too, were the keratin plates armoring her chest and the bony ridges on her neck. Her wicked curving horns, however, were silvery, as were the three crescent-shaped blades at the tip of her tail.

Dorian gulped. Not a pit wraith at all.

"Dragon!" Dorian's voice came out a full octave higher than normal. "That's a dragon."

Tai replied with a stiff nod. She, like Dorian, seemed torn between fascination and terror. And judging from her expression, she was thinking the same thing he was. *If that's a dragon, does she have a rider?* He thought of Callahan and his dragon, and his sense of apprehension grew.

The dragon stood about half again as tall and twice as long as a well-bred Adenthulian draft horse. But she looked fragile, somehow, too spindly, like a delicate sculpture of glass. Dorian was hardly in fighting shape, but he suspected he could do actual damage just by slamming into her. Then again, he couldn't ignore the danger of those tail blades.

«Why would we want to hurt each other?»

The dragon dragged herself forward with agonized desperation. Magical energy dragged behind her in a silver-white stream of sparks.

"She's hurt," Dorian said.

«Yes. And unless I stem the flow of magical energy, I fear our bond will be a short one.» Her mindvoice came more clearly now, but so did her pain, like a discordant note in a symphony.

"Bond?" Dorian asked. "What does that mean?"

The dragon grunted in combined pain and, it seemed, irritation. «I committed a grave offense against my kind, in answering your Summons. The leader of my clan saw fit to punish me. I consider myself fortunate I did not suffer worse.»

*Bond. Summons.* Was this dragon... had the spell worked, after all?

Heart racing, he focused on the creature's injury, racing through the sigils and spell patterns he knew. He wasn't a trained Healer, not like Sullivan, but he might improvise. "Let me see... if I use a connection rune to knit the skin back together..."

"Dorian, that's dangerous," Tai warned.

«It will do no good, anyway,» the dragon said. «This physical form is an extension of yourself.» She looked at Dorian's soft, exhausted body, and plainly found him wanting. Twitching her tail, she explained, «You can no more Heal me than you can Heal yourself. It simply does not work that way.» She cocked her head slightly to the right in a puzzled gesture. «But surely you must have known that, if you knew how to cast the Summons.»

Dorian felt the heat rise to his face. How in the Void was he supposed to know about dragon Healing? There'd been almost no contact between humans and dragons for centuries.

«As I said, I am in rather dire straits,» the dragon said, «So perhaps you might staunch the bleeding?»

Dorian blinked. "But if I can't do magic—"

«Something mundane, you foolish human,» the dragon snapped in reply.

"Oh. Right." Dorian scrambled to recall what he'd learned of basic first aid. "Um. That glowy white stuff. That's blood, then, um, is it?"

«Effectively,» the dragon said. She cocked her head in puzzlement. «How is it you do not know these things?»

Dorian handed Tai his athame-torch and unsheathed his regular, non-magical belt knife. He bit his lip awkwardly as set about removing his shirtsleeve. It would be easier if he simply removed the shirt, but appearing shirtless in front of both Tai and the dragon was simply a bridge too far. So he ripped loose the sleeve, then removed the ties from his lace-up collar, and used those things together to set and bind the dragon's wound.

"That's fine Vatean silk you just cut up," Tai said.

"At least this way, it's useful," Dorian said.

«With all due respect,» the dragon said, twitching her wicked bladed tail. «When you cast the Summons, I had the impression you knew what you were doing.»

«Not sure where you got that impression,» came the sour voice of Hematite.

The dragon breathed out a puff of golden sparks, puzzlement turning into outright indignation. «And just what in the Eternal Void is that?»

«Ah,» Dorian said. «Dragon, meet Hematite. Hematite, meet... um, sorry, I don't actually know your name.» *Gods and Ancients.* In all his childhood daydreams about meeting a dragon, he'd never imagined it being this uncomfortable.

«My name does not translate well into your limited human tongue,» the dragon replied, no longer bothering to hide her disdain. «I suppose, for our purposes, you may call me Solaris. But never mind that! This is unacceptable!» Solaris swished her tail back and forth in obvious agitation. «You dare to cast the Summons, knowing full well that your spirit is already—» If she could have, Dorian had a feeling she would have spat the last word — *«Occupied?»*

"Erm," Dorian said, swallowing. "I didn't exactly know what I was doing."

The dragon said nothing for a long moment, a fierce battle clearly raging in her mind. Finally, with strained, practiced patience, she said, «No matter. To lower myself to accept the bond of a human is abominable enough. To bond with a human so weak as to render me but a dry twig in a windstorm, that is even worse. What more is a demon, except just another minor humiliation?»

Dorian burned with a humiliation of his own. First, he was a disappointment to Xander and the crew, now he was a disappointment to this dragon, as well. But none of that changed the fact that she was injured and clearly desperate.

Gingerly, he took the dragon's fragile leg, and bound the wound with what was once his shirt sleeve. To his relief, the magical bleeding stopped.

«To be honest, I never understood why humans insist upon covering themselves in fabric» Solaris said, almost conversationally. «But this provides some improvement. You have my gratitude.»

"You're... you're welcome," Dorian said.

Tai cleared her throat, causing Dorian to flush once more. Years with Hematite had taught him that people found it rude when he communicated telepathically without them. "Sorry, Tai," he said. "Um. Tai, this is Solaris. Solaris, ah, this is Tai."

«Well met, human,» Solaris nodded in respect.

"You can talk to her?" Dorian asked in surprise.

«I can speak to other humans, but only when we are in proximity,» Solaris said. More tail twitching. «Or if she holds your dragonstone.»

*Dragonstone.* Dorian examined his pendant in awe. The blue aetherlight washed out the stone's red color, but he was almost certain it was the same color as Solaris's scales.

"That must be why the color changed," he said, awed. "That's what that spell did! I was summoning you!"

«Moon and Stars,» the dragon complained, «You really know nothing about dragons, do you?»

"Apparently not," Dorian said. "The truth is, I cast that spell because... well, I was desperate too, if you must know." He scratched his neck. "I found the spell in my father's old journal, with just a note saying 'To beg for aid.' And to be honest, I could've used some aid right then. But I, um, didn't, ah, actually know what the spell did." He winced.

"You cast a spell without knowing what it did?" This time it was Tai's turn to look horrified. "Void Eternal. It could've blown up in your face?"

"Yeah, well, like I said," Dorian said. "I was desperate."

Solaris huffed in indignation, several sparks escaping her nostrils. «Are you telling me,» she said, «That I have committed the greatest possible act of blasphemy known to my kind, been named anathema to my kinfolk, and been injured and nearly killed because of a spell that was cast... by accident?»

Dorian's throat felt dry. "I'm... sorry?" He swallowed an unhelpful mouthful of saliva. "But I, um. In my, uh, defense, you didn't have to accept the bond." His heart pounded. He just knew he was being out of line. "No dragon has answered a Summons in over a thousand years? Why now? Why me?"

Solaris let out a stream of orange-gold sparks. «As I said. I was desperate.» But then, more kindly, she added, «I know what I saw within that circle.» For the first time, he sensed the wild, desperate hope that roiled beneath her standoffish exterior. «I looked into your soul.»

Dorian folded his arms over his chest, feeling exposed. He wasn't sure he liked the idea of his *soul* being open for the dragon's perusal.

«As well you should not,» Hematite said. «You are my bonded human! Mine!»

"I'm sorry." Dorian said, ignoring the demon's newfound possessiveness. "I still... I still don't understand."

«It will be faster, I think, If I show you.»

And then, all around him, the world faded to black.

## CHAPTER TEN
# DRAGON MEMORIES

Solaris watched the other dragons with longing. The ghostly, transparent creatures swirled and darted under the light of the full moon, casting a vibrant aura of color and light.

It was the Ceremony of New Light, when one deity ceded their throne in the sky, and the next came to take their place. A solemn time, but a time for celebration, too.

Unfortunately, the last thing Solaris felt like doing was celebrating.

It should have been her up there in the star-strewn sky, welcoming Lady Kyrizzian as she took Lord Meroneth's place. Now, Solaris despaired she would ever get that chance.

«You need to be patient,» Celestian had said.

«Your chance will come,» Borealis had reassured her.

«You are simply not ready yet,» had been Elder Meteor's final verdict.

Not ready yet. *Not ready yet.* The words bounded back and forth in her mind like thunderbolts in the underclouds. She had easily out-flown Borealis and Meridian in the Trials. Yet they were up there, and she was down here.

Why? What would it take for the others to see her value?

«You are young,» Elder Cirrus had tried to explain, with a bit more poise and diplomacy than Elder Meteor. «The youngest of our clan. Far too young for a moondance so dangerous and volatile as New Light.»

*Too young*, always too young. But *Moon and Stars*, she was almost fifty years old! She had watched the seven gods ascend and descend their starlit throne seven times each! And besides, her friend Celestian flew his first New Light when he was only forty-three. So why? Why was she not good enough?

«It is not a matter of who is good enough,» came Chronicler Nocturne's gentle mindvoice.

«Chronicler!» Solaris raised her tail in greeting.

Despite her sullen disappointment, she was glad to see the black and silver dragon. He was the only member of their clan who ever really seemed to treat her like a proper dragon and not some errant fledgling. He couldn't take part in the Moondance either, though for vastly different reasons.

«They only seek to protect us,» Nocturne said, but with no small amount of regret.

Solaris twitched her tail in irritation. At this rate, she was going to be encased in crystal by the time she was seventy.

Nocturne replied with an understanding chuckle. «Come with me. I know a good vantage point to watch the Moondance.»

Nocturne led Solaris to an outcropping next to a waterfall on the edgecliffs. Multihued rainbows of magic reflected in the silver-light foam of the falls.

«Meteor will be furious to find us so far out here,» Solaris said. Past the outcropping, there was nothing beneath them but the constant roiling clouds, lit at random intervals by stray bolts of lightning. Down there was the domain of wraiths, the domain of the Void. Deadly peril, even to a dragon.

«There can be no adventure without risk,» Nocturne said.

Solaris smiled. «For someone charged with carrying the memories of the entire clan, you certainly can be irreverent, Chronicler.»

«It is because I am the keeper of our legends that I am so irreverent, little one.» Nocturne chuckled. «I know the way things once were, and the way they could yet be again, if we let it.» He paused, contemplative, trying to decide whether to say more. Finally, he concluded, «Elder Meteor is too overcautious by half. Come. See the dance from here.»

Solaris had a feeling that a critique of Meteor was not what Nocturne originally intended to say, but she decided not to press the issue, and followed him out above the clouds. She laughed despite herself, feeling exposed, feeling defiant. From out here, the light of the moon dancers shone brighter. The dragons glowed with their own light, and the light of the gods. Their dance was a storm of power and magic.

Solaris watched Borealis dart after a bolt of magical energy — and miss. Solaris winced. The energy dissipated and vanished, lost to them forever. The Moondance wasn't just supposed to look pretty. They needed to gather all the energy they could if they wanted their clan to survive another year. Solaris would not have missed. Moon and Stars, she should be up there too. She *deserved* to be up there, too.

«It has nothing to do with your skill or ability,» Nocturne said. «It has everything to do with the fact that Meteor and the others are too cowardly and hidebound to see the obvious truth in front of them.»

«Unwise,» Solaris said, «To speak of the Elders like that.»

«Have you noticed,» Nocturne said, «That with every passing year, the Moondancers gather less energy?»

Solaris tilted her ghostly transparent wing. Nocturne was the Chronicler, so she trusted him to know the raw numbers of it. «It seems like we had more energy in the past,» Solaris admitted. «But perhaps it is because they let dim-sparks like Borealis do the Dancing instead of those of us who defeated them in the Trials.»

«Do not be censorious,» Nocturne said with gentle reproach. «Borealis flies as proficiently as any of the Ancient Ones, and better than some. But these are not the Ancient Times.» He shook his head.

Solaris let out a snort of ghostly sparks. «I thought much-vaunted Ancient Ones did everything better than we do.»

«Not at all,» Nocturne said. «They did not need to.» The Chronicler craned his shadowy neck towards the sky. «Something is wrong with the Lunar Nexus. Something is preventing energy from passing through.»

«Impossible,» protested Solaris. «The Lunar Nexus has stood since the dawn of time!»

«Do you not find it odd,» Nocturne said, «That we have had no new dragons in almost fifty years?»

Solaris's ethereal snout narrowed into a draconic frown. That *did* seem odd. She had few memories of her infancy in the Spirit Realm, before she crossed the Lunar Nexus to take her chances in the Physical. Solaris was the last of her clan to cross through. Solaris had always been the last to cross through. But that was seven Cycles ago. the others were all only a Cycle or two apart. Why had Solaris been the youngest for so long?

«It is because there is not enough raw magical energy to maintain a new dragon on this side,» Nocturne said. «While the Nexus has stood for countless ages, no one has maintained it for over a millennium.»

Solaris felt a prickle of unease. She knew what maintaining the Lunar Nexus entailed. «You fly dangerous skies, Chronicler.»

«A dragon with a rider flies better than a dragon alone,» Nocturne said.

«Flew better! Past tense!»

*Moon and Stars,* Solaris thought. This talk was going to get Nocturne killed. And maybe Solaris, too, if only by association.

«The entire world may be in danger, Solaris,» Nocturne said, raising his ghostly tail. «Together with humans, I believe we can still save the magic. Apart, however, I fear there is nothing but doom for both races.»

«You must not speak of this to anyone, least of all Elder Meteor.»

Nocturne chuckled. «Believe me. I do not yet nurture such suicidal impulses. But you, perhaps, I thought might understand.»

Solaris twitched her tail in annoyance. «I will not report you,» she allowed. «You well know I would never do that. But I do not know what you expect me to do! Humans, Nocturne. The last time one of us got involved with humans...»

She cut off, pushing aside the painful memories. Twenty-one years ago, three Cycles, close to half a lifetime. Solaris recalled it as clear as if it happened yesterday. Nightflame, Starfire, and Cloud, all killed for their base treachery. Meteor killed Starfire and Cloud right away, but Nightflame, the Elder captured. To make an example.

«I have reason to believe,» Nocturne said, «That Starfire and Cloud might not be as dead as Elder Meteor would have us believe.»

«Impossible.»

«There are... rumors. Circulating among the Chroniclers of the other dragon clans. Rumors of a secret location, where dragons and humans still work together.»

«Nocturne, I mean it.» Solaris was well and truly terrified now. «Speaking of these things will get you killed.»

«Continuing to ignore humanity will get everyone killed!» Nocturne shot back.

«You do not know that,» Solaris tried to make him see reason. She did not think she could stand it if Elder Meteor executed Nocturne, the only dragon in the clan who ever bothered to be nice to her.

«And besides,» Solaris added, «If there are secret blasphemers out there, why have they not fixed the Lunar Nexus?»

«Perhaps they do not yet know how,» Nocturne said. «But if there is one thing I have learned about humans in my studies, it is that they have a knack for figuring out how to do things they once could not.»

Three days later, Solaris flew in intricate loops and spirals in the open sky, trying and failing to dispel the anxiety that had settled in the back of her mind.

Was there any truth in what Nocturne had said? Would she be able to fly better if she bonded to a human? *No.* She refused to consider it. If Meteor did not kill her, the humans surely would. Humans were not to be trusted.

Solaris was not aware, right away, when disaster struck.

If she had been down in the valley with the others, she herself might have fallen victim to the chaos. Then again, if she had been there, she might have been able to make a difference. But she was not. And she did not.

As it was, the prickle of anxiety with in her grew. Unease turned into fear, which grew into genuine terror. And only then did she realize those feelings were not coming from herself.

As fast as her ghostly wings would take her, she darted back towards the valley.

To Solaris's horror, the entire mountainside was on fire. Even in her ghostly form, she recoiled from the searing heat. Below, she saw one section of the valley spared from the flames, but it gave her little comfort. The iridescent shimmer of a protective magical barrier flickered in the firelight. That could only mean one thing.

There were humans in the valley.

They stood on the ground next to ornithopters made of wood and steel and aether silk, a crude mimicry of draconic flight. They carried angry torches, flickering flame illuminating greedy human faces. Ghostly draconic figures scattered bin their presence, but they, too, were trapped in the magical barrier. They dared not risk the inferno. The fear and terror of two dozen panicked dragons reverberated across the vale.

«No!» Solaris cried out in horror as she plunged through the magical barrier. To her great relief, she passed through unharmed. But she knew she was far from safe.

She found Nocturne, flapping his wings against the chaos.

«What is happening?» she asked, frantic, desperate.

Nocturne laughed a ragged, bitter laugh. «It seems I was wrong, and you were right, dear child,» the aged Chronicler said. «Humans are not to be trusted.»

Next to the humans stood Borealis and Celestian. Only three nights ago, she'd watched them with envy as their ethereal forms danced under the moon. Now, they waited at the humans' sides, obedient, their scales glittering like gemstones in the firelight. Solid. Docile. Bonded.

The lead human, a pale, blue-eyed man, traced a spell circle into the air. The human sigils glowed lurid blue, providing stark contrast to the surrounding flame.

There was something oddly compelling about those sigils. Something beautifully hypnotic, piquing Solaris's interest, making her want to fly closer. She clearly was not the only one. One by one, entranced, the dragons of the vale passed through the circle and emerged solid on the other side. Meridian. Northstar. And, to her horror, Solaris herself.

«No,» she thought, «This is not right.»

And yet, that thought came from far away. A silly thing, really. She had to fly into the circle; it was the only logical option. The most natural thing in the world.

*Wham.*

Nocturne slammed into Solaris, knocking her free of the spell's terrible grasp. Solaris flared her ethereal wings. Still incorporeal, thank the gods. *Moon and Stars*, that was close!

Short-lived relief turned into horror as Solaris watched the spell take hold of Nocturne instead.

«No!» Solaris dove to block him, as he had blocked her, but it was too late. She watched, helpless, as his midnight black scales and silver wings solidified, joining him together with a human bond he neither wanted nor asked for.

"Ah, now you are mine," said the pale human, stroking Nocturne with a twisted form of affection.

«Nocturne!» She flew to him, but he took a swipe at her with sharp, metallic claws. With a crackling of magical energy, his solid form met with her spiritual one, sending her reeling backwards.

«Why—»

«You must flee,» Nocturne told her. His mindvoice felt like it came from the other end of a long tunnel. «This human, Janus Callahan, controls my actions. Please. Go.»

The horrific spell circle abruptly winked out.

"We will be back," the human called Janus Callahan promised to the others, "When we have gathered more dragonstones. Do not think to resist us."

And just like that, the humans climbed upon their ensorcelled dragons and took off into the sky. They left the ornithopters arrived on behind like so much litter, but it didn't matter. Once the barrier failed, as it would without the humans to maintain it, the flames would destroy them, too.

Solaris turned frantically towards the rest of her clan. At least some of them remained. At least Solaris was not wholly alone. «We have to do something! We have to stop them!»

«Do?» Elder Cirrus radiated bitter amusement. «There is nothing we can do against the forces of humans and their twisted magic. That is why we have avoided them all these long Cycles.»

And it was, Solaris realized with dismay, true. Nocturne had been right in his own way. An unbonded dragon was no match for a bonded one. Solaris felt the Nocturne's superior strength the moment he struck her.

«I will rescue you,» she vowed to Nocturne and the others as they departed. «I do not know how, just yet. But by my wings and the stars that guide me, I will find a way.»

«What do you mean there will be no rescue mission?» Solaris demanded three weeks later. She struggled to keep her outrage in check.

Three weeks ago, questioning the High Elder would have been unthinkable. But when the Elders made no effort going after their captured kinfolk, Solaris could keep quiet no more.

«You are letting your personal feelings cloud your judgement,» Meteor said in a bland, paternalistic mindvoice. «Please try to use common sense.»

«I am using common sense!» With forced calm, Solaris continued, «There are nearly two dozen of us, and only six of them. If we all band together, it does not matter if they have physical bodies, they cannot hope to—»

«We would still suffer unneeded casualties,» Meteor replied, the epitome of calmness. «I know you were close to Chronicler Nocturne, but you must admit he always espoused dangerous notions. This heresy—»

«He did not commit heresy.»

«Come now,» Cirrus, the other Elder, cut in. «We all know Nocturne was always a blasphemous human-lover. Do you honestly believe he did not choose this?»

«It is possible,» Meteor put in, «That he invited the humans to the valley.»

«Nocturne would do no such thing!» Solaris was furious that the Elders would even suggest it. Forcing herself once more to calm, she said, «Nocturne was our Chronicler. What do we hope to do without the knowledge he holds?»

«Perhaps it is better to let go of such dangerous and outdated memories,» Meteor said.

«But we cannot let his knowledge fall into the hands of

humans!» Solaris tried to convince them, even though she knew it would be in vain.

«It is too late,» Meteor said. «The humans will have already stolen what information they can from Nocturne, much to all our detriment. A rescue mission is far too risky.»

Solaris twitched her tail in agitation. «But the others! We need them! Borealis and Celestian — they were some of our best Moon-dancers.»

«I believe just last moon you called Borealis, what was it, a dim-sparked tail dragger, when I selected him for the Moondance instead of you,» Meteor put in.

Solaris lowered her head. *Yes*, she had said that. She regretted it now.

«It was an unfortunate blow against us, it is true,» Meteor said. «But not so grave a blow as we would suffer in trying to correct their Heresy.»

«But—» Solaris began.

«No,» Meteor replied, «I am afraid that for now, Nocturne and the others must go unpunished.»

For a long moment, Solaris was certain she must have misunder-stood. «Punished? What does punishment have to do with it? It was those humans who—»

«There are no excuses to engage in Heresy,» Meteor replied.

«But they did not have a choice!»

«Irrelevant.»

Solaris blew out a plume of frustrated sparks and spiraled ever higher into the clear blue sky.

She had to do something. She couldn't just let Nocturne and the others suffer as slaves forever! But what? She was only one dragon, and a young one at that. Never in her seven Cycles of living had Solaris ever felt so powerless. The very air seemed to vibrate with her frustration and despair.

Except... no. That was not it. It was not her own emotions causing the strange rippling in the sky.

«Now?» she asked, disbelieving.

She recognized this sensation. It was the same she felt when Nightflame committed blasphemy. It was the same she felt when Starfire called out, foolishly, for second chances.

The humans who came for Nocturne and the others took their bonds by force. Today, however, a human tried to procure a bond the old-fashioned way — by asking nicely.

Dragonkind's most solemn rule was to ignore the Summons when they came. But Solaris felt reckless, defiant. She reached out and touched minds with the human on the other side.

Solaris once assumed all humans were the same. Arrogant, entitled fools, each convinced that somehow they would be the exception, they alone could overturn a thousand years of sacred dragon law.

This human, however, was different. He was as far from arrogant as she could imagine. Almost everything about him reverberated with self-doubt. Yet there was a desperate sort of determination in him, too. A quiet spark in his soul that could, with time, be fanned into flame.

And then, in his memories, she saw another human face. Pale and cold, with eyes like chips of ice.

The human on the ornithopter. The man who took Nocturne.

She could tell from the depths of her soul that her would-be summoner hated and feared this man, too. The summoner and Solaris shared a common enemy.

Solaris decided in an instant. She knew if she took even the briefest moment to consider, courage would fail her.

«I accept!» she declared. «I accept the human Dorian Valmont as my bond!»

She felt the energy pour through her as if struck by lightning. Her ruby scales and golden wings solidified. Far away in the land called Adenthul, the human's dragonstone turned red to match her scales. And yet, Solaris did not feel powerful, the way she thought she might if she bonded. She felt exposed, as if a gust of wind might send her tumbling into the underclouds.

«Solaris,» Elder Cirrus said, «By the Moon and the Stars, what have you done?»

«What must be done.» Solaris spat out sparks of defiance.

«There are no excuses for Heresy,» Meteor repeated.

The rest of Solaris's clan attacked.

# CHAPTER ELEVEN

# FLIGHT

The vision ended, and the cavern re-materialized around Dorian. At some point, he'd sat down against the cavern wall. The spiky ends of the aether crystal dug into his back.

"They... they were the ones that hurt you," Dorian said, rising shakily to his feet. "Your clan-mates. They... they hurt you because of me." Guilt and shame welled up within him.

«Enough of that,» Solaris said. «I chose you of my own free will. Do not forget that.»

Tai rolled her eyes. "Blaming yourself for the dragon's injury is probably the most *Dorian* thing you've ever done." But then she laughed. "Void, boy. First you're able to read a magic book, then you're the lover of a queen, and now you're a dragonaut too? Of course you are."

Dorian flushed and scratched his neck. It sounded ridiculous when she listed it out like that. He was just an awkward boy from Adenthul. Not some kind of hero. Not a dragonaut. But Solaris came to him out of desperation.

Solaris needed Dorian's help to free the other dragons. But how in the seven Voids was he going to do that?

«Ah. Well. I suppose there is no reason that you should know,» Solaris said. She swished her wicked tail slowly back and forth, thinking. «There are many ways to sever a dragonaut bond. The most obvious way is to kill the human, naturally.»

Dorian blanched.

«If you are squeamish about such things,» Solaris continued, «You could always destroy the dragon's body instead.»

"Um," Dorian said. "Wouldn't killing your friends sort of defeat the purpose?"

«Destroying their physical forms would not kill them,» Solaris said. «It would only sever the bond. We are not so fragile as you humans.»

"Right. Well, um, I... I appreciate you coming for me. But... I think maybe we've both made a mistake. I... wasn't in my right mind when I cast that spell. And..." he swallowed, hating himself. "I'm not sure I can help you."

More tail twitching. «Even a human such as you is better than no human at all.»

Dorian wasn't so sure about that. But rather than arguing further, he said, "I suppose we won't be saving anyone unless we can find a way out of these catacombs."

«Ah,» said Solaris. «With that, I can help. Come with me.»

They followed the dragon through the corridors, eventually reaching reached a massive open space that had probably once been some kind of great hall. Sunlight — glorious sunlight — filtered in through cracks in the ruined dome. Dorian didn't think he'd ever felt so relieved to see the sky.

«There it is,» Solaris said. «Our way out.»

"How are we going to get up there?" Dorian asked.

Solaris let out a spark of impatience. «We will fly, obviously.»

Dorian's heart leapt with a combination of excitement and terror. "Fly? On... on your back?"

Solaris spread her golden wings with an impatient flick of her tail. «My understanding is that *dragon riders* actually *ride* their dragons.»

"Well, yes, um, sure," Dorian said. "But I don't... I mean... There's both Tai and me here, and, I'm no good at riding gryphons, and..."

«I am not a gryphon,» Solaris scoffed. «Just get on.»

Apprehensively, Dorian climbed onto the dragon's back. He didn't know what else to do, so he held onto the ridges on the back of her neck for purchase.

A moment later, Tai climbed on behind him with considerably more grace. Dorian felt all too keenly aware of his body as she moved up close to him and grabbed onto the hem of his shirt. She smelled like cinnamon.

«Void Eternal,» Solaris complained. «You are heavy.»

"I know that," Dorian grumbled. "Thanks."

«You leap to do her bidding,» Hematite complained, «When it is I who have been with you all these years.»

Dorian felt a pang and reached out to reassure his demon. But Hematite's tirade cut off at once as soon as Solaris launched into the sky.

Dorian gasped. For all of Solaris's claims that she wasn't a gryphon, Dorian assumed flying on one was like flying on the other. But he was wrong. This, thank the Ancients, was nothing like flying on a gryphon. This was something deeper. He felt the wind against her scales, experienced the energy of her wings taking flight. It took him a moment to realize why the sensation was familiar.

"This is just like the linking!"

«Of course it is,» Solaris said. «Your skyships are but a crude imitation of our magic. This is the very core of our essence.»

Like the Linking, however, it was a lot of effort. Through their connection, he could feel her wings straining from exertion. Even this short flight was a challenge for her. And for Dorian, too. He heaved for breath. Why was he short of breath? He wasn't even doing anything. At that moment, facing down Callahan and his minions seemed a tall order indeed.

*I told you, Hematite's mindvoice said. You are helpless on a real adventure.*

«That was not the demon,» Solaris said. «That was just your own insecurities.»

The dragon gathered her energy and pumped her wings hard, and together they rose further into the sky.

"Zekador's poorly fitting pants," Xander swore as he made his frantic way up the crumbling staircase. And then, for good measure, he added, "Meroneth's balls. Kyrizzian's teats. Valgren's left toe!"

"Calm down, Xander," Hildegard said, though she looked frantic herself, her rich auburn hair flying free of her bun. "They can't have gone too far."

"Maybe." Xander was unconvinced. True, Dorian and Tai didn't seem like the types to cause much trouble, but the abandoned Ancient fortress was enormous. They could search for days and still not find them.

"Typical," he said, "Typical, typical, typical. I only had care of Cyrus Valmont's son for two weeks, and already I've gone and lost the boy. *Nahiira's sphincter!*"

And not just Dorian, but Tai, too. Why did she have to get mixed up in all this? *Void, void, void!*

"They're aeronauts, not children," Hildegard said. "They know what they're doing."

"Maybe," Xander repeated. True enough, Tai had a good head on her shoulders. She wouldn't steer Dorian towards trouble. But Dorian himself?

He took a deep breath and forced himself to think rationally. Hildegard was right. Dorian wasn't a child. But he wasn't a seasoned aeronaut either. He remembered the exuberant child he'd met once or twice during his long years of friendship with Cyrus. And he considered the awkward, timid young man the boy had become. Honestly, Xander didn't know what to make of Dorian.

"Over here," Hildegard said. "This collapse is recent. See all the dust in the air?"

"Sweet Ancients." Xander rushed over, dreading what he might find.

"Calm down or you'll cause another collapse," Hildegard warned. She put her hand on his arm. "There're footprints in the dust, see?" She shone her aether lantern into the chamber.

Sure enough, two sets of footprints led towards the chamber exit. This only made Xander feel marginally better. "They walked further into the ruins?"

"I think I have an idea which way they might have gone," Hildegard said. "Follow me."

She led him up a long narrow spiral staircase towards the back side of the ruined fortress. "Sorry," Hildegard said, "But this is the safest route, even if it is longer."

"So long as we find them before another piece of the castle collapses down on their heads," Xander said.

"Your crew members are fine," Hildegard repeated. But her platitudes did nothing to ease the nightmare scenarios running through Xander's mind.

"They're my crew members. I'm responsible for them. And you yourself said how dangerous the old fortress is! I don't understand how you can be so calm about this."

Hildegard shook her head. "You saw how Dorian acted. You know as well as I what he'll find in that fortress."

Despite the desert sunlight, Xander felt a chill. *Yes.* He knew. Or at least, he suspected. Part of him even thrilled at the possibility. But the more rational, adult part of him refused to even consider it. He'd had his hopes raised and dashed before, after all.

"Don't pretend you're not at least a little excited." Hildegard flashed a self-satisfied smile.

*Gods above,* that smile again. It was like they were back to being ten years old.

"We're not children anymore," he grumbled, more to himself than to Hildegard.

"Neither are they, Xander," Hildegard said. "You are not their father, no matter how much you may wish it."

Xander ran a nervous hand through his damp and sweaty hair. Gods above, was that what he was doing? Trying to set himself up as their father? He felt a certain responsibility towards everyone in his employ, of course. But it was different with Dorian. Dorian was Cyrus's son. Was he overstepping some unstated boundary?

"So you really think Sylvia's going to contact us?" Xander asked, changing the subject. Personally, he had his doubts. "Much as I'd love a nice little family reunion, she's wanted little enough to do with me in the past. I don't see how that might have changed."

"Everything has changed," Hildegard said. "Surely you can see that." Her mouth turned into a mischievous smile. "Unless you want to come fully back into the fold. Then everything would be so much easier."

Xander barked a bitter laugh. "I'll do that when Meroneth's Halls catch flame."

Hildegard sighed and shook her head. "The boy has a right--"

"The boy," Xander snapped back, "Has benefited precious little from Sylvia's meddling, and I doubt that'll change soon. That woman has done us all a huge favor by leaving us alone, as far as I can tell."

"And Callahan?" Hildegard asked. "What, we just let him conquer all of Aeris? End the magic like he wants, plunge us down beneath the underclouds to live among the Orith and the Iriya?" She smirked bitterly and turned the corner into a half-collapsed corridor. "Can't imagine your shipping business will do so well then."

Xander ground his teeth. "Of course, I don't want Callahan to destroy the magic. But Valmont -- he's just a kid. With time, he might become a passable aeronaut, but—" he waved his hand and shook his head. "The Order would eat him alive and spit him back out."

Hildegard frowned and shook her head. "Don't think I didn't notice what the boy had around his neck."

So. It was back to that. The topic Xander longed to avoid. "No," he said, "I imagine not."

Hildegard ran her hand along the gold chain of her own necklace. Hildegard's shirt obscured the pendant, but Xander knew what it looked like, anyway. He had his own, once. A dragonstone, just like Valmont's. Though Hildegard's would be gray and inert, while Dorian's was red and active. *Alive.*

Xander sighed. *Yes.* He knew what it meant. To claim otherwise was just obstinate. Still, he shook his head and said, "He's not ready."

Hildegard pursed her lips. "Perhaps not. But can you make him ready?"

Xander shook his head and spread his hands in a helpless gesture. "I don't know," he said. "One day. Maybe. But only if he wants to. I've attempted to teaching him the sword, but he has little interest. And the one time we had him in the Linking... I don't know."

Hildegard wrinkled her nose. "That bad, huh?"

"No," Xander answered at once. "He... has potential. But not much drive to use it. He's... not his father."

Hildegard rested her index finger on her dimpled chin, face quirking into a knowing smile. "I can think of someone else who seemed inadequate in his father's shadow."

Xander bristled. "That's different," he said, even though he knew it wasn't. His hands curled into fists. "Gods and Ancients above, I want to protect him. For him to learn on his own terms, in his own time. Not to send him off to the bloody slaughter, all on the Order's whims."

"A dragon wouldn't choose someone unworthy," Hildegard said.

Xander grunted. It seemed bizarre to him that a dragon would choose anyone at all, much less Valmont. But what did he know?

"Where is this mysterious dragon, anyway?"

"I'd say right about... ah!" Hildegard gestured ahead, looking far too self satisfied.

"Wha?" Xander asked.

They came to a halt on a parapet overlooking another ruined section of the castle.

"Just wait for it," Hildegard said.

A moment later, a dragon, solid and ruby scaled, burst out of the ruins, frantically beating her golden wings.

"Sweet Ancients."

The scarlet serpent came to a staggering landing on the parapet, depositing an exhausted-looking Dorian and Tai at Xander's feet. The dragon wavered, and from what looked like a bandage on her leg, Xander surmised she was injured. Dorian and Tai, for their parts, looked disheveled and covered in dirt, and Dorian's shirt was missing its sleeve. But otherwise, to his great relief, they looked unharmed.

"She followed us out," Dorian said with an awkward, nervous smile. "Can we keep her?"

# CHAPTER TWELVE
# THE VOID

The days leading up to Saedra's nameday drained away like
ale from a leaking keg.

Dorian's time with the princess had been the happiest
of his life. But his happiness, it seemed, came with an expiration
date. On the second of Spark Moon, Saedra would turn twenty. Then,
she'd be legally old enough to rule Kasanarae. She'd marry Bradford,
and the happy couple would return to her homeland for coronation.
And that would be the end. Dorian would never see her again.

Moons ago, Dorian entertained a fantasy that Saedra would
invite him to come home with her. Not to be her husband, of course.
But to be... a friend. A companion. But Dorian had nowhere near the
courage to broach the topic himself, and as the weeks wore on, the
princess remained stalwartly silent about the future. Lately, the
princess seemed to avoid Dorian altogether. After being near insepa-
rable almost a year, it came as a jarring surprise when she found
more and more excuses to stay apart. He wished he knew what he'd

done to offend her. And yet he also couldn't help fearing something even worse was afoot.

Tension and wrongness settled over Callahan Manor like a fog.

Lord Janus Callahan skulked about the manor with a permanent scowl on his face, snapping at the servants for minor infractions. Even Bradford looked thoroughly browbeaten. Dorian knew well to avoid the manor lord when he was in this kind of temper. Once, years ago, Lord Callahan threw an expensive vase at the wall because Dorian sat incorrectly at the Unfurling Ritual. The only sure way to avoid Callahan's wrath was to stay out of the way.

Dorian retreated to his usual refuge of the manor kitchens. He kneaded dough, peeled potatoes, even scrubbed the occasional pot. This might not protect him from the miniature storm cloud that was Janus Callahan, but it least it kept him busy.

"Dorian, there you are," said a frazzled-looking Stewardess Tahlia on the afternoon before the feast.

Dorian froze, sure he was in for yet another reprimand.

"I hate to ask, but could you deliver Lord Callahan his tea?"

Worse than a reprimand. There was little Dorian wanted to do less than meet the manor lord face to face. But defying Tahlia Weatherbee was never something he considered a genuine option.

"I'd do it myself," Tahlia said, "But there's this thrice cursed feast to prepare for. Zekador's pants. It seems like just yesterday we were all getting ready for Saedra's arrival. And now it's time for her to leave."

*Why do you have to remind me?*

His heart settling somewhere around his boot heels, Dorian put together the tea tray and trudged up the long spiral staircase to Callahan's tower study. His hand shook slightly as he knocked on the door.

No answer.

He knocked again.

"Ah, My Lord? It's Dorian. I have your tea."

Still nothing.

Dorian wavered with indecision for several long moments. Returning the tray to the kitchen and leaving it to someone else was a tempting prospect. But if Callahan expected tea and didn't get it, the gods only knew what he and his temper would do.

Finally, trembling, Dorian tried the doorknob. It was unlocked. Heart thudding, he pushed it open with an audible creak.

"My Lord?" he asked.

Dorian blinked in surprise as he crossed the threshold.

The Janus Callahan Dorian knew was a man who liked to keep everything in neat, organized little rows. But that could not be further from the vision of chaos he saw strewn out before him. Magical trinkets tossed about at random intervals. Books haphazardly unshelved and left open. Everywhere Dorian looked, there were papers, so many papers, flung about the room as if a Voidstorm descended upon the study.

"What in the Void?"

«Dorian,» Hematite said with an air of genuine fear. «What is that?»

Dorian looked in the direction the demon pointed with his fiery tale.

And then he dropped the tea tray in shock.

Scones scattered off of the platter as scalding water spread across the cold stone floor. But Dorian hardly noticed. Shaking, he bent down and picked up a rumpled, discarded page.

It was a spell he'd copied from the grimoire. One he'd shared with Saedra. One they'd both sworn to keep secret. A dangerous spell. Maybe the most dangerous. He picked up more pages, found more spells. His spells. Saedra's spells.

"This is—" he stammered. "This is—"

The door creaked open once more. On instinct, Dorian dropped the page into the spilled tea water.

"What in the Void are you doing?" Lord Callahan leant forward and snatched the page off the ground, drying it off with a lace cuff. He sent Dorian a cold, challenging stare.

Dorian fought back panic. "Nothing, sir. I just... wanted to deliver you your tea, sir." He looked down at the fallen tray and winced.

"I see you've done as commendable a job as ever." Callahan sneered. "Now leave."

Dorian's heart pounded in his chest. There had to be some kind of catch. Callahan wouldn't just ask him to leave. Eventually, he was going to face punishment. The only question was how severe.

"I didn't... I saw nothing..." Dorian stammered, his mouth working faster than his brain.

"*Go*," Callahan repeated.

Dorian didn't need to be told again. But as he hurried down the spiral staircase, one thought was at the forefront of his mind. If Callahan was letting Dorian go, it was because he considered Dorian beneath his concern. And that must mean he was planning something much worse for everyone.

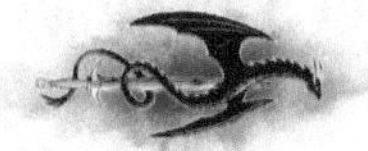

Dorian's insides roiled with terror as he sat down at the feast. Up at the high table, Saedra looked serene and somber, and beautiful as ever. She wore a new gown he hadn't seen before, this one glittering silver. Dorian wore the same uncomfortable suit he'd worn to her arrival feast. It seemed itchier than before, more restrictive. He kept tugging at the collar, his chest tight, finding it difficult to breathe.

If Bradford and his cronies greeted him with any of their usual animosity, Dorian barely noticed. He wondered why Bradford hadn't yet merited a promotion to the high table. He was about to marry the princess, wasn't he?

Dorian looked hopefully up again, trying to catch Saedra's eye. As she had all week, though, she seemed to deliberately ignore him. His heart stung, wondering what he'd done wrong. Lord Callahan, however, met Dorian's gaze with icy contempt, and Dorian sank lower in his own uncomfortable chair.

Even Saedra's sudden hurtful indifference was secondary in Dorian's mind, next to his encounter with the Manor Lord. How had Callahan gotten those spells? Worse, what did he plan to do with them?

Dorian couldn't even remember what sort of food they served at the feast. The entire affair passed in a daze, like he was floating high above, watching, detached. It might as well have happened to somebody else.

Finally, the aether lamps dimmed, and everyone grew quiet, as Janus Callahan stood to make his announcements.

"Nearly one year ago today, Kasanarae graced us with the most honored of guests, one who has brought our town much prestige: the First Princess of Kasanarae, Saedra Alansae Adrienne Penregon Kasani."

Saedra stood, silver gown glittering. She beamed at the crowd, but once again, refused to meet Dorian's eyes.

"Today, as you know, is her twentieth birthday, and therefore the day that she will leave us. She is now old enough to become Queen in her own right, and shall return to Kasanarae where she shall claim the crown that has been hers in all but name since the day her elder brother died, twelve years ago."

Dorian might not have noticed if he hadn't spent the past year in close intimacy with the princess, but he could tell by her posture that she was distinctly uncomfortable. *Oh Saedra,* he thought woefully, *What is going on?*

"It is, therefore, with a heavy heart that I must announce that I shall no longer serve you as Viscount of Frostvale. That duty shall now pass to my son, Bradford Callahan."

"What?" Dorian gasped, and he was not the only one. Many startled mutterings rippled across the hall.

Bradford looked so shocked he nearly spilled his wine. This was apparently news to him, too. But he recovered quickly, sweeping his goblet into the air and declaring, "It will be my honor to lead you all!"

"The reason for this," Callahan continued, "Is that I shall accompany the Princess Saedra to Kasanarae to become her wedded husband, to be coronated beside her as king of that prosperous nation."

Dorian dropped the dinner roll he'd been about to eat. As it fell to his plate, his stomach plummeted to the floor. Startled whispers spread through the hall. Bradford no longer simply looked surprised. The older boy's face was a white mask, mouth agape.

"I thought *you* were going to marry her," Dorian whispered.

"So did I," Bradford replied, voice trembling.

Saedra wore a well-practiced smile. But her cool gray eyes held a look of grim resignation. The leaden lump that sat in his stomach all week grew with the sting of betrayal. Was this why she'd been avoiding him? Why had Saedra kept this from him?

"Enough." Callahan's command shot through the crowd like a bolt of lightning. Immediately, the feast-goers became silent once more. "This alliance with Kasanarae will bring great wealth and prosperity to Adenthul in general, and Frostvale in particular. But I will have none of you think she is the only one to offer anything to this union. I am no mere beggar. No, I think, quite the opposite." With a sudden, fluid motion, Janus Callahan unsheathed his ornate silver athame. "I shall now show the full might and power of House Callahan."

Dorian's breath caught in his throat. He should have known this was coming ever since he saw the scattered papers in Callahan's office. *Oh, gods and sweet Ancients,* he should have known.

Dorian and Saedra had never quite figured out how to cast most of his father's spells. As far as Dorian was concerned, that was a good thing. Cyrus hid them for a reason. But Janus Callahan had depths of arcane knowledge that went far beyond that of a typical country lord. Dorian should have known he'd be able to figure it out.

Dorian waited with looming dread as Lord Callahan carved sigil after sigil into the air. In the precise order Dorian feared, in the exact positions Dorian knew he would. There wasn't enough ambient magic. Callahan shouldn't have been able to do it. But he did, all the same. Dorian watched with helpless horror as his cold-hearted foster father cast a spell lost to Cyrna for a thousand years. A spell so feared and hated that even its name was a curse.

"*Void.*"

"Watch your language," Bradford chided.

"I wasn't swearing," Dorian replied.

*Only stating a fact.*

The aether lamps in the hall abruptly blinked out, leaving only the flickering tabletop candles to illuminate the frightened faces of the party-goers.

For a long moment, there was only stunned silence. Then Dorian heard a startled cry and the sound of shattering glass.

Stewardess Tahlia, usually so level-headed, dropped the wine decanter she'd been carrying and fled the room, face in her hands.

"It's gone," Bradford said, looking more distraught than Dorian had ever seen him. "The magic is all gone."

Dorian examined his own athame with fascinated horror. Even the blue aether crystal on the hilt had gone out. But Dorian did sense *some* magic. Hematite's magic. He didn't like to draw from the demon; it was dangerous for both of them. But it came in useful in emergencies, and Dorian could think of no bigger emergency than being surrounded by the Void.

«May I?» he asked the demon.

«If you must,» Hematite allowed.

Taking a deep breath, bracing himself, Dorian drew a tiny amount of power into his athame. Even that small amount made his insides feel like they were on fire. He doubled forward in sudden, sharp pain. But the power came, as he knew it would, and the sigils etched into the blade glowed blue.

Corynne Beckett watched him intently, her well-groomed eyebrows slightly arched. "Well now, isn't that interesting?"

"Are you all right?" Bradford's eyes were wide.

"He's going into a demonic fugue," Graigor said. He sounded almost excited by the prospect.

"Should we call the Healer?" Bradford wondered worriedly.

"I'm... fine," Dorian gasped. "No Healer."

"It's not a fugue," Corynne said. "Look."

Shaking slightly, Dorian showed the others the glowing blue runes on his spell knife.

"Abomination," Graigor Beckett said.

But Corynne shook her head and said, "He's got access to magic when the rest of us don't. If that's abominable, then I want to be an abomination too."

Graigor opened his mouth, perhaps to argue, but at that moment Lord Callahan started speaking again.

"Magic is failing." Janus Callahan's voice was cold and direct, like an edge of naked steel. "This we have known for Cycles. While the wisest Magi in their Towers have wasted time with sigils and dusty tomes, every year, the lands of Aeris lose more and more elevation. But I am here to tell you they are going about it entirely the wrong way." He slashed his athame once more and magic returned to the room. The aether lamps sprung back to life, bathing the room in a warm and reassuring glow. Dorian felt like he'd just resurfaced after nearly drowning.

Callahan continued. "The Ancients before us harnessed the very flow of magic itself, forging an empire that lasted millennia. That power was lost to us, once, but I, Janus Callahan, have reclaimed it. And with it, the might of my kingdom shall be unstoppable."

# CHAPTER THIRTEEN

# HARD TRUTHS

*PRESENT DAY*

It was a tense crew that returned to the skyship *Phoenix* after departing from Greystone Citadel. Dorian's excitement over meeting the dragon steadily mounted into fear, then panic, and then finally despair as he realized the full magnitude of what he'd done, and what he yet had to do.

«I suspect you have now realized,» Hematite said to Solaris, «That you have chosen the wrong human to do your bidding.»

«That remains to be seen,» Solaris replied, but he could tell by the dragon's stiff posture that she was inclined to agree.

So was Dorian. He wasn't just the wrong person for the job; he was possibly the worst choice on all of Cyrna. How was he supposed to liberate six dragons from Callahan's service? Dorian could barely even hold a sword!

One thing was certain. He couldn't leave the crew now. He might've disappeared into anonymity on his own, but Callahan could scarcely fail to notice a dragon. And Dorian couldn't just abandon Solaris, either. Not when she was desperate and exiled. *No.*

He had to stay with Solaris, and the two of them had to stay with Xander and the others. Dorian could only hope that Xander's new cloaking device worked as well as Hildegard promised it would.

For as disastrous as the past few weeks had been, Dorian was growing fond of the crew. He had very few friends in the world, and they, it seemed, were the closest he was likely to get. But he could not ignore the tension that settled over them all after they left Greystone.

Captain Xander was usually an easygoing enough employer (except during those thrice cursed sword lessons). But lately, he snapped at minor offenses and jumped at small noises. That was, of course, when he could be bothered to run the ship at all. Xander spent most of his time locked up in his stateroom, drinking whisky and brooding over gods knew what. Fortunately, Tai and the others seemed to know enough to keep the ship running without him, but it was hardly professional behavior, and everyone was on a short fuse.

The entire crew felt pulled tight, like a bowstring about to release. Or at least Dorian assumed this was how pulling a bowstring must feel. Like many things growing up, archery had been Bradford's thing, not his.

The loosing of the proverbial arrow came three days later, as a mug of ale. It thunked down with such force that some of the foamy brown liquid spilled onto the wooden galley table.

Dorian blinked. "Wha?"

Sullivan stood over him, arms crossed, and nodded expectantly at the beverage.

"For... for me?" Dorian asked, examining the wooden mug.

"We're going to have a drink together as a crew," Sullivan said, "And we're going to talk."

"What's this about?" Xander asked, taking a reluctant sip before crossing his arms.

"You all came back from Greystone with a living dragon, and yet you're all moping about acting like someone died," Falgar said. "Is anybody gonna take the time to explain what in the skies is going on?"

They all looked at each other, silently urging the others to speak first.

"I have been pulled into things," Captain Xander finally said, "That I find far better left alone. However, I should not let that impede the running of the ship. And for that, I apologize." He coughed and took a sip of his drink.

Falgar, however, did not appear impressed. "All due respect, Captain, we didn't just mean you." He waved an impatient hand towards Dorian and Tai. "You two. Who shat in your breakfast?"

Dorian blinked. "What in my... what?"

"A dragon," Falgar repeated, gesticulating wildly. "A bloody Kassoria-cursed dragon! You should celebrate, calling every bard you know, posing for your statues and your portraits. Instead?" He gestured at the sorry crew seated around the round galley table. "Valmont, you're the most miserable excuse for a dragonaut I've ever met."

"Technically, he's the only excuse for a dragonaut you've ever met," Sullivan pointed out.

Dorian shook his head. "Falgar's right, I'm afraid. But see, the thing is, I'm not a dragonaut. I can't be a dragonaut. Not a proper one. Gods know I'm a hopeless at every single thing the dragonauts used to prize. A master aeronaut? Ha, look at me, I can't even—"

Yet another angry slam of a beer mug against the wooden table, this time, from Tai.

"That," she said, "Is exactly your problem."

"My ... problem?"

She flared her wings. "'Look at me, I'm Dorian Valmont! I'm so sad and pathetic! Woe is me, all I've got is a dragon and a magic book and the love of a Queen! Boo bloody hoo!'" She waved her hands in frustration. "Void Eternal, it's like you want to be a failure!"

Falgar's mouth fell open, and Sullivan widened his eyes. Even

Xander looked up from his mug with something of a stunned expression.

Too shocked to answer right away, Dorian took a sip of ale. Somehow, it tasted like dust. He at last opened his mouth to speak, but the only words that would come out were, "I, um, ah..."

Tai, however, hadn't finished with her tirade. "You want to fail," she repeated. "That's it, isn't it? You. Want. To. Fail. I think you're afraid. Afraid you might have to actually do something for once and not just hide behind your own self-pity." Her wings flared, scattering black feathers across the common area. Falgar defensively covered the top of his mug.

"That's not... I mean... it isn't..." was the best Dorian could manage in response.

"You've got a real potential as an aeronaut, you know," Tai said. "You're good with sigils and your instinct for air currents is unbelievable. But none of that matters because you've," she jabbed her finger at him, "Decided. To. Fail. Well, fine. If you're so determined to fail, then fail. See if I care." She spun towards the door and departed in a cloud of feathers.

The rest of the crew watched in stunned silence. Dorian would not have been more shocked if she had slapped him. Face burning, he took another swig of beer.

The others eventually dispersed, but Dorian sat there for some time, contemplating the yeast dregs in his mug, while Tai's words echoed in his mind like continuous physical blows.

*"You've decided to fail."*

*What does she know? She hasn't been through what I have. She doesn't understand me at all.*

«That is the spirit,» Hematite said.

But it wasn't true. Dorian knew it wasn't deep down.

Tai's words stung, not just because they were harsh, but because she was right.

Dorian was terrified. Not of skyships and dragons, not even of

Callahan. But of his own inadequacy. Of what he needed to do. Who he might need to become.

Who was that? Who was he now? Did he even know? Who did he *want* to be?

"Right. Okay." He took a deep breath and downed the paltry remnants of his mug.

Dorian stepped outside onto the upper deck and took in the cool evening air. The first stars of dusk shone in the purple-gray sky. As a gust of wind ran through his hair, Dorian realized he didn't want to leave this behind, not ever. He might not be much of an aeronaut or a dragonaut, but whatever came next, he was glad he hadn't stayed behind in Thlarknia.

He clutched his dragonstone pendant. The stone thrummed in his hand, warm to the touch.

«Solaris?»

«Ah, the human speaks.»

Solaris struggled against the wind as she circled down, then fell to a graceless landing on the deck. Dorian winced.

"Are you all right?"

«Still not used to this landing business,» Solaris said with a note of wounded pride. Although Sullivan had been able to Heal most of her injuries, she was still feeble and easily tired. Dorian felt more than a little feeble and easily tired himself.

"I wonder..." Dorian frowned. "You said... you said you're an extension of me. Right?"

«That is my understanding,» Solaris confirmed.

"So..." Dorian bit his lip, not sure how to put it. "Is that why you're so—" he gestured at Solaris, "Like that? Is it because I'm so—" he waved towards himself, "Like this?"

Solaris snorted, a few sparks drifting up into the darkening evening. «You need to understand,» she said. «That I am as new at this as you are.» She swished her tail back and forth. «However... the dragons of old were said to take on their riders' traits. And I think I see some of that, with the two of us.»

Dorian's shoulders slumped. "I knew it."

«It is not all bad,» Solaris amended. «You, I sense, are a thoughtful human of above-average intelligence.»

"Um," Dorian said, not feeling thoughtful or intelligent. "Thank you?"

More amused sparks. «Since we have bonded together, I find I can think more clearly. Analyze problems from different angles. I am, alas, also more keenly aware of all the ways things could go wrong. My natural inclination is to be impulsive, so this is quite new to me. But I am still myself. Your presence does not override my nature. Simply... enhances it.» She twitched her tail. «I suppose it holds true for other traits, as well. You are clever, but with little in the way of physical strength to draw upon. I am, by extension, the same.»

«Is that such a bad thing?» Hematite put in. «If we must face Callahan and his minions, could we not merely outwit them?»

Solaris bared her teeth. «I forgot you were still here,» she said to Hematite. «Anyway. I said he was above average. Not a strategic genius.»

"Thanks for that," Dorian grumbled. Then he sighed. "Callahan has six well-trained dragonauts, and we just have ourselves. I'll take whatever paltry advantages I can get." He swallowed, half dreading the answer to the question he knew he must ask. "Solaris, if... If I got stronger, would you get stronger, too?"

Solaris paused for a long moment. Finally, she said, «I believe so.»

Dorian let out a long breath. "Right," he said. "Okay." He ran his hand down the dragon's spine, taking in the warmth of her beautiful, fragile ruby scales. "I guess I know what I have to do now."

Solaris inclined her head in acknowledgement, while Hematite projected his dismay. Then, before he could change his mind, Dorian made his way down to the cargo hold.

Tai sat cross-legged, leaning back against a stack of wooden crates. A small cordoned off section of the cargo hold was reserved for the crew's training equipment, but it was also a decent place to sit and read.

Ceiling-mounted aether lamps cast a flickering light on the lurid red cover of the accounting ledger she'd helped rescue from Greystone Citadel. Who knew such a loudly colored book could hold such boring material? If there was anything mysterious or important hidden within the lines of old purchase orders, Tai couldn't discern it. There was nothing down here to distract her from her own frustration.

*Savior's Wings, she thought miserably. When am I going to learn to control my temper?*

She knew she was sulking. Worse than sulking. She was behaving like a petulant toddler. Anger didn't motivate her outburst, only jealousy. Petty, petty jealousy.

Tai couldn't stop thinking about that night seven years ago when her younger brother achieved his first flight before she did. She'd reacted the same way, with a thrice-cursed temper tantrum. But she'd been only thirteen. One could forgive her for being immature. Now she was supposed to be an adult. She hated this envious part of her nature, the resentment curdling in her stomach like sour milk. She hated milk, too, but that was neither here nor there.

She was, she admitted, fond of Dorian. He was generous and compassionate and baked excellent pie. She liked the way his eyes lit up whenever someone mentioned flight sigils. In the rare instances when she could coax him out of his shell, he had a boyish enthusiasm she found both endearing and infectious.

But now he'd bonded to a dragon. Not enough to be admitted to the crew with no qualifications, but now, an honest-to-the-gods dragon. Dorian was nice enough, sure, but what in the Void had he done to make the gods decide he deserved all that?

Still. It wasn't Dorian's fault, was it? And it certainly wasn't a personal slight against Tai. She knew she was being unfair.

Tai heard the creak of the trapdoor, followed by someone climbing down the ladder into the hold. She didn't need to look to know who it was.

"Dorian." She lowered her wings.

"Listen," he said, "About before."

"I'm sorry," Dorian and Tai said at the same time.

Tai blinked. "Why in the Void are *you* sorry? I'm the one who was out of line."

Dorian gave a small, sad smile and picked up a random dumbbell off the training rack. He flinched, put it back, then selected a lighter one. He did nothing with it, just bit his lower lip and examined it like a puzzle he needed to figure out. "You weren't out of line," he said at last.

Tai snorted. "Of course I was."

He frowned, but said nothing more. He raised the weight towards himself in an awkward movement that was halfway between a curl and a triceps extension.

"Did you mean what you said?" Dorian asked finally. "Or were you just being nice?"

Tai's mouth fell open of its own accord. When words finally returned to her, she said, "I thought I already told you. I don't say things just to be nice. But even so. I cannot see where you got *niceness* out of all that."

Dorian snorted, then scratched his neck. "Well. Um. I mean. You said I had... I had potential, for, um, reading air currents and things. You, um, seemed to indicate that I might actually..." Dorian swallowed and tried again. "See... um... I guess I was just wondering... did you also mean what you said a few days ago? Do you really believe I can become a competent aeronaut?"

"I've already said that I do," she said.

"Could you teach me?" He blurted it out, full of nervous energy. "I mean, all of it, the sigils and stuff, but also things like strength, and endurance, and... and whatever else I might need in order to fly without collapsing." He blushed furiously and inspected the dumbbell in his hand. "I, uh, realize that sounds like a lot. It's just... I'm so utterly incompetent, I don't even really know where to... start?"

"I—" Tai began, but she realized she didn't have an answer. She was barely out of apprenticeship herself. How could she teach a complete novice? And yet, his blue eyes shone with such desperate, hopeful longing, she couldn't help wanting to lend a hand.

Even as she struggled for an answer, her mind raced with ideas and plans. He already had a good foundation with sigilwork; getting him up to speed on that aspect ought to be simple enough. Physical fitness would be a greater challenge, but if he worked for it, it wasn't insurmountable.

"Why me?" she asked. "Surely Sullivan, or Captain Xander..."

"Xander's the Captain. That would be... I don't know. He's trying his best with the sword lessons, but I don't want to bother him for more." He scratched his neck nervously. "As for Sullivan... I'm not sure. I guess maybe I'm still ashamed about getting his arm broken. But maybe..." he swallowed. "I think maybe I asked you because I didn't think you'd suffer my excuses."

Tai laughed. "You're not wrong."

Dorian offered a tentative smile, but then his expression became grave again as he continued inspecting the dumbbell. "The thing is... Lord... I mean King Callahan... he's got Solaris's friends and family. I think he's gonna use them for something terrible. Ending all magic, maybe."

Tai rose her eyebrows. "Ending all magic? That's quite the accusation. Why would he do that?"

"So he can control what little remains, I think," Dorian said. "He's... one of those people who's not happy unless he's in control. But the point is, I can't... I can't just let him get away with that.

Solaris needs my help. She sacrificed a lot to answer my summons. But... I'm useless to her the way I am now."

"So do you wish to be a warrior, or an aeronaut?" Tai wondered.

Dorian slumped his shoulders and spread his arms. "Both, I guess. I just thought, maybe if I could fly worth the Void, maybe the rest of it might not seem so..." he shrugged. "Insurmountable."

"I think dragons and magic and the fate of the world are a tall order for anyone," Tai said, contemplating her words. "But what about you? What do you want?"

"What I want doesn't really matter."

"To the Void, it doesn't. Humor me." She fixed him with a penetrating stare.

"Fine, fine." His eyes met hers. Gods, but he really had the most gorgeous eyes. His answer came out as a reverent whisper. "*To fly.*"

"All right," she said, dusting her hands on her trousers. "I'll help you."

His face lit up like the morning sun. But he put his hand on his neck, nervous, too. "You will? That... that'd be good. Like I said, I... really do not know what I'm doing."

Beads of sweat were forming on his face, and his arms quivered. He'd been ineptly curling the dumbbell for the past minute without pause.

"Stop that," Tai said, half amused, half concerned. "You're going to hurt yourself. Here." She took the dumbbell from him and placed it gently back on the rack. "Let's start with the basics."

Dorian swallowed, squared his shoulders, and clutched his dragon pendant. "Right. Okay. I'll try," he said. Then, he added, "Thank you, Tai. For... for agreeing to help. Really. I--"

Tai smirked and tapped him on the shoulder. "See how much you thank me tomorrow, eh?"

# CHAPTER FOURTEEN

# ENDINGS AND BEGINNINGS

*ONE MOON AGO*

Dorian and Saedra sat across from each other in the empty gaming parlor, exchanging furtive glances. It seemed hard to believe that they'd once shared such intimate closeness. Now they could barely talk to one another.

A million questions ran through Dorian's mind, ranging from accusatory to desperate. None of them seemed wise to voice out loud. He didn't want to confirm he had suspected all along.

Saedra never cared about him. Not really. How could she?

"I thought you were supposed to marry Bradford," he said. It was the only thing he could bring himself to voice.

Saedra avoided his gaze. She stared instead at the glossy parquet inlay on the card table. "Would it be better if I had married Bradford?" Her voice sounded hollow, devoid of its usual vibrancy.

"I don't know." Dorian's voice cracked to his shame. Of course, he didn't want her to marry Bradford, but he'd gotten used to the idea. Bradford could be arrogant and boorish, but he was at least nice to the people he found useful. And he was handsome. With Bradford, she could have found some measure of happiness.

Janus Callahan, though. The elder Callahan was cruel and cold and power-hungry. He refused to even mention the name of his previous wife. What sort of husband would he be to Saedra, a woman younger than his son?

"He's so *old*," Dorian said.

A small, wry smile appeared on her lips. "He wasn't my first choice." Her expression turned grave again, and she looked exhausted, older than her twenty years. "But it would have been foolish, I'm afraid, to marry your brother."

"He's not my brother."

Saedra stood, pacing around the fire-lit room. Outside, snow fell against a steel gray Adenthulian sky. Winter was well and truly upon them, the golden summer days of their secret affair nothing more than a treasured memory.

"I know you must hate me," she whispered.

"I don't hate you," Dorian said. But he couldn't hide the hurt and confusion from his voice. Before he could stop himself, he blurted, "Did you give the Void spell to Lord Callahan?"

Saedra stared at the flickering firelight, gray eyes shining with grief and regret. "No," she answered after a long hesitation. "But I'm afraid I always knew I would have to betray you." She picked her wine goblet up from the card table, examined it, and took a long sip.

"You... never intended to use the spells to restore Cyrna's magic," Dorian guessed.

Saedra sighed, drinking more wine. "I did," she said, "But... not in the way you're thinking."

"Then what were you trying to do?"

She downed the rest of her goblet in one gulp. She grimaced, took a deep breath, and said, "I planned to use the Void to thin the veil into the spirit realm. My goal was to restore the demons to Aeris."

Dorian blinked several times. He glanced over at Hematite, who lay curled up next to the hearth like a sleeping cat. "I, um, hate to be the one to tell you this, but there are, ah, already demons in Aeris."

"Not," Saedra replied, "Enough of them."

Whatever lies Saedra told him before, they all seemed a lot more plausible than this. A thousand questions ran through his mind, but the best he could come up with was, "Why?"

"I thought it was the only way to save the magic," she said. "The demon-possessed can draw power from their demons, even when ambient magic fails."

Dorian didn't know where to begin. Saedra likely underestimated just how difficult it was to draw energy from a demon. People wouldn't accept demons as a substitute for ordinary magic. There'd be uprisings in the streets.

"But Callahan has other ideas," Saedra continued. "I fear he wants to end all magic entirely."

Dorian shuddered. "You mean he won't do anything to stop the decline?"

"No." Saedra drew in a long breath. "I mean, he wants to destroy it. Decisively. Permanently. As swiftly as possible."

"Void Eternal," Dorian swore. "Why?"

Saedra sighed and poured herself more wine. "To consolidate power on his own terms. I suppose I misspoke. He will leave some magic intact — that which he alone controls. I will stop him if I can. That's why I agreed to marry him. Or part of the reason." She stared at her goblet, defeated. "I love you, Dorian. But my first loyalty is, must always be, to Kasanarae."

*Say something useful, you big dolt.* Dorian's brain seemed to have been wiped clean. After a long hesitation, he asked, dumbfounded, "You... love me?"

Saedra set down her goblet and sat beside him, taking his hand in hers. "Of course I do. Surely you know that by now." Her gray eyes met his blue ones, shining with sincerity and sadness. "Gods know, I never wanted things to turn out this way."

"But... but you can't love me." He was blithering like a fool now, but he didn't care. "I'm nobody! I..."

"Oh, my dear, sweet, foolish Dorian." She cupped his face in her hand and kissed him, gently but passionately, one last time.

Saedra broke away from him and glanced towards the door. She bit her lower lip, then squared her shoulders.

"I want you to have this." She reached behind her neck and unclasped her necklace. She dropped the heavy pendant in his hand, the gold chain falling behind it like wine into a goblet.

"You're... you're giving me this?"

"I want you to have it," she repeated. She closed her eyes, breathed, then opened them again. "You need to understand that some things are more than they appear. Yourself most of all. If you remember nothing else of our time together, I hope you'll remember that."

He examined the heirloom, feeling the weight of it in his hands. Saedra's last gift to him. The most precious item he owned. He did not know, at that moment, just how precious.

Dorian circled his thumb around the odd gray stone in the center, feeling a thrum of power, magical energy just out of reach. And then, like an aether lamp igniting, he understood. The item's worth didn't come from gold or the jewels of the setting at all. It was the stone in the middle. Dragonstone. Saedra just handed him an Ancient dragonstone.

The sound of footsteps approached, and Saedra drew away from him. Dorian felt a stab of panic, but it was only Duchess Vivienne.

"Our carriage is ready, your Highness," the burly woman said from the doorway.

"I guess this is goodbye." Dorian's throat felt dry.

Saedra gave his hand one last affectionate squeeze. "Goodbye for now." She kissed him one last time on the forehead. "Give Hematite my regards."

*TWO WEEKS LATER*

Dorian ran the gold chain through his fingers, feeling hollow inside.

He wasn't sure what made him do it. Desperation, maybe, or despair. He'd lost everything else that gave his life meaning, so he did the only thing he could think of.

He cast one of his father's spells.

Dorian knew he'd been foolish. He didn't even know what the spell was for. Only that it required a dragonstone, and now Dorian had one of those, and that his father's notes mentioned "To beg for aid." Saedra would have been furious. Hematite *was* furious. But Saedra wasn't here, and not even Hematite could talk him down from his sudden impulsive need to do something, anything, no matter how reckless.

«And what,» Hematite asked in the aftermath, «Did you think was going to happen?»

Dorian wasn't sure. Did he think that somehow, miraculously, magic would sweep across all of Cyrna, halting the Voidstorms and restoring the might of the Ancients? Did he suppose the spell would somehow give Lord Callahan a change of heart, and cause Saedra to come running back into Dorian's arms? Most realistically, Dorian suspected the spell was going to blow up in his face.

But while he was preparing the spell, for the first time in weeks, Dorian felt hopeful. He had something to look forward to. But now it was done, and the result was... nothing.

He had felt something, at first, in the moments after casting. A sense of connection, the knowledge that he was one life among many. But then, as soon as it started, it was over, and Dorian felt no different from before. In some ways, he thought, that was worse than if it had blown up.

Dorian leaned against the stone wall, staring miserably up at the hanging copper pans. Distorted by the gleaming metal, he saw his reflection. He thought he looked sloppier than usual, round face covered with the unkempt reddish stubble of several days' growth. What was the point in grooming himself? What was the point of anything?

Only two weeks had passed since Lord Callahan departed for Kasanarae with his new bride-to-be, but everything had changed around the manor. Stewardess Tahlia never returned after running away that fateful night, so in the intervening fortnight, it seemed like half the manor staff had resigned. The newly minted Lord Bradford spent most of his time in his father's study — Bradford's study, now — and he seldom ventured into the rest of the house. Dorian supposed he ought to feel relieved, but mostly, he felt lonely.

«There must be something else we can do,» Hematite said.

Sighing, Dorian lifted a hand pie off the cooling rack and examined it. One good thing about half the manor leaving, he thought. Nobody complained about his forays to the kitchens. The new servants didn't know who he was, and they didn't care.

Dorian smiled sadly as he took in the scent of freshly baked apples and almonds. It occurred to him he could leave. Make a life for himself. Try to stop Callahan on his own. Maybe figure out the rest of his father's journal and restore the magic.

«You'd rather cold and wet adventure?» Dorian asked the demon.

«No,» Hematite admitted. «And yet...»

Dorian shook his head sadly. They were just one person and a demon. What power did they have against Callahan and his wicked magic? Shaking his head in resignation, he raised the pie to take a bite.

"Dorian Valmont!" Bradford's voice rang through the kitchen.

Dorian was so startled he dropped the pie. He watched, transfixed, as it tumbled downward and landed with a splat, golden-brown apples spilling out onto the cold stone floor.

"Ah, sorry about that," Bradford said.

Still momentarily poleaxed, Dorian looked at the mess, then back at Bradford. The young lordling looked like something of a mess himself. Bloodshot eyes, disheveled hair, and a wrinkled shirt marred his usually tidy appearance. A whiff of peaty whiskey on his breath suggested he'd been drinking.

"May I... help you? My Lord?" Dorian finally asked as he scrambled to fetch a wash rag.

"Please," Bradford said. "Bradford. Just Bradford."

"Sure." Dorian frowned, scooping the remains of the pie into the compost bucket. "Bradford."

"Come walk with me." Somehow it sounded like both a request and a command.

Once he'd removed the evidence of his pie to his satisfaction, Dorian grabbed his woolen overcoat off a peg near the servant's entrance. He sucked in his gut to fasten the brass buttons, then followed the young lord outside, ignoring the freezing rain. The orchard, so full of life when he used to walk here with Saedra, now stood like empty white skeletons against the gray sky. The icy ground crunched beneath their feet.

Bradford took a deep breath. "May as well get to the point. First of all, it was me who gave those spell notes to my father. I snuck into your room and stole them out of your writing desk."

"Oh," Dorian said. Perversely, his first reaction was relief. Saedra hadn't betrayed him. But why was Bradford telling him this?

"My father ordered me to do it. I didn't know what the spells did. I didn't know he would do... *that*." Bradford shuddered. "I apologize, for what it's worth. But you should know. My father also ordered me to kill you."

"Oh," Dorian repeated. He supposed he ought to feel afraid, but he felt nothing at all. "Why?"

Bradford sighed and ran his hand through his messy hair. "You know how I've spent our entire childhood insisting you're not my brother?"

"Yes…"

"Well." Bradford shrugged. "I lied."

Dorian blinked. "Wh… what?"

"I'm your brother."

Dorian gazed up at the naked branches, struggling to find words. "How… Callahan's not… he can't be… unless… is Cyrus your father too?"

Bradford chuckled. "No," he said, "We're half brothers. Different fathers. Same mother."

"L… Lady Callahan?"

Dorian's heart hammered in his ears. He remembered the smiling woman in the portrait in the library, with her curly brown hair and wide blue eyes. *We never talk about Lady Callahan. Void Eternal.* Was that why she was a forbidden topic in the manor? Because she was Dorian's mother?

Bradford nodded. "Cyrus was Father's friend, and he and Mother… well… the betrayal drove Father mad. He hates you for existing, for reminding him. For a long time, so did I. However…" he shook his head, and wiped an icy raindrop off his shoulder. "It's time you knew the truth."

Dorian leaned against a tree trunk for support. His mother was Lady Callahan. It seemed impossible to believe, and yet, deep down, perhaps he'd always known.

"And… and now he wants to kill me." Dorian frowned. "But he could have done that anytime. Why now? Why send you?"

Bradford wrinkled his nose in distaste. "Truth is, I'm not sure what changed his mind." His grim smile held a bitter irony. "Perhaps as your father was a threat to his first marriage, he considers you a threat to the second."

Dorian let out a long breath. "Wh… why are you telling me all this? Why not just kill me and be done?"

Bradford shook his head. "I'm not going to kill you, Dorian."

"But you said…"

"Just because father ordered it doesn't mean I'm going to *do* it."

Bradford scoffed. For a second, some of his usual swagger returned. But then he grew serious again. "But you need to get out of here, or my father will just send someone else."

"But..."

"As it happens, you're in luck. Captain Xander is in town with his skyship. He's an old family friend, but no friend of my father's, not anymore. He says he'll take you on, but you have to leave today." Bradford wrinkled his nose. "Might want a bath first. And some fresh clothes. But please try to hurry."

Dorian could only stare at his brother — his *brother* — as he tried to process the torrent of information. Grasping the cold tree trunk for purchase, he struggled to his feet. "I... a ship. Yes. Thank you." He'd allow himself to panic later once he'd processed everything he'd just learned. But at the moment he was too stunned to do much else but numbly agree. "Just... um... why are you helping me?"

Bradford gave a pained smile. "I know I can't make up for all the things I've done," he said. "But I want to do all I can to make things right. I've... I've been a complete bastard to you. And I'm sorry."

Overcome with every emotion at once, Dorian did not know what to say. So he blurted the first thing that came to mind.

"Technically," he said with a weak laugh, "It seems *I'm* the bastard."

At that moment, unbeknownst to Dorian, the dragonstone around his neck turned from gray to red.

# CHAPTER FIFTEEN

# TRAINING

*PRESENT DAY*

Dorian wasn't sure when he first realized he enjoyed his training.

He liked the other parts of being an aeronaut. He found the spell sigils intuitive, and he loved being in the Linking — at least until he got too tired and fell behind. The physical aspect, however, continued to be a thorn in his side. Convincing his body to catch up with his mind seemed like an impossible task.

Still, Solaris was counting on him, so he endured it with a martyr's grim resolve. He got up every morning and did the thrice cursed training under Tai's tutelage, heaving for breath, muscles on fire, every moment like agony.

Progress was slow, but there was progress. Weeks turned into moons, and his body grudgingly responded. Over time, the impossible turned into the challenging, and the challenging became trivial.

Tai, grinning all the while, presented him with newer, harder challenges. Her wicked grin used to fill him with a dread. More and more, however, he found he looked forward to it more than almost any other part of the day.

One sunny morning during the Radiant Moon, he found himself in the cargo hold doing bench press under the watchful eyes of Tai, Solaris, and Hematite.

"Just... one... more... rep," Dorian grunted to himself as he pushed the heavy bar off his chest. He heaved a massive sigh of relief as he re-racked the bar with a clang.

"That's a new record," Tai said. He almost dared hope she looked impressed.

Dorian both laughed and panted, taking a long swig from his canteen. "Would you look at that."

He ran his hand along the silver-black iron bar, marveling at the weighted plates on either side. Only three moons ago, he'd considered himself doing well just to move the empty bar. Today's load would have seemed impossible those twelve weeks past. He felt a little thrill of accomplishment well up within him and grinned despite himself.

«Yes, yes, we are all very pleased with ourselves,» Hematite said churlishly. «Now may we perhaps leave and do something more productive with our time?»

«Not quite,» Solaris said. «He still has to do legs, after all.»

Dorian's happy little bubble punctured. "Ugh. Legs."

He hadn't realized he'd spoken out loud until Tai playfully punched him on the shoulder. "Lower body work is the most important there is! You could have biceps the size of Greystone Citadel, and it won't mean a spark in the Void if your enemy can simply knock you off your feet."

"I know, I know." Dorian was well aware of the benefits of squats and lunges. But by the Ancients, they could be uncomfortable.

«Hear me out,» Hematite said, «You could end the training session early and go back to finding a magical solution to stopping King Callahan.»

Dorian sighed and shook his head. The demon must despise the training sessions indeed, if he thought studying his father's hated journal was a better alternative. Dorian supposed he couldn't blame the creature. Hematite experienced every physical sensation Dorian did, even the unpleasant ones.

No matter how he turned it over in his head, however, Dorian couldn't think of any way to rescue Solaris's kinfolk without both learning to fly better and learning to fight better, and both things required strength.

«I know it's irritating,» Dorian said. «But come on, it's not that bad, is it? It's only until we beat Callahan. After that—»

Well, Dorian had trouble visualizing life after Callahan. For the moment, becoming competent enough to stop his stepfather was all that mattered.

«I understand it is necessary,» Hematite sighed. «I just wish that it were not. Life used to be so much simpler.»

«I guess,» Dorian allowed. But Dorian found he didn't want to return to those simpler times.

Training was hard, no doubt about it. The feeling afterwards, though, the sense of accomplishment, was not something he wanted to give up.

«If I did not know better,» Solaris interjected, «I would say you are enjoying yourself.»

«Yeah,» Dorian replied with an awkward smile. «Maybe I am.»

«Hmph,» came Hematite's response. «You are not fooling anyone, you know.» This he directed at Solaris, not Dorian.

«And what is that supposed to mean?» the dragon asked.

«You do not care if he is enjoying himself or not,» Hematite replied. «You only care that he is useful.»

«That is not true,» Solaris protested, though he could sense through their bond that Hematite had hit a nerve. «It is not true,» she repeated, defensiveness tinged with guilt. «I care just as much about our bond as you do.»

«Of course you do,» Hematite said. Dorian could feel the sneer in his mindvoice.

Tai cleared her throat. "Leg day, remember."

"Right, of course." With a resigned smile, Dorian started loading plates onto the squat rack. To his bonds, he said, "If you two would stop arguing, I've got squats to do."

He scratched his neck in consternation. His mind was a crowded place these days.

Dorian was just about to position the barbell on his shoulders when the trapdoor swung open and Falgar came swinging down the ladder.

"Heyoo," he declared in a voice more cheerful than it had any right to be.

"What did you do, Falgar?" Tai's mouth formed into a smirk even as she crossed her arms in exasperation.

"I'm wounded that you think so little of me." Falgar placed his hand over his heart. "Sullivan volunteered to cover my shift in the Linking, so I thought I'd come down here and pump some iron." He raised his arm in an exaggerated flex. "Alas, I see the equipment's already occupied."

«Tell Falgar he is welcome to it if he wants,» Hematite said. Dorian ignored him.

"We can take turns if you like," Dorian said instead.

"Could do." Falgar moved to the rack on the wall and selected not a dumbbell, but one of the wooden practice swords. "Must say, Valmont, you've been training pretty hard lately."

"Suppose so." Dorian felt his cheeks turning pink.

"Was wondering if you wanted to put some of that training to the test, and spar with me?" Falgar brandished the practice blade with an elegant flourish.

Dorian opened his mouth. "Spar with you? I mean... sure. But I think you're going to sweep the floor with me."

"Sweeping the floor is your job, Cabin Boy," Falgar said. "Anyway, at the rate Captain says you're improving, I expect you to put up a proper fight."

Dorian felt a rush of warmth. "Cap... Captain said that?"

Xander was never forthcoming with praise, but he didn't seem to complain about Dorian's technique as much anymore, which Dorian took to be a good sign. At the very least, Dorian no longer dreaded their sword lessons.

"Oh, I don't expect you to win or anything," Falgar said. "I'm just curious to see what you can do."

"Oh." Dorian swallowed. "All right."

Tai clasped her hands together. "Oh, this'll be fun to watch."

Dorian fought down an upwelling of panic. He hated the idea of losing in front of Tai. He was curious, though, to see if he'd improved at all.

«It is just like training with Xander,» Solaris said. «Do not worry so much.»

Dorian thought this was a lot easier said than done, but the dragon sent warmth and comfort, and it made him feel a little better.

"All right." Dorian selected a practice sword from the rack. "Let's get this over with."

Only a few seconds into the fight, Falgar jabbed Dorian hard in the shoulder.

"Gah!" Dorian jumped backwards in surprise and pain.

«Dorian!» Solaris shouted in sudden alarm.

"Void, mate, I didn't mean to hit you so hard," Falgar said.

"No, no, I'm fine." He rubbed his shoulder. With a rueful smirk, he said, "This is going well."

He raised his sword to block Falgar's next attack. Dorian's too-tight shirtsleeve strained under the movement of his upper arm, but he brushed the wooden blade aside. Barely. But he hesitated before coming in for the attack and lost the opportunity.

«I know, I know, I'm trying,» he mindspoke in response to Solaris's obvious dismay.

«He is skilled, but he favors his left side,» Solaris said. «If you are careful and look for an opening, you may strike him.»

«Left side,» Dorian acknowledged.

Gathering himself, Dorian planted his feet in a relaxed fighting stance. It surprised him a little how easily it came to him now. He had a long way to go, but his fighting stances were improving. That was something, wasn't it?

Unfortunately, while Dorian wasted precious instants admiring his own footwork, Falgar seized the opening and prodded Dorian hard in the side.

"Owww!"

Falgar charged again. Dorian blocked. Falgar recovered and came in for another attack. But — *yes* — Solaris was right. Falgar favored his left. Abandoning hard-practiced footwork, Dorian charged.

This time, he might well have hit his mark, if not for his shoddy form. Instead, he tripped on the hem of his trousers and barreled forward, dropping his practice sword just in time to catch himself.

"Oof."

Falgar jabbed Dorian lightly in the stomach with his practice sword. "You're dead."

"I'm dead," Dorian agreed.

Ignoring both Hematite's smugness and Solaris's worried disappointment, Dorian rose unsteadily to his feet. "Well. That could've gone better."

"Honestly wasn't bad," Falgar said.

"Falgar's right," said Tai. "You'd've had him for sure if you hadn't tripped on your trousers. Tighten your belt, won't you?"

Blushing, Dorian inspected his belt and pulled it tight. It landed well past the grooved notch where the belt buckle had once settled.

"I thought I just tightened this." He scowled at it in personal offense.

Tai tried and failed to contain her laughter. "Yes, well, that can happen when you spend your every free moment training. Come to think of it, mend your clothes, too. Those pants hang off you like you're ill."

Dorian's face burned, and not just from the exertion of the match.

The thing was, he didn't think he looked any different. The

reflection that blinked back at him in the washroom mirror every morning looked much the same as it always had. He ate heartily at mealtimes — gods knew he was always hungry these days — so why were his pants falling off? And why, paradoxically, did his shirt feel so tight, especially in the shoulders and upper arms?

"Let's spar again," he said, eager to change the subject. "I think I can beat you this time."

Falgar smirked. "I know. But we're landing in Sanorska this afternoon, and we need all hands in the Linking." His grin widened. "That means you, too."

This, at last, was enough to make him forget his embarrassment. The Linking was Dorian's favorite part of life on board the *Phoenix*. But more than that, the fact that he was told, and not asked, to take part in the landing meant that the others saw him as a real member of the crew.

"I look forward to it." Adjusting his belt again, Dorian said, "But landing isn't for another three hours. We have time for one last bout."

Falgar laughed. "Sure, sure. But what about the rest of your training session?"

Dorian blanched. "You mean leg day? But I thought…"

"That I'd let you skip it? What kind of friend would I be, then?"

Dorian snorted. Well, stronger legs meant stronger foot work, which he could use to beat Falgar in a rematch.

"Very well, very well." Dorian turned towards the loaded bar.

# CHAPTER SIXTEEN

# SANORSKA

They disembarked in Sanorska to a sweltering summer afternoon.

Dorian stepped off the gangplank and wished he could look every direction at once. From up in the sky, the city's golden spires and crystal domes shone like a legendary treasure chest. Down here in the thick of it, it reminded Dorian of nothing so much as an overflowing anthill.

Dorian stared, overwhelmed, at the press of people milling about the skyport, surrounded by the tallest buildings he'd ever seen. The crew had visited many cities and towns over the past three moons, but none came close to approaching Sanorska. As Dorian descended the narrow gangplank, he breathed in the sticky, fragrant air. The cloying scent of flowers did not quite mask the intermingled odors of cook fires, sewage, and refuse.

Sullivan sucked in a deep breath. "It's good to be home."

"Smells like rotting piss," Falgar observed. Then, quickly, he amended, "In a good way."

"I've got to meet with a contact in the sky quarter," Captain Xander said. "I ought not to need any help, so you can have liberty for the day. Be back by tomorrow morning, and I'd prefer not hungover. Though my hopes are not high." He jangled a fat leather purse. "Right. Money."

He counted out coins and handed them out, first to Sullivan, then to Tai, and finally to Falgar. Dorian hung back awkwardly and tried not to feel jealous.

"Well, don't just stand there, Valmont. Come, collect your pay."

Dorian started. "Me, Sir? I thought..."

"You do your share of the flying, you get your share of the coin. I'm not a tyrant."

Dorian's hands trembled as he accepted the coins. It was a modest sum, appropriate for a novice with little experience. But Xander thought Dorian was competent enough to receive pay. Dorian felt a bizarre urge to cry, but luckily resisted the impulse.

"A word, though, if you will," Xander said.

"Certainly, sir." Dorian bit his lip, buoyant mood deflating. The captain looked grave. Dorian wondered if he was in trouble.

"My connection on the other side of town claims to work for the Order," Xander said. "With luck, we may get rid of all those pesky documents crowding the cargo hold."

"That's good, isn't it? They're the ones who made the cloaking orb for the *Phoenix*?"

"They did," Xander confirmed, but his face drew into a deep frown.

Dorian frowned, too. He had seen neither claw nor scale of Callahan's dragonauts in the three moons since they left Greystone, and he knew Hildegard's cloaking device was to thank. With the device, he could sometimes forget he had a powerful enemy. He could pretend he was just a normal apprentice aeronaut with a normal career in the sky. It couldn't last, of course. These happy days on the *Phoenix* were only the calm before the proverbial storm. Dorian knew that.

However, it was only because of the Order's intervention that he had the time he had. Why did Captain Xander speak of them with a combination of fear and contempt?

"If you'll forgive me," Dorian said, weighing his words, "I'm still not sure I understand what the Order even is."

Xander chuckled. "I suppose it's time you knew. The Order of the Silver Dragon was its full name. It was a secret society I used to belong to when I was young and foolish. Your father was a member, too. And your mother. And... Callahan."

Dorian felt a knot in his stomach. "I... see, sir."

Xander hadn't finished. "Our little club had many lofty aims, from rediscovering lost Ancient magic, to forming innovative new spells of our own. Chief among those goals was convincing dragonkind to forgive humanity for the heinous betrayals of the past. In short, to revive the dragonauts."

The pendant under Dorian's shirt thrummed, and his heart beat faster. "And... and now I'm a dragonaut. You want me and Solaris to come with you, sir?"

"What?" Xander asked. "No. Void, no. I want you to stay well away from them."

"But—" Dorian began.

"Listen, boy," Xander said, his tone low and serious. "If the Order finds out you bonded a dragon, they'll never let you leave their secret headquarters. You and Solaris will spend the rest of your days being poked and prodded while they try to figure out how your magic works. That's assuming they don't simply turn you right into King Callahan. Word's bound to get to him, regardless, if I flaunt to everyone in town that there's a dragonaut on my crew. I trust Hildegard, mostly, and my sister, sometimes. The rest might as well be pit wraiths for all my confidence in them."

Dorian let out a long sigh. He wished more than anything that they could trust the Order, that there were people out there who understood the dragon bond, who could help him. However, he knew Xander was right to be cautious. The risks, for now, simply outweighed the rewards.

With great reluctance, he removed his dragonstone pendant.

«Sorry, Solaris,» he said, but her wordless response showed she understood.

He fastened the necklace in the most secure inner pocket of his belt pouch, hoping, praying, that it would be safe there. A dragonstone would stick out to the people who recognized it, and if what Xander said was true, to be seen wearing one would be more dangerous by far. He couldn't save Solaris's friends, after all, from the confines of a laboratory.

"Valmont!" Falgar waved Dorian over. "We were just about to get some food. Want any?"

Dorian's spirits brightened immediately at the sight of his friends. "*Obviously.*" He patted his stomach and grinned.

They found some public benches, pleasantly shaded under a thick tree with broad, flat leaves.

"Lots of street cart vendors around here," Sullivan said, "Only, if you want the good stuff, order in Sanorian, not the trade tongue."

"Pity that none of us speak Sanorian," Falgar said.

"I'm from here," Sullivan said. "Of course I speak Sanorian. Anyway, I'll do the ordering. Spiced stew, okay? I know a guy who makes great spiced stew."

"Sure," Dorian said, "Do you need coin?"

"Nah," Sullivan said, "My treat."

He hurried off before any of them could protest.

"Spiced stew it is." Tai grinned and ruffled her wings, making herself more comfortable on the bench. The dappled sunlight partially illuminated her face in a way that Dorian found fetching. Realizing he was probably staring, he glanced away.

"Say, Valmont," Falgar said.

"Mmmm?"

"That princess of yours."

*Right. Saedra.* He shouldn't be ogling Tai at a time like this. "She's queen now. But what about her?"

"Well... I mean... Void, I'm going to sound like an arsehole."

"Never stopped you before," Tai chimed in.

"Go on." Dorian smiled despite himself.

"Well," Falgar said, "She's up there for you, ain't she? I mean, being royalty and all. Not that you're like, bad, or anything. I just figured a princess, you know, wouldn't run in the same circles."

"Meroneth's balls, Falgar," Tai said.

"All I'm saying is, it seems a little unfair that this guy gets to bury the weasel with the queen of Kasanarae, and I can't even get a single date."

"Again with the weasels," Dorian said, blushing furiously.

"You can't get a date because you're obnoxious," Tai said.

"So," Falgar continued, ignoring her, "What I mean is. If, in theory, *I* wanted to bury the weasel with someone high above my station, would you have any advice to, like, you know, woo them?"

Tai choked on a mouthful of water from her canteen. "Who in the Void are you trying to woo who's above your station?"

"None of your thrice cursed business, that's who. Anyway, I was talking to Valmont."

Dorian's face burned. "I'm, um, really am not the person you want to ask about this kind of thing. But, ah, well, with Saedra, I suppose I just sort of, um, shared her interests. Did nice things for her." *Also, copied down dangerous Ancient magic that got us all in a lot of trouble.* "I... I mean... it just sort of happened."

Falgar opened his mouth, but just then Sullivan arrived, laden with several mugs full of stew, and Falgar rushed up to help him.

Dorian was skeptical, at first, about eating stew in this hot weather, but he found himself pleasantly surprised. The stew's spicy flavor somehow made the humidity more bearable. For a time, sitting there, enjoying a meal with his crew-mates, it was easy to forget about dragons and demons and the mysterious Order.

"So, ah, what did people have planned for the afternoon?" Dorian had never had shore leave in such a large city before.

"We could go see the dancers at the Gilded Rose." Falgar crossed his wiry arms and smirked. "My treat. It's payday, after all." He glanced at them each in turn, but his gaze seemed to land longest on Sullivan, gauging his reaction.

Sullivan blanched, and he tugged on the cord of his lace-up shirt. "That's... certainly one possibility. And I appreciate the offer. But the city has much to offer. Surely we could..."

Falgar mussed his own sandy hair and said, "Come on, Sullivan, they're supposed to be the best in Aeris! I've heard they have legendary... talents." He wiggled his eyebrows meaningfully.

Tai raised her own eyebrows. "Talents, eh?"

"They are very... talented," Sullivan allowed.

"Then that settles it." Falgar clapped Sullivan's burly shoulder. "Sullivan and I will go see the dancers."

"I never said—" For a large, muscular man, Sullivan looked like a frightened rabbit caught in Falgar's talons.

"You joining us, Lunstrum? Valmont?" Falgar asked.

"Certainly not, but have fun." Tai gave her hand an airy wave.

"Well, this is a change," Falgar said. "No lecture about the wickedness of our lecherous ways?"

"You're both adults." Tai shrugged and turned towards Dorian. "I suppose you'll want to go with them."

"I... I hadn't thought about it." Dorian felt his face reddening once again. *I'd hoped to spend the afternoon with you,* he almost said. But thank the Ancients, he had the sense not to blurt that out. What even made him think it?

Unbidden, he pictured Tai the way she looked when they crossed practice swords, raven wings flared, sweat glistening off her smooth brown skin, tight black jerkin showing off her lithe, muscular form. *No, no, no!* He must not think that way, not about Tai. He loved

Saedra. He should think about Saedra, instead. With dismay, he realized he had trouble recalling her face.

"Legendary Dancers," Falgar intoned, bringing him back to the
present.

Dorian gulped. "I'm sure they're... that is... I'm sure they're very
good. But I, ah, needed to, um, ah..."

Tai, winged goddess she was, came swiftly to his rescue. "He has
a girlfriend, remember? Royalty, even."

"Yes." Dorian clung to the excuse. "Saedra wouldn't like it. Yes."
He doubted Saedra would give a spark in the Void if Dorian saw the
dancers, but he'd take whatever out he could get.

*Saedra. I love Saedra.* He reached in his pocket and clutched his
dragonstone, her last gift to him, and forced himself to remember
her. Her smile, her laugh, her bright silver eyes. Why was visualizing
her face so hard suddenly?

"So then," Falgar said, "I assume you'll be up to some nice, tame,
royal-girlfriend-approved activities for the afternoon?"

Dorian's face was so warm he thought it might be in real danger
of bursting into flame. "I... I um... I sort of hoped I might buy
clothes."

"It's true." Falgar steepled his fingers. "Your royal girlfriend may
wish to see you naked, but I don't. Nothing personal. Just not my
type. I like you anyway, mind."

"Zekador's poorly fitting pants, Falgar," Sullivan admonished.

"No," Falgar said, "*Dorian's* poorly fitting pants. Ancients, haven't
you been paying attention?" He jabbed his thumb in Dorian's direction. "How's he ever supposed to best me at sparring if keeps tripping on the hems?"

Dorian buried his face in his hands, wondering if it was possible
to die from embarrassment.

Dorian would much rather just figure out the alterations for the
clothes he already had. He hated shopping for clothing. It was
uncomfortable, humiliating, and often fruitless. But it was increasingly clear that he needed clothes better suited for life in the sky.

Besides no longer fitting, he also was running low on shirts that weren't frayed or torn. Even the newly forming callouses on his fingers posed a hazard to some of the more finicky silks.

"There's bound to be aeronaut's clothier in town," Tai said. "Most of the big cities have them. They have a decent selection of pre-made clothes, since the bulk of their customers are just passing through."

"You should go to Ruon's, down in the market square," Sullivan said.

"Great!" Falgar said, "It's settled, then. You two go shopping. We're going to the Gilded Rose. Sullivan, you coming?"

Sullivan looked like he'd been more comfortable when he'd had a broken arm. But he nodded and departed with Falgar.

Tai laughed and shook her head. "Falgar, Falgar. What will we do with you?"

"Is there, um, something going on between you two?" Dorian tried to keep his tone casual. He thought of Falgar's attempt to ask for romantic advice. Had he meant Tai? Why did that prospect give him such an upwelling of jealous indignation? He had no reason to be jealous.

Tai, however, snorted a laugh. "With Falgar? Oh, *Void* no. I don't court crew members. Besides. Falgar's like... like my brother. A very annoying brother." She lowered her wings, and for a moment, looked inexplicably sad. But she recovered quickly, and said, "Let's go to Ruon's, shall we?"

Dorian felt relief mingled with disappointment. She wasn't courting Falgar, but she wouldn't court any other crewmember, either.

«Saedra,» Hematite reminded him reproachfully. «You love Saedra.»

"Yes," Dorian agreed, "Let's go."

# CHAPTER SEVENTEEN

# SHORE LEAVE

Sullivan kept a firm grip on his sword hilt as they marched the dusty streets of the Rat Quarter. He realized what he was doing, and, embarrassed, let go. How many years would it be before he outgrew his old prejudices? Part of him worried he never would.

True, strutting through the Rat Quarter in the dead of night wearing fine silks was probably a good way to find yourself at the point of a dagger. At present, though, the noonday sun shone bright, and Sullivan wore only plain aeronaut's homespun. He noticed that passers-by cast wary glances *his* way.

*He shook his head with a bitter smile. I've become one of the dockside toughs Mother warned me about. What she would think if she could see me now?*

His mother would not see him now. Sullivan intended to make bloody well sure of that. Hence crossing the Rat Quarter instead of Silk Row or the Sky District.

Falgar, for his part, moved with the effortless grace of someone well used to traversing city streets unnoticed. The lithe Vatean lacked Sullivan's size or raw power, but conveyed obvious athleticism in every step. He kept his linen sleeves rolled to the elbows, displaying nicely muscled forearms.

Sullivan drew in a deep breath and let it out. "Are you certain there's northing else you want to do while we're in Sanorska?"

Falgar crossed his arms. "'Course not. The dancers at the Gilded Rose are legendary."

Sullivan grunted his assent. The ladies of the Gilded Rose *were* renowned for great beauty. By the narrow standards of the Sanorian fashionable elite, anyway.

Sullivan didn't fault his friend for liking that sort of thing. He, however, could think of about a hundred better ways to spend the afternoon than in a stuffy, smoky theater, watching scantily clad performers advertise their breasts like some hedonistic banquet for infants.

Sullivan supposed it didn't matter so much how he spent the afternoon, as long as he spent it with Falgar.

*You are seven kinds of fool, he chided himself.*

He wondered when things had changed. He never used to feel this way about Falgar. *Falgar*, by the Ancients. At first, the aeronaut's biting wit and casual irreverence grated on Sullivan's nerves. Over the past few moons, however, he'd come to realize there was no real cruelty in Falgar's ribbing. Deep down, Falgar cared for his friends. And he made flying look good, too.

Falgar was also Sullivan's crew-mate. They had to work together every day. To desire anything but a professional relationship was beyond base buffoonery.

They spoke little as they walked past the dilapidated tenements of the Rat Quarter. Stale urine and cook fires permeated the muggy air, but Sullivan thought he caught another scent, wafting along the breeze. The cloying sweetness of rosewater.

*It can't be*, he thought. Not here. Not in the Rat Quarter, of all places. Not her, either. Plenty of women wore rosewater-scented perfume. It had to be someone else.

But it was her, and she was here. Sarena stood outside a dusty herb seller's shop, chatting with a man in a stained apron. She carried herself with the practiced poise and confidence of the Sanorian elite. Although she dressed plainly, the quality and cut of her linen fabric dress showed greater wealth. What was Sarena Damaring doing in this part of town?

Sullivan froze in his tracks, casting about for a place to hide. Exposed, like a mouse in an open field. To run would only draw the predator's attention.

"Eh?" Falgar asked. "Why'd you stop? What's the matter?"

The woman's head snapped, hawk-like, towards them. Her eyes narrowed as if trying to remember where she'd seen them before.

*Sullivan's heart pounded. She won't recognize me. She can't recognize me.*

Sarena opened her mouth to speak. "Don't I—"

Falgar put his hand on Sullivan's shoulder. His touch shot aether through Sullivan's veins.

"Sorry, you're thinking of someone else. Must hurry along. We're going to be late if we stand here all day." Falgar gave the woman a polite nod. "Afternoon, Lady."

"Good... good afternoon." Sarena stared after them, perplexed.

Once they were out of earshot, Falgar's face broke into a wide grin. "So. Who was she, then?"

Sullivan sighed. He considered evading the question. But this was Falgar he was talking to. Falgar wouldn't rest until he had the entire story. "Her name's Sarena Damaring. She was my fiance."

Falgar's hazel-green eyes widened with delight at the scandal. "You were engaged?"

Grateful that his dark skin obscured his blush, Sullivan nodded.

Falgar laughed. "She must not've been much invested in the relationship. She looked like she hardly knew you."

She was not the problem, Sullivan thought. "It was many years ago. I was a soft, scrawny kid dressed in fine silk. I didn't expect her to make the connection." *At least I hope she didn't.*

Falgar snorted. "Scrawny? You? Can't picture it."

Sullivan shrugged. "Years of hauling cargo crates put an end to that. There's a portrait in my old family home, if you don't believe me." Sullivan almost laughed, imagining how his parents would react if he brought Falgar over for a cordial visit. "Although they probably burned it when they kicked me out."

Falgar's face fell. "You never told me why your parents kicked you to the curb."

"No. I didn't."

Falgar rolled his eyes.

Sullivan sighed. If he was going to tell anyone, it may as well be Falgar.

"They kicked me out for refusing to marry Sarena Damaring. Her family had a lot of money."

Falgar snorted. "You let a fine woman like that go? What, was she demon possessed?"

*This cannot be happening.* "There's nothing wrong with being demon possessed. But… oh, if you must know, I was already in love with someone else."

"Ooooh, scandalous!" Falgar's eyes lit up, and he folded his hands. "Well, go on, go on. Who was she?"

Sullivan took a deep breath. "His name was Trevor Wainwright."

Falgar's expression was blank, making it impossible for Sullivan to discern his reaction. "I hear little of Trevor Wainwright now. What happened? Is he… did he…"

"He's alive, if that's what you mean. At least as far as I know." Sullivan's heart lurched at the painful memories. "I was young and foolish and unprepared for what it meant to give up everything for love." He shook his head.

The younger Sullivan had been a pampered, spoiled brat. Poor Trevor Wainwright had been a god among demons to put up with Sullivan for as long as he did. But even gods had their limits. Trevor was married, last Sullivan heard, and had a handful of kids by now. There was no sense lamenting what might have been.

Falgar put a sympathetic hand on Sullivan's shoulder. "Oh, dear.

Well, if it's any consolation, you're far from the first person to make mistakes where love is concerned." He put a hand on his chiseled jaw. "You know, I don't fancy the Gilded Rose much after all. Know any good taverns around here?"

Sullivan gave a hesitant smile. "One or two."

Falgar bowed and extended his arm as if Sullivan were still a nobleman. "Then please, lead the way."

Dorian had been to several markets since joining the *Phoenix* crew, and he often frequented the quaint market square back home in Frostvale. But none of them compared to a bustling metropolis like this.

They walked past stalls of bright silks, glittering jewelry, and exotic fruits. One stall sold actual, living gryphon cubs, who wrestled playfully in a straw-lined enclosure. Dorian tarried, taking in delicious aromas from the pastry seller's cart, but, still full from lunch, continued on his way.

He could not, however, resist spending a silver on a new scabbard for his athame, and he also spent several of his replenished coins on a selection of rare and exotic baking ingredients.

"Great prices here," he said as the seller wrapped up a bundle of dried lavender and candied elderflower for only six coppers each.

"Glad to see that just because you're a proper aeronaut now, you won't stop baking for us," Tai said with a grin.

"Never," Dorian vowed, hand on his heart. "I know the real reason the crew keeps me around."

«And thank Meroneth for that,» Hematite intoned.

"Enough of that, now." Tai punched Dorian's arm. "Your contributions are many and manifold."

The people in the market were as diverse and fascinating as the wares for sale. Sanorians and Kasani milled with Vateans and Pazai, and even Orith like Tai, with luxurious plumage reaching almost all the way to the ground. And then — Sweet Ancients, was that an Iriya with spiral ram's horns curling behind his ears? He'd only heard of them in stories. But there weren't just hominids at the market.

Floating among their mortal counterparts, circling and darting and snapping up bits of silver-white energy, were demons. Several dozen, maybe more. Some flitted from mortal to mortal, while others, the larger ones, attached to a single favored person. Dorian's fellow demon-possessed went about their business, as if so many demons together were commonplace.

«Do not stare,» Hematite said. «It is rude to stare.»

"That," Tai said, "Is a lot of demons."

«At least you and I would fit in here,» Hematite said. «Perhaps we could stay. I am certain Solaris can manage on her own.»

«Nice try,» Dorian replied.

Inwardly, however, he worried. He'd never known demons to congregate in such large numbers before.

"This is the place," Tai said.

"The... the place?"

"Ruon's. The clothier."

"Right. Clothes." Dorian fiddled with the frayed edge of his silk cuff.

"If you don't mind," Tai said, "I'm going to visit the hair cutter across the street. I'll meet you out here afterwards."

"Hair cutter?" Dorian was perfectly capable of going in the shop by himself, but he felt cut off, unmoored, at the prospect of Tai's departure. *Ridiculous*, he told himself.

Tai nodded. "I prefer to keep it short, so it doesn't get in the way when I'm flying." She tugged on the ends, which fell most of the way down her neck. "I see yours is getting long, too. Did you want to get yours cut?"

"Oh! I'm not sure..." Dorian ran his hand through his own copper mane. It was about the same length as Tai's, and he'd never let it get this long before. But he liked the way it felt when the wind ran through it in the Linking.

"You don't have to," Tai said, laughing. "I'll meet you afterwards, okay?"

She touched him on the shoulder, and Dorian felt a sudden rush of energy spread across his entire body.

Dorian took a nervous breath and stepped into the clothing shop. *Just a store*, he reminded himself. *Nothing to fear.* The jingling of a bell alerted the bald, well-dressed shopkeeper to his presence.

"Welcome," the shopkeeper said. "I am Ruon, purveyor of fine aeronaut's attire. How may I be of service?"

"Ah, hello. I, um, need a belt. And trousers and a waistcoat. And shirts. If you have them. In my size. That is." Dorian scratched his neck. Couldn't he behave like a normal human for once and not some bumbling buffoon?

Ruon, however, nodded without comment. "Do you know your measurements?"

"Um…"

Ruon made a *tsk* noise and produced a measuring tape from his desk drawer.

Forty humiliating minutes later, Dorian's money pouch was lighter, but his rucksack was heavier with not just trousers and tunics, but three additional sets of clothes and a sturdy frock coat of grayish blue wool.

He'd just finished handing Ruon his coins when the clothier said, "Haven't I seen you around here before?"

"Um, no, I don't think so."

"Hmm," Ruon frowned. "Are you certain? I could have sworn…"

"This is my first time in Sanorska," Dorian said. "Unless you spend a lot of time in Frostvale."

"Frostvale, Frostvale…" Ruon's frown deepened, as if trying to place the name. "In Adenthul." His eyes widened with recognition, and Dorian felt a sudden chill run down his spine.

The bell chimed, and the door flew open. Tai, hair shortened, scrambled in.

"We have to go."

"Wait—" Ruon began.

Before the clothier could finish, Tai grabbed Dorian by the arm and ushered him into the street.

"Tai!" Dorian complained. "What—"

"That," Tai jabbed her thumb at a nearby wooden notice board.

The first thing Dorian saw was a black-and-white sketch of Captain Xander, hard-faced and shaggy-haired, with several days' stubble decorating his rough square jawline. Next to it was another sketch of Dorian's own face. Perhaps Dorian *had* lost weight recently, or else the sketch artist exaggerated his roundness. But there was no mistaking him. Beneath the images stood bold block letters in several languages. The topmost, in the Kasani trade language, said, "WANTED for HIGH TREASON against EMPEROR Janus Callahan Penregon Kasani Sanorsk."

"Emperor?" Dorian yelped.

Dorian heard clanking metal and looked up with a sinking stomach. A full guard patrol made a beeline towards them.

"I guess Callahan found out I'm not dead."

Tai nodded. "I think maybe we should run."

# CHAPTER EIGHTEEN
# FIGHT OR FLIGHT

Dorian heaved for breath. The sound of his pounding heart and his footfalls on the cobbles drowned out all other sounds as he and Tai sprinted through the streets of Sanorska.

Dorian tried to shout the occasional "'Scuse me!" and "So sorry!" but mostly, he needed all his air for breathing.

Thank all the Gods and Ancients he'd started running laps on the *Phoenix's* upper deck. He might not be about to win any foot races, but three moons ago, the guards would have been on him in a second.

«We still cannot outrun them for long,» Hematite said, and Dorian knew the demon was right.

They compensated for his lack of speed by taking frequent turns. This worked for a time, but they couldn't keep running forever. A large red-haired man and his winged companion barreling down the street at top speed were bound to get attention, even in a diverse city like Sanorska. Drenched in sweat and panting in desperation, he struggled to think of plan.

They rounded yet another corner into the wealthy section of

town. Dorian noted a banner labeled "Silk Row" as he sprinted by. Pedestrians in vivid clothing looked up from their shopping deliberations as Dorian and Tai barreled past them. *Definitely* distinctive-looking.

Dorian's eyes landed on a stall selling ornate polished rapiers on a red velvet blanket.

"Tai," he panted. "I'll... borrow... one of these swords. And... and..." he fought to catch his breath. "Try to... to fight the guards... you go... fly... back to the ship... warn the others."

It was a terrible plan, and he knew it. He was a poor runner, and an even worse swordsman. And he was out of energy. But what choice did he have?

"*Go.*"

"I can't!"

"This is no time... to be noble," Dorian huffed. "At least... one of us... should escape."

But Tai shook her head. "No. You don't understand. Literally, I can't." She twitched her wings. "These wings don't work, Dorian!"

Dorian blinked. *Tai couldn't fly?* Come to think of it, he'd never seen her do so outside the Linking.

The sound of clanking armor returned, followed by the wing-beats of gryphons.

Dorian heaved a heavy sigh, still fighting to catch his breath. This looked like the end of a line. No runner could outpace a gryphon. Not much could, except...

"Oh!" Dorian palmed his forehead in sudden realization. "I am such a fool." He shoved his hand into his belt pouch and retrieved Solaris's dragonstone, which he slung over his neck.

"What? What are you doing? Why did we stop? We have to—"

"You can't fly." Dorian grinned despite his exhaustion. "But I can."

«I was wondering when you would call.»

Startled cries came from the passersby as the red dragon swooped down into the middle of the crowded street.

«Ah,» Solaris said, as if in pleasant surprise. «This is more like it.»

Solaris spread her golden wings. Dorian and Tai wasted no time scrambling onto her back.

Falgar examined his long-stemmed wine goblet. Gold-leaf filigree stood out against the green glass, sparkling like an emerald in the flickering lantern-light. These Sanorian taverns put every dockside bar back home to shame. Too bad the beer selection was so lackluster. The dry wine wasn't bad, though.

"It figures," Sullivan said with an ironic twist of his mouth, "That on the day I should think of my family for the first time in years, we end up at a tavern drinking their wine."

"*Their* wine?" Falgar asked.

Sullivan nodded. "My family owned vineyards. I learned quite a lot about the winemaking process, growing up, but it's been years. My knowledge of biology extends mostly to the healing arts."

"I never knew that," Falgar said, intrigued.

Sullivan snorted dismissively. "To tell you the truth, I never thought our wine was any good. Harsh, our grapes, compared to the Vatean varieties."

Falgar chortled. "Gods know I could never afford Vatean wine. Now. Vatean beer. Vatean beer is a proper common man's drink. I could regale you with the virtues of Vatean beer all day long."

"The Adenthulians claim to be the masters of hops and barley, but they're uninspired compared to Vatea." Sullivan put a finger on his firm chin. "I've thought of making beer, you know. I know a bit of fermentation from the vineyards. But I always liked beer better, much to my parents' chagrin."

*Sullivan's parents didn't care for many of his preferences, did they?*
*Falgar thought ruefully.*

"You should try brewing," Falgar said. "There's room in the cargo hold for a cask or two, and the Ancients know Xander wouldn't mind saving some money. Hops and barley are cheaper than beer."

"Perhaps I will." Sullivan inspected his drink with renewed interest.

"So," Falgar said, would-be smooth. He suppressed a grimace. *So?* "You don't like women at all? Or just not that Sarena woman?"

Sullivan took a long sip of wine. "I like women just fine," he said. "I just don't wish to bed any of them."

Falgar made it all the way to adulthood before he learned some people were only attracted to *one gender*. With all the world of attractive people out there, it seemed absurd to dismiss so many of them. But he supposed people couldn't help who they liked.

He examined his wine, casting about for something witty and clever to say. For all his boasting, Falgar was never especially good at flirting. He'd bedded three individuals in his twenty-three years, two women and one man. A reasonable count, he supposed, but far fewer than he claimed.

"Sorry about the Gilded Rose and all," Falgar said. "Shame they don't have a Gilded Rose for fellows."

"They do." Sullivan twirled his shirt lace around his finger. "I mean. Not that I ever frequented such a place." Clearing his throat, he added, "We could've gone, though, to the Rose. I'm sorry if you skipped it on my account."

"Nah." Falgar shrugged. "Wouldn't've been any fun if you weren't enjoying it."

He opened his mouth to ask Sullivan about this intriguing Gilded Rose for Fellows when the tavern door swung open.

An armored city garrison guard strode in, and the hairs on Falgar's neck stood on end. Growing up in the mean streets of Tremaine, he learned to have a healthy distrust of the garrison.

"Where are the two aeronauts from the *Phoenix*?" The guard demanded, hand on the hilt of his broadsword.

"Here—" Sullivan began, before Falgar kicked him under the table.

"Don't go giving us away!"

"But we're not in trouble," Sullivan said.

"Not yet, we're not," Falgar said, eyeing the guard.

Unfortunately, the guard noticed. "You there. What ship are you from?"

"The *Winds of Fortune*" Falgar lied, giving the name of the ship he'd served on before the *Phoenix*.

The guard's eyes narrowed. "Let me see your papers."

"We're not here to cause trouble," Falgar said. He held out his right hand to show he was unarmed while he reached for his aeronaut's license with the other.

The guard snatched up Falgar's paperwork and examined it. Then, almost casually, he backhanded Falgar. For a second, Falgar was so shocked he didn't even realize what had happened. He teetered backwards, nearly falling off the barstool.

"What are you doing?" Sullivan's eyes were wide, his voice a full octave higher than normal.

"It's a crime to lie to the garrison," the guard said.

*Void*, Falgar thought. He must have given the man his *Phoenix* paperwork instead. So much for handling this the peaceful way.

The guard hit him again, harder this time. Stars danced in front of his eyes. "Where. Is. Dorian. Valmont?" He punched out each word like an individual sentence. And then he hit Falgar again. Then again, and again, and again.

"Stop it!" Sullivan cried. "Let him go!"

"I don't take orders from traitor Valgrenites," the guard snarled.

Falgar staggered to his feet and reached for his sword. He needed to fight back, not just sit here useless. But floor swayed beneath him, the walls spinning. He hadn't had *that* much wine, had he?

He collapsed back down, clinging to the circular table for

purchase. He tasted blood in his mouth. *That can't be good.* He wondered if he'd lost any teeth. Sullivan would never find him attractive if he lost all his teeth. The guard wound up to punch Falgar again.

Wham. Fist met flesh, but neither fist nor flesh belonged to Falgar. The guard staggered backwards. It took Falgar a second to process that Sullivan had just punched the guard in the face. Sullivan might not be as well-armed as the soldier, but he carried much more muscle. In his arms. *Well-armed.* In his dazed, pain-addled state, Falgar started giggling.

Sullivan stared in shocked horror, from Falgar, to the guard, to his own fist, back to Falgar. "I hit a guard," he said. "Oh, Void Eternal, I hit a guard. I can't believe—"

The tavern doors swung open once again, and Captain Xander staggered in, short of breath.

"Falgar! Sullivan! Thank the Ancients. We — Oh, Void."

The soldier, recovered from Sullivan's assault, lunged towards the captain. But Xander dodged and tripped the guard with a sweeping kick beneath the knee. *Captain fights well for an old fellow,* Falgar thought.

"Let's go!" Xander motioned towards the door.

Falgar wanted to obey, but when he tried to rise to his feet, he wavered and toppled over.

"I've got you," Sullivan said. He hoisted Falgar over his shoulder as if he were a sack of laundry.

"You have nice shoulders," Falgar slurred.

The world faded into blackness.

The city shrank behind Dorian and Solaris, gryphon-mounted guards hot at their wingtips. Dorian's heart thudded in his ribcage.

Together, he and Solaris flew, swiftly and with purpose, faster and farther than he ever had before.

He knew he ought to feel afraid. And he did, in a distant, abstract way. But as he and Solaris spiraled ever higher into the warm summer sky, a sense of rightness settled around him. This was what he was supposed to be doing. This was where he belonged.

It took him a moment to realize that some of those feelings came not only from himself, but from Solaris.

"You're enjoying this!"

He felt a stab of embarrassment from the dragon. «Do not be ridiculous. We are in terrible danger.»

But through their bond, neither of them could hide their genuine emotions.

Dorian clenched his teeth in determination and flew harder, higher, desperate to create distance between themselves and their pursuers.

Three moons' practice in the Linking smoothed out the awkwardness of their initial flight. Dorian and Solaris moved together as one. They may be a far cry from the easy, fluid grace of the Ancient dragonauts of legend, but they were flying. *Sweet Zekador above*, they were actually flying!

The unmistakable twang of a bowstring hit Dorian like a bucket of cold water. As fast as they flew, the gryphon-mounted knights were still close behind. He could hear the beating of their white-feathered wings.

Taking Solaris into an awkward roll, he dodged the arrow, barely. Tai screamed and clung to his shirt for dear life.

"Sorry, sorry!" Dorian's voice was high as he and Solaris desperately fought to right themselves. He regained control just in time for the gryphon knight to loose another arrow. This time, it struck true.

Pain jolted down Dorian's back. Solaris's back? It didn't matter. His pain and Solaris's pain were the same.

Dorian screamed and fought for another burst of speed. It did no good. The gryphons were gaining on them. The knight drew his bow and loosed again. Dorian dodged, but too slow. The arrow grazed across Solaris's face, sending a stream of silver-white energy trailing behind them.

"Come on, come on, we're nearly there," Tai whispered in a terrified litany as she clung to him. Was she hit? He couldn't risk turning around to look. Heart tight with worry, he kept flying.

Another arrow hit them, piercing Solaris through the tail. She and Dorian cried out as one. Their opponent loosed another arrow, then another, faster than Dorian could comprehend. He couldn't even dodge. He clung to Solaris and flew with an urgency he hadn't believed he could possess.

Blessedly, mercifully, he saw the skyport up ahead. He could even pick out the distinctive squat form of the *Phoenix* tethered to the docking pillar.

*Not much more, not much more.*

An arrow lanced across Solaris's wing like a fire made solid. Dorian screamed. With a desperate prayer to the goddess Nahiira for her protection, he kept flying.

Every wing stroke was agony now. Tears streamed down Dorian's face, but he didn't care. He wanted to quit. To surrender, accept arrest, anything to make the pain stop.

*No.* He couldn't do that. What would happen to Tai and Solaris if he did?

Through her pain, the dragoness almost laughed. «You think of me… at a time like this?»

The world faded around him. Soon, there was nothing except for Solaris and the pain and the narrowing tunnel view of the *Phoenix* ahead.

Somehow, by luck or determination or Kassoria's own grace, they made it to the ship. Dorian, Tai, and Solaris skidded and tumbled to a halt atop the wooden deck.

"Valmont! Lunstrum! Thank Zekador." Xander sprinted up towards them. He had the docking rope in his hand already, pulling hard to disengage from the pillar. There was no time to waste.

The ship lifted off of the platform, leaving the gryphons behind in the wake of the aether engine. They were, for the moment, safe. Though how long that would last, Dorian didn't know.

Exhausted and terrified, heart threatening to burst from his chest, Dorian leaned over the railing and vomited. He watched with detached horror as the remains of his stew rained down on the land below. Grimacing, he took a swig of water.

Across the deck, Sullivan hunched over Falgar, muttering worried imprecations and deftly carving healing sigils into the air.

Tai rose to her feet and dusted herself off. To his great relief, she looked uninjured. That same relief died, however, when he saw the others.

"Falgar!"

Dorian struggled to his feet and lumbered towards his friend. Half of the aeronaut's face was swollen in a colorful patchwork of bruises. A stream of blood dripped from the corner of his mouth.

"What happened?" Dorian asked, forgetting his own discomfort.

"Ran afoul of some garrison soldiers," Sullivan said.

"Sull'van punched him," Falgar slurred. "Was brill'ant."

"Don't talk, I need to focus," Sullivan said. To Dorian, he added, "You're not hurt, are you?"

For the first time, Dorian inspected his own wounds. What had a moment ago been burning agony now receded to a dull ache. An enemy arrow had grazed his upper arm, tearing the linen fabric of his brand new shirt and drawing blood. But other than that, he remained blessedly uninjured. Which meant that Solaris —

"Meroneth's balls! Solaris!"

He spun around and sprinted back towards the dragon. No less than four arrows protruded from her ruby scales. Silver-white spirit energy dripped down onto the deck beneath her. She swayed unsteadily, tried to stand, and collapsed again.

"Oh, no." Solaris was his dragon, his bond, his partner. He should have thought of her first. He should have flown more carefully. He should have... *he should have...*

«It is all right,» Solaris said. Even though their shared pain gave lie to the words, he could feel her sincerity.

"No." Dorian's heart was a hummingbird trapped in his chest. "No, it's not bloody all right! It's—"

"No time," Captain Xander barked. "We may have escaped those gryphons, but if they don't send an attack sloop after us, I'll eat my boots. Lunstrum! Valmont! Linking!"

Tai cast a nervous glance first at Dorian and Solaris, then at Falgar and Sullivan. She frowned, nodded, and dove into the glowing blue circle.

Dorian, however, stood, horrified, powerless to make himself move.

«The dragon will be all right,» Hematite said, but he didn't think he'd ever heard the demon sound so worried before, especially not over Solaris. «She will recover. Dragons are strong and arrogant and self-assured in their superiority. For one to fall to something such as arrows would be ludicrous.»

Hematite sounded like he was trying to convince himself more than Dorian. Was he actually concerned for his rival?

"Linking," Xander repeated, "Now!"

Dorian shook his head. "But — Solaris — I need to — I should —"

"No time!" Xander shouted, before diving into the Linking circle himself. "Falgar's out of commission and Sullivan's busy. It has to be you."

«Go,» Solaris prodded him, urgent. Over the railing, he saw knights approaching on skimmers and ornithopters.

"Void." His oath came out in a raspy whisper. Every inch of him trembling, he stumbled into the circle.

# CHAPTER NINETEEN

# TOGETHER

Thinking back, Dorian had no idea how they got out of Sanorska alive. Already exhausted, sick with worry over Solaris and Falgar, it seemed impossible that he could fly at all.

But fly they did, and steadily, the metropolis gave way to the outlying towns and villages, then farmsteads, then wilderness. Only when they passed Sanoria's edgecliffs, and the vast expanse of underclouds lay out beneath them, was it safe to Unlink.

"Solaris!" Every muscle in Dorian's body screamed as he half-stumbled, half-crawled onto the deck. "Solaris!"

He sprinted to his dragon so fast he almost tripped over the chicken Henrietta, who gave an aggravated squawk and nipped at his ankle in return.

«I am all right,» Solaris said. «Your friend Sullivan removed the arrows and Healed me while you were escaping.»

"Sullivan did," Dorian repeated, heart pounding. "It should have been me. I should have—"

Solaris twitched her tail impatiently. «I already told you back in Greystone, dragonauts cannot Heal their own dragon. Besides.

Sullivan is the ship's Healer. It is his job. Your job was to fly, and you performed it commendably.»

Dorian couldn't help but smile a little. *His job was to fly.* He liked the sound of that. Unfortunately, her words failed to hide the bone-deep worry thrumming through their bond like a discordant note. *I've failed again,* he thought. *No matter what I do, I'll never be good enough.*

«That is not—»

"Meroneth's cold and shriveled left testicle," Falgar joined in. Sullivan's healing had cleared most of the bruises from his face, but he still looked paler than usual, and more than a little exhausted. "Anyone want to explain to me why we just got chased out of Sanorska by a bunch of angry soldiers with sticks up their arses?"

"Right," Xander said. He looked tired, and older than his forty-two years. "Let's have a beer while I explain. On second thought, I'm bringing out the single malt. We're going to need it."

The others nodded and made their way downstairs to the common area, but Dorian lingered on the deck. He knew he'd have to face his crew-mates soon, but his dragon was his priority. He turned his attention back to her.

To Dorian's great relief, Solaris didn't seem to have suffered any lasting damage. She sprawled on the deck, glittering in the evening light, leaving no sign she'd been shot full of arrows.

Dorian recalled the first time he saw Solaris, frail and injured, like a gust of wind might break her. Now, however, even freshly healed from multiple arrow wounds, Solaris looked comparatively hale. She was still slender, willowy, and it surprised Dorian that she could safely carry him. But she didn't look fragile. Not like before. Was Dorian's initial prediction accurate? Was she getting stronger because he was? Or was this simply a normal part of dragon growth and recovery? It heartened him to see it, either way.

"Solaris." Dorian expelled her name like a sigh. "I'm so glad you're all right. You were amazing back there. I should have flown better. I'm sorry. I—"

«No.» The dragon reverberated with concern and worry. Even...
guilt? She hesitated for a long moment, before saying, finally, «It is I
who owe you an apology.»

"Oh!" Dorian said. "Um, no you don't. I mean, I'm sure it's fine,
whatever you think you did."

Solaris tilted her scarlet head towards the setting sun. «I have
been abysmal to you. Treated you with disdain. Foisted expectations
upon you that you neither asked for nor deserved.»

Dorian swallowed and scratched the back of his neck. "Hey, but I
mean, you're desperate to save your friends. I can understand that."

Solaris shook her serpentine head. «You have trained so hard,
worked so hard. You are changing so many things about yourself, all
for my sake. To rescue *my* clan-mates. This has never been your fight,
yet you work tirelessly and without complaint.»

"I seem to recall plenty of complaints," Dorian said, but he
smiled, too.

Solaris tossed her head in obvious agitation. «Today they could
have killed you. You shrug it off, but I saw one of those arrows hit
you, too. And you humans are much, much more fragile than we
dragons. It was... wrong of me, to force this upon you.»

Dorian's breath caught in his throat. That was what was bothering the dragon? He took his time to respond, choosing his words
carefully.

"Solaris," Dorian said, "I hate Callahan too. He's keeping dragons, sentient, self-aware beings, as slaves. That's wrong whether or
not you personally know them. Of course I have to do something if I
can. And as for the rest of it. You want to know the truth?" He gave
her a shy, conspiratorial smile. "I love it. I love learning how to be an
aeronaut. I love flying with you. Even the strength training. Yes, even
leg day. Don't tell Hematite."

«I can hear you, you know.» Hematite, who'd been oddly silent
during their escape, responded with a snort. Dorian noticed for the
first time that while Solaris looked haler and heartier, Hematite
looked somehow diminished.

"I've been quite the poor bond to to you, haven't I?" Dorian said, now turning his attention towards the demon.

«Do not worry about me.» Hematite brushed off Dorian's concern. «I am feeling under the weather, that is all. Anyway, I have known a dragon or two in my time, and the thing you must understand about them is they are positively moon-blinded where freedom is concerned. They value it above anything else, to a wholly irrational degree. Even I can see that Janus Callahan's actions are abominable.»

This did little to allay Dorian's concerns. He needed to do a better job looking after both his bonds. But he put on a brave face and said, "There now, see? Even the demon wants to help."

Solaris looked at Hematite like she'd never seen him before, and then gave a burst of melodious, good-natured mirth. «You mean what you said?» she asked Dorian. «You really enjoy all of this?»

"Oh, yes," Dorian said. "I mean. I could do with less danger and mayhem, let's be honest. But..." he smiled wistfully and stared out at the orange-pink sunset. "I have never felt more alive."

Solaris's relief washed over Dorian. Relief and... something else. Admiration? «Your flying today was... incredible. I do not believe I could have outflown those gryphons on my own. It was your flying skill, not mine, that won our way to freedom. You have gone well above and beyond what I had any right to ask of you, to ask of any human.»

Feeling warm, Dorian allowed himself a self-indulgent moment to bask in the glow of her praise. Solaris was pleased with him! She was actually pleased with him! For a brief, irrational moment, he wanted to dance giddily around the deck, to the Void with his exhaustion.

«I would like to remind you,» Hematite said, «That I approved of you the entire time.»

With a quirk of a smile, Dorian said, «You were worried about Solaris too. Don't pretend you weren't.»

At that moment, Tai emerged from the forecastle. "Are you coming? Everyone's waiting."

"Oh," Dorian said. *Right.* His human companions. *Can't forget those.* "I'll be right there. Sorry about that."

He scratched Solaris one last time behind her horns, then hurried to join the others.

His crewmates gathered around the round wooden common room table.

"Whiskey?" Xander brandished a crystal decanter as soon as Dorian sat down.

"Th... thanks," Dorian said. He'd had nothing stronger than feast day wine before, but the Ancients knew he could use it today.

Xander poured what seemed like a generous measure. Dorian took a sip. It reminded him of the kitchen hearth at Callahan Manor, all wood smoke and flame. Warm and comforting, but liable to burn him, too.

"All right," Falgar said. "Do either of you want to tell us why there are wanted posters with your faces plastered all over Sanorska?"

Dorian squirmed in discomfort. "I don't know how he found out I'm still alive. But surely his reach ought not extend past Kasanarae..."

Xander's expression was grave. "I imagine," he said, "That it has something to do with this."

The captain placed a yellowed parchment flyer down on the table. Sullivan picked it up, and Dorian leaned in closer to look. His heart wrenched as he saw the pen-and-ink drawing of Queen Saedra's face. The artist captured every detail perfectly. Gods and Ancients, it had been more than a hundred days since he saw her last.

Dorian's beloved queen stood beside a hard-faced Callahan, both of them dressed in elaborate regalia. Dorian's stomach turned to ice at the sight of his stepfather, and he took another sip of whiskey to warm it. He'd not realized before now what a relief it had been, these past two moons, being away from that man.

Dorian jerked his eyes away from the image and read the headline. "Kasani Ruler Named Emperor Following Sanorsk Surrender."

Sullivan's hands shook. "Sanorsk... surrender." Sanoria was Sullivan's homeland. Dorian suspected the news hit him particularly hard. "It says here that King Sanorsk surrendered with no hostilities."

"I guess it's good no one died this time," Tai said. "But I don't think every nation's going to surrender as easily."

Dorian's stomach twisted in knots. "Callahan has access to... terrible magic. Gods. Do you think he could use the Void as a weapon?"

Xander nodded gravely. "This could mean bloodshed worse than the War of the Magi. It's no wonder King Sanorsk was so quick to give in."

A leaden weight settled in the pit of Dorian's stomach. And here he'd been feeling so pleased with himself. He'd gotten stronger, sure. But what was a paltry bit of strength against the combined might of Sanoria and Kasanarae? What use was he against someone who could bring entire nations to their knees?

«Do not despair,» Solaris said. «If you are the man I think you are, then together we will find a way.»

Dorian was not at all certain he was the man Solaris thought he was, but the dragoness's obvious faith brought him back, just slightly, from the precipice of despair.

Falgar crossed his arms. "Doom and gloom aside. I still want to know what in the name of Kyrizzian's drooping right teat this has to do with Valmont and the Captain!"

"Kyrizzian's drooping right teat?" Sullivan raised his eyebrows.

"It's an expression." Falgar waved a dismissive hand.

Dorian sunk into his chair, feeling lower than the underclouds. They were going to find out, eventually. Might as well tell them now. "Callahan... wants me dead."

Briefly, he told them about the grimoire, about Saedra, about the Void and the demons and Callahan's plans to end all magic.

"I should've left the crew back in Greystone, but I was so desperate to learn to fly, and then Solaris came along, and we had that cloaking device, so I thought... It was selfish of me. I'm sorry I involved you all in this. I had no right. Maybe... maybe I'd better leave. Next time we make landfall. I've caused you all enough trouble."

"Like the Void, you will!" Tai said.

"She's right," Sullivan agreed. "If Callahan wants to end all magic, it's something that affects all of us."

"Can't make money flying a ship if there ain't no flying," Falgar said pragmatically. "But besides. We're in this together. If you think we'd just dump you off to face this on your own, what friends would we be?"

Dorian took a hasty gulp of whiskey and almost choked on it as he fought back a sudden upwelling of tears. Never, not once in Dorian's entire life, had he ever had friends who said things like that.

Xander cleared his throat. "If you think this doesn't involve me, then I assure you, you're very mistaken. I was on that wanted poster too, in case you'd forgotten. Besides. My sister would come out of hiding just to skin me alive if I left you to face Lord Callahan without help." He gave a small smile, but it soon gave way to a serious expression. "However, there's something else you all deserve to know."

The crew of the *Phoenix* looked up at him in worried curiosity. Dorian didn't think he'd ever seen the captain look so grave before.

"It wasn't just because of Valmont here that those dragonauts tracked us down." Swallowing, Xander brought out a cloth-wrapped bundle. "I think they were looking for this."

They all leaned close over the table as Xander un-wrapped the bundle.

Tai's hand flew to her mouth. "Is that what I think it is?"

Dorian felt a frantic tug on his connection with Solaris, as if their bond was a rope suddenly snapped taut. Fear and anger, the likes of which Dorian had never felt from the dragon, plunged into his heart like an icepick.

«That is an abomination.» Solaris's mindvoice was cold.

Even Hematite stirred with distaste as he looked upon it.

"What... what is it?" Dorian asked, half fascinated, half horrified. From where Dorian sat, it didn't look evil or dangerous. It looked like the ornate silver hand mirror that used to rest on his dead mother's abandoned vanity table. In place of glass, however, lay a flawless flat sheet of iridescent blue aether. Dorian thought he might get lost staring into the object's crystal depths. It drew him in, hypnotic. He rocked his head back and forced himself to look away. No wonder Solaris and Hematite were afraid of it.

"It is called the Moon Glass, and it's an Ancient artifact of unfathomable power," Xander said.

"It was used to sink Orith," Tai said.

"Void," Dorian swore. He edged away from the artifact as if it were a poisonous serpent.

"I might have... stolen it," Xander admitted. "Twenty years ago, when I left the Order. The point is, I have it, Callahan wants it. My primary goal is to ensure that Callahan does not get it." He took a long sip of whiskey. "Obviously, this puts you all in a lot of danger. The *Phoenix* isn't a prison ship. The rest of you are free to go." He took another sip. "I... apologize for not telling you sooner."

"I'd never abandon a crew in danger," Sullivan said, sounding affronted and a little hurt.

"We already said we'd stay," Falgar said, crossing his arms.

"Honestly," Tai said, smirking. "First a secret dragonaut, and now the Void-cursed Moon Glass? Any other skyship crew would be terribly boring after this."

"Granted," Falgar added, "I fully expect you and Valmont to stick your necks out for me next time I'm in trouble. Fair's fair."

"Of... of course," Dorian stammered, not sure whether he was more shocked that the Captain carried a continent-sinking artifact in his back pocket, or that his crew-mates, somehow, didn't hate him. "But... but if we're criminals now, what about shipping contracts? What are we going to do for money?"

Xander chuckled. "We do still have the cloaking device. Do you have any idea how valuable invisibility from scrying is for a smuggler? Do not assume I've always been such an upstanding citizen. I still have my contacts in the underground. No, boy, don't you worry about that. Leave it all to me."

Dorian squirmed nervously and traced the knots on the wooden table. His crew-mates just showed they would risk arrest and worse for him. He didn't feel like he deserved it, but it meant the sky to him all the same.

What sort of person was he if he didn't trust them in return?

"There's something else," Dorian said. His voice caught in his throat, and his heart hammered. "If Callahan has access to all these dangerous spells, then the rest of you need to at least know what we're up against. I think it's time I shared what's in the Grimoire."

# CHAPTER TWENTY

# THE SINKING OF THE SPIRE

Dorian stood in the tepid mists of the *Phoenix's* shower, waiting for the feeble water pressure to clear the soap from his bulky frame. He swore he could get cleaner just standing outside in a light drizzle. It wasn't raining, however, and water was a precious commodity on board a skyship, and supplies didn't come cheaply now that they were on the run. Dorian still had to get clean somehow.

The aether-heated shower was a clever device, but finicky, too. Too often it broke down at just the wrong time, leaving Dorian covered in suds and grasping for towels. *Gods*, how he missed the steam baths back in Frostvale. Probably the *only* thing he missed about Frostvale.

Ah, well, any shower was better than no shower, and Dorian endured because he wanted to be clean and presentable when he saw Tai this evening.

«Not that I am one to discourage hygiene, but Tai sees you every day,» Solaris pointed out, «And usually when you are drenched in sweat.»

"Ack!" Dorian turned off the water and grabbed for a towel. It wasn't a big towel, so faced with the choice of exposing his manhood or his rump, he awkwardly held it in front and blushed furiously. "Are you *watching* me?"

The dragon seemed perplexed. «Of course not. I am up on the deck. There is no room for me in your small bathing room. But we are bonded. We are always connected so long as you wear your dragonstone.»

Dorian reached for the pendant around his neck. Usually, he took it off when he bathed, but in his haste to get clean and ready, he'd forgotten. "Yes. But I didn't think you'd, um, be present. While I'm bathing."

«Why not?» Solaris asked, genuinely confused. «We bathed together in the Vatean lakes just last moon.»

"That was swimming. It's different."

«I cannot see how.»

Dorian's face burned bright. "Well, I wasn't naked, for one."

Solaris was both amused and perplexed. «So you wish for me to only speak to you when you are covered in fabric?»

"Er, yes."

«Humans are strange.» Then Solaris's amusement gave way to annoyance. «Does Hematite not speak to you when you are bathing?»

«Of course not,» Hematite said. «I have some respect.»

"Gyah!" Dorian tried to wrap the towel tighter around himself. So Hematite was here, just being quiet. *At least Hematite is male,* he thought, more to himself than to either of his companions.

«Gender,» Solaris telepathically scoffed. «What a useless human concept. First, I have no desire to mate with you, or any human. Second, many humans mate within their own gender, your friend Sullivan, for instance, so the entire concept of segregating—»

"Wait. *Sullivan* does?"

«*Moon and Stars* you are oblivious.» Above, Solaris let out a long stream of sparks.

"Huh."

Dorian shrugged and then pulled on a fresh set of clothes. After shaving his copper stubble, he gave his reflection a cursory glance in the reflective metal sheet that served as a mirror.

Dorian had long ago come to terms with the fact that he'd never be especially handsome. This didn't bother him as much as it once did, but he couldn't pretend to be overjoyed about it. So he avoided mirrors, in general.

Today, though, he lingered a touch longer, pulling his neck-length copper hair out of his eyes, and tried a few experimental facial expressions. *No*, he thought, it was no good. He was unlikely to enthrall Tai with his looks. Perhaps he could still impress her in other ways.

«My understanding is that the human royal Saedra found you attractive,» Solaris pointed out. «It is entirely possible that the Orith Tai might, as well.»

«Correct,» Hematite agreed, «And that is why you should think about the woman you claim to love, not entertaining fancies of another.»

«My love life is neither of your business,» Dorian said, even though he knew they were both right.

Dorian loved Saedra. Didn't he?

Why did it feel like he was always trying to convince himself?

«It is natural for you to compare the two,» Solaris said, «When you are thinking about doing with one what you so often did with the other.»

Dorian's face burned. «Void Eternal, Solaris!»

«What?» the dragon retorted. «Surely I may talk to you, now that you are covered in fabric.»

«Yes, and I will stay that way, thank you.»

«I only meant studying from the Grimoire,» Solaris said.

Dorian's face turned redder still. "Oh. Right."

Hematite chuckled. «He thought you meant *mating*,» he told Solaris in a teasing tone.

Dorian shook his head in consternation. Ignoring both of his bonded companions, he stopped by his cabin and scooped up the blue covered Grimoire under his arm. Solaris and Hematite both had a point, though. Dorian felt things about Tai that went beyond the boundaries of ordinary friendship.

They'd been studying together every evening for more than a moon now. Sometimes Falgar and Sullivan joined, but they didn't seem to take to it as much as Tai did. The Orith aeronaut, however, took to learning Cyrus's spells like a gryphon took to the sky.

But tonight was different. Tonight, Dorian was equal parts excited and afraid. Tonight, finally, Dorian would teach Tai to cast the Void. The most dangerous spell of all. He trusted Tai to do the right thing with the information, but still. It required an immense amount of trust. Doing this with Tai felt almost as unfaithful to Saedra as if he *were* bedding her.

«Saedra mated with you while engaged to another human, and then wed yet another human still,» Solaris pointed out. «She has long ago surrendered the right to expect fidelity from others.»

«I say they are both bad influences on you,» Hematite said. «Saedra and Tai. And Solaris, too.»

«That's awfully misogynistic of you to dislike every woman in my life,» Dorian said. «Besides. I thought you liked Saedra.»

«I did. I do.» Hematite hung his head. «So much has changed. So fast.»

Dorian felt his annoyance replaced with concern.

Hematite had, at least, not diminished any further since their escape from Sanorska, but nor had he regained any of his former vigor. Dorian and Solaris thrived in the sky, but the demon, it was abundantly clear, did not. Dorian sent Hematite a thin silver-white tendril of spirit energy, by way of apology.

Dorian sighed. «Hematite... I know you don't... approve. Of my training. Becoming an aeronaut.»

«Do not forget learning the sword,» Hematite replied. «I also disapprove of the sword.» More seriously, he added, «Lord Meroneth sent us demons to Cyrna to protect the humans. How in the Void am

I to do that, when you are all so stubbornly determined to bring about your own demise?» Hematite's blue flames guttered, and he forced himself to calm down. «There was nothing wrong with our lives back in Frostvale. We were safe and comfortable. Now we are constantly on the run, sore and exhausted, and for what? So that you can try to convince the world you are someone you are not?»

Dorian's stomach twisted. Was that really what he was doing? Trying to prove he was someone he wasn't? It was true he was still leagues behind the others, as both an aeronaut and a swordsman. But life in the sky felt right, somehow. He'd never been content with his life in Frostvale, not really. Safe and comfortable, he might have been, but not happy.

Dorian didn't want to go back to the way things were. Just thinking about it made him sick, a leaden lump in his stomach. But Hematite hated it here. And the demon had been a friend to Dorian, back when almost no one else would. Surely he owed it to Hematite to take him home.

«Where, I wonder, does your own happiness fall into all this?» Solaris said.

Dorian expected Hematite to snap back at the dragon, but the demon stayed quiet for a long moment. «Dorian's own happiness matters, though not, perhaps, as much as his safety. However, Solaris's companions should be freed. On that, at least, we are all in accord. After that... I do not know. I have never shared a bond with a dragon before. I fear that this is a new ground for all of us.»

«How very accommodating of you,» Solaris said. Her mindvoice held an affected tone of sarcasm, but deep down, Dorian could tell she actually meant her words.

Something passed between Hematite and Solaris, then something strangely profound. But whatever it was, it belonged in the realm of magical beings, and not mere humans, so Dorian could not understand it.

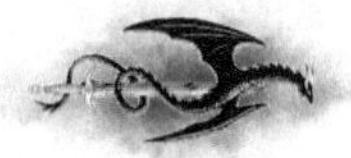

When Dorian arrived in the common area, Tai was not alone waiting for him. Captain Xander and the rest of the crew sat around the circular wooden table, all wearing stony expressions.

Dorian gingerly set his book down. "Why do I feel like I've been summoned to a tribunal?"

"You're not in trouble," Xander said, though there was a hint of resignation in his voice. "No more so than the rest of us, at any rate."

"So a great deal of trouble, really," Falgar said.

"Might be *slightly* more trouble than the rest of us." Tai's brown eyes were alight with worry. "Have a seat."

Dorian sat, and Xander poured him a jot of whiskey from the half-empty decanter on the table. Dorian accepted it and took a sip. He coughed and sputtered as the fiery liquid attacked his throat. He didn't think he liked whiskey very much. Beer was one thing, but whiskey he was beginning to associate with bad news.

"So what happened?" Dorian asked once he'd regained his voice.

"I received a communication via aether transmitter," Xander responded. "Using a special secret encoding used by the Order."

Dorian felt himself instinctively leaning closer. "From your sister?"

In the moon following their hasty departure from Sanorska, they'd seen neither hide nor hair of this mysterious Order. Dorian wondered if Xander's sister was even still alive.

Xander's frown deepened. "Maybe. Could also be from Hildegard. Or any of the others I haven't spoken to in Cycles." He took a hefty swig from his tumbler. "Or it could be a trap."

Dorian took another tentative sip from his own glass. *No*, he thought, this was not his favorite beverage. "So... what's got everyone so worried?"

"Here's the transcript." Xander handed Dorian a cheap, lumpy piece of paper inscribed with Captain Xander's cramped but neat handwriting.

*Dorian read out loud. "You're going to find out eventually, but I figure you'd better hear it from us first. Last night, Callahan's dragonauts sunk a spire in the Dragon's Fangs."*

Dorian put down the missive and looked up at the others, shocked.

"But... but how? I thought he needed that Moon Glass thing."

"Keep reading," Xander said.

*Dorian obliged. "Sources close to the Kasani throne have reported that King Callahan has hoarded aether stone for moons now. Enough, perhaps, to gather the astronomical amount of energy needed to do this. But we can not rule out the possibility that he has used other sources as well."*

Dorian blanched. "Other sources? What does that mean?"

Xander's mouth narrowed. "The Moon Glass is a powerful magical amplifier, but there are other ways of getting the requisite energy," he said. "It might be worth finding out if Callahan still has all six of his captive dragons."

Dorian felt a tight knot of fear in the pit of his stomach, and he knew it came from Solaris.

"You think he sacrificed one?" Dorian said, feeling cold. "Would Callahan stoop that low?"

"I do not know the depths to which Callahan would stoop," Xander said.

*Dorian exhaled. "Meroneth's balls." He continued, "Sources close to the Order report that you have a rogue dragonaut serving on board your ship. — Well. That source'd be Hildegard, I suppose. — I cannot stress enough the danger you are in. Callahan will do everything in his power to gain that dragon for his own followers. Please, with all haste, report to my contact at the Star and Garter Inn in Goose Head to await further instruc-tions. Your safety, and the future of all Aeris, may depend on it."*

Dorian took another sip of whiskey, and this time he didn't even mind the taste. "Don't... hesitate to be dramatic, do they?"

Xander's expression darkened. "'Await further instructions.' As if we'd come at their beck and call."

Dorian bit his lower lip. "I don't know," he said. "Maybe we should listen to what they have to say. This all looks a lot bigger than anything we can handle on our own. Gods. If he can sink one spire, how long will it take before he sinks the rest of Aeris?"

"The cost to do that is much higher than the magic to sink a single spire," Tai said. "He'd need the Moon Glass, and more dragons, to start."

Dorian let out a long breath. "Ending the magic indeed. Zekador's poorly fitting pants."

Xander's shoulders slumped, resigned. "I'll go meet them at this bloody tavern," he said, "But you're not coming with me."

"What?" Dorian asked. "Why not?"

"Because it might be a trap, snot-for-brains," Falgar said.

"Falgar is right, if a bit crudely put," Xander said. "You stay hidden on the ship. Once we know it's safe, you can come join us."

"I don't like it," Dorian said, crossing his arms.

Xander shook his head and drained his glass. "I don't think any of us like any of it."

# CHAPTER TWENTY-ONE

# GOOSE HEAD

"How's it looking, Lunstrum?" Xander asked.

Tai gave the silvery line one last tug. "Took some damage after the last Voidstorm, but should get us through to Goose Head, no problem." She smiled and shook her head. The crew had improved across the board, it seemed, in terms of safety and efficiency. Dorian's clever sigilwork hadn't hurt, either. They made a good team.

Good thing, too. The Voidstorms had only increased in frequency. Just last week, a storm nearly knocked them out of the sky. If they'd faced it a few short moons ago, it probably would've blown them to pieces. This time, however, they held together. It was testament, she thought, to their improved collective strength as a crew.

Dorian grunted in consternation as he pulled his own line taut. "I know why I can't come with you," he said. He paced the deck, restless, checking the knotwork on the lines he'd triple-checked already. "But Zekador help me. I can't stop Callahan by hiding forever. I need to do something before he sinks yet another country."

"He can't sink countries," Xander said with a dismissive wave of his hand. "He sank one spire, and it took near all the power he had. Posturing, nothing more."

Tai, however, agreed with Dorian. Callahan's message couldn't have been clearer. *Do as I say, or next time it might be you.*

"Well," Dorian said, "If that missive really was from the Order, I still think I should come along."

Xander nodded at Dorian with something almost like respect. He shook his head, though, and said, "I don't think I need to remind you, you're not much use stopping Callahan if you get arrested and executed before you can even get near him. Your face is all over every wanted poster between here and Kasanarae, in case you'd forgotten."

"No." Dorian slumped his shoulders. "I hadn't forgotten."

Tai felt it was now her time to interject. "Forgive me, Captain," she said, "But *your* face is all over those wanted posters, too."

Xander smiled. "I appreciate the concern, but I'll be fine. Lucky for me, I can cast Illusion."

Xander twirled his athame, then carved a handful of sigils into the air. He walked through the circle, then, a moment later, emerged with his hair turned gray and shortened to a crewcut. He also grew a short gray beard to match and wore an eyepatch over his left eye. "Now I look the proper smuggler."

"Not bad," Tai admitted.

"My sister was always the Illusionist in the family, but I can hold my own." Xander gave a modest shrug.

"Why not cast Illusion on Dorian, too?" Tai asked.

Dorian gave a blithe smile. "'A personal illusion cast on another will always blur and fade,' as my old governess used to say. It's one of those spells you really have to do yourself." His smile turned into a grimace. "I'm afraid I've... never been any good at it."

To Tai's surprise, Xander actually laughed and clapped him on the shoulder. "Nothing to be ashamed of, boy. Your mother was a genius at Illusion. But your father? Absolutely hopeless. Best mage of his day, and couldn't make a rope look like a serpent. Bad luck, I suppose, that you ended up on his side of the family tree."

This seemed to cheer Dorian up. "Here I thought the man had no flaws."

"Well, he chased off after Lord Callahan's wife," Xander grumbled. "Like father, like son, I suppose."

"Captain!" Tai wasn't sure whether to laugh or be outraged on her friend's behalf.

Before any of them could respond, however, Sullivan came over, asking, "Valmont, I hate to ask, but can I get your help to wrestle Henrietta and Mrs. Pennyfeather back into the coop?"

"Right away!" Dorian cast an apologetic shrug in Tai's direction, then jogged across deck to help Sullivan.

Tai watched them work for a moment. Dorian fell over in his attempt to corral Mrs. Pennyfeather, who seemed desperate to make a bid for freedom. He recovered himself with much flailing of arms, and both men laughed.

Xander laughed, too, but he wasn't looking at the chickens.

"Just what, Sir, is so funny?" she asked, bringing herself back to the present.

"You and Valmont." Xander's face twisted into an amused smirk.

Tai crossed her arms, wings cocked. "What about me and Valmont?"

"I see the way you look at him."

Tai's wings flared. She most certainly did *not* look at him in any particular way.

Granted, he wasn't bad looking. She liked his bright eyes and his ready smile. Gods above, he had a pleasant smile. He was also intelligent, and determined, with a boyish enthusiasm she found infectious. And just when, she thought as she watched him work, had his shoulders gotten so muscular? His forearms, too.

She shook her head. His *forearms*? *Zekador's pants*. Bad enough to develop feelings for any crewmember, much less Dorian. Falgar would never let her hear the end of it.

"He's just a friend," she said. Then she sighed. "It's just... he's one of us now. He laughs and jokes with the crew. It didn't use to be like that."

Xander responded with a knowing smile. "One could say the same about you."

Tai tensed. "I beg your pardon?"

"You always held yourself apart from the others," Xander said, staring over the railing at the busy skyport below. "But ever since Valmont arrived..." he shrugged. "You seem more open, I suppose, now."

The captain was right, she realized. She was fond of this crew, not just Dorian. She'd almost come to think of them as family. Her heart clenched, and she looked over the side.

*Like a family.* Yes. Tai had served on a crew like that, once. She'd also promised herself that she'd never let herself get too close with her crew-mates again. Would she get hurt again? She didn't want to believe it of this crew. And yet, she wasn't sure her heart could stand to find out.

Goose Head Settlement was too big to be called a town, but Tai didn't think it qualified as a city. Rather, it was a haphazard collection of buildings grown out of some no-longer-insignificant outpost in the Pazai-Thlarknian borderlands. Ramshackle tents and huts lined the dusty streets stacked atop each other on creaky wooden platforms.

Tai recalled reading that Goose Head was an unofficial center of trade between the warring nations of Pazarae and Thlarknia — a haven for smugglers. And on first glance, that was exactly what it looked like. But the more Tai saw, the more she became certain that they'd find no smuggling work here.

There were soldiers about. Many soldiers. Pazai in uniforms of green and blue, Thlarknians in brown and gray, Kasani in blue and silver. What were Kasani doing all the way out here? Nothing good, she was sure about that. There was tension here. It was so thick she could almost taste it in the crisp Autumn air.

A blue-clad soldier looked straight at Tai as she passed and then waved to get his companion's attention. The companion looked in their direction and nodded. Tai walked faster, head bowed.

"Stop it," Xander said. "You're just going to make us look more conspicuous." He ran a frustrated hand through his shaggy brown hair.

His *non-Illusioned* shaggy brown hair.

*Oh no.*

"Void," Tai said, her voice a full octave higher than normal. "Actual Void! Your Illusion isn't working because this entire area is thrice-cursed Voided!"

They made to run, but soldiers were on them in an instant.

"Stop right there!"

A gauntleted arm pulled her close, crushing her breasts and wings.

For a moment, the world stopped. Tai felt powerless and small in his iron-tight grip, the sour stench of yesterday's ale still on his breath.

"No need to be afraid," the soldier said. "We just want to talk."

*Like a demon's promise, you do.*

She let out a defiant scream and kicked at her captor, hard. She cared little where the kick landed, just so long as it did. Her boot contacted steel armor. It probably hurt her foot more than it hurt the soldier. But the force was enough to loosen his grip. She seized the opening and lurched downwards, slipping through his grasp to freedom.

"Hey!" the soldier reached out and grabbed the end of her left wing, tearing out a handful of feathers. *Useless thing.*

Tai sprinted around a corner, and another, frantic for a place to hide. There, outside the greengrocer's shop, she saw it. A loosely stacked pile of rotting refuse.

*Wonderful.*

Not giving herself time to think better of it, she took a deep breath and dove. Not a moment later, her pursuers came sprinting past, not sparing the barest bit of attention to her malodorous hiding spot. Tai waited, heart pounding, until their footprints faded from earshot. Her face wasn't on the wanted posters. Would they even care about hunting her down? But that wasn't the case for Xander and the others. Her heart pounded with worry.

Once she was certain it was safe, she climbed free of the pile, flicking a bit of potato peel out of her hair. *Disgusting.* Looking both ways to make sure they hadn't followed her, she made her way back the way she came.

*Please let the others have escaped, she prayed to all seven of the gods. Oh, please oh please oh please...*

The gods did not see fit to answer.

At the end of the alleyway, her breath caught in her throat. She pressed against the far wall, desperate not to be seen. Falgar, Sullivan, and Xander lay motionless in the street, surrounded by soldiers. The slow up and down movements of their chests were the only indications they were alive. At least there was that. But what had knocked them out? With the area Voided, nobody should have been able to cast magic.

Her answer came with the sound of wingbeats.

Two mounted dragons, even bigger than Solaris, descend into the alleyway towards her unconscious friends. *Breathtaking creatures,* she thought, but that only heightened her terror. These had to be some of Solaris's enslaved kinfolk, and that meant their riders worked for Callahan.

A muscular, strawberry-blonde woman dismounted from her golden dragon's back and turned her athame in her hands with a satisfied smirk. The sigils on the blade still glimmered blue from recent spellwork.

*Dragonauts can cast magic in the Void.* She remembered that now, from reading about them as a child. She wondered if Dorian knew that. She wondered if it might be useful. But Dorian was safely back on the ship, and she intended for him to stay that way. She had to figure out how to help the others on her own.

The other dragonaut dismounted. She assumed the dark-haired figure was a man, though he faced away from her, so it was hard to tell. He wasted no time tossing Falgar and Captain Xander onto his indigo dragon's back as if they were nothing more than sacks of flour. He then helped the other dragonaut tie Sullivan's bulkier frame onto the gold dragon. Tai felt a flare of indignation. To use dragons as common pack mules! *Focus, Tai,* she told herself. *Rescue your friends first, then maybe we can help the dragons.*

With Tai's friends attached, the dragonauts remounted their dragons and launched into the warm afternoon sky. Tai marked the direction of their flight and followed.

She took back alleys through the town to avoid notice, holding her athame at the ready. It may be useless for spellwork here in the Void, but it was still a serviceable blade. *Gods and Ancients.* She wished she'd thought to bring a proper sword.

The dragon's path through the sky led to a fortified encampment on the edge of town, surrounded by a high palisade wall. Crawling with Kasani guards, with mounted gryphon knights watching the skies high above. But Tai's eyes landed on a wooden scaffold just outside.

She almost laughed as she climbed up. Probably part of some construction project, but at the moment, Tai didn't care what it was for. If these Kasani would deign to allow Orith immigrants into their ranks, they might not have overlooked such a glaring security flaw. Tai might not be able to fly, but she inherited the light, durable frame of her Orith ancestors.

Without allowing herself a moment to think it through, she squared her shoulders and leapt off the scaffolding. The ground rose at an alarming speed, and on not-quite-Orith-born instinct, she threw out her hands to catch herself. Blood and dirt ground together into her palms. But she was inside, and she was mostly uninjured. She stood up and dusted herself off.

"No one can take a fall like an Orith."

Her satisfaction, however, was short-lived. Now that she had a minute to think about it, she realized the guards could barely fail to notice an Orith girl careening off the palisade wall. *Good, good. Definitely one of your better plans.*

Sure enough, for the second time that afternoon, she heard the unmistakable sound of wingbeats from above. It was the indigo dragon from the alleyway, the one whose rider handled her friends so carelessly. The creature came to a soft landing not a gryphon's length from Tai, tight corded muscles glittering under scales of purple and blue. Even as terrified as she was, the creature's beauty took her breath away.

The dragon's rider dismounted with effortless grace, brushing nonexistent dust off his gleaming silver epaulets. If she'd thought the dragon was frightening, that was nothing compared to the dragonaut.

*No.* Tai's stomach dropped to her boots. *No. It can't be.*

He'd faced away from her when she saw him in the alleyway, so she hadn't recognized him then. But now she recognized everything about him, from the set of his shoulders to the shape of his nose. The enemy dragonaut had glossy black hair, pale green eyes, and a face so handsome it almost hurt to look at him. She never thought she'd see that face again. She'd never *wanted* to see that face again.

And yet, here he was, gorgeous as ever in the enemy's uniform. And here was Tai, beaten and bloody and covered in garbage. *Just perfect.*

"Hello, Tai," he said, flashing that dashing, arrogant smile of his.

Tai fought back the bile that rose in her throat. "Hello, Kadmin."

# UNWELCOME VISITORS

Dorian's practice sword hit the dummy with enough force to send it swinging. Dorian ducked to avoid his adversary's whirling arms. He might have felt proud of his maneuvering, but he knew it wasn't because of quick reflexes. He'd simply faced the dummy enough times to know exactly how it would react.

"And I win again." Dorian sighed and slumped his shoulders.

Solaris, sprawling across the depressingly empty cargo bay floor, eyed him with amusement. «I have heard,» she said, «That there are spells that can make the practice dummies fight back with considerable skill.»

"That'd be nice," Dorian sighed. He wondered vaguely if his father's grimoire might contain any information about how to enchant a practice dummy. That would at least be something to do.

"Who knew being on the run from certain doom could be so boring?"

Ever since their hasty departure from Sanorska, Dorian dreaded having to make landfall. In the sky, he had flight rotations and training and the day-to-day chores of running the ship to keep himself busy. Though he feared Callahan in a distant, abstract sense, he could honestly say he was happy on board the *Phoenix*. In the sky, he was free.

On land, however, it was different. Staying cooped up on the ship might help him avoid arrest, but it felt like a different kind of prison. And perhaps it was Dorian's imagination, but today Captain Xander and the others seemed to be taking longer than usual to return.

He'd done all he could to keep occupied while he waited for his friends. He'd scrubbed the upper decks until they shone. He'd completed an entire strength training circuit. He'd then gone up to the galley and assembled individualized hand pies for all of his crewmates.

Ingredients were sparser now that they were on the run, so most everything they cooked was some combination of potatoes and carrots from the ship's garden beds. But Dorian had enough herbs and spices left from the market in Sanorska that he could customize quite a lot. Unfortunately, to his dismay, the aether stove wouldn't start, and the stasis chamber that kept ingredients fresh was on the fritz as well. Dorian had been forced to leave the uncooked hand pies in a makeshift stasis circle of his own, and he dreaded informing the captain that their galley equipment needed repairs.

So, with baking no longer an option for the time being, he'd returned to the cargo hold to try a few swings against the practice dummy.

After all that, the others still had not returned.

Dorian paced the cargo hold, trying to shake off his frustration. He hated this feeling. While everyone else got to explore the town and do productive work, he was stuck here, being useless.

*Again.*

«You never used to be this restless,» complained a petulant Hematite. «I do not suppose it will do any good for me to suggest you stick to the things you are good at.»

Dorian sighed. "You mean like sitting in the kitchens at Callahan Manor and feeling sorry for myself?"

«Not feeling sorry for yourself, no,» Hematite said. «But there are other places you can avoid Callahan. It has always been said that if someone needs to disappear, Goose Head is the best sort of place to do it. Study sigils. Start a bakery. Study sigils and start a bakery. Bake enchanted muffins.»

"I can't bake enchanted muffins," Dorian said, running a frustrated hand through his shoulder-length copper hair. "I'm on wanted posters all throughout Aeris."

Dorian sighed again and sat down against a row of wooden crates, staring up at the hanging aether lamps. Practicality aside, perhaps Hematite was right. Perhaps he was kidding himself, thinking he could be an aeronaut. All his hard work, his constant training and practice, and he was still stuck in the cargo hold like an unruly child.

«Well,» Hematite said, «At least we can make this interesting. Solaris, I bet you four units of spirit energy that Dorian defeats the practice dummy in three blows this time.»

Solaris twitched her tail in obvious interest. «Five units,» she allowed, «That he does it in one.»

Dorian looked at the spirit beings, half amused, half perplexed. He didn't even know they could trade spirit energy as betting currency. But before he could face the dummy again and prove which one of them was right, the heavy sound of footfall sounded on the gangplank.

Dorian felt a surge of hope. Were the others finally back?

*No.* Dorian felt a chill as he heard the distinctive clang of armored boots. None of his crew-mates wore armored boots.

"Oh," he said, throat dry. Hematite faded into Dorian's demonic aura, but Solaris remained in plain sight on the cargo bay floor. "Oh, no."

In a panic, he yanked off his dragonstone and shoved it into his belt pouch. Solaris faded to ghostly energy. "Sorry, Solaris." He knew she would understand.

"Skyship *Phoenix*," a cruelly delighted masculine voice came from the other side of the cargo bay door. "Sweet Meroneth. We've been looking for you for a long time."

Dorian's breath caught in his throat. They knew the ship's proper name. That shouldn't have been possible. Had Hildegard's cloaking device stopped working?

The door slid open of its own accord, revealing a burly, intimidating man. He wore chain mail armor and the silver and blue tabards of the Kasani sky navy. A demon, smaller than Hematite and whipcord thin like a ferret, clung to the soldier's shoulder, blue flames enveloping violet hide.

Dorian swallowed his panic and put on what he hoped was a convincing smile. "Ah. Yes. Hello. Um. How can I help you?"

"I've got a warrant to inspect your cargo," the soldier said with palpable smugness.

Dorian's eyes widened, and he felt the heat rise to his face. "I... um... that is... no smuggled cargo... no!"

"Who said anything about smuggling?"

«Meroneth bless you, Dorian, but you never were any good at lying,» Hematite said.

The soldier almost looked amused as he casually brushed past Dorian, sweeping his gaze around the cargo hold. The demon leapt off his shoulder and began sniffing at the cargo crates. Apparently finding the one she wanted, she signalled for her bondmate to follow.

"Though now you mention it, these aether crystals sure don't look on the level." The soldier grinned at Dorian with the expression of someone who'd just found a gold coin in his shoe. "Where's the rest of your crew, anyway?"

"They're... they're not here."

"Pity," the soldier said. "Illegal aether crystals are small change, but if I bring Callahan your captain, I can retire to a palace in Vatea." The purple-skinned ferret demon circled several times around Dorian and cocked her head towards the soldier, blue flames flaring high. The soldier's eyes narrowed, then widened again. "Well, I'll be Meroneth's favorite uncle," he said. "You're him, aren't you?"

"That depends on who you mean by 'him'," Dorian said weakly, though he had a feeling he already knew. A bead of sweat rolled down the side of his face.

The purple ferret demon climbed back up onto the soldier's shoulder, and her flames guttered and flared once more. They must have exchanged something telepathically because the soldier's wicked grin widened and he said, "Oh, indeed." He turned to Dorian, still grinning that evil grin. "Amethyst here informs me that your captain and your friends are already in custody."

Dorian's heart lurched. So that was why the others hadn't returned yet!

"Now I just need to collect you, and it'll be quite the hefty payday for old Silas."

And so Dorian acted without thinking. Still holding the wooden practice sword, Dorian lunged forward and hit the man, Silas, on the head, hard. This gave Dorian enough time to shove his hand in his belt pouch and loop Solaris's dragonstone back over his neck. Solaris bloomed into physicality, breathing sparks right in the soldier's face. Silas screamed and staggered backwards, falling clumsily off the side of the gangplank. Dorian winced at the sound of clattering armor.

"Do you... think he'll be all right?"

«I imagine he will live,» Solaris said. «Excellent strategy dismissing and summoning me back.»

«Strategy or dumb luck,» he said, heart still racing. Dorian sprinted across the hold, towards the wooden arms crate. He threw open the lid and seized the first weapon he saw.

The sword's handle glittered in the lamplight, dragon-shaped golden hilt bedecked with blood red gemstones. Not a sword for one looking to avoid attention. It was probably meant for ceremonial purposes, or to hang on some rich lord's mantle. But it was well-balanced and sharp, and the perfect length and weight, as if forged for Dorian alone. Dorian wondered vaguely why such a thing was in

Xander's arms chest, but he had little time to worry about it, nor did he have time to be picky.

Fancy sword in hand, Dorian scrambled onto Solaris's back and took off into the crisp autumn air. Despite his terror, a feeling of euphoria washed over him.

*Sweet freedom.*

Now that he was airborne, he could think more clearly. His friends. He had to save his friends. But where were they?

*Oh, I don't know, he thought to himself. How about that big fort over there with all the Kasani banners?*

Solaris replied with a grim draconic smile. «Seems like a good place to start.»

They took off in the fortress's direction. Joined with Solaris, he felt as aware of her body as he felt of his own. He gripped Solaris's neck ridge with one hand, and his sword with the other, and desperately hoped he wouldn't have to fight anyone in the sky.

*Void*, he wasn't even ready for a sword fight on the *ground*. But his friends were in trouble. At the very least, Dorian had Solaris had the element of surprise.

«I may be doing something very foolish,» he told Solaris.

«Almost certainly,» Hematite quipped.

«Perhaps,» Solaris agreed. «But I know as well as you we have no other choice.»

They attracted little attention as they soared through the crisp autumn air towards the fortress. Dorian had assumed a dragon would be obvious, but if anyone noticed them at all, they simply nodded acknowledgement and went back to their business.

Far fron relieved, Dorian's fear mounted. If dragons flying over-head weren't surprising, it was probably because they were commonplace. That meant some of Callahan's dragonauts were here in Goose Head. *Better and better.*

Still, he couldn't quite feel miserable, not when he was flying with Solaris. *Gods and Ancients,* at least he was off the ship. At least he was *doing* something.

«Here is the fortress,» Solaris informed him. They flew around the enemy stronghold in a high, wide circle. He saw no sign of the other dragonauts yet, but nor did the guards and soldiers below show Solaris much interest. That all but confirmed in Dorian's mind that the other dragonauts were here. Of course, they'd know Dorian wasn't one of them if they paid him the slightest bit of scrutiny. If Dorian could pass himself off as a Kasani dragonaut, he wouldn't have needed to be in hiding all this time.

Dorian brought Solaris to a soft landing in an empty alleyway near the loading docks. Despite his heightened nerves, he felt a rush of pride. Neither of them could have landed so gracefully a few moons ago. He jumped nimbly down from Solaris's back, then ducked behind a stack of crates while Solaris took back off into the sky. His heart raced, but so far, he didn't think anyone had noticed him. Thanking Solaris, he removed his dragonstone and put it in his pocket. While he'd been lucky so far, the other dragons would notice her presence eventually. Solaris faded into spirit form, and already, Dorian missed her comforting presence.

«If you like, I can pretend to be Solaris,» Hematite said. «Look at me! I am a dragon! I think I am better than everyone else because I can fly.»

«Oh, ha ha, hilarious. Solaris does not sound like that.» Dorian took a deep breath, squared his shoulders, and readied himself for the task at hand.

The Kasani fortress seemed like a disorganized place. Haphazard tents outnumbered the more permanent structures almost three to one. The Kasani must have moved here in a hurry. *Why*, Dorian wondered. To shut down the smuggling trade? It didn't seem likely. What did Callahan care about goings on halfway across Aeris?

«You forget we are near Thlarknia again,» Hematite said. «The archaeologist Hildegard warned us that Callahan had interests in the Thlarknian aether mines.»

«Yeah,» Dorian said, frowning. «Sinking entire islands can't come cheaply.»

«Control the aether, control the world,» Hematite said.

Dorian couldn't help worrying there was something more to it. Something he was missing. But for the time being, his priority had to be finding his friends.

Years of bullying at the hands of Bradford and his cronies meant Dorian was good at keeping his head down. Ensuring that the hem of his frock coat covered his sword hilt, he took care to make himself as unassuming as possible, all the while searching frantically for any place that might hold his friends.

"You there!" A sharp woman's voice shouted in his direction.

Dorian's heart sank. They couldn't recognize him already! *Void Eternal*. It wasn't like he was the only stocky redhead on all of Cyrna! Dorian pulled his coat closer to himself and kept walking.

"Hey! Don't ignore me." The voice sounded annoyed now. "Oh, for the Ancients' sakes." Before Dorian could react, the woman grabbed his arm and dragged him into an unoccupied tent.

"What — what the —"

His captor, wearing a silver and blue Kasani military jacket, glared at him through sharp green eyes. She looked oddly familiar to Dorian, but he couldn't imagine where he'd met her. The only Kasani soldier he'd ever met was Saedra's guardswoman, the duchess Vivienne, and this certainly was not her. His captor had tan, freckled skin, and a mane of copper-brown hair only a shade or two lighter than Dorian's own.

"What," she demanded with barely suppressed fury, "In the name of the Ancients do you think you're doing?"

Dorian blinked. A lie came to him, unbidden. "I, um, work here," he said. "As a baker. For the soldiers."

A flimsy lie, though the best he could manage. Surely if she sent him back to the kitchens, the other bakers would notice he didn't work there and know him for an impostor. If he could even find the kitchens.

The familiar-looking woman, however, looked thoroughly unconvinced. "Like the Void, you are. Bakers do not carry around convincing replicas of Ancient dragonaut swords."

Dorian flushed.

«I knew grabbing that ostentatious sword was a poor idea,» Hematite complained.

Dorian knew it was hopeless, but he grasped for a lie, anyway. "It's, um, a family heirloom. But I came to Goose Head to, uh, sell it. To feed them. The family, I mean. They're, uh, starving."

*Zekador's pants*, he thought. Couldn't he come up with something even a bit more believable?

"Dorian," the woman said with an exasperated sigh, "Please cease with the gryphon dung. I was friends with your parents, remember? I know your family isn't starving."

Dorian blinked.

"Friends... friends with my parents?" Then, suddenly, he remembered where he'd seen her before. "Oh, I know who you are. You're Hildegard Weatherbee. You were at Greyst—"

"Not so loud," Hildegard said, looking frantically around. "Meroneth's balls, boy. Half Callahan's army is desperate to find you. What in the name of the Ancients are you doing walking right into his base?"

"I... um... they captured my friends... but... wait a second. What are *you* doing here?"

She sighed, tugging on the ends of her auburn hair. "Looking for you, as it happens. Bradford just about had a panic attack when the *Phoenix* popped back up on the scrying mirror."

"I knew there was something wrong. That soldier... Wait. Bradford? You're in contact with my brother?"

Hildegard nodded. "He was the one who sent that encoded

message. When none of you showed at the Star and Garter, he feared the worst, so he sent me in here to get a look around."

"Is Bradford affiliated with the Order?"

"Yes, and no," Hildegard hedged.

"Why did the cloaking device stop working?" Dorian asked.

Hildegard grimaced. "If I were to guess? Not enough magical energy. This whole area's Voided. They keep enough magic at the sky docks to allow skyships to come and go, but not much else. Did any of your other aether devices stop working when you landed?"

"Yeah, they did," Dorian said, thinking of the broken aether stove and stasis chamber. "Listen, you've got to help me. Those soldiers arrested Captain Xander and the others. I only just barely got away. I'm trying to rescue them. Clearly," he sighed, "I'm not doing a spectacular job at it, as you found me out in the first five minutes."

Hildegard tossed her head in annoyance. "I bet Xander tried to use Illusion in a Voided area. Brains of a sky puffer, that one. I always told him not to rely too much on that spell, but does he listen?"

"It's, uh, good to see a friendly face, at least," Dorian said. Though the way Hildegard glowered at him, her face could hardly be called friendly. "I mean, I'm glad you found me, instead of getting caught by a real Kasani soldier."

"Bloody lucky, that." Hildegard sighed and inspected him up and down. "You look well, at any rate. Life in the sky seems to agree with you. Though I notice you have lost weight." Her eyes narrowed. "Xander hasn't been starving you, has he?"

"What? No, of course not. I've just been, ah, training. A lot." Dorian's voice came out defensive, but there was also a hint of pride, too. Just a little.

Hildegard clapped him on the shoulder. "Let's put that training to use and bust our friends out of here."

# CHAPTER TWENTY-THREE
# PRISONERS

Tai scowled and ran the plush towel through her short black hair. The soft fabric felt wonderful, just like the bath had felt wonderful. It was all so *bloody* wonderful. Tai hated it.

She was a prisoner. Gods and Ancients help her. She was *Kadmin's* prisoner. The very idea made her sick. That he'd allowed her a bath and a fresh change of clothes mattered little; it made things worse. Now she owed him, Ancients help her. She didn't want to owe that rat bastard anything.

Well, she sighed, at least she'd cleaned off all the garbage. She shook her head forlornly at the change of clothing laid out for her. The baggy gray wool dress was too big and lacked the cutouts necessary for her wings. She flattened her wings as far as they could go against her back and pulled the shapeless garment over her head.

Tai sighed again at the familiar frustration. Her inability to fly made her an outcast in her homeland. Her difficulties fitting into unaltered Aerish clothes reminded her she'd never really belong here, either. *Well*, she thought, self-pity would not get her out of this prison cell. She gathered herself as best she could, looked around, and assessed her situation.

As prison cells went, she supposed this one wasn't so bad. The locked room more resembled an inn than a dungeon. She had a private bath, a comfortable bed, even a pot of tea on the end table. She poured herself a cup and took a sip. Lukewarm. So throwing scalding tea in Kadmin's smug rat face was out of the question. She smiled anyway at the mental image.

As if summoned by her thoughts, Kadmin let himself in with a casual turn of a skeleton key.

*Gods.* He looked just like she remembered him, but *more*, somehow. His fine, dark blue jacket was tailored perfectly to his athletic frame. He had silver filigree embroidered on his cuffs. Was that part of the standard Kasani uniform? Or was Kadmin just showing off? Shifting uncomfortably in her scratchy woolen smock, Tai fumed that of course Kadmin Bloody Crowley would have silver bloody filigree.

"I hope," Kadmin said with that thrice-cursed smile, "That you have no complaints about the accommodations."

"They're... fine," Tai said, grudgingly.

"I should certainly hope so," Kadmin said. "They're mine, after all."

Tai's heart froze. "Yours?"

"Of course." His grin widened. "I would not put you in one of the regular holding cells."

Tai ground her teeth. He locked her in his room? His *personal* room? The implication made her blood boil. She would've preferred just a regular prison cell. And he had the nerve to look at her like she was supposed to be grateful.

"I sense you're less than happy to see me," he said.

"I can't imagine why you might think that."

"Now Tai," he said, waggling his finger like she was a naughty schoolgirl. "You know that tongue of yours will get you in trouble one day."

Tai glowered, but said nothing. *See? I can be quiet.*

Kadmin laughed that infuriating laugh of his. "Gods Above,

surely you still can't be mad about what happened between us. Sweet Natlanti, it's been two years! Please, I must know, why are you here?"

It took all of Tai's willpower not to claw his smug face off. *Of course I'm still angry, you arrogant piece of gryphon shite.* Two years was not such a long time. But something Kadmin said gave her pause.

He'd asked Tai why she was here. That meant there was a chance, just a chance, that he didn't know already. And why should he? Her face was not on all those wanted posters. After her initial escape into the midden heap, the soldiers hadn't bothered pursuing her at all.

The beginnings of a plan took shape. It had only a slim chance of working and required swallowing every ounce of pride she possessed. But it was worth a shot.

"You're right," she said in her best placating voice. The words tasted like bile in her mouth. "It's wrong of me to cling to my anger like that. I apologize. Fact is… I wasn't expecting to see you here. But… but maybe it's better this way. Maybe we can help each other."

"My, my, Tai Lunstrum, admitting she's wrong? Things have changed in two years."

*You have no idea.*

"As they have for you." She smoothed her hair in a way she hoped looked flirtatious, then batted her eyelashes a couple of times. Did people actually bat their eyelashes when they were flirting? *Savior's wings,* the man was going to see right through her. "A dragonaut, now, are you?"

Kadmin's face lit up just a fraction. "Oh, yes. I've bonded the dragon Celestian. Truly a fine dragon, the finest of all the dragons, I should think. Celestian was reluctant at first to be pressed into service, but he's come around to my way of thinking."

"Yes." Tai nodded vigorously, clinging tightly to the opportunity that presented itself. "Yes, I see why Celestian would."

"Now, granted, he still will not grant me a dragonauts' sword, but ah, well. We can't have everything we want in life, can we?"

Kadmin flashed a toothy grin, and Tai fought to keep composure.

Those were the same words he said to her on the day she received her rejection from the Academy three years ago. *"We can't have everything we want in life."*

"That's true," she said with forced calm. "We can't always have what we want. But..." *Oh, gods, I hate this, I hate this,* "That's why I'm here. I heard the Kasani value persistence, so I decided to make myself known to whoever's in charge, and demand they reconsider their position on not admitting foreigners." She crossed her arms and met Kadmin's eyes with defiance.

Kadmin burst out laughing, and Tai was certain the game was up. "My, my," he said, "That is audacious! As it happens, I am the one who's in charge of this base. You've *certainly* got my attention." His grin turned predatory. "You always were a lovely one, Tai Lunstrum. Breaks my heart to see you dressed as a prisoner."

Well. There was her opening. Time to cast all her chips on the table. She took both his hands in hers, and fixed him with her most imploring, doe-eyed gaze.

"Then see me dressed in a soldier's uniform instead," she said. "You and me. Serving Kasanarae. Together. Like it always should have been."

Kadmin's smile almost, *almost* looked genuine. Curse him and his smile to the depths of the Void. "You know I'd rather see you in nothing, darling."

Tai's prayed he didn't notice how tightly she clung to a fistful of her robe, to prevent her fist swinging for his face instead.

"I can't play favorites, you know. You'll start out cleaning chamber pots. But work hard, and you'll advance. Well, come now, let's get you a uniform. We can even cut little holes for those wings of yours."

"Right!" Tai hoped she didn't sound too surprised. "That's good."

*Meroneth's balls,* she thought. This was actually working. She supposed the one good thing about men like Kadmin was they were startlingly easy to manipulate, so long as you flattered their ego. Now Tai just had to keep her temper in check — a tall order at the best of times — and figure out how to get her friends out of here.

Kadmin tapped a bracelet on his wrist in a distinctive drumbeat pattern. Tai recognized it as a smaller version of the signal beacons aeronauts used to communicate. Probably, somewhere on the base, someone wearing a similar bracelet felt the same pattern buzzing against their wrist. Tai knew a moment of fear. Was he calling in for reinforcements? But if that were the case, he would've just left her locked in the room.

"Flight Leader Kadmin!" a woman Tai recognized as the other dragonaut jogged up to them and gave a crisp salute.

"Good, Ashe, you're here," Kadmin said. "This is Tai. She'll be joining up. Please find her something to wear from the women's quarters, won't you? Tai, this is Ashe Valerian, my second in command, but you'll be referring to her as Lieutenant, Lady Dragonaut, or simply Ma'am."

Ashe snorted. "I'm useful for more than just accessing the women's quarters, you know. Anyway, I was actually just looking for you. You're needed in the Questioning Chamber." Her face twisted into a grim smile. "I think your friend Zachary Falgar is ready to talk."

Kadmin drew in a sharp breath and turned his gaze towards Tai. *Oh, no.* Tai's heart raced.

Kadmin might be an arse, but he was no fool. He'd known Falgar back in the old days, too. For all three of them to be here at the same time strained all bounds of plausibility.

"Oh, wow, Falgar," Tai said with a weak laugh. "Haven't seen him in a long while."

Several agonizing moments passed while Kadmin continued to stare at her suspiciously. "Keep an eye on the recruit," he finally told Ashe, his jaw set in a grim line. "I suppose I don't need to remind you not to let her near any of the restricted areas."

"Of course, Flight Leader," Ashe said. She saluted and gestured for Tai to follow.

Tai tried not to look too frantic as Kadmin departed. Falgar was in danger, and likely inadvertently just blew Tai's cover. She wracked her brain for another plan, but came up empty. At least Kadmin hadn't locked her back up. Yet. But how to shake her new escort?

Ashe guided her through a locked door into a utilitarian building that was, presumably, the women's quarters. She then thrust open a wooden chest and searched through several folded squares of tan fabric before roughly handing one to Tai. "Put these on. Ah, I suppose you'll need one of these, too." She rummaged through a drawer and retrieved an athame, the tarnished blade etched with sigils.

"You'll have to use that to cut the wing holes. Shouldn't fray the fabric too much for today, but I recommend getting them tailored at the earliest convenience. Should do for the time being, at any rate."

The tan-colored tunic and breaches were scarcely any better quality than the woolen robe, but at least she could move around in them. After she'd made the alterations, she pulled the tunic over her shoulders and looked around desperately for some way to cause a diversion, so she could lose this Ashe woman and go off looking for her friends.

Diversion came without her help. A rumbling sound echoed across the base. A skyquake?

*No. Worse.*

Tai and Ashe rushed outside the building just in time to witness what had to have been the base's entire stock of gryphons, a cloud of dust and white feathers in their wake. The creatures' eyes rolled with fear and fury.

"Oh, Meroneth's balls," Ashe growled, reaching for her own athame and brandishing it towards the sky. A moment later, her golden dragon swooped down to face the gryphons head on. "Go get Kadmin."

"Eh?" For a moment Tai was too stunned to act.

"Now, recruit!" Ashe shouted, leaping onto the dragon's back.

Tai couldn't decide if it was good fortune or bad that granted her exactly what she wanted, while putting her in real danger of getting clawed and trampled to death. But it didn't matter. She'd take what she could get.

"Kyrizzian's great sagging teats," Falgar said. "I didn't expect to find you here, Kadmin."

Falgar ought to have guessed his former friend would be one of Callahan's supporters. Kadmin was from Kasanarae, and he was always something of a jackass. Still, there was being a jackass, and then there was enslaving a dragon. Even Kadmin should've known better than to stoop that low.

Kadmin's angular face scrunched into a perplexed expression. "Can't say I expected to find you here, either," he said. He paused just a beat before continuing, "Kyrizzian's great sagging teats?"

"Yeah, well," Falgar said. "Your teats'd sag too, if you were older than time itself."

Kadmin smirked. *To the Void with that smirk.* Kadmin was always a good-looking son of a demon. Falgar remembered how jealous he used to get, the way he and Tai carried on. It was too bad he was such a miserable piece of gryphon shite.

Kadmin ran his hand lovingly down the smooth wooden end table, on which laid an impressive array of knives, chisels, and other instruments of pain. "I'd much prefer not to have to use these on my old friend."

"Uh huh," Falgar said. "So you'll continue pretending to be my friend if I talk. Got it. I can be reasonable." Falgar had no intention of being reasonable, of course. But he'd make up whatever he needed in order to buy time.

Kadmin glowered. "We'll see about that. Very well. Is Tai Lunstrum with you?"

Falgar kept his expression carefully blank. "Kadmin," he said, "We've been over this. It's not my job to keep track of every single one of your exes."

Kadmin grunted. "Where is Dorian Valmont?"

"Oh!" Falgar said. "Is he your ex, too?"

Kadmin ground his teeth. "Stop being a pit wraith."

"Perhaps he crawled up your bum."

*Well. So much for being reasonable.*

Kadmin slapped Falgar, hard. Void Eternal. It was like Sanorska all over again. Smarting from the pain, Falgar said, "Fine, fine. He went to the market for some cheese."

This was a lie, of course. But the longer he kept Kadmin talking, more time Dorian had to charge in on his dragon and rescue them all. The poor sweet bastard not only lacked self worth, he also completely lacked a sense of self preservation. Between that and his almost obnoxious compulsion to always do the right thing, Falgar knew Dorian would come to the rescue. Falgar just had to buy him time.

"Why so eager to find him, anyway? I mean, he's kind of a dolt, isn't he?" *Sorry, Valmont,* he thought. *I don't actually think you're a dolt.*

Kadmin scoffed. "You cannot tell me you've been traveling him for this many moons and not know what he's capable of."

Falgar laughed and shook his head, giving his friend another fierce mental apology. "Zekador's Pants, no. This is Valmont we're talking about. He doesn't know an aether sail from a bedsheet, and probably thinks you're supposed to hold the sharp end of a blade."

*Sorry, Dorian, sorry, sorry.*

It would just be Falgar's luck if Dorian did charge in for the rescue at that moment, and then it would be a Voidstorm with a broken-winged gryphon to convince the poor bastard that Falgar didn't actually think all those things. But if he could convince Kadmin of Dorian's incompetence, it could only help them all in the long run.

Kadmin sighed. "I believe this is the part where I remind you I'm the one asking the questions. But I'll indulge you this once. Your friend is bonded to the demon Hematite. I don't suppose you have any idea what that implies. You never were much of a mental heavyweight."

"Now that's just cruel," Falgar said with mock levity.

Privately, Falgar thought of the first time Dorian joined them in the Linking. Hematite had done something. Falgar was pretty sure that Voidstorm should have blown them out of the sky. But somehow, Hematite stopped that from happening. Hematite had saved their lives.

It would be nice if these people intended to use that ability for good, but Falgar was nowhere near naïve enough to believe that. Kadmin and his buddies were the ones who provoked that storm.

"How many of you dragonauts are there, anyway?" Falgar wondered.

"Again, I remind you. I am asking the questions," Kadmin said. "So tell me this. Is it also true that your friend Dorian Valmont is bonded to the dragon Solaris?"

"I know nothing about that," Falgar lied. "But I doubt it, you know? He's a bit of a dolt, but he's a nice guy. He wouldn't just brainwash a proud magical creature into a mindless slave." Falgar waggled his eyebrows in Kadmin's direction.

Kadmin's mouth twitched and Falgar worried perhaps he'd gone too far. Kadmin was surely to go straight for the torture tools now. But he only said, "Celestian is not a mindless slave."

"Oh, good," Falgar said. "Celestian joined you out of her own free will, then. That's great! Congratulations!"

Kadmin's mouth-twitching intensified. He looked like he was chewing on several potential retorts. Finally, he said, "We believe the dragon Solaris *did* bond of her own free will. To Dorian Valmont."

"Don't see why she'd want to do that." Falgar shrugged in his bonds. "Like I said. Kind of a dolt."

Kadmin ran his hand over his face. "I can see this is going

nowhere." He sounded regretful. "Believe it or not, I never enjoyed causing pain." He moved to the table, but instead of one of the more sinister blades, he grabbed a plain, wooden-handled athame. He turned it over in his hand, inspecting it. "This shall be all I will need, I think. Falgar, tell me, old friend. Have you heard of the magic of Extraction?"

*Oh, Void.* It would be better, in some ways, if Kadmin simply tortured him.

"That's illegal," Falgar said, with a boldness he didn't feel. As if legality mattered to someone like Kadmin.

"King Callahan grants exceptions to those who need it," Kadmin said. His mouth twisted into a sadistic grin. "And come now. The dangers really are overstated. It won't *necessarily* burn out your brain, or leave you a drooling vegetable. It doesn't *always*—"

Not a moment too soon, an alarm, magically magnified, sounded throughout the base.

"What the—" Kadmin lowered his athame in consternation.

"Kadmin!" Tai Lunstrum burst in the door, panting for breath.

Falgar's eyes widened. "Tai?"

She looked disheveled and rather frightened, dressed in a poorly fitting uniform, a single mismatched white feather sticking haphazardly out of her black wings.

"Kadmin. Sir." She reported with a crisp salute. "Ashe just sent me. The gryphons are stampeding. You're needed right away."

"You were told to stay with Ashe," Kadmin said harshly. "How do I know this isn't some kind of trick?"

"I was just sent to warn you," Tai said, eyes narrowed. "Hardly my fault if you choose not to listen and get clawed to death."

Kadmin sneered, his expression betraying a fierce internal debate. At that moment, however, a high pitched *Keeerrrrrr* sounded from outside the questioning chamber, and a golden-furred, white feathered gryphon barreled its way through the tent canvas, slashing razor sharp lion's claws and knocking over the table. The creature let out an outraged cry as the metal tools tumbled to the floor.

"Meroneth's balls!"

Falgar was keenly aware that he was bound to the chair in the face of an out of control rampaging predator.

Tai whipped out her athame and flung a burst of air magic in the gryphon's direction. The spell caught Kadmin full in the chest.

"You!" the enemy dragonaut gasped, before he and the gryphon collapsed together in a pile of fur and feathers. Batting her own feathers in panic, Tai grabbed a heavy metal key and shoved it into Falgar's bonds.

"Run!" she shouted as soon as the handcuffs clicked open.

"But what about you?" Falgar asked.

"I can take care of myself. Run!"

He didn't need to be told a second time.

Dorian's heart pounded, as much from adrenaline as from fear. "We did it," he said. "I can't believe we actually set loose all those gryphons." He paused, catching his breath. "They'll... they'll be okay, right? I mean. We didn't scare them too badly. Right?"

"They should be fine," Hildegard said. "Let's go find the others."

He followed Hildegard away from the rampaging feline birds, still casting wary glances over his shoulder as they screamed and clawed.

"Prison is this way," Hildegard said. "I can pick the locks when we get there. Most of the guards should be busy trying to quell the gryphons. If any come by, fight them off, okay?"

*So casual. Fight them off. Because I can just do that with my excellent sword skills. Right.*

"Listen," Hildegard said as they made their way to the outer wall. "If you and your friends get out of here in one piece, come join up with Bradford's rebellion."

"Bradford's... rebellion?"

Hildegard nodded. "Lord Bradford's been working to undermine his father for close to a year now. Smuggling aether to people who need it. Sabotaging Callahan's supply chains. That kind of thing."

Dorian felt an upwelling of affection for his half-brother. They'd had their differences growing up, but to his surprise, Dorian missed him. Saving Dorian's life must not have just been a fluke, if Bradford continued to defy his father. At least he was doing something, not staying cooped up on a ship like Dorian.

«You are not cooped up on a ship right now,» Hematite pointed out, in a tone that made it clear he would prefer otherwise.

Dorian let out a grim chuckle. «You're not wrong. I need to do more, though, not just keep running away.»

As soon as Dorian turned the next corner, however, thoughts of Bradford were driven from his mind.

"Oh," Hildegard said, coming to an abrupt halt. "That wasn't there before."

They stood in the shadow of a massive skyship, nearly twice as large as the *Phoenix*. The polished mahogany hull gleamed with silver and gold accents. It was the banners, fluttering in the wind, however, that caught Dorian's eye. A rich blue dragon, perched atop a silver moon.

Dorian gulped. "That's the royal moon dragon of Kasanarae."

Hildegard's eyes were wide. "What do we do?"

Why was Hildegard asking him? Suddenly, Dorian felt foolish and helpless. So far, other than the soldier at the dock, nobody had connected him with the image on the wanted poster. If King Callahan himself were here, though, he would recognize Dorian in a second.

"I suppose we should hurry," he heard himself saying. No matter what complications Callahan threw in the way, Dorian's top priority had to be rescuing his friends.

Footsteps approached them from the other side of the nearest building.

"Isn't that your Orith friend?" Hildegard whispered.

"I'm sorry," Tai's voice whined, sounding terrified and small. "I was only trying to hit the nearby gryphon. I never meant to attack you, you know I'd never do such a thing."

"N... no way," Dorian said.

"You expect me to believe that?" The man accompanying Tai looked more than a little disgruntled, his black ponytail half fallen out of the cord that bound it, with several white feathers sticking out. Fresh blood dripped from a wound on the otherwise smooth planes of his chiseled face.

"Everything's going so wrong," Tai said, sounding to all the world like she might cry. "I only wanted to make things right. That rat, Falgar, coming between us once again." She batted her eyes seductively and snuggled up close to the soldier.

"Even if that's so," Kadmin said, clearing his throat, "You have to be stronger than this if you have to succeed in the Kasani guard."

"Oh, I will, Kadmin, I will!"

*Zekador's poorly fitting pants,* Dorian thought. Why was she simpering to this man? Tai Lunstrum did not simper. This had to be an act.

Tai looked up and met Dorian's eyes for a moment. She gave her head the barest shake in the soldier's direction, her brown eyes begging him to understand. Dorian let out a small sigh of relief. Definitely an act. What was her plan? Was Dorian about to ruin it?

"What is it, recruit?" the soldier asked Tai. He drew his arm away from hers, suddenly all business.

Tai folded her wings and bit her lip, as if to feign nonchalance. "Thought I saw someone I knew, but it was only my imagination."

The soldier turned and looked at Dorian and Hildegard. "You two," he said. "I haven't seen either of you around here before. You're not one of my soldiers. Speak."

"Lieutenant Weatherbee, sir." Hildegard didn't miss a beat. "I just transferred here from Azure."

"Hmm," Kadmin said. "And you?"

"I work in the bakery, Sir," Dorian said.

The soldier's eyes narrowed. "Pretty fancy sword for a baker." He looked down at Dorian's exposed sword hilt, and his eyes suddenly widened. "That's a dragonaut's sword! Gods above! Ha, I knew if we nabbed your captain, you couldn't be far behind. We've been looking for you for a long time, Valmont."

The soldier drew his own blade.

"Kadmin, don't!" Tai blurted.

"You'll find if you wish to join us, Tai, that sometimes being a warrior requires offending your delicate sensibilities." The enemy soldier, Kadmin, raised his sword and spun towards Dorian.

Not just any soldier, Dorian realized as he rushed to defend himself. The dragon-shaped pendant at his throat indicated that Kadmin was a dragonaut, too. Dorian felt the sudden weight of how outclassed he was. Callahan wouldn't recruit a dragonaut who wasn't an expert swordsman.

Kadmin brushed Dorian's blade aside with casual ease. Dorian liked to think he'd improved over the past eight or so moons, but what was that compared to this man's years of training?

Dorian stepped backwards to avoid Kadmin's riposte, but for the second time, tripped on the hem of his pants.

*Again? Really?*

Kadmin charged forward and drove Dorian to the ground. With clinical proficiency, he stepped on Dorian's chest and placed the sword tip against his throat.

"Did Solaris give you that sword? Pity. You clearly didn't earn it."

"S... sword?" This was a mistake. The tip of Kadmin's blade nicked his throat, drawing a tiny droplet of blood.

More footsteps approached, and the sound of arguing voices. "I already told you, I was rather preoccupied with the thrice cursed bloody thing attacked me!"

Dorian's breath caught in his already terrified throat. That sounded like the soldier he'd confronted on the *Phoenix*.

"You didn't think to collect the artifact after he left?" This was a woman's voice, authoritative, like the ringing of a temple bell. And achingly, achingly familiar. She turned around the corner and beheld what must have been a somewhat startling scene of Dorian pinned to the ground. "What is the meaning of this?"

"Your Majesty!" Kadmin drew back from Dorian and dropped to a knee. A couple of beats later, Tai and Hildegard followed.

Dorian thought he should kneel, too, except he was already on the ground.

Eight moons since he'd seen her last. She'd changed little in that time. She was still as poised and beautiful as he remembered.

"Saedra." Dorian's voice came out with a strangled gasp.

# CHAPTER TWENTY-FOUR

# REUNIONS

"You may rise," Queen Saedra Penregon of Kasanarae said. She spared Tai and the others on the barest passing glance before focusing her gaze on Dorian.

"Saedra," he said again. He seemed to have forgotten his command of the Kasani language.

"Dorian," Saedra whispered in a tone like a prayer. "By all the gods, it really is you."

She extended her hand to help him up. Awkwardly, Dorian rose to his feet.

Dorian marveled at how small and soft Saedra's hands were. He'd forgotten about that. He was suddenly aware of his own hands, rough and calloused from moons of hauling skyship lines and practice swords and training equipment.

How many times had Dorian dreamt of their reunion? Now the moment was here, and all he could think about were the callouses on his hands.

"It's... good to see you again," he finally said.

Her honeysuckle scent wafted towards him, sending him back to stolen hours in the library, in the carriage house, in Dorian's late mother's dusty, disused bed chamber. For the briefest of moments, it seemed like no time had passed at all.

Her silver-gray eyes shone with worry and concern, as she said, "Oh, my dear, sweet Dorian, what have they done to you?"

"Done to me?" Dorian dusted himself off, checking for wounds or injuries. Once he determined he was unhurt, he said, "Nothing, thank the gods. You intervened before that man Kadmin could gut me like a skypuffer. Thank you for that, by the way." He cleared his throat awkwardly. "Enough about me. What about you? Are you all right? Has Callahan hurt you?"

Saedra shook her head. "No, no, of course not." Her expression looked stricken. She cupped her right hand around the side of Dorian's face, running her smooth fingers down his cheek and neck, tucking a strand of copper hair behind his ear. "But you," she whispered. "Oh, you poor dear, how you must have suffered."

"Suffered," Dorian repeated, as if tasting the word. He'd been on the run for moons now, fearing for his life. Much of his life in the sky had been difficult. But Dorian couldn't make himself describe any of his time on the *Phoenix* as suffering. "I... I don't know about that."

"I should never have left you behind," Saedra said. "I should have convinced Callahan we needed you alive sooner. You could have lived with us in the palace. We would have honored you, we would have..." she trailed off, and shook her head. "Instead, I left you to the mercy of vagabonds and worse, afraid for your life, half-starved... oh, my dear Dorian, I don't know if you can ever forgive me."

"Forgive you..." He blinked several times, trying to clear his head. This wasn't going at all the way he'd hoped. "I'm not half starved ... Why does everyone keep insisting that I'm starving? Vagabonds and worse? What?"

He hazarded a glance towards the others, though what they could say or do to help, he did not know. Tai stared at Queen Saedra with a stricken expression. Hildegard stood at attention, to all the world the consummate soldier. The soldier from the *Phoenix* glanced around uncomfortably, probably wondering if he'd be in trouble if he left. Only the dragonaut, Kadmin, kept his shrewd eyes on Dorian, his hand still clasped around his sword hilt.

"You poor, poor dear," Saedra said again.

Somehow, Dorian had thought, or perhaps only hoped, that if he saw Saedra again, she would find his exploits impressive, praise him like he was the hero from a tale. He supposed that was foolish. He had done nothing impressive so far, not really. All the same, for her to pity him was almost too much to take.

"I'm fine, really," he said. "It's... it's not so bad, living on the ship, kind of nice, even. There's... there's flying, and my friends, we—"

Saedra shook her head and pulled him into a tight embrace. The rest of Dorian's stammered protest died on his lips. Though it seemed ludicrous, at a time like this, he was most conscious of his stomach poking out over his waistband. *I am* not *half starved.*

"Well," Saedra said. "I can't fix the past, though gods know I wish I could. I can, however, fix the present. Everything will be all right now."

"It... it will?"

"Of course it will!" She clasped his hand. "I've already convinced my Lord Husband that you're more use to us alive. He listens to me, sometimes, you know. I can bring you back to Kasanarae! You can help me. There's so much of the Grimoire that needs to be translated. Ah, we can restore poor Hematite to his full strength, and you to your full strength, too."

"I'm actually stronger now than I was when all this started," Dorian said, but she ignored him.

"We can be together. Isn't that what you want?"

Suddenly, Dorian didn't know.

"But... you're Callahan's wife." Gods above, why couldn't Dorian think clearly around this woman? He felt like he'd just downed half a bottle of Xander's best whiskey.

"Don't worry about Janus," Saedra said with a dismissive wave of her hand. "I only married him for politics. I may take whatever lovers I choose."

From what he knew about Janus Callahan, Dorian doubted this. He hazarded a glance towards the others and was relieved to see that Tai and Kadmin both wore faintly revolted expressions, though likely for very different reasons.

If Saedra cared, however, she didn't show it. Instead, she caressed the side of his face once more, and said, "Things can finally be like they were before."

*Like they were before.*

Dorian felt like someone had doused him in cold water. He didn't want to return to a time before the *Phoenix*, before Solaris, before Xander and Falgar and Sullivan and Tai. *Tai.*

He looked at Tai and her brown eyes met his blue ones. They swam with some indiscernible emotion, and she shook her head, just once. That was enough. Dorian knew he could not return to his life before.

«I fear you are correct,» said Hematite, sounding sad, resigned. «We cannot. Oh, how I wish we could. But you and I both know that would not be right.»

Dorian shook his head. "I'm sorry, Saedra. Things are different now."

"Dorian," Saedra said, "If you come with me, you could be a dragonaut. Isn't that what you've always wanted?"

"Eh?" Dorian asked. Did Saedra not know he was already a dragonaut?

"With you, we could finally complete Callahan's Flight," Saedra said. "He'd have a full complement of seven, just as it was in the Ancient days."

"J... join Callahan's flight?" Had Saedra completely taken leave of her senses? Revulsion coursed through every fiber of Dorian's being.

"You still have the pendant I gave you, yes?" she asked.

"Yes, but—"

"Surely you know what it does."

"Yes, but—"

"Then we shall find and capture you a wild dragon! Kadmin here can teach you how to control them. I think you'll find it's very easy, isn't it, Kadmin?"

"Your Highness, are you sure this is wise?" Kadmin asked through gritted teeth. He seemed to find the idea of working with Dorian as distasteful as Dorian found the idea of working with Kadmin.

Dorian placed his hand against the belt pocket where Solaris's dragonstone lay hidden. He longed to grab it and summon Solaris, to show them all what a real dragon bond looked like. But an imaginary voice that sounded like Captain Xander warned him not to tip his hand. He didn't know why Saedra didn't seem to know about Solaris, but he wasn't about to squander an advantage, no matter how small.

An expression of remorse crossed the Queen's face. "Sometimes," she said, "We must do things we would otherwise find distasteful, for the sake of the greater good."

Dorian shook his head. "This is wrong, Saedra."

Saedra shook her head. "If you're sure. Then I'm afraid you leave me no choice. It would be better to have you willingly. But we shall have you, all the same."

Dorian felt a chill and moved his hand instinctively to his sword hilt.

"Please, Dorian, please understand I am doing this for your own protection and for the good of Cyrna." She turned her attention back towards Kadmin. "Dragonaut Kadmin? Seize him."

Dorian had no chance to defend himself. Faster than Dorian thought was possible, the other dragonaut grabbed hold of Dorian's sword arm and pulled him into an iron-tight wrist lock.

"Let him go!" Tai screamed.

Kadmin snorted. "You like him, don't you? Ha! Tai, I'm disappointed. Surely you can do better than this lowlife."

"You —" Tai reached furiously for her athame, but Hildegard put a warning hand on her shoulder.

"Maybe," the archaeologist-turned-rebel said through gritted teeth, "We don't get court marshaled for drawing a weapon on a superior officer."

"But he—" Tai began.

"*Superior officer,*" Hildegard said again.

"You, Lieutenant," Saedra said, noticing the stripes on Hildegard's fake uniform. "Where is Corporal Silas?"

"He left, your majesty," Hildegard said.

"Incompetence," she spat. "Ah well. You and that recruit go find Dragonaut Ashe. Tell her we've apprehended the prisoner. Dragonaut Kadmin? Take Dorian to my skyship."

"But—" Tai protested again.

"Now, now, 'recruit'," Hildegard said, "We don't question orders around here."

Hildegard put her arm around Tai's shoulder and all but shoved her away. Tai shot one last look back at Dorian, with an expression of abject misery.

Xander paced his cell, running his hands through his shaggy brown hair. Oh, he'd gone and made a mess of things. He'd really screwed up this time.

*A message from the Order.* How ridiculous. What had made him think it would be so simple? Sylvia never did anything in a straightforward way. Even if his sister was involved, was this her plan? To let him rot in a Kasani prison cell at an outpost on the edge of nowhere?

*Thanks, dear sister. Thanks a lot.*

Although it felt good to channel righteous fury towards his absent sister, he knew it was pointless. None of this was her fault.

No, most likely, Callahan's people sent that letter themselves, hoping to lure Xander into a trap. The self-styled Emperor was the leader of the Order once. He knew all the proper codes to use. Fool that he was, Xander fell for it.

He leaned back against the rough stone wall and stared at the ceiling. He needed a drink. Or ten drinks. He wondered if anyone was going to bother to so much as feed him. He supposed a cup of wine would be too much to ask for.

As if on cue, the lock clicked with the sound of a turning key.

"About time one of you came by to check on me," Xander said. "Don't suppose I could have some food?"

"No," said a familiar voice, "But how's some freedom sound?"

"Falgar!" He rushed to the barred window to behold his employee. The wiry aeronaut twirled a thick metal keyring around his finger, while his burly companion Sullivan looked on with amusement.

"Thank the Gods you're both all right," Xander said. "How in the Void did you get out?"

"Tai rescued me, then I got Sullivan out," Falgar said. "Whole base is in chaos. Bunch of gryphons flying around, and then the queen showed up."

Xander blinked. "That's... a lot. And... Tai... wait, where is Tai?"

"Tai's here," came Tai's voice. She rushed up to the prison cell, looking disheveled, accompanied by an auburn-haired woman in a Kasani uniform. Xander blinked and did a double take. "Hildegard? What are you doing here?"

"With any luck, saving your arse," his old friend said with a reckless smirk.

Tai shook her head. "Kadmin's got Dorian, sir."

Xander blinked. "Who the Void is Kadmin?" He shook his head. "Never mind that. What is Dorian doing here? I told him to stay on the ship."

"I know that, sir," Tai said. "But he's in trouble, and we have to help him!"

"I'll go, sir," Sullivan volunteered at once.

"Wait a second," Falgar said. "By yourself? Why can't we all go?"

"Because you," Sullivan gestured at Falgar, "Know that Kadmin guy. And he," he then gestured Captain Xander, "Is on every wanted poster this side of Azure. I, meanwhile," he gestured at himself, "Was dragged in by association. I doubt anyone will recognize me out of context."

"Do it," Xander said. They had little time to deliberate. "Get Dorian and meet us back on the ship. Meanwhile, the rest of us need to find a way out of here."

"I can help with that, sir," Hildegard said at once.

"Can you, now?" In Xander's long experience, Hildegard's plans caused more problems than they fixed. But beggars, as the saying went, could not be choosers.

"I'm demon possessed, Sir," Hildegard said. "That means I can use magic in the Void."

"You're what?" Xander demanded. "When in Valgren's name did that happen?"

"Oh, some time ago," Hildegard answered evasively.

Xander glanced at her through his peripheral vision, looking for any sign of a demonic aura. Hildegard stood, her hands held behind her back, and sure enough Xander caught a lurid blue aura of blurry demonfire.

Xander frowned. Something about that demonfire didn't look right. A suspicion crossed his mind — *could it be? No, surely not.* He shook his head and pushed his suspicion to the back of his mind, and forced himself to think about the task at hand. He knew whatever Hildegard was hiding, it'd do no good to ask about it. Hildegard and Sylvia were cut from the same cloth in that respect. People like them needed secrets the way most people needed air.

"All right then," he said, surrendering the point for now. "Demon possessed. So how's that help us?"

"Means I can cast magic in the Void. I don't claim to be the best Illusionist in the world," Hildegard added, in the closest she ever came to an apologetic tone, "But I can cast a chameleon glamour convincing enough to keep us hidden until you get back to your ship. After that, we can talk more at length."

"Let's go," Xander sighed, "Before the entire base comes down on us."

Kadmin's grip was iron tight as he frog marched Dorian towards the landing platform. Saedra's flagship loomed above, glistening cannons pointed in his direction. It had none of the homey comforts Dorian associated with the *Phoenix*. This ship was all gleaming metal and sharp edges.

"You don't have to do this, Saedra," he implored the Queen.

Saedra, however, only shook her head. "I wish it could be another way."

He thrashed violently in one last desperate attempt to free himself of Kadmin's hold, but it did no good. Even after all Dorian's training, Kadmin was still so much stronger than Dorian, so much the superior fighter. He outclassed Dorian in every way.

He recalled, one afternoon during training, when Tai tried to teach him how to break out of various holds and takedowns. Despite her compact size, she was impressively skilled. He'd done pretty well at them, too. But now when it mattered, the only memory he could conjure was the combined embarrassment and rather pleasant feeling of having Tai's arms around him.

«Not helpful right now,» Hematite said. But then, the demon added, «Neither, granted, is my complaining about it.»

"Dorian!" The sound of Dorian's name and heavy footfalls accompanied Sullivan as he sprinted onto the landing platform.

Kadmin looked up in surprise, and he loosened his grip on Dorian's chest the barest amount.

Then, finally, Dorian's training returned to him, and, seizing the distraction, stomped hard on Kadmin's foot and slid out of the chokehold to safety. He rolled out of the way and then unsheathed his sword and settled into a fighting stance.

"Dragonaut Kadmin," Saedra said in a too-pleasant tone, "Far be it from me to tell you how to do your job, but why is the prisoner still armed?"

"My hands were rather full, if you didn't notice," Kadmin said. "Besides, I didn't think he'd be a threat. I mean, look at him."

Dorian considered at that moment that there were advantages to being underestimated. But he couldn't wallow in his satisfaction for long. Kadmin lunged for Dorian, and in his haste to get away, Dorian almost tripped and fell again. He caught himself, barely in time.

"Sullivan, run!" Dorian shouted.

"I'm trying to help you!" Sullivan drew his own weapon, stalking towards Kadmin with the practiced ease of a well-trained swordsman. For a second, Dorian felt a rush of hope. If he and Sullivan worked together, they might, might just stand a chance at getting out of here.

More footsteps approached, revealing several ordinary soldiers and a tall woman in a dragonaut's uniform. Dorian's heart surged with horror. These soldiers might be under orders to capture Dorian alive, but they had no such compunction against killing Sullivan.

Dorian couldn't waste any more time. He plunged his hand into his belt pocket, wrapping his fingers around the warm, solid mass of his dragonstone.

«Are you sure about this?» the dragon asked from high above.

«Keeping you a secret does no good if we're dead,» Dorian replied.

Solaris nodded in acknowledgement, then dove, breathing out a shower of golden sparks.

"What the — you!" Kadmin tucked and rolled out of Solaris's way.

"Come on, Sullivan, let's—" Dorian began, but he cut off, breath caught in his throat.

With Dorian distracted, the second dragonaut drove Sullivan to the ground. He lay sprawled on his back, his opponent's sword poised above his chest, ready to plunge.

*One step, two steps, three.* Dorian heard only the sound of blood rushing in his ears as he sprinted, sword in hand, toward Sullivan's fallen form. With reflexes born from moons of hard training, he swung his blade in a smooth arc, landing with full force against the enemy dragonaut's neck.

The sheer momentum of the swing carried Dorian's blade through skin and bone and sinew. Then the resistance stopped, and Dorian continued falling forward. Frantically, he flung his blade aside. His weapon hit the ground with a clang, just as Dorian landed on top of Sullivan in an awkward tangle of limbs.

In his shock, Dorian didn't quite register what had just happened. All he could think of was that afternoon, several moons ago, when Sullivan pulled Dorian out of a Voidstorm.

"By the seven gods, if I broke your arm again, I swear I'll—"

"No, no, I'm all right," said a dazed-sounding Sullivan, sitting upright.

Dorian breathed a sigh of relief, but it was short-lived.

Queen Saedra stared, face pale, eyes wide with horror, at the fallen dragonaut's head. It lay several arm's lengths away from the rest of her body, still wearing an expression of mild surprise as it gazed lifelessly up at the sky.

"I... did that," Dorian said. His voice sounded hollow and emotionless, and like it came from the other end of a long tunnel. Mere moments ago, the dragonaut's head had been attached to her body. And now it wasn't. "Oh... oh sweet Ancients."

"Ashe!" Kadmin rushed towards his companion, his face a mask of horror as he beheld her headless form. Then he turned towards Dorian, sword drawn, mouth twisted into a snarl of hatred and fury. "*You.*"

Dorian sat frozen in place, powerless to stop Kadmin's charge.

Solaris charged in front of Dorian and knocked Kadmin out of the way with a deft swipe of her claw.

«Get on!» she said. «Hurry!»

Dorian still couldn't move. Thankfully, Sullivan could. The burly aeronaut hauled Dorian onto the dragon's back and scrambled up behind him. *Gods above,* he was strong.

Once Solaris launched into the sky, Dorian found he could at least think again. But part of him wished he couldn't.

"That other guy, Kadmin, still has a dragon too," Sullivan warned. "We need to fly hard if we want to get out of here."

Dorian took a ragged breath and nodded. *Flying. Yes.* That much he could do. Choking back tears, he flew.

All Dorian wanted to do was keep flying forever. They escaped the fortress; it was true. But it was a lot less easy to escape the memory of that dragonaut's empty eyes staring up at him from the bloodstained ground. The way he'd ended her life as easily as chopping carrots in the galley. That he wasn't sure he'd ever escape.

# CHAPTER TWENTY-FIVE

# MOVING FORWARD

Tai paced the *Phoenix's* deck, straining her eyes against the Autumn sunset sky.

Xander checked his pocket watch with a worried expression. "Only a matter of time before the authorities get here on their skimmers."

"We can't leave them behind," Falgar said.

"No," Xander agreed. "No, I wouldn't dream of it. Just... Meroneth's balls. I hope they get here soon."

Tai clung to the railing and willed her friends to return to her faster. It had taken all her willpower to keep from crying when she'd come to the ship and found, in the galley, a neat dragon-powered spell circle containing custom-made pies for each of them. Gods help her, he'd made *custom pies*. And now he and Sullivan might be captured or worse before they even got to try them.

*They will come back. They have to come back. Oh please, please sweet Kyrizzian Lady of Love and War, bring them back.*

Kyrizzian, for once, must have been feeling merciful, because at that moment, she saw them.

"There!"

A crimson spark, barely visible against a coral sunset, grew larger with every moment. Finally, Solaris skidded to a rough landing on the wooden deck. Dorian and Sullivan tumbled, exhausted, off of her back.

"Dorian!" She rushed and flung her arms around him. "Oh, thank all the gods and Ancients. Are you all right? Did they hurt you?"

He wasn't bleeding, at least, and Solaris wasn't gushing spirit energy like last time. She took that to be a good sign. But there was a dazed, haunted sort of look in Dorian's blue eyes. He squeezed her hand and, with a sad smile, said, "I'm sorry I made you worry."

Sullivan rose swiftly to his feet. "We've got at least one dragonaut on our tail, and I don't even want to think about who else. If we hope to get out of here, we'd better fly, and fast."

"Sullivan's right," Xander said. "Linking, now!"

They all scrambled to obey, even Dorian, who she thought looked a bit punch drunk. They cut their ties with the town of Goose Head and made their frantic way towards the relative freedom and safety of the open sky.

Once above the wild underclouds, with Hildegard's cloaking device once more in operation, the authorities would have a lot harder time tracking them. Yet, as Tai tried to relish the feeling of the wind in her feathers, another thought occurred to her.

This was a more personal worry, nowhere near as dire as life and death, but it settled like a lump of ice in her stomach. She thought of the worry she'd felt just a short while ago, waiting for Solaris to return. She thought of the sheer, joyous relief she felt when they landed, and she ran to embrace Dorian. *Only* Dorian.

Sullivan was her friend too, wasn't he? She had worried about him, and she was relieved to find him alive. Of course she was. In the moment of truth, however, her only thoughts had been for Dorian.

Perhaps it wouldn't have bothered her, had she not just seen Kadmin — that living reminder of what happened when she let emotions impede good common sense. But she had, and she did, and that was when she realized her mistake.

She'd gone and done it. She'd broken the promise she'd made to herself when Kadmin left. She was overjoyed at Dorian's safe return, not just because he was her friend, but because she was hopelessly in love with him.

And that was an absolute disaster.

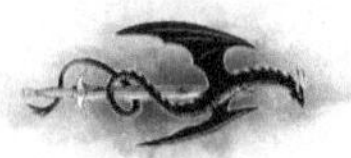

Dorian kneaded his hands through the dough in frustration. *Too watery.* Why was it so watery? He was supposed to be good at this. At least, in this one thing, he thought he could count on his skill. And yet, the dough was too watery. He supposed it didn't matter. It wasn't like he was going to taste it, anyway. All food and drink, it seemed lately, turned to dust in his mouth.

«I tried to warn you,» Hematite said, seeming just as ill at ease as Dorian felt. «This is what adventuring is. This is why I wanted to keep you safe.»

Dorian shook his head and stared blankly at the bowl of watery dough. The demon was right. He should have listened. It had been different when it was only his own life at stake. Now... He buried his face in his hand.

Dorian was supposed to be happy. They'd escaped. They were back on the ship. They were alive. Yet all Dorian wanted to do was cry.

He added some more flour to the mixture and thought wistfully about the last time melancholy descended upon the *Phoenix*. Back when he and Solaris first bonded. Back then, it was his own inadequacy that made him miserable. He'd spent the past several moons trying to correct that inadequacy, and this was the result?

He almost wished Tai would come in and give him another telling off. At least then she'd speak to him. Since their departure from Goose Head, she hardly spoke to anyone, answering questions in monosyllables, or not at all. On the rare occasion she even deigned to look at him, her brown eyes were always unmistakably sad, and a little scared.

Dorian thought he had a pretty good idea of what she was thinking. It was the same thing Hematite thought. Indeed, the same thing Dorian thought. The thing behind the look of horror in Queen Saedra's eyes, just before the end. The word that repeated nastily in his mind, over and over.

*Murderer.*

The image of the dragonaut woman's head separating from her body ran through his head, over and over. One moment, she'd been alive and breathing. The next, her head formed a smooth arc in its trajectory towards the ground. *Murderer.*

For close to a year, now, he'd been trying so hard to become the sort of bond Solaris deserved, to become the person he thought he was supposed to be. But it was all a lie. There was no glory or honor in this. Besides. Saedra preferred him the way he was before. She'd as much as said so.

*Ah*, said a tiny voice in the back of his head. It sounded like Solaris, but he knew it was only his own thoughts. *Which version of yourself do you prefer?*

That was the problem, wasn't it? The truth of the matter was, he enjoyed learning the sword. Not as much as flying, perhaps, but he liked it all the same. He relished the thrill of mastering new techniques. He adored doing what he couldn't do before. He loved sparring with his friends. But none of it had been *real* before. There'd been no *severing of heads.*

Could he be an aeronaut without being a swordsman? Maybe. It was a risky proposition. Aeronauts, all aeronauts, needed to know how to defend themselves. He'd be a liability on any crew if he couldn't. If there was one thing Dorian was sick of, it was being a liability.

Still, what other choice did he have? Surrender to Callahan and help him enslave dragons and sink Aeris? Unthinkable. Get a job as a clerk or a baker in some remote village, and live a life devoid of magic or dragons or skyships, hoping Callahan would forget about him? Possibly, but the thought left him feeling hollow.

"That's enough self pity for one day."

He looked up to see Falgar carrying two mugs of ale. Lost in his misery, Dorian hadn't even heard the man enter.

"All right, Valmont," Falgar said. "Put that dough in stasis before you ruin it worse, and have this instead." He brandished a mug of frothy ale.

Dorian raised an eyebrow. "Drinking to escape my problems? Are you sure that's wise?"

"Nope," Falgar said, taking a long swig of his own. "But we're gonna do it, anyway. Last time the entire crew was all doom and gloom like this, having a beer together helped. So. I'm gonna try that again."

Dorian smiled sadly and took a drink. *At least it isn't whiskey.* "I appreciate the gesture," he said, "But this isn't like last time." His voice caught. "I killed someone, Falgar. I killed a woman."

Falgar frowned. "Does it matter that she was a woman?"

"No. Yes. I don't know." Dorian shook his head. After considering, he added, "I'd be just as upset if I killed a man."

"She would have killed you, if given the chance," Falgar pointed out.

Dorian shook his head. "Saedra said Callahan wants me alive."

Falgar shook his head. "And what about Sullivan?" There was a slight frostiness to his tone now. "Didn't you say she was trying to kill him?"

"Yes," Dorian said, hesitantly. "But—"

*Wham.* Falgar slammed his fist down on the table with such force that Dorian skittered backwards, knocking his mug off the table in the process. Foamy brown ale spread out onto the wooden floor.

"What the — what in the *Void*?"

"It sounds to me," Falgar said, "That you value the life of that woman — that scumbag of Callahan's who enslaved a dragon — more than you value Sullivan's."

Dorian gaped at the man, thunderstruck. "I — what — of course I don't! That's not—"

"Then why," Falgar said, "Are you acting like you wish you let her murder one of our best friends?"

Dorian flinched. "No! No, I don't wish that, never that."

«Is one life more valuable than another just because one of them is your friend?» Hematite wondered.

"You saved Sullivan's life," Falgar said. "From the way he tells it, you were bloody heroic about it, too. You wish that absolute jackass of a dragonaut were still alive instead?"

Dorian stared in stupefied horror as the spilled beer pooled around his scuffed leather boots. Both Falgar and Hematite made strong points. One life wasn't worth intrinsically more than another. But what about what they did with them? Sullivan was a Healer. He saved people. Ashe was the one who brought murder to the table.

«'She started it?'» Hematite asked. «That is your defense?»

Dorian shook his head. He didn't know if he'd done the right thing or not. Simply standing back, though, and letting Sullivan die... *No.* He couldn't accept that.

"I didn't think... Oh, Falgar, I'm sorry. Of course I'm glad Sullivan's alive. I just... I hated killing that woman, Falgar. Gods forgive me, I hated it."

Falgar's expression softened considerably as he put a hand on Dorian's shoulder. "That's good," he said.

Dorian blinked. "Is it?"

Falgar nodded. "If you ever get to where you don't hate it, then we'll have a real problem."

"But you just said—"

"It's entirely possible to hate something and still find it necessary," Falgar said. He collected a second beer mug and re-filled it, then handed it to Dorian before setting about to clean up the mess. "Sorry I scared you there, mate."

"It's all right. I deserved it," Dorian said. Letting the barest hint of a smile cross his face, Dorian asked, "Sullivan really said I was heroic?"

"Very dashing," Falgar confirmed. "A real knight in shining armor. Void, I'd give my right arm to be the one who saved Sullivan. You did, though, and for that, you have both our gratitudes."

Dorian smiled despite himself, but then he frowned again, the leaden weight reappearing in his stomach. "If I'm some kind of hero and not just a murderous monster, how come Tai won't even talk to me?"

Falgar shook his head in disgust. "Oh. That. Believe me, Valmont, that has nothing to do with you. Believe it or not, you're not the root cause of everyone's problems in the world."

"I'm not?" Dorian flushed. "I mean. Of course I'm not. But... what's wrong with Tai, then?"

Falgar shook his head. "Should've thought it was obvious. It's that Kadmin bloke."

"Kadmin?" Dorian asked, perplexed. "The dragonaut?"

"You mean you don't know?"

"Don't make me feel worse," Dorian complained.

"All right, all right. Well. It's not really my story to tell. The thing is, me, Tai, and Kadmin, we all used to serve on the same ship together. Kadmin and Tai — well, he broke her heart. But like I said. Not my story to tell."

Dorian nodded morosely. So. It was as he feared. Kadmin was the sort of man Tai liked.

"I thought I said not to make me feel worse."

"Go talk to her if it's that important to you," Falgar said. "She's down in the hold, rearranging the cargo. Just, I'm tired of everyone on this ship acting like they're bloody demon-possessed."

"I am demon-possessed," Dorian pointed out.

"Sure. But you don't have to act like it."

«Rude,» Hematite said, but for the first time in days, the demon almost seemed amused rather than churlish.

Dorian wasn't sure he wanted to talk to Tai right now. However, he was equally certain he didn't want to stay here in the galley, trying to get dough to cooperate when it clearly didn't want to.

"Yeah," he sighed, finishing his beer and standing up. The chair made a scraping noise against the galley floor as he pushed it in. "Yeah, I suppose I'd better." He made to leave, then turned around. "Hey. Falgar. Thanks."

"No problem, mate," Falgar said, leaning back on the wooden chair and steepling his fingers. "Glad I could make you see reason."

Dorian found Tai in the cargo hold, grunting as she pushed a crate of aether stones back towards the hidden compartment.

"Need help with that?" he asked.

"Thanks," she said. As he helped her hoist it off the ground, she added, "Unfair. When did you get stronger than me?"

"I'm not," Dorian said, blushing. Though perhaps, strangely enough, he was.

They set the crate down, then moved the false wall back into place. "I told Falgar and Sullivan we should have hidden those stones the second we got them," she complained. "Instead, those inspectors found them, and look at the mess they caused."

Dorian thought the soldiers had been more interested in him than the aether, but he decided not to say anything. "Listen..." Dorian gulped. "Falgar... told me. About you and Kadmin."

As soon as Dorian said the words, he regretted them. Tai's expression lowered into a scowl. "How much did he tell you?"

"Nothing specific!" Dorian waved his hands. "Just that you and him... that you were... that you used to..."

Tai sighed and lowered her wings in resignation. "I was young and foolish and thought I was in love." Her wings shook of their own accord. "I gave up everything for him. In the end, he treated me like I was nothing. I'm sorry, Dorian. I shouldn't... I shouldn't take all this out on you."

"No, no, it's okay," Dorian said. He wanted to put a comforting hand on her shoulder, but he knew that would be inappropriate. "He hurt you. That much is obvious." He took in a sharp breath. "I'd really rather not kill anyone again if I can help it. For him, though, I might have to make an exception."

She rewarded him with a sad smile and took his hand and squeezed it. "Thanks, Dorian. That means a lot, believe it or not. But I..." she looked away, her eyes fixed somewhere on the wall.

"I don't want to ruin our friendship," he blurted, face burning.

Tai relaxed, her smile becoming more genuine. "Oh, Dorian," she said, "Of course we're still friends." She made a great show of cleaning her fingernails with the tip of her athame before asking, "I must ask... how did you get away from Kadmin? Last I heard, he was quite an accomplished swordsman."

"Solaris saved me," Dorian said. He swallowed back an enormous upsurge of guilt at the thought of his dragon, who he'd been ignoring for the past several days. In his misery, he'd thought he didn't deserve to partner with a dragon. However, he owed Solaris his life a thousand times over. She deserved better than for him to ignore her.

«I do not always care for the dragoness, but that was rather rude of you,» Hematite said.

"Doesn't Kadmin have a dragon, too?" Tai asked.

Dorian nodded. "I think if I'd delayed even a moment longer, he would have caught us. It was mostly Sullivan's clear head that got us out in time." He barked a bitter laugh. "I'm afraid Kadmin and I both kind of froze up after I—" he swallowed. "When I killed the other dragonaut. Ashe Valerian." If he was going to live with the fact that he'd killed her, he at least wanted to remember her name.

"Yeah, I've been wondering about that," Tai said. "The way you and Sullivan described it, you took off her head in one blow. Is that true?"

*Ashe Valerian's lifeless head sprawled on the ground, eyes staring vacantly up at nothing...*

Dorian shuddered. "Yeah. That's pretty much how it went."

Tai bit her lip. "It's just that... I know you don't want to talk about it, but isn't cutting off a head, you know, difficult?"

Dorian shrugged. "You know, in the heat of the moment, I wasn't really thinking about that much."

"I just didn't think we had any swords in the armory sharp enough to take off a head in one blow."

"Well... I mean... the sword was pretty sharp. And ostentatious. I grabbed it because it was the first thing I saw. The handle was all gold and shaped like a dragon. Pretty ridiculous, right?"

"A dragon?" Tai's eyebrows shot upward.

"Yeah," Dorian said, "With some kind of ruby on the hilt."

"Can I see it?"

Dorian frowned. "I, um, sort of threw it away."

In all the chaos following Ashe's decapitation, he'd forgotten to collect his discarded sword. He was sure Xander would be furious about him throwing away something expensive.

"You threw it away," Tai repeated, shaking head in consternation.

"It didn't, like, belong to Tovian Eagleheart or something, did it?" Dorian asked, stomach sinking.

"Probably not," Tai said, "But if it's what I think it was... I might have heard of such a thing. In an old book I have. I can go get it. In the meantime, I think you should talk to Solaris."

"Solaris?" Dorian asked. "Why?"

Tai shot him a penetrating glare. "Don't you think you should just talk to her, anyway? I mean Void Eternal, hasn't it been, like, three days?"

"Fair point," Dorian sighed, slumping his shoulders.

"Anyway. I'll go get that book. I'm serious, though. You need to hear about the sword from Solaris, not me."

Dorian reached into his belt pouch and produced his dragonstone. He looped it over his neck, feeling the bond with Solaris snap back into place. Solaris flew through the wall and rematerialized in the cargo hold.

«Finally done sulking, are we?» Solaris asked. There was more warmth than reproach in her mindvoice.

"I'm sorry, Solaris," he said at once.

Solaris bowed her serpentine neck. «Once, many years ago, a dragon in our clan made a foolish mistake that caused the deaths of two other dragons. I was... asked to take part in his execution.» She lowered her head. «As the youngest of my clan, it usually fell to the older dragons to do that grisly work, but Elder Meteor felt it would be... educational.» Solaris twitched her scarlet tail back and forth. «I reacted much the same way you did. It is never a pleasant thing to take the life of another, even when it is necessary.»

Dorian ran his hand down her golden neck ridges. "That must have been awful," he whispered. "I'm sorry... I'm sorry I neglected you."

«You did nothing wrong,» Solaris lowered her scaly forehead against his chest, radiating warmth and affection. «I am glad to have a partner who does not relish unnecessary violence. You should know, however, that in killing Ashe Valerian, you have severed her bond with her dragon, Meridian. Meridian flies freely once again because of you. And for that, you have my gratitude.»

"The dragon!" In the depths of his misery and self loathing, he'd all but forgotten that Ashe Valerian was a dragonaut. "Meridian is free now, because... because of me."

*Sweet Ancients*, Dorian thought. How could one action make him feel such pride and guilt at the same time?

«Although I will say,» the dragon said, half teasing. «You ought to have taken Queen Saedra up on her offer.»

"Eh?" Dorian asked, perplexed.

More seriously, she said, «It would have been extremely risky, so I suppose I am glad you did not. But we could have gone to Kasanarae as spies, and freed the other dragons from within.»

Dorian blinked several times. Now she mentioned it, it seemed obvious. "At the moment, I just couldn't believe Saedra would ask me to do anything so abhorrent," he admitted.

«And I adore that about you. Ah well, there is no use dwelling on what we might have done.» Solaris paused, considering. «Before we proceed, I need to know something.»

"Of course," Dorian said. "Anything."

«You have been a better partner than I had any right to ask for or expect,» she said. «Even all those moons ago, when we escaped Sanoria, I feared I demanded too much of you. You assured me, now, that I did not. I must know. Has that changed? Knowing what you know now, about what this bond has already cost you, do you wish to continue? There are... ways to sever the dragon bond, without killing the rider. But I cannot promise that our journey will not lead to more fights where it is your life against another's.»

Dorian reached out towards Hematite, but the demon shook his head. «This is not a choice anyone can make for you. Not Solaris, and not me. Only you can decide.»

Dorian considered, and then let out a long, ragged breath. "I don't like killing people. I hope I will never come to enjoy killing people. But..." But Meridian was free because of him. Despite his guilt, despite everything, that knowledge filled him with a golden glow he could not banish. "Saving people... saving your companions, the other dragons..." His hands balled into fists. "Yes. Of course. I want to continue."

«Then let us be certain. If you would kindly fetch another sword from the arms crate. A cheaper one would be better, or at least make your captain happier. Any sword will do, however.»

"All... right."

Dorian felt a prickle of apprehension over what his dragon might want a sword for, but having just decided to trust her, he did what she asked without question. He opened the arms cabinet, scanning around for the least impressive sword he could find. He found it near the back, dull and rusted, the leather wrapping on the hilt scuffed and torn.

"Here you go. I hope it's not too cheap-looking."

«Not at all. It is perfect. Put it on the floor, now, if you will.»

Dorian set it down with more reverence than the battered old blade probably deserved. Then, instinctively, he backed away.

It was a good thing he did, too, because without warning, Solaris let out a stream of golden flames.

"Ack!" Dorian scrambled further back. "What are you doing? This is a wooden ship!"

When Solaris finished, however, the floor of the cargo hold appeared undamaged. The sword was gone. In its place, glittering in the light of the aether lamps, was another golden blade identical to the one he'd left behind.

«It worked,» Solaris said, and the sheer amount of relief, joy, and affection she sent towards Dorian nearly drove him to his knees.

"I... ah... How did you do that?"

Dorian waved his hand over the dragon-shaped hilt, confirming it was cool to the touch before lifting it off the ground. He marveled once more at how it felt sized and weighted perfectly for his sword arm.

"I knew it!" Tai dropped, grinning, down through the trapdoor, carrying a battered clothbound book under her arm. She leapt down, foregoing the ladder as usual, and flipped it to a page depicting a woodcut print of a sword. It looked just like the one in Dorian's hand.

"It's a dragonaut sword," she explained.

"The symbolic weapon of the most favored and revered dragonauts of old," Dorian read out loud from the page. He blinked. "Favored and revered?" He set the sword down again for fear he was dirtying the artifact with his grubby, unworthy hands.

Solaris inclined her serpentine neck in confirmation. «It is old magic, even by the standards of our kind. The spell will only work if the bond is deep enough, if the human and dragon respect each other as equals, and not one merely a tool for the other.» She snorted more sparks. «It would surprise you how rare that was, even back then.»

"According to this," Tai read, "It's keener and stronger than any ordinary steel, and never needs to be sharpened. That's probably how you could take off Ashe's head so easily." At Dorian's wince, she added, "And it can also cast spells."

"Cast spells?" Dorian asked. "Like what, a giant athame?"

Experimentally, he traced a single flame rune into the air. The fireball exploded with such force that Dorian fell backwards.

«Now who is being reckless on a wooden ship!» Hematite chided, while Tai stomped out a stray ember.

"Sorry," Dorian said, "I, uh, didn't expect it to be that... effective."

«Perhaps *flame* should not be the first spell you think to cast,» Hematite said. But as nothing had actually caught fire, he seemed more amused than reproachful.

Dorian looked at the blade with a combination of fear and awe. Then something else occurred to him. "And... and the other one..."

«It was just after our escape from Sanoria,» Solaris admitted, a trifle sheepishly.

"That long ago?"

Solaris nodded. «You had just told me all those things, and I was so... relieved. So I thought to myself, 'I wonder if I could,' and at first it seemed like nothing happened, but there was... a seed of power, I suppose, growing in the sword. I thought, perhaps, as our bond grew stronger, so then would the sword's power.»

"You created this one in about five seconds," Dorian said, gazing at the new sword with awe.

«Yes well,» Solaris said. «Our bond has strengthened greatly since then.»

Dorian blanched as another thought occurred to him. "Void! The other sword! After you put in all that work, I just left it there!"

Had he just delivered a powerful weapon into enemy hands?

«It will have reverted to an ordinary blade by now,» Solaris said with an air of total nonconcern. «Firm our bond may be, but I believe I can only create one dragonaut's blade at a time. Besides. Celestian and his slaver will never share a bond such as the one we have.»

"Such a bond as... I... oh," Dorian said. He examined the sword with newfound reverence. "You... you really think I deserve this?" Tears started pricking at the corners of his eyes. He *would* not cry, he would *not*!

«Of course I do,» Solaris said. Then, more teasingly, she added, «Do mind you don't carelessly throw this one aside.»

"I... of course not. I promise." The tears flowed now, and there was nothing Dorian could do to stop them. But for the first time in several days, he also smiled.

# CHAPTER TWENTY-SIX

# BRADFORD

"This is a disaster," Dorian said as he riffled through his half-forgotten leather rucksack. "This is a complete and utter disaster!"

Tai came to a halt outside his cabin door. "Is everything all right?"

Dorian felt the heat rise to his face. "Oh, no. I mean yes. I mean, it's nothing." He sighed and slumped his shoulders. "It's stupid."

Tai's mouth quirked into a smile. "Try me."

"We're meeting with Lord Bradford in less than a day."

"What's so disastrous about that?" Tai asked. "I thought we all agreed it was best to answer Hildegard's invitation."

"We did," Dorian agreed.

"Then what's the problem?"

In one hand, Dorian held up a voluminous silk shirt, still bereft of a sleeve from when he tried to bandage up Solaris. In the other, he held a much more practical linen tunic, battered and frayed and, embarrassingly, stained with sweat under the arms. "The problem," he said, "Is that I have *nothing to wear.*"

Tai looked like she wanted to laugh, but schooled her face into a serious expression.

«Fabric,» Solaris said with a draconic sigh. «Why is it you humans place so much value in fabric? Why not just cover yourself in the same fabric you always use?»

"He's a lord," Dorian said. "I can't just wear any old aeronaut clothes to meet a lord."

"Isn't he also your brother?" Tai asked.

"Yes, but —" he spread his arms in frustration. He did not know how to explain Cycles of awkward family dynamics to her, not when he barely understood them himself.

"Well, let's see," Tai said. She let herself into the room and began searching his trunk. She held up a sky-blue tunic for inspection, then tossed it aside. "That one's far too big for you." She inspected an off-white linen one, but wrinkled her nose at a mended tear near the shoulder, surrounded by a red-brown stain. "Is that blood?"

"Arrow wound. From when we escaped Sanorska."

Tai made a disapproving "*tssk*" noise and set the garment down. "What about this one?"

She held up an eggshell-colored woolen shirt, one he purchased at Ruon's all those moons ago. It was in good condition, and recently re-tailored. But Dorian grimaced anyway.

"It's got a tea stain, right below the collar."

"I'd say that's a sight better than a bloodstain."

Dorian shook his head. He didn't expect Tai to understand. But the memories played in his mind with vivid clarity, of Bradford and Graigor teasing him for the stains on his shirts, gleeful at any evidence that Dorian was as slovenly as they believed him to be. His hands shook as he clutched the garment. "I can't."

Tai's expression shifted from one of mild amusement to one of concern. "Are you that afraid of him?"

Dorian let out a long breath. "I'm not sure if afraid is the right word." He clutched the stained shirt in his hand, as if it were a life-line. "I just... Bradford and I weren't... close, growing up. The opposite, really. We couldn't stand each other. But then... then he saved my life. He got me this position on the *Phoenix*. I owe him for that. No matter what happened between us before, I'll always be grateful for that."

Tai bit her lip, clearly not sure what to say. She instead settled for putting a comforting hand on his shoulder. The gesture made him feel a little better.

"I just wish I knew what to expect. He saved my life, so does that make us friends now? Or are things just going to go back to—" he shrugged — "Whatever we were?"

Dorian still didn't feel emotionally recovered from his disastrous reunion with Queen Saedra. And now, only a few days later, he was supposed to see his brother. It was all too much, too soon.

"I guess I thought, I don't know, if I wore my best clothes, tried to make a good impression, he might not... he might..."

Tai squeezed his shoulder. "Rebel leaders can't expect to get far if they dismiss people for not wearing fancy clothes. Now come on. We're about to make the final approach. You can worry about dressing to impress once we get there."

Dorian nodded, stood up, and tried to put on a brave face.

At least there was nothing quite like the Linking to soothe his ragged nerves.

The Kasani Spires, more colloquially known as the Dragon's Fangs, formed a labyrinthine cluster of cone-shaped islands in the skies just west of Kasanarae. Respectable crews avoided this area, and for good reason, because Dorian had never faced a flight so challenging. Sweat beaded on his forehead as he moved the *Phoenix* between the drifting stalactites and stalagmites, praying to all seven of the gods that they wouldn't hit anything.

It was these hazards that made the spires a haven for miscreants — pirates, smugglers, and, in this case, rebels against Callahan's empire. If anyone wanted to hide, the treacherous Dragon's Fangs were the place to do it. Still, Dorian found it hard to forget that Callahan himself sunk one of these spires, not even a moon ago. Was Bradford's base as hidden as he thought?

*I hope we're not making a mistake.*

Dorian clung to the magical link between himself and the ship. Avoiding the spires allowed for no margin of error. It was exhausting work, but it also distracted Dorian from his nerves. Besides, tricky or not, it was a breathtaking bit of flying.

The great stone spires floated around them, cloaked in clouds of mist amidst the backdrop of a glorious blue Autumn sky. Some spires boasted waterfalls, pouring down on the clouds below. As they passed, Dorian felt the cool spray of water against his skin.

From a distance their target looked innocuous, just another spire among many. But Dorian soon saw a myriad of tethered skyships hiding in the mist. Dorian felt sure the mists must result from Illusion magic. Perhaps Bradford himself cast the spell — he always had a natural knack for it. Dorian smiled ruefully, recalling an afternoon in the library, his head full of daydreams of Princess Saedra. Another lifetime, now.

As they approached, Dorian also noticed that most of those mist-cloaked ships had their guns aimed at the *Phoenix*. The hairs on his arms stood on end.

Xander flashed their signal beacon, an encoded message in a cypher Dorian didn't recognize. The rebels seemed to accept it, however, because they flashed a signal in return and allowed the *Phoenix* to approach.

Captain Xander nodded in acknowledgement, then took out his athame to cast the sigil for long-distance communication.

A curt, angry voice reverberated through the Linking, "Who are you? State your purpose."

Dorian froze. He knew that voice. "Graigor Beckett?"

If Dorian's childhood tormentor was here, that didn't bode well.

"State your purpose or I blow you out of the sky," Graigor repeated.

Dorian ran his hand over his face. *Gods*, that man was an arse.

"Captain Xander Kane and crew of the *Phoenix*," Captain Xander said. "Here to parlay with Lord Bradford."

"*Phoenix*, you say." And for the first time, Graigor's voice sounded uncertain.

Someone — a woman, from the cut of her uniform — joined him on the watch post. Hildegard? Dorian couldn't quite tell from the distance. Whoever she was, however, Graigor's posture and manner shifted, suggesting that she must be someone important. The man and woman exchanged words Dorian couldn't hear with much hand-waving and gesticulation.

Graigor turned back to his communication circle and said, "I have been informed that you are to be allowed to dock. You are to be considered invited guests of Lord Bradford himself, with all the privileges therein. It is also requested that you join His Lordship for tea."

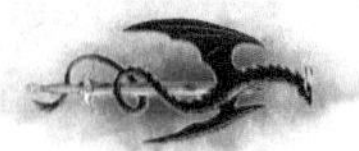

Dorian had hoped his nerves might settle now that he was here. But now he felt worse, heart pounding in his chest, jumping at every small noise.

*Bradford.* For the first time in almost a year, he was going to see Bradford. Not just Bradford, but Graigor too. *Oh, gods, oh, gods.*

Graigor himself spoke little as he led them down the twisting labyrinth of stone tunnels. This was just as well for Dorian, who'd expected more of the man's snide comments and ill-natured ribbing. Hematite, who disliked Graigor as much as Dorian did, crouched deep inside Dorian's spirit, incorporeal, demon flames lowered as far as they would go.

«I do not like this,» Hematite warned.

«You and me, both,» Dorian replied.

Bullying Dorian, however, seemed to be far from Graigor's mind. Indeed, other than turning around occasionally to make sure they were still following through the blue aether-lit corridors, he barely acknowledged they were there at all. Dorian tried to keep track of all the twists and turns, but it was no good. He only hoped that these rebels had good intentions, because he didn't think he'd ever find his way out of here on his own.

Graigor finally stopped outside a chamber. Flickering golden aether-light, not blue like in the hallway, shone invitingly from the chamber entrance. "Wait here. Bradford will be with you momentarily."

Graigor gestured them to enter the room, and Dorian's breath caught in his throat. If not for the rough stone cavern walls, he might've thought he'd stepped straight back home into Callahan Manor. Bloody Ancients, that was the table from the gaming parlor with the parquet inlay. Why had Bradford dragged that all the way here? Achingly, Dorian recalled sitting across from Saedra, discussing the Void and other forbidden topics.

He tugged on the collar of his frock coat, trying and failing to hide the tea stain. He wished he could've found a better shirt. It hadn't been so bad in the dim blue aether light of the hallway, but here in this cozy sitting room he was sure it was the first thing the others would notice. He wished he'd been able to freshen up more. *Oh, gods,* what on Cyrna would Stewardess Tahlia say?

«Tahlia is not here,» Hematite pointed out gently, «And this is not Frostvale. Though I wish you'd thought to purchase some silks in the last market town. You always did look rather fetching in them.»

Dorian snorted. "Fetching" was not the term he would have used.

«Fabric again,» Solaris scoffed. In his mind's eye, he saw her breathing sparks of annoyance.

«What is wrong with fabric? It is soft and versatile and lovely.

What is the point of bonding with a human except to feel the sensation of soft silk?»

«You are serious.» Solaris laughed. «You bonded Dorian because you enjoyed the feeling of human fabric?»

Hematite sounded a little embarrassed. «Their fabric, and their food, and their beverages. Ah, and firelight. There is nothing quite like the warmth of a human fire.»

«I see,» Solaris said, well and truly mirthful now. «What of the wind on your scales, the wild freedom of the sky beneath you, and the satisfying rush of exertion?»

«Those are… also pleasant,» Hematite admitted with grudging hesitation. «Even the thrice cursed training. Afterwards, mind, not during. Especially the lunges. Meroneth save me, I hate the lunges. I am sorry, but human knees are simply not meant to bend that way. But the rest is not so bad.»

«Nor, in turn, is fabric» Solaris replied. «But I still will never understand it.»

Both of Dorian's bonds laughed. Dorian couldn't help but smiling too, glad for the distraction from his own ragged nerves.

Bradford swept into the room a moment later, carrying a tea tray.

*Serving tea?* Dorian didn't think he'd ever seen his older brother serve tea before.

Dorian noted an array of miniature scones, and his stomach gave an involuntary rumble. Far too late, Dorian realized he hadn't eaten all morning. As he wanted to reach for one of the delicate pastries, however, he forced himself to stay his hand. *Do not be gluttonous*, a Janus Callahan-sounding voice reprimanded in his head.

"Sorry I'm late, Graigor. Ryslen ran a bit long giving her latest report." Bradford looked flustered, but otherwise much as Dorian remembered him — handsome and self-assured. Long gone, though, was his carefree attitude. He wore a grim expression, and dark circles lined his pale blue eyes. He dressed simply, too, in plain but well-made linen and soft leather breeches. Dorian felt himself instinctively relax, just a fraction. At least Bradford wasn't wearing silk.

Bradford set the tea tray down on the table and turned his attention to Captain Xander.

"It's good to see you again," Bradford said.

The two gripped each other's hands and then patted each other on the shoulders, a gesture of friendship between equals. Dorian's eyes widened in surprise at the show of familiarity. Bradford had gotten Dorian his position on the *Phoenix*, so it followed logically that the two of them must know each other. Bradford was part of Dorian's old life, though, and Captain Xander part of his new life. It was strangely jarring to see them come together.

"I fear I've landed quite a deal of trouble on your head," Bradford said with a grimace. "I'm glad to see you safe, at least for the moment."

"Trouble, *fah*," Xander waved a dismissive hand. "This is the most fun I've had in Cycles. And Dorian here has been the model apprentice."

Dorian flushed despite himself.

Bradford regarded Dorian, and his face blossomed into a smile of genuine pleasure. "My dear brother! So good to see you again." He drew Dorian into a warm embrace.

"Ah, hello," Dorian said, awkwardly patting his brother on the back.

Graigor, who Dorian had almost forgotten was still there, let out a sort of choking noise and looked at Dorian as if he'd never seen him before. "You," he said, followed by, "*Brother*?"

"Ah, yes, about that." Bradford ran a sheepish hand through his curly brown hair. "Turns out he is my brother, after all." To Dorian, he said, "I must say, you've, ah, changed since last we met. I dare say Graigor here didn't even recognize you."

"Of course I did," Graigor protested. "He's just all — dressed like a common aeronaut, that's all." He crossed his muscular arms in self defense.

"I—" Dorian stammered, blushing deep crimson. He tugged on

his collar, accidentally revealing the tea stain. He dropped his hand at once.

Bradford responded with a good-natured laugh. "At least some things are still the same. Graigor, if you could kindly give us a moment."

Dorian thought Graigor might argue, but he simply nodded, still staring at Dorian as if his hair were on fire. "Of course. I'll be at the guard post if you need me, my lord."

Once Graigor had departed, Bradford set about pouring cups of tea. He handed one to Captain Xander, then to Tai, then Falgar and Sullivan, and finally to Dorian.

"Scone?" Bradford proffered the small porcelain plate.

"Oh," Dorian said, "No thank you."

"Dorian's watching his figure," Falgar said with a smirk as he took a generous bite of his own scone.

"*Falgar*," Sullivan chided.

At the same time, Bradford smiled faintly and said, "I can see that."

Face burning, Dorian took the scone and set it on his saucer. "There."

"I suppose you're wondering what all this is about," Bradford said, more seriously.

Dorian took the tea, and sipped it carefully, lest he have another stain to match the first. It tasted good; much better than the cheap tea they had on board the *Phoenix*. Nutty undertones, and a sweet spice he didn't recognize.

"Um, yes," Dorian said. "Hildegard said... she said you were looking for me?"

"For some time now," Bradford said. "You've not exactly been easy to get ahold of."

"Comes with being on the run from the law," Dorian said.

Bradford smirked and took a sip from his teacup. "It does, that. We have a common goal, that of stopping my father. But... I admit my motives aren't entirely selfless."

"A selfish nobleman?" Falgar asked. "Shocking."

"Falgar." Sullivan buried his face in his hand.

Bradford spread his hands, not denying the accusation. "First, I must know. Are the rumors true? Have you bonded a dragon?"

Dorian searched Bradford's expression, but saw only eager excitement, no hint of duplicity. He then looked over at Captain Xander, and his crew-mates, and finally inspected his own bond with Solaris. One by one, they nodded their assent. They couldn't continue on their own anymore. Sooner or later, they were going to have to trust someone.

Dorian sent a telepathic signal to the incorporeal Solaris, and she materialized there in the middle of the room, narrowly avoiding knocking over the tea tray with her thick bladed tail.

«My apologies,» she said.

"My word," Bradford said, his blue eyes wide with awe. "She's even more beautiful than I imagined."

Solaris preened.

"In order to stop my father," Bradford continued, "We need to give the people something to rally behind, something that gives them hope. The tyrant's estranged son might garner some sympathy. The tyrant's former ward, however, wronged and out for revenge, flying alongside a dragon of his own? That is a cause to inspire the masses."

"So you want," Dorian began, setting his teacup down, "For me to be your rallying banner?"

"That is the general idea, yes."

Dorian paused. "But ... but the people wouldn't rally around me, would they? I'm nobody."

Bradford scoffed. "Give yourself some credit, dear brother. You've successfully evaded my father's forces for close to a year now, and if even half the rumors surrounding you are true, you have bonded a dragon, earned a dragonaut's sword, and defeated Ashe Valerian in single combat."

Dorian flinched. "Er, yes, well... That was... I got lucky, that's all. It wasn't a fair fight."

"It's not for me to decide how you feel," Bradford said, stirring his tea. "However, you should at least understand how it's perceived. We've enjoyed some minor triumphs over the ordinary soldiers, but against the dragonauts, we're practically powerless. And until we defeat them, there's no hope of stopping my father."

"So these dragonauts of Callahan's," Xander said, "How many are there, exactly?"

"Six," Bradford said. "Wait, no, five, now Ashe is gone." He counted them off on his fingers. "There's my father himself, of course, and then there's Ambrose Barclay. Absolute dolt of a man, Ambrose. I suspect the only reason he's still alive is because his dragon has more than enough sense for both of them. More's the pity. Anyway, then there's Kadmin Crowley. You met him at Goose Head as I understand it, and of course you know Graigor's sister, Corynne Beckett."

Dorian nearly spit out his tea. "Corynne?"

He tried and failed to imagine the haughty young woman riding a dragon. Then again, *he* was a dragonaut, and that concept was no less absurd.

Bradford looked slightly mournful. "I knew she'd never forgive me after I broke our betrothal, but I never thought she'd enslave a dragon." He took a bite of his own scone and swallowed. "The last, it pains me to say, is the Duchess Vivienne, Queen Saedra's cousin and guardswoman. I find it hard to believe that she would stoop to such levels, but she's a clever woman, and always has a backup plan. I hope that in the end she may prove an ally to us after all." Draining the last of his tea, he added, "But ah, perhaps that is merely a dream on my part."

Dorian nodded and took a bite of his scone. The tart cherry flavor was delicious, but not enough to offset the shocking news. He hadn't been close to Duchess Vivienne in the same way Bradford was, of course, but he'd always liked her. Once during their long stay, she'd even come to Dorian's defense after Graigor's usual taunts. Try as he might, he couldn't imagine the stout, good-natured woman, with her fierce sense of justice and consummate fair-mindedness, taking any part in the enslavement of dragons. Then again, he'd never have believed it of Saedra, either.

"Have you… been in contact with Saedra since you left Frostvale?" Bradford asked, perhaps sensing the direction of his thoughts.

"Yes," Dorian said, his stomach doing an uncomfortable flip-flop. "She was at Goose Head. She was…" he debated how much he should tell Bradford, but his face must have betrayed his feelings, because Bradford nodded in pained understanding.

"She knew all along what my father had planned," Bradford said. "About the stolen dragonstones. The plan to enslave the dragons. All of it. And gods help me, I was part of it too." Bradford's hand clenched into a fist, while he buried his face in the other hand. "Every moment of the past year I have spent trying to rectify that mistake. And yet I still fear it will never be enough." He shook his head and regained his usual composure. "There's one thing Saedra did that made no sense to me, though. Janus intended one of those stolen dragonstones for her. Void, she already owned the thing."

"But she gave it to me," Dorian said. He thumbed Solaris's dragonstone, feeling the connection with his dragon.

"She gave it to you," Bradford confirmed. "And prevented my father from getting a full Flight of dragons. But why? What did she hope to gain? Why help you, then stand by your enemy in all things?"

Dorian shrugged morosely. He didn't know the answers any more than Bradford did. "She was always so kind to me. Guess I was pretty foolish, to think it meant… more."

"I think she cared for you, in her way," Bradford said. "One thing I learned about her during our ill-fated betrothal — she always put her country first. Interests, friendships, romance, they all took the backseat to her all-consuming duty. It's why I found her so dull, back in those days." He shook his head with a rueful smile. "She's with my father because she thinks he's the one best positioned to help Kasanarae. I fear she's wrong in this, but I've given her no reason to listen to me." He shook his head. "The important thing is, she gave you that dragonstone. In defiance of her husband. So perhaps she cared for you more deeply than you know."

Dorian nodded gratefully, but couldn't think of anything to say. He knew Bradford meant to reassure him, but he wasn't sure what to feel. In a strange way, his bond with Solaris meant more to him than his short-lived romance with the princess ever had, and it felt strange, almost disrespectful, to have the two of them so inextricably tied together.

"We are straying from the point," Bradford said, taking another scone. "Ashe Valerian killed ten of our best soldiers and still got away with her life. And yet, you, Dorian, bested her."

"I got lucky," Dorian repeated. He picked up his scone and took a bite. "I just got lucky."

"Lucky or not, those dragonauts have been real thorns in our side," Bradford said. "We need your help, and we need it badly. As a figurehead, yes, but as a fighter, too. Best weapon against a dragonaut is another dragonaut. Believe me when I say we would not spend your life unwisely."

"But you would spend it," Tai interjected, scowling.

"Not if I can help it," Bradford said bluntly. "However, we are at war. Everyone should be aware of the risks. What do you say? Will you be our sword and our banner?"

"He isn't a sword or a banner, you dolt, he's a person," Falgar chimed in.

"That's right," Xander said, crossing his arms. "What do you offer him in return?"

Dorian felt a rush of warmth at his friends coming to his defense, but he raised his hand to forestall more arguing. "Bradford already saved my life. I'm the one who owes him."

"So what, you don't get a choice?" Tai shook her head, clearly unconvinced.

"Of course, he has a choice," Bradford said. He met Dorian's eyes, his expression imploring. "I won't ask you to do anything you're not comfortable with."

Dorian sighed and examined the willow patterned teacup. It was, he noted, from the same set he'd dropped in shock that fateful afternoon moons ago in Callahan's study. Apparently, not all the cups were broken after all.

«Solaris? Hematite? What do you think?»

«I cannot in good conscience encourage you to do this,» Hematite said. «I fear with all my being that it will end in your death. And yet...» He continued hesitantly, choosing his words with utmost care. «I know you will do what is right.»

Solaris was a swirling vortex of equal parts hope and terror. «For once,» she said with a nervous laugh, «I almost agree with the demon. I cannot ask you to take this risk.» Yet shining hope for her draconic family radiated through their bond..

Dorian decided at once. «We freed Meridian. We'll free the others, too.»

"I hate the idea that I might have to kill more people," Dorian said out loud. He took a bite of his scone and swallowed. "But a lot more people are going to die if Callahan's allowed to continue. So. If there's anything I can do to stop him, I'll do it." He almost smiled. "Besides. I was getting kind of bored cooped up in the cargo hold. I'm tired of running away."

Bradford laughed and clapped him on the shoulder. "You do not know how glad I am to hear it. I'd see where you stand as a swordsman. Spar with me this evening?"

"Oh!" Dorian said, uncertain. Bradford had been a champion fencer, back in Frostvale. "I... suppose I could."

"Excellent!" Bradford leaned across the table to clap Dorian on the shoulder. "Meet me at six bells."

Dorian arrived a few minutes early to the training grounds.

"This is impressive," he said.

Solaris and Hematite both sent agreement; hers enthusiastic, his grudging.

The rebels had equipped their training ground with free weights, fully enchanted sparring golems, and wooden practice swords of varying lengths and weights. Who was funding this whole operation? The Order? How much gold could they possibly have? Dorian took a few of the wooden blades down, giving them each a couple of swings before settling on the one that felt best.

Off to the side in corporeal form, Hematite's blue flames flickered in obvious distaste. «I enjoy the flying and even the lifting of heavy things, but I will never, ever, enjoy the sword.» He drew in a long breath and let it out, his blue flames guttering. «However,» he conceded, «Even I can see that this is important to you. Just I beg you, from the depths of my soul, do not allow yourself to become consumed in violent rage.»

Dorian frowned. He enjoyed sword fighting. He could admit that much. It was the killing that twisted his stomach in knots. «Don't worry,» he said, «I think on this, at least, we agree.» He just hoped it stayed that way.

"Ah, good, you're here." Bradford swept in, dressed in a smartly padded fencing vest. "You'll want one of these, too." He tossed a similar quilted garment in Dorian's direction.

Dorian caught it, then glanced at it, dubious. He'd fared well enough these past moons, just accepting the scrapes and bruises from the practice blades. He wrinkled his nose. This article of clothing smelled faintly of someone else's sweat.

Bradford grimaced. "We'll try to get you your own gear, but aside from the occasional supply drop from the Order, we have to rely on smuggling for almost everything."

"So you are in contact with the Order," Dorian said.

"More like they're in contact with us," Bradford said. "The Dragonmar wants to see my father stopped as much as we do. But there are ... reasons she cannot interfere directly."

"Dragonmar?" Dorian asked.

"That's what the Ancient Dragonauts called their leader. The Order... likes to abide by tradition."

"Did this Dragonmar person pay for all this?" he gestured at the expansive training area.

To Dorian's surprise, Bradford's face turned a faint shade of pink. "That," he admitted, "Is from my own personal coffers."

Dorian shrugged it off, for now, and pulled the protective padding experimentally over his shoulders. To his surprise, it fit well enough.

"If you think all this is necessary," Dorian said. "Let's get started."

The vest turned out to be necessary. Dorian liked to think he'd improved in the past year, but he was still no match for Bradford. The vest did little to protect his ego, but at least it protected Dorian's chest.

Inadequate though Dorian might be, he noticed his brother's moves were sometimes repetitive. Bradford also spent a lot of time on elegant flourishes. Noting that, Dorian saw a rare opening and seized it, jabbing Bradford in the upper arm.

"I did it!" Dorian blurted, half-shocked. "I hit you!"

Bradford responded with a good-natured laugh. "That you did. Gods Above, you're pretty good at this."

"You don't have to be sarcastic," Dorian grumbled, taking a swig from his canteen. "I hit you once for, what, the sixteen times you hit me?"

"I'm not," Bradford said. He took a drink of his own. "I've been training with the sword since I was eleven years old. You've done it for, oh, what now, eight, nine moons? Considering the gap in our experience, that you can hit me at all is… quite impressive. Give it a couple of years, and it wouldn't surprise me if you were one of the finest swordsmen on Cyrna."

Dorian flushed. "The finest — no — surely not."

Bradford smiled as he leaned against a training dummy. "I just regret the years my father wasted insisting you weren't to be taught fencing. I would have liked to have had you for a sparring partner when we were younger."

"You… you would have?" All the years Bradford tormented Dorian, all the years Dorian longed for acceptance and was denied it. And now Bradford wanted him as a sparring partner?

«Bradford's father is a cruel man, but he was right in this, I am afraid,» Hematite said. «I understand the necessity now. But in those days, if you had tried to learn the sword, I would have had to fight you with all I had. There is a reason you do not find many accomplished sword fighters who are also demon possessed. Meroneth sent us to Cyrna to keep humans out of trouble. Stabbing one another is about as troublesome as it gets.»

Dorian shuddered. His friendship with Hematite was strained enough as it was. Dorian didn't want to know what would've happened if he'd tried to learn the sword when their bond was new and Dorian himself was young and inexperienced.

How different would his life had been, if he'd had Bradford for a friend, and Hematite as an enemy? Dorian examined the possibility and wasn't sure he liked the answer. But the Bradford and Hematite of his boyhood were not the Bradford and Hematite of today.

"Bradford." Dorian bit his lip, unsure how to proceed. "That is… why did you finally defy him? Why now, after all these years?"

Bradford shook his head sadly. "I've not given you much reason to think well of me, have I?"

"Um." Dorian considered how to answer without being rude.

Bradford shook his head again. "It's okay. The way we treated you was nothing short of monstrous." His hands curled into fists. "I should have tried to put a stop to it. Instead, I made it worse... I was part of it... I..."

Dorian frowned and examined his practice sword. It was true; he had vanishingly few positive memories of his time with Bradford in Frostvale. He couldn't pretend otherwise. But Dorian also found he was loath to jeopardize any relationship they might have, moving forward.

"Do you really think he'll do it?" Dorian asked, electing to change the subject rather than confront his complicated feelings. "End the magic, I mean. Sink..." he swallowed. "Sink Aeris?"

Bradford examined the handle of his wooden practice blade, frowning deeply. "It's worse than that." Sighing, he elaborated, "Queen Saedra might have saved us all by giving you that dragonstone."

"Don't you think you're exaggerating a bit?" Dorian asked.

Bradford smiled sadly. "I don't wish to under-emphasize your value," he said, putting his hand on Dorian's shoulder. "But what I speak of goes deeper than either of us as individuals. In giving the dragonstone to you, she prevented Callahan from having a full Flight of seven."

A knot of fear settled in Dorian's stomach. "Saedra... wanted me to go join them. She wanted to complete the Flight after all."

Bradford nodded. "It seems she is fully on my father's side now. I wish it weren't so. But I am thankful, so thankful, that you didn't go with her. Because one thing I can tell you, Dorian. My father will do anything to get a seventh dragonstone. Anything."

"Why... why does it matter if he has seven?" Dorian wondered.

Bradford steepled his fingers and closed his eyes, contemplating his words. "My spies believe he has uncovered the methods of creating Moon Glass," he said at length.

Dorian felt his insides turn to ice. Through his bond, he felt Solaris's combined fear and hatred.

"That... that mirror looking thing? The one—" he cut off abruptly. He wanted to trust Bradford, but senselessly blurting out that his captain kept a priceless and dangerous Ancient artifact under a false bottom in his desk drawer seemed unwise. "That's what the Ancients used to sink Orith."

"Not just the Moon Glass," Bradford said. "But seven sacrificial dragons."

Dorian felt like someone had doused him in icy water. "He's going to *kill* them?"

«There is a reason,» Solaris said gravely, «Why my kind consider it highest heresy to bond with yours. Why joining with you was such a terrible risk.»

Dorian nodded. "The Great Betrayal." He'd read the history books. "The Ancients sacrificed dragons to sink Orith and Iriya. Did he ... did he kill a dragon to sink that spire?" His heart raced as he thought of who it might have been. Borealis? Northstar? Surely not Nocturne. Through his bond with Solaris, though, Dorian felt like he knew them all.

Bradford, however, thankfully shook his head. "No, no," he said. "He just used an astronomical amount of aether. And destabilized the economy of half of Aeris to do it, mind. But to sink a full-sized landmass like Kasanarae or Eastland or the Northen Reaches takes ... more."

With gut-clenching clarity, the pieces fit together. It was almost laughably simple. "I can draw magical energy from Solaris," Dorian said. "I could do it with Hematite, too, but it always made me feel sick. But with Solaris, I can just sort of... draw power. As much as I want. Enough to ... enough to sink all the lands?"

"Not by yourself, no. But with a full flight of seven, and the Moon Glass on your side? Yes, I'm afraid so."

"Void," Dorian said. He ran his hand through his sweaty copper hair.

«For all your talk of freedom and consent, you dragons give too easily,» Hematite complained. «Any demon worth his flames knows to let go of the host and retreat to the spirit realm before that happens. We can always return to the host later, when it is safe.»

«Most dragons would release the bond after such a heinous betrayal,» Solaris replied. «If they have the choice. Do you think my kinfolk are where they are now because they consented?»

Dorian's heart sank as surely as Orith had done all those centuries ago. "Void," he swore again, more vehemently.

Bradford looked sympathetic, but unsurprised, at Dorian's reaction to the revelation. "The good news is, even if he procures a Moon Glass, he still needs a full flight of seven dragons to complete the ritual. Right now, thanks to you, he only has five. So that buys us some time, thank the gods."

Dorian nodded and examined the hilt of his wooden practice blade. "Let's spar some more."

"Again?" Bradford asked, looking surprised.

«I know what you'll say,» he privately apologized to Hematite. «Violence only begets more violence.»

Once again, Hematite carefully considered his words. «I cannot claim I approve. But it was not just your friend Tai's people who the Ancients sent beneath the clouds. We demons, too, have suffered the consequences of that event.»

"Spar with me," Dorian repeated. "You're a lot better at this than me, and I need all the practice I can get." Dorian took a deep breath and drank from his canteen. "Callahan needs to be stopped, and those dragons need to be rescued. He can't get away with this, and I will be cursed to the Void if my fear or incompetence lets him."

# CHAPTER TWENTY-SEVEN

# THE REBELLION

orian thanked the cook in the mess hall, trying his best to hide his dismay at the dry bread and watery soup. It wasn't the cook's fault supplies were low, and Dorian didn't want to appear ungrateful. He realized what a grandiose gesture it was for Bradford to bring out the tea and scones on the afternoon of their arrival. The thought made Dorian uncomfortable. He didn't want to be on the receiving end of any such extravagance. However, he also couldn't deny the fact that he was hungry. Ravenous, even.

His training here among the rebels was even more intense than his training on board the *Phoenix*. To his mild surprise, he was able — if only just — to keep up with the others. Gods help him, though, it left him hungry enough to eat an entire gryphon.

Well, dry bread and watery soup was all he was likely to get, so he took it with as much gratitude as he could muster and looked around for a place to sit in the wide empty cavern the rebels used for a mess hall. To his slight disappointment, he didn't see any of his friends. Falgar and Sullivan were flying ornithopter patrol, while Tai was helping the mechanics with skyship maintenance. Dorian had no idea where Xander or Bradford were. Off somewhere being busy and important, he supposed.

He made to find an empty table to sit by himself when a feminine voice chimed, "And just where do you think you're going, Valmont?"

Dorian stopped and turned towards the sound of the voice. "Ah, hello, Hildegard." He waved awkwardly while careful to balance his wooden tray. He had little enough soup that he didn't want to risk splattering it. She sat at the long wooden table alongside several other rebels, among them Graigor Beckett and a burly dark-haired youth Dorian hadn't met.

"Well, don't just stand there." Hildegard beckoned him over. "Come sit down, for the Ancients' sakes!"

"Oh." Dorian swallowed back a wave of apprehension. "All right."

Hildegard scooted over on the bench to make a spot for him, and he sat down at her side. He knew it was irrational of him to feel so nervous. He and these rebels had been working together, after a fashion, for almost a moon. It was about time he sat down and got to know them. Sitting here now, though, with the others watching him like he was an exotic creature from Saedra's royal menagerie, hearkened too closely to those long, uncomfortable banquets he used to endure back in Frostvale.

At least back then, there'd been more to eat than watery soup.

«There is nothing wrong,» Solaris chided him, «With making new friends.»

«Provided,» Hematite added with a more cynical cast, «They wish to be your friend for the right reasons.»

"So," the dark-haired man — Randyl, Dorian thought he was called — said, leaning forward with his chin on top of his hands. "Is it true you killed Ashe Valerian?"

Dorian flushed and dipped his bread in the soup. "Ah... yes... I did, but..."

"Prodigious," Randyl said. "Absolutely prodigious. I faced her once, you know. Barely got away with my life. Got this scar to show for it." He rolled up his linen shirtsleeve and revealed an angry red mark along his muscular bicep.

"That's... very impressive," Dorian said.

"Well, not as impressive as killing the woman." Graigor gave a hearty guffaw. "Lobbed her head right off, from what I've heard." To the others, he said, "I knew Valmont, you know. Back in Frostvale. Grew up together, we did. Always knew this one was meant for great things. Always knew."

Dorian sank down on the bench, wishing he could disappear. If Graigor Beckett had ever thought Dorian was destined for greatness, he had a strange way of showing it.

«It seems I was wrong,» Hematite said, surprised, almost mystified, to find himself capable of being incorrect.

«Oh?» Dorian asked.

«All those moons ago, when you said you thought they'd be nicer to you if you changed yourself. Do you remember?»

Dorian squirmed. «Suppose so.»

«Well,» Hematite continued, «I insisted they would not. But you are a far different man than you were back then, and they are being nicer to you. So. It seems I was mistaken.»

«Wish you weren't,» Dorian replied. In a twisted sort of way, he thought he would have a lot more respect for Graigor if the man had continued to be rude to him.

Solaris let out a draconic sigh. «The human called Graigor is a blowhard and a scumbag. However, the rest of these rebels mean you no harm. It might do you well to open up to them.»

"So tell me," Randyl said. "What's it like to fly on a dragon?"

This, at least, Dorian was happy to answer. His mood lightened as he explained how they worked together as one being. He described the feeling of air thermals beneath Solaris's golden wings, the rush of wind and magic in his hair, of the near-religious feeling of closeness to which skyship Linking could only provide the faintest echo.

"You need to trust each other more than anything else," Dorian concluded. "I think that's maybe the most important thing Solaris and I have learned this past year. How to trust each other."

Trust, he realized, was what Dorian was missing in his interactions with the rest of the rebellion. And to his dismay, he did not know how to go about bridging it.

The others listened with rapt attention, admiration bordering on awe shining in their expressions. Dorian squirmed a bit and took another spoonful of soup. Their regard made him uncomfortable. He wasn't used to getting this sort of reaction from people, and he wasn't sure he liked it.

"Tell me about that Orith girl," said a dark-haired woman. Dorian thought her name was Ryslen.

"Oh, Tai?" he said, glad to turn the subject away from himself. "She's great. She's the ship's mage on board the *Phoenix*. That means she's in charge of—"

"No, no." Ryslen tossed her hair back with a melodious laugh. "I mean. Is she your lover?"

Dorian felt his face turning bright red. "Tai? Oh, oh no, we're just friends."

Ryslen seemed to brighten at this news. She leaned across the table towards him, folding her arms in a way that emphasized her breasts. Dorian looked to the side, blushing.

"Surely," she said, "You must have a lover, though?"

"I... ah... um... that is..." Dorian didn't know how to respond. He supposed it was time to give up the notion that there was anything between Saedra and himself, especially after Goose Head. But he couldn't for the life of him fathom why Ryslen was asking such a thing.

«Oblivious human,» Solaris said with a peal of draconic laughter, «She asks if you have a mate as a way of implying that *she* would like to be your mate.»

Dorian felt the heat rush to his face. «What? Me? Why?»

Solaris only laughed.

Dorian tried to wrap his head around the idea. *Was* Ryslen

flirting with him? Should he try to flirt back? He wasn't even sure he knew how to do that. Or if he even wanted to. Ryslen *was* attractive, the type of pretty girl who never gave him a second glance back home in Frostvale. Then, however, his mind drifted to thoughts of Tai's intelligent brown eyes and lithe, compact muscles, and he found himself frozen with indecision. He hadn't been lying. Tai was his friend and nothing else. He ha no reason *not* to flirt with Ryslen. So why couldn't he bring himself to do more than gawp at the poor woman like some kind of aether-stunned sky puffer?

"It's... complicated."

"It always is."

Dorian thought Ryslen looked a little disappointed as she returned to her bowl of soup.

Dorian exhaled. *Fool, fool, fool.* Why did he feel so wrong-footed? Hadn't he spent his adolescence longing for the respect and approval these rebels now accorded him? Why did receiving it make him feel so miserable?

Dorian's friends on the *Phoenix* knew him when he was nobody, and, despite initial misgivings, befriended him all the same. They watched him struggle, and they helped him, and in time, he helped them in return. They'd earned each other's regard through sharing laughter and tears and heart-pounding terror. Perhaps, with time, he could share such closeness with these rebels. They weren't there yet, though. How could they ever reach that point?

They all looked at him like he was some kind of hero out of a legend. Like a story come to life, not a flesh-and-blood human with hopes and fears and flaws. How was he supposed to build a friendship on that? He wondered if any single person among them would have spared him more than a sniff of disdain when he was nothing more than Callahan's insecure, pudgy, unwanted ward. Graigor Beckett hadn't. What about the rest? How would he ever know?

«There is no sense in holding a grudge against someone for what they *might* have done,» Solaris pointed out.

Hematite, however, disagreed. «You should seek friends who like you for who you truly are,» he said, «And recall that I was your friend first.»

He was almost relieved when Bradford approached, geared up for gryphon flight.

"Braaaaaad!" Graigor drew out the nickname. "Come to join your humble followers, almighty leader?"

"Afraid not, Graig." Bradford smiled, but there was a serious expression in his cool blue eyes. "I need a word with my brother."

Dorian swallowed the last of his soup and stood up. He was relieved for an excuse to get away from the others.

"What do you need, sir?" Dorian asked.

"How many times must I ask you to call me Bradford? No matter. Scout has sent word. There's a lone dragonaut on patrol near Crimsonrock. If we hurry, we can mount a surprise attack. So what do you say? Want to free a dragon?"

Dorian stood a little straighter. He and Solaris had been practicing a difficult maneuver that he hoped ought to help free the dragon without killing the rider. So far, though, he'd not had the opportunity to test it. "Eager to do so, sir," he said. Then he amended, "Bradford."

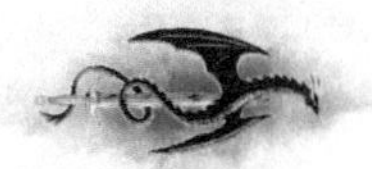

The wind gusted through the openings in Dorian's helmet, creating a faint ringing sound. Dorian silently cursed his brother for making him wear the thing. He didn't mind the rest of the mail and leather armor, but the helmet got in the way, and heightened his already tense nerves.

«We can do this,» Solaris reassured him. «It is just like training.»

Dorian wasn't sure if she was trying to convince him or herself. But Dorian gathered his courage all the same and stared through the helm's eye slit to the vibrant pink and orange sunset ahead.

*Just like training.*

They'd spent the better part of the past two moons practicing this maneuver. Dorian recalled being bloodied, bruised, and sent to the Healer more times than he could count, all in the course of their practice. By now, Dorian half thought he could do it blindfolded. *Good thing, too,* he thought ruefully, given how much this thrice-cursed helmet obscured his vision.

But training was one thing. Actually doing it, and on such short notice besides, was another thing altogether. No amount of preparedness stopped his stomach from turning itself in knots as he approached the lone dragon and dragonaut flying far ahead.

"Why is she by herself, anyway?" Dorian mused.

«Perhaps she is here without permission,» Solaris suggested.

"You mean working against Callahan?"

Solaris emanated agreement. «It would reassure me to know that at least some of my kinfolk are in the hands of humans who sympathize with the rebellion.»

"Maybe," Dorian agreed, but something still didn't sit right. He recalled Bradford suggesting at a meeting weeks ago that he suspected there was a dissenter in Callahan's ranks. His argument had been that if all the enemy dragonauts were working together, they'd have done even more damage by now. But Dorian wasn't so sure. Corynne used to be Bradford's friend. He thought the rumors of a dissenter were just wishful thinking on his brother's part.

Still, he was glad for the command to capture Corynne alive. The memory of Ashe Valerian's head leaving her body still haunted Dorian's nightmares. He didn't want to do that again. Not if he could help it.

Tai pulled up below him on her sleek, silver ornithopter, snapping him out of his reverie. The long, narrow flying machine reminded Dorian of a giant dragonfly with gossamer aether wings.

Dorian's heart gave an involuntary little leap as he saw her there, jet-black feathers spread against the breeze. *Gods,* how he missed her. She'd been so busy lately, working on skyship maintenance with the rest of the rebels. Dorian entertained a moment's fancy about asking Bradford if he could learn about skyship maintenance. But he knew what Bradford would say. Dorian's duties for the rebellion were elsewhere.

As one, Dorian and Solaris soared, a bright red and gold streak against the coral-colored evening sky. As he did so, he felt like he was leaving his fears and anxieties back behind him in the Dragon's Fangs. Despite everything, he laughed with delight. He couldn't think of a better way to spend the evening than soaring into the glorious sunset on Solaris's back.

Corynne Beckett and her captured dragon Borealis flew alone, as the scout predicted they would. Again, Dorian wondered why. He felt, like an itch he couldn't quite scratch, that there was some vital piece of information he was missing.

«We can work through all that later,» Solaris said. «For now, we have a job to do.»

«Right.» Pushing his misgivings aside, Dorian took Solaris into a dive towards the other dragonaut.

"What the!" Corynne yelped as they approached at speed.

Dorian held himself steady to Solaris's harness and unhitched his feet from the stirrups, pulling himself onto the dragoness's shoulders. He crouched in as low a squat as his armor would allow. Despite his nerves, he grinned. Just a few moons ago, Dorian would have broken poor Solaris's neck, followed swiftly by his own.

"Who's there? Is that you, Vivienne? Meroneth's cold and shriveled balls, I told you, I can do this myself." The enemy dragonaut's words relayed in an instant, from Corynne to her dragon to Solaris to Dorian. Despite the howling wind, he heard her as clearly as if he were right next to her.

"Don't think I've ever heard you swear before, Corynne," Dorian said.

"Wait. You're not Vivienne. Who in the Void are you?"

Dorian took several deep, nervous breaths. He tried to think of Corynne in the abstract, an enemy dragonaut, not the girl he'd grown up with. Just in case this all went wrong. Just in case he had to kill her.

Steeling himself against the fear that coursed through him like the wind through his helmet, Dorian raised his dragonaut's sword and drew a single sigil in the air. Flame.

The sword caught fire.

Before Dorian could change his mind, he leapt off of Solaris's back, wind and flame turning him into a blazing comet in the cool evening air. He raised his flaming sword, not against Corynne, but against the dragon. Fire and steel sliced through scales and bones and sinew.

Corynne screamed. The dragon screamed, too. *Oh, gods.*

*It won't kill him*, Dorian reminded himself, for what felt like the hundredth time. *It doesn't work like that for dragons.* But Dorian had to fight back the urge to vomit as his sword sliced through the draconic flesh. Corynne's scream shifted from one of fear to one of pain. Corynne trembled as she lifted her pale hand to her neck. He knew from experience that she felt everything the dragon felt. *Oh, oh gods. What are we doing to them?*

«Stay with me, Borealis!» Solaris breathed a stream of sparks in the other dragon's direction. Rather than flinching back, however, Borealis basked in it. *Healing fire?* Dorian wasn't sure how Solaris did it, but somehow, the gift of her magical energy dampened his pain. There was so much about draconic magic, he realized, that he didn't know.

«Sol... aris?» Borealis asked, bewildered.

Dorian's blade came to a halt just over halfway through the dragon's sturdy neck. Borealis was, Dorian mused in a detached way, much harder to decapitate than Ashe Valerian. Dorian hung in midair by the hilt for a moment that seemed to last an eternity. But it was enough.

Borealis faded to a translucent dragon-shaped cloud. The emerald stone at Corynne's throat turned gray.

Dorian's sword fell the rest of the way through the ethereal creature, as did Borealis's startled rider. Both Corynne and Dorian plummeted.

"Solaris!"

«Right here!»

The dragoness swooped under Dorian, and he landed with a thud and clank of armor. He winced. It had been so much more graceful when he did it in training.

Meanwhile, Tai pulled her ornithopter into a steep dive, roughly scooping up the stunned rider before she could fall further. *Corynne Bloody Beckett.* Dorian wondered what had made the prim and proper banker's daughter want to join Callahan's dragonauts.

The ghostly form of Borealis gratefully inclined his serpentine neck, once more intact in his ghostly form, and then darted off towards the open sky.

"Why didn't you let me fall?" he heard the stunned Corynne demand of Tai, through their distance communication spell.

"My friend up there has a problem with killing people," Tai said as she bound the fallen dragonaut's wrists. "I, however, do not, so you'd better cooperate, or I'll not hesitate to shove you off this ornithopter."

They returned to the base to the sound of tumultuous applause. All around the hovering, mist-cloaked spire, rebels watched from ship decks and balconies. Dorian gave an awkward smile and wave, but inside, he burned with embarrassment. He supposed he was glad, this once, that his helmet obscured both his fake smile and his familiar blush.

His smile when he dismounted, however, was genuine. Dorian removed the hated helmet and ran a hand through his shoulder-length, sweat-soaked hair. Heroes in stories always seemed to have perfect hair when they took their helmets off. Dorian's hair was wet and lank, but at least it was free now.

"We did it!" Tai threw her arms around him. Dorian felt himself warming up all over, but then she drew back, embarrassed. "Good flying."

Dorian laughed despite himself. *Yes*, they had done it. They'd freed Borealis and captured Corynne Beckett alive. Callahan's dragonauts were down to four. *By all the Gods and Ancients*, they'd done it!

"You know," Dorian said with giddy euphoria. "I can't believe that worked."

"Ha!" Falgar strode onto the landing platform and giving him a clap on the shoulder. "That was the most reckless bit of flying I've ever seen in my life. Brilliant, mind. But reckless."

"You really ought to be more careful," Sullivan said. "I fancy myself a skilled Healer, but even I can't bring you back from the dead."

Xander, however, took a different view. "A docked skyship is safe," he quoted the proverb. "But that's not what skyships are for. Well done, Valmont."

Dorian felt his face go redder still, but this time pride mingled with embarrassment. The adulation of the other rebels felt awkward, but the Captain's praise was something else. "Thank you, sir. But Tai was the real impressive one, catching Corynne like that."

Tai stood off to the side, removing her flying gear. If the rebels' admiration for Dorian made him uncomfortable, he imagined it must rankle her even more. *For good reason*, Dorian thought, it *wasn't* fair. She was the one who deserved admiration, not him. The rebels were all so excited to have a dragonaut on their side, but Dorian couldn't have accomplished anything without Tai's help.

Dorian felt the joy of his daring rescue of Borealis ebbing a bit. He'd seen so little of Tai since they came to the Dragon's Fangs. He didn't want their friendship to drift apart. Not when he owed her so much.

Xander nodded. "Indeed, Lunstrum, brilliant flying. Your best yet, maybe. Ah, not that the other times weren't good."

Tai beamed at the captain. "You should have seen the look on that dragonaut's face when I caught her."

Dorian's smile faltered. "How is Corynne?"

"In custody," Xander said, his expression turning grave. "Bradford's seeing to her now. Along with Graigor. Her brother, you know."

Dorian felt the hairs on the back of his neck stand on end. Somehow, he'd all but forgotten that Graigor was Corynne's brother. "You don't think Graigor... I don't know... is going to set her free or something, do you?"

"That guy gives me the creeps," Tai asked. She twitched her wings, running a nervous hand through her hair.

Dorian felt a flash of anger. "He hasn't bothered you, has he?"

Tai grimaced. "Not exactly. But... He keeps watching me. Whenever we're in the same room, his eyes are always on me, almost like... almost like I'm a quail he wants to hunt." She ruffled her feathers in dislike. "But I always thought I was just my imagination. But if you think there's something off about him too..."

Dorian fought back his jealousy. "With the rebellion, you mean? No, not really. He's just..." he waved his hand, unable to express in mere words just why he disliked Bradford's best friend. "We were not friends as children, no matter how much he wishes to insist otherwise." Dorian gave a long sigh.

"He is an enemy dragonaut's brother," Sullivan said, frowning.

"Yeah, but Bradford's Emperor Callahan's son," Falgar pointed out. "He can't hold Graigor's family against him without looking like the world's biggest hypocrite."

"You're probably right." Just because Dorian didn't like the man, didn't make Graigor a traitor.

"It's the sister I'm worried about," Falgar said. "Isn't it suspicious that she was off there flying by herself? What if bringing her here is some kind of trap? I just hope letting her live doesn't come back to bite us."

"You knew her back in Frostvale," Sullivan said. "What sort of person was she?"

Dorian considered. He'd considered her shallow and vain, back then, but she usually wasn't as mean to him as Bradford and Graigor. She was the type who laughed at their jokes but never joined in. He never would have considered her the type to become a dragonaut. "You know," he said, "I don't think I knew her very well at all."

Had they done the right thing in sparing her life?

«Of course it was,» Hematite said.

«Your compassion is something I admire about you,» Solaris added with an exasperated sigh. «For once, I suppose, I agree with the demon. She must answer for her crimes. But not with her life.»

"It will be fine," Dorian said.

He just wished he could make himself believe it.

# CHAPTER TWENTY-EIGHT

# ONE STEP AHEAD

Dorian tumbled forward into the mud, narrowly avoiding the enemy ornithopter as it zoomed overhead.

"This way!" Sullivan shouted.

Dorian scrambled to his feet, spitting out grass and dirt.

"Void," Dorian swore. "The one time I don't wear the thrice cursed helmet..."

He took off at a run, not caring how much noise he made as his feet pounded through the sticks and rotten leaves of the winter woods. He dove behind a skeletal tree to dodge a blast of magical fire, to find Falgar shared his hiding spot.

"Just a supply run, they said," Falgar panted alongside them. "It will be easy, they said."

"What I want to know," Sullivan remarked, "Is how Callahan's forces have been tracking us. Seems like no matter where we go, they're on us like aether flies on a Thlarknian pit wraith."

Dorian reached for his sword hilt, but didn't draw. He had a sinking feeling he might know, but he didn't dare voice it yet. *Corynne.* Was she communicating with Callahan's forces somehow?

«Do not be ridiculous,» Solaris reassured him. «We confiscated everything on her person. We keep her prison cell Voided at all times. There's no way she can communicate with the outside.»

«Maybe so,» Hematite replied, far more cynically. «But what is it you are always saying about humans?»

«That they are skilled at figuring out how to do what they previously could not,» Solaris allowed. «But still—»

The dragon cut off at the sound of of shouting ahead. Dorian drew his sword with a ring of metal, but it was only Hildegard riding on the back of her gryphon.

"Got the crystals." Hildegard looked triumphant, but Dorian noted she was splattered with blood. *Her own, or someone else's?*

"Are you all right?" Dorian asked.

"Me, personally? Grand," she said, with an expression that could have been a grin or a grimace.

"Tai and the others?" he asked. Tai had been with Hildegard, securing the aether cache. If she'd gotten killed or captured... He fought the urge to vomit that morning's breakfast all over the muddy ground.

"She made it safely to the tunnels and is overseeing the transport of the crystals," Hildegard said. "Lucien and Ryslen are with her."

"Thank sweet Zekador." Dorian breathed a sigh of relief. "What about the others? Graigor? Randyl?"

"Graigor reported back to the base already. Randyl... didn't make it."

Dorian's heart lurched. "Randyl, no... Oh, Void Eternal."

Randyl, who'd enthusiastically shown Dorian the scar on his bicep. Randyl, who only ever wanted to be friends. Dorian recalled how wary he'd been around the other dark-haired man, how standoffish. *Gods, I was such an arse.* Dorian wiped away a stray tear that made his way down his mud-splattered face.

"Anyway, we're to return to base and be quick about it," Hildegard said.

"*Right.*" *Mourn later. You're not out of danger yet.*

"Is that dragon of yours ready?" Hildegard asked.

«Of course I am,» Solaris said, swooping down in the clearing and motioning for Dorian to climb on. He allowed himself a tiny self-indulgent moment to admire what a powerful creature she was, dwarfing Hildegard's gryphon. A far cry from the frail creature he'd found in the tunnels beneath Greystone Citadel.

"We stay here a minute longer and we'll be up to our eyeballs in Kasani soldiers," Hildegard said.

"Right." He leapt onto Solaris's back and took off into the chill winter sky. Beneath him, he still saw evidence of the Kasani soldiers in pursuit. *Oh, gods, I hope Tai and the others get back okay.* Fighting back a painful tightening in his chest, he said, "Randyl. Gods. I'm sorry."

He thought back to what Sullivan said earlier. Sullivan was right. This couldn't have been a mere coincidence. The Kasani knew to expect them. And this was far from the first smuggling run where this had happened. Callahan's forces just seemed to always know what the rebels were going to do. It was like they were one step ahead.

Dorian didn't know if it was because of Corynne or not, but someone was leaking information to their enemies. And if it was Corynne, then this meant the entire fiasco was Dorian's fault.

Bradford straightened his silk brocade coat and ran a hand through his curly brown hair. He usually only wore his nobleman's clothes when he traveled back home to his holdings in Frostvale, but today he wanted to make a good impression. He flashed his most charming smile before the mirror, but shook his head, resuming a grim expression. It did no good, pretending nothing had changed. Everything had changed.

Taking a deep breath and drawing himself to his full height, he marched down the corridors to the cavern they'd sealed off as a makeshift prison. He felt a slight tingle as he passed through the barrier of the Void. Even though he knew to expect it, the abrupt vanishing of the ambient magic still set his teeth on edge.

There, sitting primly on her makeshift cot, was Corynne. Seeing her felt like coming home. The good parts and the bad.

It was easy to recall why, in another life, Bradford assumed he'd one day marry his best friend's sister. He'd never found her as captivating as Saedra's guardswoman — he doubted he'd ever feel that way about anyone ever again. But Corynne had always been gorgeous in her own way.

Moons of training as a dragonaut had turned Corynne's soft curves into tough, whipcord muscle. While it would be a long time before she was as burly as someone like Vivienne, Bradford couldn't deny the effect was rather fetching.

Bradford entertained a moment's fancy of Corynne and Vivienne, together in their fighting leathers, tying him up and — *Not appropriate, Bradford,* he reprimanded himself.

"It's good to see you, Corynne."

Corynne raised her head in a dignified manner, removing a stray golden lock from her face. "Come to mock me some more?"

"Not to mock you, my dear," he said in what he hoped was his most charming voice. "Never to mock you."

Her blue eyes narrowed. "That response itself mocks me."

Bradford sighed. She was acting exactly as he feared she might. "For what it's worth, I'm sorry," he said. "I never meant things to turn out the way they did between us."

"You never meant for it, and yet, here we are."

Bradford cleared his throat. "I was hoping you'd help me with something, is all. We need not remain enemies." He knew as soon as the words left his mouth that they would do no good.

Corynne laughed. "And why, in the name of all the Gods and Ancients, would I help you?"

Bradford sighed. "Your freedom," he said. "And... and for the sake of what we once were."

This was the wrong thing to say. Corynne's second scoff was even more derisive than the first. "*What we once were*," she repeated. "And what would that be, exactly? A sham, a farce, a passing dalliance to be tossed carelessly aside the moment some tartlet of a foreign princess entered the picture?"

Bradford felt his shoulders slump. "You know I didn't have any choice in that."

Another snort. "And her harlot of a guard? Did you have a choice in that?"

"Vivienne's not a harlot." Bradford bristled, but took a deep breath and forced an even tone. "I... never meant to hurt you," he repeated, though why he thought it would do any good, he didn't know. "I was... a different person, back then."

To his surprise, this garnered a reaction. "We've all changed," she said, expression pensive. But then her face twisted into an ironic smile. "That brother of yours, especially. Is he single?"

"I'm... certain I don't know," Bradford said delicately.

"Hmm," she leaned against the wall, staring up at the faint blue glow of the aether lamp. "Not vehemently denying that he's your brother? My, my, you have changed." She frowned, fiddling with something underneath the sleeve of her plain homespun dress. "You know, I'm kind of surprised you're running this little rebellion, given you never had the guts to stand up to your father before."

Bradford cleared his throat again. "Yes. Well."

"Seems almost a pity I have to put an end to it." She said the words so conversationally that at first, Bradford almost didn't register them.

"Put... put an end to it?"

"I took quite a risk, you know. If your brother had killed me up there in the sky, my dragonstone would have fallen into the underclouds, never to be seen again. And Callahan would have been *furious*."

"Yes," Bradford coughed. They'd confiscated Corynne's dragon-stone, naturally, when they apprehended her. Bradford kept it in his personal lockbox. Privately, he hoped they might use it towards coaxing another dragon to join their side willingly, and bond with a rebel, but Bradford knew such matters had to be handled delicately. "I can imagine Callahan must be quite upset to have lost it."

"It matters little." Corynne cocked her neck and shrugged her muscular shoulders. "He'll have it back when he overruns the base, I am certain. And Emperor Callahan will richly reward me."

"Over... overruns the base?" Bradford felt a chill run down his spine.

"I'm honestly impressed you were stupid enough to fall for it," she said. "Surely you must have been a little suspicious. Lone drago-naut, out flying patrol all by her little self." She pouted out her lips slightly. "It's true I disobeyed my emperor when I did it, but if the result is leading him to you, I'd say the rewards are well worth the risks."

Only then did Bradford see the blue gem on the bracelet around her left wrist, glittering in the torchlight.

Bradford drew in a sharp breath. "An aether beacon! But we severed your dragon bond and your chamber is Voided. How—"

"Foolish boy," Corynne said. "You know almost nothing, do you?"

Her blue eyes flashed. Except... Corynne had green eyes. He gasped as he saw blue flame reflected behind her gaze. Behind her, so hazy as to be almost invisible, loomed a creature of vivid forest green, cloaked in blue flame.

"Meet Malachite," she said with a twisted grin.

"You're... you're demon possessed," Bradford sputtered. "You bonded a demon *and* a dragon."

"Naturally." Corynne examined her fingernails. "I got the idea from your brother. When your father cast the Void at Saedra's leaving feast. Dorian tried to draw magic from his demon. Didn't you remember?"

"How did you get a signal beacon past the guards?"

"Swallowed it and shat it back out, obviously," Corynne said with a casual flick of her wrist.

Bradford blinked several times. Dainty, uptight Corynne, who hated the way horses smelled and refused to walk in the orchard because she might get dirt on her shoes? "I guess we *have* all changed."

"I have enjoyed toying with you," Corynne purred, catlike, "But now you've figured me out, I'm afraid the game is up."

She tapped a distinctive pattern on the crystal. A pattern Bradford knew too well, from his own aether-sent communications with Lady Sylvia. It was the code transmitting their location.

Bradford swore, then dashed into the corridor. The first person he encountered was Hildegard, still dressed in riding gear and marching purposefully away from the gryphon aerie.

"Hildegard!"

She raised her hand into a hasty salute. "My Lord!"

"We're evacuating the base," he said without preamble.

"Evacuating? Of... of course, sir. Evacuating where?"

Bradford ran a nervous hand through his curly hair. In his panic, he'd not given much thought to where they would evacuate *to*.

*Void Eternal, where else?*

"We're... going to ask the Order for help."

Bradford had only one reason to trust the Dragonmar, and about a thousand reasons not to. But the one outweighed the thousand. It *had* to.

"Send an aether signal to Cloudfire," Bradford commanded Hildegard. "Tell Lady Sylvia to expect company."

# CHAPTER TWENTY-NINE

# THE BATTLE OF THE DRAGON'S FANGS

Behind them, the spires of the Dragon's Fangs receded. Ahead, there was nothing but clouds. Clouds, and the city of Cloudfire. Dorian recalled Tai telling him all about the mountaintop Orith city. The liminal place between the sky and the underclouds, the only part of lost, sunken Orith to reach the sky. It was the only place tied to Orith where skyships could land.

There, Bradford promised them, they would find safety until they could regroup and resume the fight against Callahan. But even that reassuring news was not enough to quell the tempest inside Dorian's soul.

Dorian concentrated all of his will on the effort of flying. The wind in his hair, the glowing motes of magic, the strain of his muscles as he swam through the Linking. These sensations alone prevented him from dissolving into a sobbing mess.

*It's all my fault.* The thought ran through his mind, again and again, a never-ending chorus. *We're forced to flee because of me.*

Dorian doubted the other rebels would think he was much of a hero now. But he didn't fear their disdain. He could handle disdain. He was *used* to disdain. But how many would die because of his poor judgement? *Randyl. Lucien.* Maybe even Hildegard. He'd spared Corynne's life, but in doing so, how many of his friends had he condemned to death?

*No matter what I do, he thought, I always get people hurt or killed.*

*No.* Dorian couldn't think about that. *Mustn't* think about that. Far more important to protect those who remained. He couldn't undo what had happened, but at least he could make sure as many people survived as possible.

Bradford appeared in the Linking, forcing Dorian out of his glum reverie.

"Oh!" Bradford stared out at the expansive vistas of floating islands below them. "Sweet Ancients, we're, ah, rather high, aren't we?"

He looked paler than usual, and rather like he might throw up.

Dorian felt a smile threatening at the corner of his mouth, cracking through his fear and guilt. "You've never been in the Linking before?"

"I've flown on gryphons," Bradford said, a trifle defensive, "But this is something else entirely."

Dorian let a genuine smile cross his face. "It's wonderful, isn't it?"

Bradford grimaced, looking in terror at the space of empty sky beneath him. "Not quite the word I would use, but I'm glad you like it." He straightened himself and cleared his throat. "Dorian. Xander. I need a word."

"Right," Xander said, "Our young lordling might piss his pants if he's in the Linking much longer, so Tai, Falgar, Sullivan, you take things from here. I trust you have our escape well in hand."

"I would *not* piss my pants," Bradford said, once the three of them emerged back on the deck. But he looked vastly relieved to have solid wood beneath his feet again, and he still looked a little green.

Bradford stared pensively at the darkening sky, running a finger along the smooth, red wood of the *Phoenix's* railing. "I've... not been entirely honest with you two."

"There's a shock," Xander grumbled, but without true malice. "Figured you must have secrets. Hard to lead a rebellion without keeping some things from some people."

Bradford sighed. "Yes, but this time I fear my mistake might have cost us dearly. The truth is... soon after my father left with Queen Saedra, I received an unexpected visitor." He hesitated, sucking his teeth as he considered what to say next. "By the name of Sylvia Kane."

Xander nodded. "I figured that must be the case."

"She's there," Bradford said, "In Cloudfire. That's who, I very much hope, will take us in."

"Well, she'll have to listen to us," Xander mused. He paced the length of the deck. Carefully, he said, "You know who she is? You... understand the implications?"

Bradford drew in a deep breath, then let it out. "Yes."

"Um." Dorian swallowed. "Sorry, but... *I* don't understand the implications."

Xander and Bradford exchanged wary glances.

"She wanted me to fight Callahan." Dorian got the impression that Bradford was side-stepping the question. "I would have done so anyway, of course. But the Order isn't supposed to take sides in political conflict. So Sylvia asked me to do it."

"Oh," Dorian said. "But... if she's not supposed to take sides... why should she help us now?"

"Because I have something compelling to offer," Bradford said. "Rather, someone. Someones."

Dorian blinked. "Who?"

«My dear rider, I adore you, but I wonder often how one so seemingly intelligent can simultaneously be so utterly oblivious,» Solaris interjected.

"Me!" Dorian yelped, but it made sense when he thought about it. "Of course. Solaris, and Hematite, and me."

Bradford swallowed. "There's something important you should know. Sylvia—"

Bradford cut off at the flashing beacon in the distance. Red for emergency. He watched the blinking pattern intently.

*Under attack. Enemy dragonauts present. Enemy must not learn fleet destination. All mounted units to action.*

"Void," Dorian swore. "All mounted units to action. That'd be me."

His stomach did a nervous flip-flop at the thought of leaving his friends on the *Phoenix* behind. But of all the rebels, he was the best equipped to fight dragonauts, and so fight dragonauts he would.

Bradford raised his hand in alarm. "Wait!"

But too late. Dorian leapt onto Solaris's back and took off into the overcast sky.

It started raining. Large wet droplets pounded one after another on the top of Dorian's head, all but drowning out the sounds of battle. As the rivulets ran down his face, he almost, almost regretted not having time to put a helmet on.

Gryphons and ornithopters darted all around in the macabre dance of battle. Among them, Dorian counted three enemy dragonauts. The only three left, save for Callahan and Nocturne themselves. One dragonaut, a stocky woman riding an enormous golden beast, was locked in fierce combat with a gryphon-mounted Graigor Beckett.

That had to be Vivienne, Dorian realized with a pang. He watched them fight for a moment and instinctively rooted for Saedra's guardswoman. He shook his head frantically, realizing how inappropriate that was, and flew on. There was little he could do for either of them just now. Graigor seemed to hold his own, at any rate, so Dorian turned his attention to the other two dragons.

The next dragon he saw was surely Celestian, so that meant—

"Kadmin."

He made to dive for his enemy, but pulled up short when he saw the other dragonaut, mounted on a sleek purple beast, bear down upon Hildegard. She was fighting one of the ornithopter-mounted soldiers and didn't see the incoming danger.

"Hildegard!" Dorian shouted, but she was too far away to hear.

*No, no, no.* His heart was in his throat. If, in sparing Corynne's life, he caused Hildegard to get killed...

*No.* He wouldn't think about that. He had to act.

*He dove towards her, all pretense of safety forgotten. Only two hundred gryphon lengths between them, only one hundred...*

"Hildegard!"

Slowly, mercifully, Hildegard turned around. So did the dragonaut.

"You!" the dragonaut, Ambrose Dorian thought his name was, turned towards Dorian. Abandoning Hildegard, Ambrose drew his sword and dove towards Dorian.

The enemy dragonaut wore chain mail armor but no helmet, his curly hair soaked in the rain. Mingled blood and rainwater streamed across his hard, menacing face.

As Dorian dove in for the attack, Solaris swiped her diamond-sharp claws across the purple dragon's face, giving the creature a wound to match his rider's. The violet dragon cried out in rage and charged for Solaris, but she and Dorian darted away in a swift barrel roll.

«I am sorry about this, Northstar,» Solaris said.

«If you free me from this monster,» he heard Northstar reply in a tense mindvoice, «I shall forgive any pain you cause in doing it.»

Ambrose wheeled Northstar around for another attack, but Dorian was ready for it. He was sure Ambrose would not have joined Callahan's dragonauts if he were a truly poor fighter. Yet Ambrose and Northstar seemed clumsy, almost cumbersome. Dorian and Solaris had no problem outmaneuvering them.

Dorian lit his dragonaut's sword aflame and aimed at the dragon's neck. He didn't manage as graceful a swipe as he had done against Borealis, but a slit throat was a slit throat. Northstar screamed. But as he faded to transparency, he nodded in thanks to

Dorian and Solaris, and streamed off to join the battle. Ambrose, eyes wide, seemed to hover midair for an exaggerated moment.

"I'm sorry, Ambrose." Dorian's second murder horrified him every bit as much as the first one. He knew nothing about this man he'd consigned to death, except that he was a dragon slaver.

Ambrose seemed to hope that Dorian would reconsider and catch him. He gazed up imploringly at them as he fell. Then an arrow soared straight through Ambrose's heart. The dead dragonaut's eyes glazed over as he descended into the cloud layer.

Dorian looked up in surprise to see Hildegard on her gryphon, crossbow in hand.

"See now, technically, you didn't kill him."

Dorian forced a smile. He appreciated the gesture, but dead was dead, and Hildegard could have saved the arrow. He nervously scanned the skies for the other dragonauts. Graigor and Vivienne were nowhere to be found. And where was Kadmin? Why had none of them tried to help Ambrose?

He found the answer almost at once. The indigo dragon, Celestian, hovered far to the west, away from the battle. Dorian's blood ran cold. The *Phoenix*. Heart plummeting as surely as Ambrose's corpse, Dorian and Solaris dove towards them as fast as their wings could take them.

It wasn't fast enough.

Dorian looked on in horror as Celestian opened his indigo-blue jaws.

A gout of flame, blue-white and hot, erupted from the dragon. The flame shot straight for the *Phoenix*, setting her aether sails ablaze.

*No. No no no nonononono.*

Dorian couldn't think. Half blind with panic and horror, he dove towards the *Phoenix*, his home, the vessel carrying almost every person in the world Dorian loved. The burning ship shuddered in the sky, but didn't lose altitude, the flames and the driving rain cloaking the skyship in mist and smoke. Maybe the rain would put out the flames on time. Maybe there was still a chance. He had to get to them. Had to help.

Hematite and Solaris both screamed in his mind, but he scarcely understood them. His own hammering thoughts drove them both out. The only thing that mattered to Dorian right now was saving his friends.

Kadmin cut across him, a streak of dark blue.

"I don't think so." Athame at the ready, Kadmin whipped out the sigils for a barrier spell, flinging them at Dorian as if they were arrows.

The spell shoved Dorian and Solaris backwards. For a dizzying moment, it was all he could do to hold on as the dragon turned end over end in midair. With great effort, Dorian righted himself, panting for breath and glaring at Kadmin.

"I believe I owe you some payback for Ashe Valerian."

"Get out of my way!" Rage and pain clouded Dorian's vision as tears mingled with the driving rain. He didn't have time to deal with Kadmin.

Kadmin, however, shook his head and smirked. "No can do, pretty boy."

*Pretty boy?* Dorian forgot all about Kadmin's mockery, however, as soon as the other dragonaut drew his sword. Dorian's chest tightened.

«No,» Solaris said. «It cannot be.»

Kadmin's sword was silver where Dorian's was gold, and the gem at the pommel was indigo rather than scarlet. Other than that, however, it was an identical copy of Dorian's own sword, perfectly balanced for Kadmin's size and strength, the hilt wrought into the shape of a dragon.

«Celestian,» Solaris accused, showering sparks towards the other dragon. «You summoned that blade for him? Willingly?»

Celestian let out a rain of sparks of his own, which Dorian and Solaris only just dodged in time. «Kadmin regrets the necessity of our coming together as much as I do,» Celestian replied. «That does not make us any less compatible.»

"Enough!" Dorian stared in horror at the *Phoenix*, cloaked in smoke. The driving rain had dampened much of the fire. The damage, however, was done. The ship shuddered and wavered in midair, showing all the signs of an aether engine in its death throes. "I. Don't. Have. Time for this!"

He charged Kadmin, sword raised. Kadmin was more than ready for it, and as the two dragonauts' swords clashed, so did dragon fight dragon, clawing and gnashing and spraying silver spirit energy.

Dorian's training with Bradford paid off. When he faced Kadmin back in Goose Head, he'd been thoroughly outclassed. This time, he held his own. For now.

Kadmin charged in for what he clearly hoped would be a killing blow. Dorian raised his sword to block him, wondering if he could withstand it, when Celestian skidded backwards.

"What the—" Kadmin gripped the reigns as he fought to stay on Celestian.

Dorian looked up in just as much surprise. Three ghostly dragons pelted Celestian with magical fire. They darted about, multihued motes of light against the overcast sky.

"I didn't know wild dragons could do that," Dorian said.

«Of course they can. Elder Meteor did it to me, remember?»

Dorian recalled streaming spirit energy and a makeshift silk bandage. For a distracted moment, he watched in awe as the dragons fought. Dorian recognized the golden dragon once bonded to Ashe, the woman he killed. Meridian, he thought her name was. And there was Northstar, the dragon he'd just freed. The third, an incorporeal figure of emerald green, was Corynne's erstwhile dragon, Borealis.

«You came back!» Solaris said, delighted.

«Of course we did,» Borealis said. «Least we could do after you freed us. Now go rescue that falling ship before it crashes into oblivion. We can hold Celestian off for a time, but even the three of us together are no match for a corporeal dragon of his strength.»

"Right! Um, thank you!" Dorian wheeled around and took Solaris into a dive towards the faltering skyship.

His breath fell short when he arrived. The aether engine emitted desperate fits and sparks, fighting to stay alive. Heart sinking, however, Dorian felt sure that it would fail at any moment. With the aether sails burned, they couldn't gather any more magic from the air, either. And without magic, there could be no Linking. The ship would not stay afloat.

"Maybe — maybe if we carry everyone to one of the other ships," Dorian thought out loud, fighting off the upwelling of panic threatening to burst from his chest.

«There is no time,» Solaris said. Already the failing *Phoenix* was descending towards the underclouds. «We must land the ship safely.»

"But if there's no magic, how can we — *Oh*," he gasped, sudden realization dawning on him.

«You know,» Hematite said, «I believe this may be the most foolhardy thing you have ever done.» But his mindvoice held none of its usual reproach. In a resigned sort of way, he almost sounded admiring.

Determination burning inside him, he and Solaris plunged towards the ship, just in time for the *Phoenix* to disappear beneath the clouds.

# THE PHOENIX AFLAME

"Come on," Tai begged of the aether engine as she cranked its heavy lever in manic desperation. "Come on, I know you have more in you. Come on, come on, come *on.*"

Tai wiped the driving rain out of her eyes, her short dark hair matted to her head like a wet, glistening helmet. Her soaked feathers weighed heavily on her back. To her left, Lord Bradford leaned over the railing, puking his guts out. She might have felt sorry for him, were they not all about to suffer much worse.

To her right, Falgar and Sullivan fought to coax some sort of power out of the burned and frayed aether sails. But Tai feared it was all to no avail. She considered herself a passable skyship mechanic, but she didn't think all the mechanical talent in the world could save the *Phoenix's* failing engine.

"Come on," she repeated, almost plaintively.

*At least Dorian got out on Solaris, she thought. At least he has a chance.*

Now that she was about to die, a sentimental part of her regretted that she'd been so distant with him these past few weeks. It wasn't his fault she had feelings for him. It all seemed so foolish now. Now, selfishly, what she wanted most (apart from fixing the engine, of course) was to see him one last time before she plunged to a fiery death.

Unexpectedly, she got her wish at once.

Solaris came careening down onto the deck, depositing Dorian, who rolled off her back with impressive grace. He sprung to his feet at once and made straight for the Linking circle.

"Dorian!" she gasped. "What — what are you doing here?"

"You bloody pit wraith," Falgar interjected, looking up from his losing battle with the sail. "You're going to get yourself killed with the rest of us."

"Nobody's going to get killed," Dorian said. Swallowing, he added, "I hope."

He unsheathed his athame and started working.

"What is he doing?" Bradford asked with wan-faced curiosity.

"Saving all our lives," Captain Xander said.

For the briefest moment, Tai allowed herself to hope. The engine sputtered and then sprung to life. The Linking circle shone vivid blue. Then, horribly, the ship gave a violent shudder as their last working aether crystal sparked and died.

*That one lasted a whole moon and a half,* she thought, in an odd, detached way. They *had* gotten better at flying efficiently. But she supposed it didn't matter, now.

Tai, already soaked to the bone, shivered and pulled her coat closer to herself. But the rain already soaked the garment through, so it offered no comfort. With the engine dead, there was nothing to stop the *Phoenix* from falling into the underclouds. Nothing but splinters of the once-proud skyship would ever reach the Orith.

Dorian seemed to pay little heed to their impending doom as he carved more sigils into the air. He stuck his tongue out in concentration.

*He's recreating the Linking from memory, Tai thought, impressed. He is excellent with sigils.*

"How are you doing that?" Sullivan wondered. "The engine's dead."

"Don't need an engine," Dorian said. "I have a dragon. Make sure the safety lines are secure." He grimaced. "This might get bumpy."

To Tai's surprise, his spell worked. The Linking Circle sprung back to life, sputtering and shaking, but functional. Without further explanation, he dove into the circle, and Solaris followed. Tai made to follow him too, but the Linking circle once more faded and died. Apparently, the makeshift circle could hold only the dragon and her bond.

"Be careful," Tai shouted, but she wasn't sure he heard her.

«All right.» Dorian breathed in and out, feeling the Linking shudder around him. «I can do this. *We* can do this.»

«Naturally,» Solaris agreed.

«If we must,» Hematite conceded.

Dorian's stomach clenched in fear, anyway. He needed to use Solaris to power the ship. What if, in trying to help his friends, he ended up harming his dragon? In response, she sent a burst of affection and reassurance.

«It will be fine, my dear human. I have more than enough power for this.»

Dorian nodded and swallowed his fear.

Every inch of him trembled as Dorian climbed on Solaris's back. Together, they took the skyship downward, into the clouds. The permanent underclouds embraced him, cold and daunting. Lightning illuminated the steel gray sky.

*Gods*, he thought, it really was like a giant Voidstorm.

And like a Voidstorm, the gale force winds assaulted him at once, without warning. The sudden gust of turbulent energy knocked the air out of his lungs.

"What — what the —" he sputtered.

Sparks danced in front of his eyes as he fought desperately to right himself. Solaris felt reassuringly solid underneath him, the only stable thing in this maelstrom. Together, they fiercely seized back control.

He'd never flown the ship while also flying on Solaris before. Now, he wondered why he'd not tried it moons ago. With the same strength and unity of purpose they displayed when flying outside the Linking, they darted between clouds, dodging bolts of lightning, fighting back against gale-force winds.

Thank the Gods for Solaris, too. Flying in the Linking was so much easier with his crew at his side. On his own, Dorian felt like he was flying with one hand behind his back. Without his dragon, he knew it would be near impossible to fly the damaged vessel at all. But together, they flew. He even dared hope they flew well.

"I can do this," he panted once more. "I can definitely do this."

If he said it enough, he might convince himself it was true.

Strangely, however, even in the storm, with his entire attention focused on the flight, he felt better. It was easier to let go of his fear, his shame, his regret. *This.* This was where he belonged, what he was meant for. The sky, the ship, the clouds, they were his lifeblood, pumping through his veins and setting his soul on fire. He laughed out loud with joy and defiance, shaking, raising his fist into the turbulent air.

Solaris thrummed with fierce pride and affection. «My dear rider,» she said, «I could ask for none better to fly with than you.»

The unforgiving skies, however, rarely rewarded arrogance. A violent whirlwind caught him off guard. Dorian fought to keep stable, but the ship twisted the opposite direction. Dorian felt an odd moment of weightlessness as the wind tossed him free of Solaris's back. He looked down and saw only clouds. His stomach plummeted, and then so did he.

«Dorian!»

The dragon dove for him, batting at the winds with her golden wings. She caught Dorian deftly by the arm with her right front claw.

«Thank—» Dorian began, but before he could finish the thought, another gust hit them. He almost thought he heard the crack of his arm breaking. For a second he was so shocked he didn't register the pain. But then it came. White-hot agony lanced through him, causing him to cry out in anguish.

«Dorian!» Solaris cried again.

She nudged her scarlet head under him, and somehow, somehow, he re-seated himself. Leaning desperately against her golden neck ridges with his one good arm, he strained to maintain control of the ship. His heart thudded in his chest and his vision began to tunnel.

«Just a bit further. Just a bit further.» He wasn't sure whose thoughts those were. They repeated over and over in his head, in tune with his heartbeat. «Just a bit further and we can rest.»

*Rest.*

That was when it occurred to him. Dorian was going to die. He might bring the ship down safely, but the effort of it would probably kill him. And in that moment, Dorian realized he didn't care.

Dorian would not let his friends die. If this was the last thing he ever did, he would not fail again. *Not this time.* If he died here, now, doing what he loved, protecting the people he loved, well then, he would consider it a life well spent.

Dorian thought he heard something carried through to the Linking from the ship below. "Dorian, you better not die!"

*Tai's voice?*

He thought he heard her say something more, but he couldn't understand it through the gale-force winds.

*I'm sorry, Tai. I don't think I can honor your request. Just please, he prayed fervently to all seven of the gods, Kassoria, Zekador, Natlanti, Valgren, Meroneth, Kyrizzian, Nahiira, all of you, please! Let my friends get down safely.*

«Stop.»

Hematite's mindvoice reverberated like a gong throughout the Linking. And as if on command, everything *did* stop. The storm, the clouds, and the ship below all slowed down to an eerie, unnatural stillness. Hematite flew out ahead of him, startlingly solid, his flickering green flames the only movement Dorian could see. Even the agony of his broken arm faded to a dull ache.

«The gods cannot hear you in this place. But I can.»

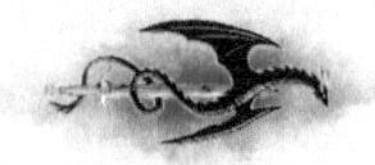

Tai watched from the *Phoenix's* deck as the ghostly forms of Dorian and Solaris fought their way through the maelstrom. She didn't see the strange way time seemed to slow down and stop within the Linking. But she saw Dorian fly. *By all the Gods and Ancients*, that man could fly.

It felt wrong, though, painfully wrong, to sit on the deck clinging to her safety harness, while Dorian did all the work below him. She imagined this was how Sullivan must have felt when he broke his arm, or how Dorian felt when he thought he thought he wasn't competent enough to become a true aeronaut.

*Well,* she thought with fierce pride in her friend, *the tables have turned on us now.*

Considering their ship was on fire just a few short moments ago, she thought they were all holding together very well. True, Bradford had only stopped throwing up because his stomach had no more contents to give. And Falgar looked more terrified than Tai had ever seen him, clinging to Sullivan while the larger man awkwardly patted him on the back. But they were all uninjured, and Tai considered that nothing less than a Mystictide Miracle.

"I must thank you, Lord Bradford, for suggesting I bring this one onto my crew," Captain Xander shouted into the storm as he clung to his lifeline. "I'd say he's proven more than worth it!"

Bradford gave a shaky smile. "He's... quite good, isn't he?"

"Guess it shouldn't surprise me," Xander said. "Given who his parents were and all."

Bradford smiled, but it turned into a grimace as he fought back another wave of illness. "Pity Mother didn't pass any of that flying skill on to me."

"You got her political savvy instead," Xander said. "Our Dorian, bless him, couldn't politick his way out of a burlap sack."

Bradford made a sound that was halfway between a laugh and a groan. "Is that why you haven't told him the truth?"

Xander moved a wet strand of hair from his face. "Truth? What truth?"

"You know full well what truth. He isn't weak," Bradford shouted through the gale. "I used to think so, but he's not."

"Weakness has nothing to do with it," Xander said. "It isn't my truth to tell."

Tai didn't intend to eavesdrop, but she listened with burning curiosity, anyway. What secret was Captain Xander keeping from Dorian? What secret was he keeping from *all* of them?

A sudden, fierce gust of wind hit them, driving off all thoughts of the captain or his secrets. She barely had time to think at all before the ship turned over on its side.

Desperate, she clutched to her safety line, ensuring the clasp was in place. She tried to check on the others, but saw nothing around her but gray and driving rain. All her regrets flashed to the forefront of her mind, all the things she didn't do or say.

"Dorian!" she cried into the gale. "Dorian, you better not die! I love you, you colossal idiot!"

The winds carried her cries into the maelstrom.

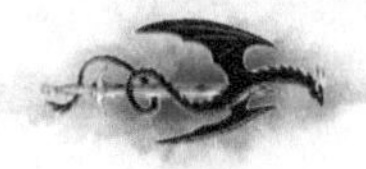

Dorian used the momentary calm to catch his breath. "What... what is happening?"

«Do you remember your first time flying in a Voidstorm?»

"We're about to die. Is this really the time to be reminiscing?"

«This is the *only* time to do so. So I ask again. Do you remember your first Voidstorm?»

Dorian nodded, perplexed. "Of course I do. It's kind of difficult to forget. I broke Sullivan's arm." He laughed weakly and looked at his own arm, hanging to the side at a useless angle. Feeling ill, he looked away. "Voidstorms appear to be hazardous to arms."

The demon smiled, revealing rows of pointy teeth. «And yet you returned to the Linking. Again and again and again. I did not approve, at first, you know.»

"Yeah," Dorian said, staring down at the clouds. "I know."

«Alas,» Hematite said, «My approval is not what is relevant. You kept flying and kept flying, until today,» he gave a telepathic laugh, «You are single-handedly flying a broken skyship through the Void begotten Wraith Clouds.»

*Wraith clouds.* Dorian felt a chill.

"Ah," Dorian said, "Well. Solaris is helping. But, um, do you suppose you could tell me what's happening? With the whole, um, time stopping, and all?"

«That depends on you.»

"Right. But, um, like I said. Kind of about to die. So I *really* don't understand why you're asking all these bizarre, vague questions."

Frustrated, Dorian urged Solaris to push the ship forward. They needed to finish passing through the storm. But Solaris didn't move. She floated eerily still; her shining blue eyes stared ahead into nothing. Dragon and ship both remained firmly rooted in place.

«Solaris?» With increasing panic, he reached towards her through their bond, but she felt distant, unresponsive.

«What did you do to Solaris?» Dorian demanded.

«Solaris is fine,» Hematite said. With something like fondness, he added, «I would never hurt her. I have temporarily created a pocket in time. But I cannot hold it much longer. You are asking me to betray all I have ever known. I need to know if it is worth it.»

Dorian gaped at him. He did not know what any of that meant. But he was almost certain he'd never asked Hematite to betray *anything*.

«Not in words,» Hematite said. «But you ask me all the same. So tell me, Dorian Valmont. Who *are* you?»

Outside the frozen time bubble, the ship violently flipped on its side.

Falgar swung from his safety line, heart in his throat, feeling a bit like vomiting. *Gods*, he should be handling this better. He'd swung over the side of the *Phoenix* countless other times in safety drills. *Zekador's poorly fitting pants,* though, he'd never watched the ship threaten to break apart before his eyes before. And in the *cloud layer,* for the Ancients' sakes. The Void-begotten cloud layer! He thought he had every *right* to be terrified out of his mind.

At least he was doing better than the Bradford upstart princeling. That boy looked even paler than usual, and Falgar hadn't been sure that was *possible*. But there on his other side was Sullivan, clinging to his safety line as calm and stoic as ever.

*Valmont will save us or he won't, the imaginary Sullivan said in his head. There's nothing we can do about it. Sullivan always said that kind of thing. Don't worry about what you can't control.*

*Falgar always hated that adage. Imaginary Sullivan, he thought,*

*Don't you see? Things I can't control are the only things worth worrying about. If I could control it, I wouldn't need to worry about it, would I?*

No sooner had the thought crossed his mind than his eyes grazed over to Sullivan's lifeline. The knot around his waist held steady. Above him, though, with a feeling of ice water shot through his veins, Falgar saw the unmistakable signs of fraying rope.

*No! Meroneth's balls. I just inspected that line this morning! No, no, no!*

"Sullivan!" he cried into the wind.

Miracle of miracles, Sullivan heard him. He looked at Falgar just as a hemp strand snapped loose, then another, then another.

Falgar let out a wordless cry and swung his own line towards Sullivan.

Sullivan shouted something that might have been, "What?"

The line snapped free just as Falgar reached Sullivan. Still screaming his desperation, Falgar seized his friend, and not a moment too soon. He strained against the weight of the muscular Sanorian, clinging to fistfuls of his clothing with more desperate urgency than he'd ever felt in his entire life.

Brown eyes wide with shock, Sullivan hoisted one muscular arm around Falgar, then grabbed their shared lifeline with the other.

"Falgar," Sullivan said. "You—"

Falgar tightened his arms around Sullivan's waist. "Don't let go of me, Sullivan," he said. "Don't you dare let go."

Falgar wasn't sure what made him do it. Perhaps the adrenaline rushing through his veins, or their impending demise. Without thinking, Falgar pulled Sullivan forward and kissed him. And for that single instant there was nowhere else Falgar wanted to be except dangling from a safety line in the middle of a perilous Voidstorm clinging to Sullivan for dear life.

Which was why, of course, Dorian Bloody Valmont chose that moment to regain control of the ship. The *Phoenix* jolted upright, and the faltering wards lurched back to life, pulling them back towards the deck in an awkward tumble. Falgar, luckily, being the lighter of the two, landed on top.

"Sorry," he said. With the swift efficiency earned through many practice drills, he unclipped the broken line from Sullivan's harness and clipped in a fresh one. "I guess I should have asked your permission before I did that."

Sullivan blinked, looking unsure, for a moment, whether to laugh or cry.

"Permission granted," he said, and pulled Falgar towards him once more.

«Tell me,» the demon repeated, «Who are you?»

Dorian let out a nervous laugh. "*You've* been living in my head for the past ten years. If anyone knows who I am, it's you."

«Answer the question.»

"Oh, for the love of the Void," Dorian grumbled. He couldn't for the life of him figure out why the demon was doing this *now*. "I'm Dorian Valmont. Dragonaut. Aeronaut. Awkward nobody from Adenthul. I like sigils, and I like pies, and I like flying. Is that what you want to hear? I've murdered two people. I've gotten countless others killed, trying *not* to murder. I got my father killed, too."

«*Wrong*!» Hematite's mindvoice bellowed. Below, the ghostly *Phoenix* shuddered.

"Okay, okay," Dorian waved his good hand. "So technically, that last one was an accident. And the... and the thing with the rebellion... I did what I thought was right. I didn't think Corynne would... I was foolish." His voice caught. "But I *still did what I thought was right*."

«Good, good.» Perhaps it was imagination, but the demon almost seemed to grow stronger, treating Dorian's answers like a food source. But Dorian saw no tendrils of shining white spirit energy between the two of them. «do you *enjoy* fighting?»

"Sometimes," Dorian admitted, hating himself for it. "I enjoy sparring. You know. For fun. The real stuff, only... only when I have to." He swallowed. "Because there are times... I think sometimes not taking action would be worse."

Hematite's blue flames intensified. «And flying? What possessed you, who broke your dear friend Sullivan's arm in your first abysmal attempt at Linking, to pursue the art with such a single-minded determination that you are taking on the cloud layer a scant year later?»

Dorian snorted. This, at least, he could answer genuinely, and without remorse. "I love it," he said. "I love everything about it."

«Oh?» Hematite prodded.

Dorian drew in a deep breath, taking in the lightning and the clouds, the swirling motes of magic, Solaris's glittering ruby scales, and the ghostly form of the *Phoenix* he pulled behind him. "When I'm in the sky," he said at last, "I no longer feel quite so broken."

Hematite radiated a powerful emotion, a mixture of sadness and pride. «The god Meroneth sent us demons to your plane, to be your guides and guardians. Our purpose is to... protect the mortals from themselves. In pursuing this goal, I have tried to make you what you are not. In the end, I failed.»

Dorian stared ahead at the eerily still clouds. In the distance, a single lightning bolt glowed, frozen in time. "You were a good friend to me, Hematite. I don't think I ever would have survived those years in Frostvale without you. Good books, warm fires, hot mulled cider, all the things we enjoyed together. That wasn't false. That *is* who I am. I love those things. But... the wind in my hair and the exhilaration of flight and the thrill of a good sparring match... that's who I am, too. It's possible to be both at once."

Hematite responded with a wave of affection and sadness. «Perhaps so, for humans. I wish... at least, there is a part of me that wishes that it were so for demons too.» His flames flickered as he continued, «All places but here, Meroneth would forbid me from helping you. Here in the underclouds, however, we are invisible to Meroneth's watchful eye.» The demon laughed. «With this final act, I preserve the spirit of my vows, if not the letter.»

"I don't understand."

Hematite shook his head. «I fear this is goodbye, Dorian Valmont. For what it is worth, I have enjoyed our time together. Though things did not turn out the way I would have chosen, you have every right to be proud of who you are. I am proud too. I ask you not to blame yourself for what I am about to do. In this, I act of my own free will.»

"Wait, what?"

Hematite's sapphire flames flared so high they almost blinded Dorian. The demon sped forward, blue fire and silver-white spirit energy trailing behind in a magnificent plume. He bore a tunnel through the clouds, an opening through which there was no lightning or turbulence. When Hematite broke through to the other side, he vanished.

«Hematite? *Hematite?*»

The demon did not respond. His presence vanished entirely from Dorian's mind.

«*Hematite!*»

The pain of Dorian's broken arm came surging back as time returned to normal.

«Dorian!» Solaris came back to him, alarmed. «What happened? I felt like... I am uncertain what I felt.»

"Hematite," Dorian gasped through the pain. "He..."

Well, Dorian wasn't sure what Hematite had done.

«He saved our lives,» Solaris finished for him, awed.

The tunnel Hematite bore through the clouds hungrily sucked them down. It was as if Hematite had pulled the plug on a washtub, and Dorian, Solaris, and the *Phoenix* were droplets of water rapidly circling towards the drain.

And then, in an instant, it was over.

The ship emerged on the other side, out of the clouds and into an empty sky. Above, bursts of lightning occasionally illuminated the billowing gray clouds. Below was the soft light of a luminescent forest, trees glowing silver.

*Orith.*

For the first time in a thousand years, a ship emerged in the skies above Orith.

# CHAPTER THIRTY-ONE

# PICKING UP THE PIECES

They emerged from the cloud layer without warning, the sky around them clearing and revealing the silver-white forests of Orith below. Tai knew from the shape of the river and the proximity to the base of Cloudfire that they must be in Toreen, close to the town where she grew up. She drew in a deep breath at the view she'd never expected to see again.

*Home.*

The *Phoenix* began its slow but adamant descent, the silver-white trees of home rising to meet them.

Dorian, in his ghostly form above them, did all he could to slow the fall, but the *Phoenix* could handle no more. With a sickening lurch, they plunged into the trees, branches cracking, splintering beneath the weight of the wooden vessel. Tai clung to her safety line.

"Oh, Void." Tai's voice was high, giddy with adrenaline.

Tai heard more than felt the crash, a terrible crunching and groaning of splitting wood. When the motion at last ceased, she rose unsteadily to her feet.

"Is everyone alright?" Tai was fine, of course; Orith could fall a considerable distance without injury. But she worried about the safety of the others.

Thankfully, however, except for a few scrapes and bruises, the others seemed in good condition. Even Henrietta and Mrs. Pennyfeather, although vexed at the commotion, seemed otherwise unharmed, letting out a long stream of clucked complaints while they picked at an overturned sack of grain.

And there, in the center of what had once been the Linking circle, red-faced, on his knees, heaving for breath, was Dorian.

"Dorian!" Bradford half-ran, half-lurched over and engulfing his brother in a fierce bear hug.

"Gah—" Dorian gasped.

"Dead," Bradford said, tears streaming down his face. "I thought we were dead for sure. Then *you* came and... and that *flying*... that was... *Zekador's Poorly Fitting Pants,* Dorian. Where did you learn to *fly* like that?"

"He learned here on the *Phoenix,*" Xander said with a note of pride.

Dorian gave a weak smile. Then he collapsed again, holding himself up with a single good arm.

"He's hurt!" Tai covered her mouth in horror.

Sullivan hurried over to inspect Dorian's broken arm. "Oh, dear. Well, let me just get this splinted up for you." He used the blade of his athame to cut open the front of Dorian's blood-stained shirt. "Doesn't seem like so long ago you and Falgar were doing this for me. This is, I believe, the second time you've saved my life."

Dorian smiled wanly. "Guess we're even now."

Sullivan snorted. "I'd say so." He pushed back the fabric and examined Dorian's arm with professional scrutiny. "Oh, dear. More than made up for it, I think."

"Is it bad?" Falgar asked, looking paler than usual.

"No, no, I can splint it up. Unfortunately, I can't cast a Healing spell down here."

"We'll need to head to Cloudfire," Tai said. "It's above the clouds, so magic works there."

Falgar blanched. "We have to go through those clouds *again?*"

Tai shook her head. "It's not so bad, around the mountain. We'll have to march through the rain and the fog, and it won't be pleasant, but it won't be another Voidstorm."

"Thank the Ancients for that," Falgar said. "And Valmont can see a Healer there?"

"Yes," Sullivan said, "Or I can do it myself."

"Good," Falgar said, "Good. Because if it were serious, and I were to ask how come you're ripping *his* shirt off and not *mine*, that would be really inappropriate."

"*Falgar,*" Sullivan chided, but he smiled, too.

Tai tried to tell herself it was only out of curiosity that she watched him work. It had nothing at all to do with the fact that Dorian Valmont was sitting there with his shirt off, glistening with sweat from the exertion of saving all their lives.

She had always, always considered him attractive. She could admit that to herself, now. However, it startled her, in that moment, just how much he had changed from the soft, pampered boy she'd turned away from the docks in Frostvale over a year ago. At that moment, all she wanted was to throw her arms around him, to bury herself in the hardness of his shoulders and chest, and the softness of his midsection, to explore every inch of him, including the sections still covered by his trousers. *Don't be a pervert,* she thought furiously. But *really.* Bad enough that he was kind, charming, clever, and made her laugh in her surliest of moods. Did he have to look like *that*, too?

*So much for not getting attached.*

She could tell him, she realized. With the *Phoenix* in shambles, they were not crew-mates anymore. He was wounded and vulnerable, yet alight with triumph and relief. This would, she realized, be the perfect time to confess her feelings. She could see, like a Kassoria-granted prophecy, how it might go. After Sullivan finished bandaging him, she would pull him aside in private, and admit that she'd been in love with him for moons. He would be skeptical, and a little embarrassed, but pleased, too. Then he would embrace her — gingerly, of course, because of his injuries — and they would kiss. It seemed so perfect, so right.

But she did not.

Perhaps being in Orith again dredged up all these unpleasant memories of her past. Perhaps it was the knowledge that, with the *Phoenix* destroyed, they were all going to be out of work and their future was uncertain. Whatever the reason, she knew with sickening certainty that if she confessed her feelings to Dorian right now, she'd never accomplish more in life than being the girlfriend of the dragonaut who saved the day. While Tai wasn't looking, Dorian Bloody Valmont had surpassed her in almost every way. Until she could prove herself his equal once more, she felt she had no place by his side.

This realization broke her heart, but she refused to live in the shadow of someone else. *Never again.*

Tai wondered, in a detached, selfish way, what she would do now that the *Phoenix* was destroyed. She thought about the long and arduous process of applying for an aeronaut's position on another ship, and realized that it *wasn't* what she wanted. She might not be willing to attach herself romantically just yet, but she *would not* abandon her crew. They *were* her crew, ship or no ship. She would go with them to Cloudfire, to meet with this Order. And perhaps, just perhaps, she could make a name for herself there.

"Oi, Lunstrum," Xander said, snapping her out of her reverie.

Tai jumped, wings flaring, scattering black feathers. "Hi!" she yelped. "I was just... just..." Just what? *Not ogling my ridiculously attractive best friend. No, certainly not!*

"We've got company," Xander said.

Blushing, she looked the direction the captain was pointing. Two flickering yellow pinpricks of light grew closer through the dim silver-white glow of the trees. Orith carrying torches, she realized.

Someone was flying towards them, probably to see what all the commotion was about.

As they grew closer, she made out their features. They were both quite young, a boy and a girl of perhaps fifteen or sixteen years. The boy had dark wings and hair to match. The girl's hair was also dark, but she kept hers short, and her wings were tawny gold. She must have Kavarian heritage to have wings like that. They flew close enough that she could hear their conversation. Their loud voices suggested they didn't care about being overheard.

"Lucky, lucky us!" the Kavarian girl said in Toreenish. "Finding this crash before anyone else does. I hope there's some good loot inside!"

"Don't get too excited, Lana," the boy responded. "We're required to check for survivors first."

"Survivors?" the girl, Lana, crossed her arms in midair. "There are never any survivors."

"I wouldn't be so sure," the boy responded. "Did that look like an ordinary crash to you? With all those flashing lights? What in the Fallen was that about?"

They flew in closer, and Tai waved her arms. "Greetings and well-met!" she said in Toreenish. It felt strange, almost cumbersome, to speak her native tongue after all these years. "As you can see, we're in a bit of trouble."

Lana did a surprised flip midair. "Fallen, Tanis, you were right!"

Tai's wings tensed as she gave the dark-haired boy a second look. Tanis? Had she said *Tanis*?

Tanis was older now, his sleek black hair grown out, his boyish features given way to adolescence. It was him, though. There could be no mistaking him. Tai's heart pounded. She almost laughed. Of all the people on all the bloody continent, *this* was the first person she met. She had to wonder if perhaps the gods held sway here beneath the underclouds, after all.

Tanis gave Tai as stunned a look as she gave him. "Savior's Wings," he swore. "Tai? Is that you?"

"If I may," Captain Xander said, "My extensive education never quite covered the nuances of the Toreenish language. Just what in the *Void is going on here?*"

Tai's wings fluttered all on their own, a nervous reflex. "Everyone," she said to the crew, "I'd like you to meet my brother."

Xander hummed the ballad of Tanazar Felanthryn to himself as they ascended the steep mountain of Cloudfire.

"You seem happy about something," Dorian observed. The young dragonaut was red-faced, but high-spirited, as they continued the long uphill trek.

"You think so, do you?" Xander asked.

But he was, at that. And why shouldn't he be? Tai and Tanis were reunited, Dorian and Bradford were reunited, and now, finally, he and Sylvia would be reunited. It was a fortuitous time for sibling reunions.

Less than a year ago, Xander had dreaded the prospect. But remarkably, how quickly circumstances could change. He couldn't wait to see the look on her face when he showed up on her doorstep with Cyrus Valmont's boy, a bonded dragon, and the leader of the rebellion. Not to mention all those documents from Greystone Citadel.

Over the past several moons, those crates had become a fixture in the cargo hold, part of the furniture, such that Xander had almost forgotten they were still there. But when they opened the wrecked cargo hold to see what might be salvaged, sure enough, there they were, the crates that held them miraculously intact. The moon glass survived the crash intact too. *More the pity*. As far as Xander was concerned, the world was better off without that thrice cursed thing.

Xander was, in truth, surprised to be so cheerful. His ship was ruined. They'd salvaged the valuables; the cargo, the aether crystals, even Xander's beloved collection of drawings. But the *Phoenix* herself was no more. Xander thought he ought to feel more upset about that.

The *Phoenix* had been Xander's ship for over three Cycles. His ship, his home, his business, his livelihood. He should feel angry, or sad. But what he felt, more than anything, was free. He'd lost a ship, but he may yet gain a family.

"What about you? You holding up all right?" Xander asked the Valmont boy.

It was two days' march from their crash site to the mountain city of Cloudfire. It was tough going, mainly uphill over rough terrain. Xander worried how his crew would take it, but if any of them struggled, they didn't complain.

"Oh, yes," Dorian said, running his good hand along a silvery tree branch. "How often you get to see glowing plants?"

He gestured at the silver-white tree branches with an obviously forced smile. The boy refused to complain, but it was clear he was exhausted.

"Ack!" Dorian gave a sudden yelp as he tripped on a shimmering root.

"Valmont!"

Dorian grabbed a branch with his good arm and clambered to his feet. "Bloody Void." He took in several slow breaths and forced himself to stand straight. "It's fine," he said, panting slightly. "I'll be alright."

Xander waved to signal the others. "We make camp here."

Dorian's eyes widened. "No!" he insisted. "No, I can keep walking. I'm really fine, really. I... I won't hold everyone back."

Xander gave an amused, yet gentle, smile. "Void Eternal, boy. We've been marching through these woods all day now. We're all exhausted. And anyway, we've made good time. I think we can take some well-deserved rest."

Dorian nodded, obviously relieved, though he tried to hide it.

While Tai chopped wood and Falgar and Sullivan got to work building rudimentary shelters, Dorian borrowed some magic from Solaris to start a campfire. He then set about one-handedly preparing supper from some local plant life they'd gathered along the way and provisions they'd salvaged from the ship.

"Should my sister not do?" Tanis Lunstrum asked in halting Kasani. "She is woman, after all."

"Zekador's Pants," Tai complained. "I'd forgotten about these bloody Orith gender roles."

Dorian smiled. "Tai's good at cooking, but I'm better," he said. "You'll like this, I promise."

"A boast, coming from you!" Falgar laughed. "Sweet Ancients, I never thought I'd see the day."

The food was good, too. Maybe Dorian's best so far, despite the limited ingredients. Or perhaps Xander simply thought so because he was in such a good mood.

After they'd eaten, Falgar and Sullivan retired together to one of the shelters. The Orith paced the outskirts of the campsite, talking among themselves in hushed, serious Toreenish. Only Xander, Bradford, and Dorian remained at the fire.

Bradford absently peeled at a branch with the blade of his athame. He dropped the pieces into the fire and watched the pale wood ignite, then shrivel. Much of the young nobleman's vigor had returned since returning to solid ground, but he was still quiet and withdrawn. Xander didn't have to think too hard to discern why. Bradford, like Xander, had reason to be apprehensive about facing the Order.

Dorian, meanwhile, sat on the ground and leaned against Solaris, thumbing through the pages of his father's grimoire. In the flickering firelight, he looked almost exactly like Cyrus, back from the dead.

"I'm sorry," Dorian said, abruptly slamming the book shut.

"Eh?" Xander asked. "What for?"

Dorian looked perplexed, like it should have been obvious. "For crashing your ship, of course. I should have—"

"Bloody Void, Valmont," Xander shook his head. Trust that boy to take even the most daring heroics and make it into something to apologize for. "We can replace ships. We can't replace lives."

Dorian looked like he wanted to argue more, but he nodded and said, "Yes. Of course. You're right." But ran his hand down his splinted arm, and said, "Sorry. I hate being injured like this. I feel so... useless."

Dorian stared morosely at the campfire, his expression anguished in the flickering light. But then he sat a little straighter, allowing himself to smile. "I never thanked you. For letting me on the ship, I mean." He leaned back against Solaris, watching the smoke and sparks rise to the perpetually overcast Orith night sky. "The past year, it's been... it's been..."

Xander smiled. "Oh, my dear boy."

There were so many things he wanted to say. Things Dorian deserved to know. But so much of it wasn't his story to tell. He cursed his sister for keeping herself cloaked in secrets and lies, even though he understood her reasons.

But there were things he could tell Dorian, things he should have done long ago.

"Do you know," he said, "Why I let you on my ship?"

"You... you were friends with my father," Dorian said, looking up in surprise. "You owed him a favor."

"That's part of it," Xander said. He stared at the flickering flames. "But do you know what that favor was? Why I owed him?"

Dorian shook his head.

Xander sighed again. "I'm not sure I ever told you before, but my *own* father used to be the Dragonmar of the order."

"Was he?" Dorian said, surprised.

Xander nodded. "Everyone assumed, when the time came, I'd be Dragonmar too. Problem was, there weren't many people on Cyrna worse qualified than me."

"I doubt that," Dorian said, with heartwarming loyalty.

Xander laughed and shook his head. "You didn't know me back then."

Bradford leaned forward, obviously eavesdropping.

"Oh, come over here," Xander said to the young nobleman. "This concerns you, too, I suppose."

Bradford nodded eagerly and moved to a nearby log.

"I was always sickly, off and on," Xander said. "None of the healers could discern why. Sometimes I'd be almost normal, sometimes I couldn't leave my bed for half a moon. When I was seventeen, Janus Callahan thought he could save me. With experimental magic. He... summoned a demon. Rose Quartz, she called herself. Don't let the friendly name fool you. I recovered from my illness, for all the good it did. But I also got possessed."

Dorian and Bradford sat closer, listening intently.

"Rose Quartz," Xander said, "Was not like your Hematite. She made no pretense of trying to be friends. If I didn't do her bidding, she made me relieve my worst memories. Over and over again."

Dorian's eyes were twin blue coins. "Sweet Ancients."

"And then Father passed away unexpectedly, and of course, he always wanted a successor who was just like him," Xander said. "Strong and brave and good with magic. I, though, was an awkward, out-of-shape demon-possessed kid with no flying talent."

Dorian dropped the stick he'd been holding. "You... you were *what*? But... but how can that be? You're the *captain*, you're an *aeronaut*, you—"

"Awkward out-of-shape demon-possessed kids can't become aeronauts, is that it?"

A smile tugged at the corner of Dorian's mouth. "Fair point."

"The thing is, I can't say I blame the Order, exactly. On one hand, you had me, who was... well, me. On the other hand, you had Janus Callahan, dashing and charming and charismatic. Void Eternal. Who do you *think* the Council was going to choose?"

Bradford's eyes looked like they were going to pop out of his head. "My father was Dragonmar?"

"Oh indeed," Xander said with a wry smile. "And wouldn't you know it, my sister, my dear, dear sister, was his biggest supporter."

Bradford's face drew into a pained expression, while Dorian's mouth fell open in shock.

Dorian closed his mouth and opened it again several times before speaking. "Your... your sister... Lady Sylvia... supported Callahan as Dragonmar?"

Xander drew in a breath and let it out. "Indeed. Mind, he got ousted soon enough, once it became clear what he intended to do."

"Enslaving dragons," Bradford said bitterly.

"That," Xander sighed, "Among other things. To her defense, even Sylvia turned against him in the end."

"Now *that* I believe," Bradford said.

"So what did you do?" Dorian wondered.

Xander shook his head. "I, ah, absconded with the *Phoenix*, and I ran, naturally. Your father, Cyrus, stayed with me through it all. He... helped me. Taught me how to fight and to fly. According to him, it didn't matter if I became Dragonmar or not. Said there was no reason I couldn't be an aeronaut, demon or no demon. At that point, I didn't even care about the Order anymore. I just wanted to prove myself *to* myself. I was awful at first. But I got better."

Dorian chuckled. "I think I might know something about what that's like."

Xander echoed his laugh. "One day, I fought against Rose Quartz, and I won. She... was gone. And I was free. But do you know, for all my relief, for all that in some ways it was the best feeling in the world, I still regretted it?" He sighed and shook his head. "Ridiculous, I know. And yet."

Dorian stared at him in obvious fascination. "I had... I did not know, sir." He stared at the fire for a long time. "Hematite... died. In the underclouds. He died saving me. Saving all of us. I'm still... not really used to the idea that he's gone." Dorian swallowed, as if fighting back tears. "He told me not to blame myself. He said... he said he was proud of me."

Xander put his hand on Dorian's shoulder. "We all are, dear boy," he said. "Hiring you to work on my ship was the best bloody decision I ever made."

Face red in the firelight, Dorian turned his attention back to the journal. He frowned, as if something crucial had crossed his mind, something of even greater import than Xander's story. "If you had a demon too, and you worked with my father, I wonder." He handed the grimoire to him. "Can... can you read this, Captain?"

"Well, of course not," Xander said. "Your father keyed all his work to Hematite's energy, so even if Rose Quartz came back, gods forbid—" he cut off abruptly. Where he'd expected blank pages, he saw sigils, notes, and magical circles, all transcribed in Cyrus's cramped handwriting. Spellwork he'd never expected to look upon again. "How in the name of the Gods?"

Dorian nodded. "Both our demons are dead. Or at least banished. But we can still read it. I think... I think maybe down here, everyone can."

Xander practically shoved the book under Bradford's nose. "Can you read this?"

Bradford blinked in surprise. "Erm. Yes?"

Xander nodded, awed and impressed. "No magic down here, so the Illusion won't hold. Makes the whole thing seem kind of useless."

*Useless.* Xander sat bolt upright.

"Captain?" Dorian asked.

Xander leapt from his seat and took off towards the wagon. Dorian, startled, jumped to his feet and quickly scrambled after him.

"Captain!" Dorian stammered. "What's going on?"

"I'll tell you what's going on," Xander said, finding the crate he wanted and hauling it out. He slid open the wooden lid and revealed the leather-bound tomes within. With the eagerness of a child at the Mystic Moon, he picked one up, blew the dust off the cover, and flipped open to a random page. Dorian, puzzled, looked over Xander's shoulder.

"Gods and Ancients," the boy whispered. He snapped his eyes towards Xander. "You said your sister used to support Callahan. Can we trust her?"

"I sure hope so," Xander said, staring at the pages in awe.

Spread in intricate, illuminated text were sigils, circles, and spells, the likes of which Xander had never seen. He eagerly flipped through the rest of the volume, revealing even more. A plethora of Ancient lost magic, the kind the Order could previously only dream of, suddenly laid out before them.

Xander drew in a sharp breath. "So this was what Hildegard wanted us to deliver to Cloudfire." He shook his head and burst into manic, uncontrollable laughter. "Ancients, help me. I hope she's on the right side. Because friend or foe, she's *certainly* going to be glad to see *us*."

# EPILOGUE

Sylvia Kane, Dragonmar of Cloudfire and leader of the Order of the Silver Dragon, sighed and adjusted her wire-rimmed spectacles. *How annoying.* She never *used* to need spectacles to read. But then, she wasn't exactly getting any younger. Pity she never bonded a dragon of her own. With her other hand, she tapped the point of her quill pen on the smooth mahogany desk and surveyed the stack of papers with dismay.

"And this is correct, Hildegard? All of it?"

The copper haired woman grimaced, a look she recognized all too well. Sylvia had been spymaster too, once. "I'm afraid so, Lady Dragonmar."

Sylvia buried her face in her hand. "Void Bloody Eternal."

Bradford and his rebels were driven from their hideout, like bats from a sinking skyship. She could only pray to all the gods that their own escape was much less ineffectual.

She forced her face into a businesslike expression. "How many survivors?"

"Forty-seven that we know about, Lady Dragonmar." Hildegard

inclined her head. "We're still waiting to hear from the rest of the skyships."

*Forty-seven.* So few. "And... and Lord Bradford?" Years of secrets, Cycles of hiding her emotions, and her voice still caught when she asked the question she dreaded the most.

Hildegard's shoulders slumped. "No word yet, Lady Dragonmar." This time it was Hildegard's voice's turn to catch. "He was last seen evacuating on the *Phoenix.*"

*The Phoenix. Xander.*

"Sweet Ancients." Never had the phrase felt more like a prayer.

"It's not all bad news, Lady Dragonmar," Hildegard said. She straightened herself, though the continued tugging on her pendant chain betrayed her nerves.

"Oh?" Sylvia asked.

"Callahan's dragonaut Ambrose Barclay died in the fighting. With him gone, the enemy forces are down to three."

Sylvia sat up straighter at this news. "Indeed? In that case, that puts us nearly on an even footing."

"Indeed, Lady Dragonmar." Hildegard looked like she was steeling herself for battle. "There is something else I haven't told you."

Sylvia's eyes narrowed, but she said, "Go on."

"You've heard the rumors of a rogue dragonaut, one who serves neither Callahan's forces nor the Order?"

"Indeed," Sylvia said. She steepled her fingers in thought. "Callahan says it's all nonsense, but I take a more pragmatic view. There's simply not enough evidence either way."

"Oh, he's authentic enough, all right," Hildegard said. "He served with us during the later moons of the rebellion. I have never seen a flyer like him. He killed Ashe Valerian and Ambrose Barclay, and he captured Corynne Beckett, thus severing her bond with Borealis. That's three enemy dragonauts he's neutralized. Single-handedly. The rebellion made no headway against the dragonauts before he came along."

Sylvia felt her eyes widen. A soldier like that would be a valuable asset, albeit a dangerous one. "I would like to meet this rogue dragonaut," she said. "Is he with you?"

Hildegard grimaced. More bad news. "Last I heard of him, he was desperately trying to save the *Phoenix*."

Sylvia's heart thudded. The *Phoenix*. The doomed ship that contained her younger brother, and, if Hildegard was correct, Bradford. *Bradford...*

"If this rogue dragonaut saved them," Sylvia said, forcing an even tone, "Then I owe him quite a steep debt indeed." She brushed her hands, donning her mask of authority. "Have your scouts be on the lookout for any skyship crashes in the area. If there's a chance, even a chance, of survivors..."

"Yes, Lady Dragonmar," Hildegard said at once. "If I may, Lady Dragonmar, what shall I tell the other survivors? The ones who are here right now?"

Sylvia let out a long sigh. "We may well have to bring them wholly into the fold. We've been using them for too long. It isn't right."

Hildegard frowned. "It's not that I disagree on principle. But if Callahan finds out we've taken in rebels, it will be tantamount to a declaration of war."

Sylvia's knuckles tightened in the sky blue folds of her skirt. She had avoided confronting Callahan for a long time. Far too long. It was bound to happen, eventually.

"Delay as long as you can," she said, choosing her words carefully. "Bring them tents, and blankets, and food from our kitchens. At least until I can meet with the rest of the council. But I fear we cannot hide in the shadows anymore. Even the local Orith have suspected that more than archaeologists and wraiths haunt the empty halls of Cloudfire. If we must re-enter the open, let us do so with a blaze of defiance, I say." With a wan smile, she added, "It's what my dear old father would have wanted."

Hildegard clutched tightly to the pendant around her neck. "And Jameson and I? Are we to come into the open, too?"

Sylvia drew in a deep breath. Once she opened this box, there was no closing it again. But it was time. "Yes," she said.

As she did so, Hildegard let go of her pendant, revealing a golden dragon curled around an orange-amber dragonstone.

"It will soon be time," Sylvia said, "For the world to know that the dragonauts have returned."

# ACKNOWLEDGMENTS

How exciting! I finally get to write one of these! Many people helped me finally bring Dorian's story to life. A thousand thanks to:

Chuck Gould, Marilyn Lary, Joshua Perme, and Henry India Holden for your patience with my incredibly messy rough draft, and for helping me level up my writing as much as Dorian leveled up his sword and flying skills. Showing up to the first meetup on a whim was the best decision I ever made.

Elizabeth Mitchell, Tom Thorogood, Hafidha Acuay, and Elise Baldwin, who have stuck with me over the years and helped me through countless iterations of Dorian's misadventures. I could not ask for better critique partners or better friends.

Luis Enrique Torres from the North Seattle Writers Critique Swap, who offered fresh perspective when I desperately needed it. Can't wait to recommend your book to all my friends!

Keylin Rivers for the cover design, and Nathan Hansen for the interior art. Your stunning artwork turns this book into a finished product I think we can all be proud of.

Matthew, for supporting this dream of mine, and for the years of cake jokes. You know what you did.

The Fitocracy community between 2011 and 2014, who taught me how the heck training the human body works, so I could finally write a training sequence with anything resembling realism.

And finally, you, the reader, for sticking it out all the way to the end of the acknowledgements. Thanks for reading my book, it means a lot!

# ABOUT THE AUTHOR

Morgan lives in Washington State with their husband, child, and an enthusiastic corgi. When not writing, Morgan enjoys lifting weights, making digital art, running, and dabbling in game development. Morgan has worked as a software engineer, science lab assistant, and cashier at a haunted tourist destination, but their first love has always been bringing fictional worlds and characters to life.

 bsky.app/profile/morgankbell.bsky.social

 facebook.com/morgankbell

 instagram.com/dragonmorganbell